AN INCH OF ASHES

DAVID WINGROVE is the Hugo Award-winning co-author (with Brian Aldiss) of *Trillion Year Spree: The History of Science Fiction*. He is also the co-author of the first three MYST books – novelizations of one of the world's bestselling computer games. He lives in north London with his wife and four daughters.

1 Son of Heaven

2 Daylight on Iron Mountain

3 The Middle Kingdom

4 Ice and Fire

5 The Art of War

6 **An Inch of Ashes**

7 The Broken Wheel

8 The White Mountain

9 Monsters of the Deep

10 The Stone Within

11 Upon a Wheel of Fire

12 Beneath the Tree of Heaven

13 Song of the Bronze Statue

14 White Moon, Red Dragon

15 China on the Rhine

16 Days of Bitter Strength

17 The Father of Lies

18 Blood and Iron

19 King of Infinite Space

20 The Marriage of the Living Dark

AN INCH OF ASHES

CHUNG KUO

BOOK 6

DAVID WINGROVE

CORVUS

An Inch of Ashes was first published as The Broken Wheel in Great Britain in 1990
by New English Library.

This revised and updated edition published in special edition hardback, trade paperback,
and eBook in Great Britain in 2013 by Corvus, an imprint of Atlantic Books Ltd.

10 9 8 7 6 5 4 3 2 1

A CIP catalogue record for this book is available from the British Library.

Hardback ISBN: 978 0 85789 817 3
Trade paperback ISBN: 978 0 85789 818 0
E-book ISBN: 978 0 85789 819 7

Printed in Great Britain by the MPG Printgroup

Corvus
An imprint of Atlantic Books Ltd
Ormond House
26–27 Boswell Street
London
WC1N 3JZ

www.corvus-books.co.uk

CONTENTS

INTRODUCTION   I

PART TWELVE   **An Inch of Ashes – Autumn 2206**

Chapter 49   The Pool in the Ruins   5
Chapter 50   Shadows   38
Chapter 51   The Veiled Light   73
Chapter 52   Islands   III
Chapter 53   King of the World   153

PART THIRTEEN   **Artifice and Innocence – Spring 2207**

Chapter 54   The Feast of the Dead   191
Chapter 55   Catherine   232
Chapter 56   The Lost Bride   258

IN TIMES TO COME…   291

Character Listing   293
Glossary of Mandarin Terms   306
Author's Note   324
Acknowledgments   326

AN INCH OF ASHES

Book Six

For Matt Acevedo,
for keeping The Gift of Stones

CHUNG KUO

INTRODUCTION

Soren Berdichev, Head of the Dispersionist faction, is dead, his spine snapped by Gregor Karr after a long pursuit that led finally to Mars. Meanwhile, back on Chung Kuo, DeVore has abandoned his old friends and forged a new alliance with the *Ping Tiao*, or 'levellers', terrorists from the crowded lower levels, who wish to destroy the City and start again.

Within the Seven there is discord for the first time in their history, sown mainly by its latest and youngest member, the obese T'ang of Africa, Wang Sau-leyan. Seen as a selfish, dissolute young man by the older T'ang, he is, in fact, a highly intelligent and cleverly manipulative politician, and his presence among them makes them weaker than ever before.

Li Yuan, heir to City Europe, has married his beloved Fei Yen, his dead brother's wife, and, at his young age, has become his father's most trusted advisor.

Kao Chen, once a *kwai*, or hired 'knife', is now a servant of the T'ang, a Security officer and a friend of Gregor Karr. Alongside the redeemed figure of Axel Haavikko, these three are chief among those fighting DeVore and his minions. One of those – an unexpected figure – is Hans Ebert. Major in Security, heir to the massive GenSyn Corporation and betrothed to General Tolonen's daughter, Jelka, he seems to have it all. Only he wants more. He wants to rule, and DeVore – like the devil he is – has decided to help him get what he wants, whatever the cost.

And then there are Ben and Kim, both still young men, who will become the premier artist and foremost scientist in Chung Kuo. Two young men who walk very different paths and represent in themselves very different things, like the two sides of the great Tao.

Historically, it is a moment of stillness, of quiet before the great storm. For the storm is sure to come now. Nothing the Seven can do will prevent it. Change is coming to Chung Kuo, like the darkest of clouds on the horizon. Who will survive the days to come? And who will go under, as the Great Wheel turns once more and the War of the Two Directions takes on a new, more violent aspect?

PART TWELVE AN INCH OF ASHES

AUTUMN 2206

The East wind sighs, the fine rains come:
Beyond the pool of water-lilies, the noise of faint
    thunder.
A gold toad gnaws the lock. Open it, burn the
    incense.
A tiger of jade pulls the rope.
Draw from the well and escape.
Chia's daughter peeped through the screen when
    Han the clerk was young,
The goddess of the river left her pillow for the great
    Prince of Wei.
Never let your heart open with the spring flowers:
One inch of love is an inch of ashes.

—Li Shang-Yin, untitled poem, 9th century AD

Chapter 49

THE POOL IN THE RUINS

Servants came running to take their horses, leading them back to the stables. Fei Yen seemed flushed, excited by the ride, her eyes wide with enjoyment. Li Yuan laughed, looking at her, and touched her arm.

'It suits you, my love. You should ride more often.'

Tsu Ma came up and stood between them, an arm about each of their shoulders. 'That was good, my friends. And this...' he gestured with his head, his strong neck turning to encompass the huge estate – the palace, the lake, the orchards, the view of the distant mountains, '... it's beautiful. Why, the ancient emperors would envy you.'

Tsu Ma's eyes sparkled and his pure white teeth – strong, square, well-formed teeth – flashed a smile.

'You are welcome here any time, Tsu Ma,' Li Yuan answered him. 'You must treat our stables as your own.'

'Thank you, Li Yuan.' Tsu Ma gave a slight bow, then turned, looking down at Fei Yen. 'You ride well, Lady Fei. Where did you learn?'

She looked away, a slight colour in her cheeks. 'I've ridden since I was a child. My father had two horses.' She turned back, the way she held her head displaying an intense pride. In a world where animals were rare, to own two horses was a matter of some prestige. Only the Seven took such things for granted.

Tsu Ma studied her a moment, then nodded. 'Good. But let us go in. Your father will be expecting us.'

Li Shai Tung was sitting in the Summer House, a small comset on his lap. Tiny three-dimensional holograms formed and faded in the air above the set, each figure giving its brief report before it vanished. Tsu Ma sat close by the old man, keeping silent, while Li Yuan went to get drinks. Fei Yen stood by the window, looking down the steep slope towards the terrace and the ornamental lake. From time to time she would glance back into the room, her eyes coming to rest on the casually seated figure of Tsu Ma.

He was a broad-shouldered, handsome man. Riding, she had noticed how straight he held himself in the saddle, how unruffled he had been when leading his horse across a fast-flowing stream, how easily he brought his mount to jump a wall; as though he were part of the animal he rode. And yet he was immaculate, his hair groomed and beaded with rubies; his tunic an achingly sweet shade of pink that was almost white, edged with black; his trousers of a blue that reminded her of the summer skies of her youth. She had seen how tightly his thighs had gripped the flanks of the roan horse; how commanding he had seemed.

Li Shai Tung finished his business and set the comset down, smiling at Tsu Ma, then at his daughter-in-law, greeting them wordlessly. Li Yuan turned from the cabinet, carrying a tray of drinks. He was host here in this room.

Fei Yen took her drink and seated herself beside her husband, facing the other men. She was conscious of how Tsu Ma looked at her. So open. And yet not impolitely.

'You're looking well,' Li Shai Tung said, looking across at Fei Yen. 'You should ride more often.'

Li Yuan leaned forward. 'She was magnificent, Father. A born horse-woman! You should have seen how she leaped the meadow gate!' His eyes flashed wide as he said it, and when he looked at his wife it was with unfeigned admiration. Tsu Ma saw this and pushed his head back slightly, as if his collar were too tight. He reached into the inner pocket of his tunic and took out a slender silver case.

'May I smoke?' He held out the case and Li Yuan nodded, looking to his father for approval. The old man said nothing, merely smiled.

Tsu Ma removed one of the pencil-thin cheroots and lit it, then inhaled slowly, seeming to relax in his chair as he did so. The silver case lay on the arm of the chair.

He watched the smoke curl up; a thin, fragile thread of heated ash. 'I must thank you, Li Yuan. Today has been perfect.' His eyes settled on the young man's face, finding nothing but open friendship there; perhaps even a degree of admiration. He was used to it; accepted it as his due. But the look on Fei Yen's face, that was different. That, too, he recognized, but kept the knowledge to himself. He raised his glass, toasting his host and hostess silently, his smile serene, sincere.

Li Shai Tung watched all, nodding to himself. He seemed well pleased with things. For the first time in months he was smiling. Tsu Ma saw this and asked him why.

'I'll tell you. When we are alone.'

The T'ang had not looked at Fei Yen, and his comment seemed quite innocuous, but she knew how traditional her father-in-law was. He was not like her own father; he would not discuss business in front of women. She set her drink down untouched and stood up, patting Li Yuan's hand, then turned to bow low to the two T'ang.

'Excuse me, *Chieh Hsia*, but I must go and change. The ride has made me tired.'

It was untrue. She had never felt more alive. Her eyes shone with a barely contained excitement. But she lowered her eyes and went quietly from the room, turning only at the door to look back, finding, as she'd hoped, that Tsu Ma's eyes were on her.

'Well?' said Tsu Ma when she had gone. His manner seemed no different, and yet the word seemed somehow colder, more masculine than before.

'Good news. Both Wu Shih and Wei Feng have agreed to our little scheme.'

Tsu Ma looked down. The development was unexpected. 'Is that wise?'

'I thought so,' Li Shai Tung continued, noting his hesitation. 'In the present circumstances I felt it... safer... to have the balance of the Council know of my plans. It would not do to alienate my oldest friends.'

Tsu Ma drew on the cheroot again, then looked up, meeting his eyes. 'That's not exactly what I meant. This whole business of covert action. Surely it goes against the spirit of the Council? If we can't be open with each other...'

'And can we?' Li Yuan's words were bitter, angry, but at a look from his father he lowered his head, holding his tongue.

'I understand your feelings, Li Yuan,' Tsu Ma answered him, smiling at the old T'ang to show he was not offended by his son's interruption. 'But Wang Sau-leyan must surely not be allowed to triumph. This way, it seems we play into his hands.'

Li Shai Tung was watching him closely. 'Then you will not give your consent?'

Tsu Ma's smile broadened. 'That is not what I said. I was merely pointing out the underlying logic of this course. Whatever you decide I will consent to, my father's oldest friend. And not only because of my respect for my father. I know you would not follow this course if there was any other way.'

Li Shai Tung smiled then looked down into his lap. 'If it helps reassure you, Tsu Ma, I will say to you what I have already said both to Wu Shih and Wei Feng. I do not wish to circumvent the Council in this matter. This is merely a question of research. A fact-finding exercise before I present my case to Council. The brief of the Project will be to study only the feasibility of wiring up Chung Kuo's population. It will fall far short of actual exper-imentation. After all, it would not do for me, a T'ang, to breach the Edict, would it?'

Tsu Ma laughed. 'Indeed. But tell me... who did you have in mind to look after the Project? It's a sensitive scheme. The security on it must be watertight.'

'I agree. Which is why I'm placing Marshal Tolonen in charge.'

'Tolonen?' Tsu Ma considered it a moment, then smiled. 'Why, yes, I can see that that would work very well.'

He met the old T'ang's eyes, a look of understanding passing between them that escaped the young Prince's notice. For Tolonen would be opposed to the scheme. He, if anyone, would be guaranteed to keep it in check.

'But see, I've talked enough already, and you still know so little about the scheme itself. Let Li Yuan speak for me now. Let him be my voice.'

Tsu Ma looked across at the young man, interested. This was why he had come: to hear Li Yuan's proposal in detail. 'Speak,' he said, his left hand outstretched, palm open. A broad hand with long fingers clustered with heavy rings. Smoke curled up from beneath the hand.

Li Yuan hesitated, then, composing himself, began, itemizing the dis-coveries they had made at various SimFic establishments: discoveries that had broken the Edict. Things meant to harm the Seven, now harnessed for their use.

Tsu Ma listened, drawing on the cheroot from time to time, his smile growing broader by the moment. Until, finally, he laughed and clapped his hand against his thigh.

'Excellent! My word, it is excellent.' He rose and went to the window, looking down the slope. 'You have my agreement, Li Shai Tung. I like this plan. I like it very much.'

Tsu Ma turned, looking back at the young man. Li Yuan was smiling broadly, pleased with himself, proud of his scheme, and delighted that he had Tsu Ma's approval. Tsu Ma smiled back at him and nodded, then turned to the window again.

At the bottom of the slope, on the terrace above the ornamental lake, a woman was walking, looking back towards the house. She wore riding clothes and her long dark hair hung loose where she had just unfastened it. She was small, delicate, like a goddess made of the finest porcelain. Tsu Ma smiled and looked away; turned to face the two men in the room with him.

'Yes,' he said, the smile remaining on his lips. 'It's perfect, Yuan. Quite perfect.'

'Who is he?'

DeVore turned to Lehmann and smiled. 'His name is Hung Mien-lo and he was Chancellor to Wang Ta-hung before his recent death.'

Lehmann studied the screen a moment longer, then turned his back on it, staring at DeVore. 'So what is he doing there?'

The film had been shot secretly by DeVore's man amongst the *Ping Tiao*. It showed a meeting Jan Mach had had that morning. A meeting he had been very anxious to keep a secret from the other *Ping Tiao* leaders.

'I don't know. But I'm sure of one thing. He wouldn't be there unless Wang Sau-leyan wanted him there. So the real question is – what does Wang Sau-leyan want of the *Ping Tiao*?'

'So Hung is the new T'ang's man now?'

'It seems so. My man in Alexandria, Fischer, thinks Sau-leyan wasn't responsible for his brother's death, but there's good reason to believe that Hung Mien-lo has been his man for some time now.'

'And Mach? Why didn't he consult the others?'

'That's Mach's way. He didn't like it when I went to Gesell direct. If he'd had his way he would have checked me out beforehand, but I circumvented him. He doesn't like that. It rankles with him. He likes to be in control of things.'

'But you think he'll deal with Hung Mien-lo?'

DeVore nodded. 'It makes sense. If I were him I'd do the same. He'll get what he can out of the T'ang. And he'll use that to keep us at a distance. To make the Ping Tiao less dependent on us. And, conversely, he'll use the alliance with us to keep the T'ang at a distance. It'll mean the Ping Tiao won't have to accept what either of us tell them to do. It'll give them the option to say no now and again. Mach will try to keep the deal with us secret from the T'ang, and vice versa. He'll try to make it seem as if the change – the strengthening of their position – comes from within the Ping Tiao.'

Lehmann was silent a while, thoughtful. 'Then why not kill Hung Mien-lo and prevent Mach from making this deal? There has to be a reason.'

DeVore smiled, pleased with his young lieutenant. He always enjoyed talking out his thoughts with him.

'There is. You see, Mach's scheme works only if we're unaware of the T'ang's role in things. If we're fooled by his tales of a great Ping Tiao renaissance. Oh, their fortunes will be on the up after Helmstadt, there's no doubt, but a deal with the T'ang could give them something they lack. Something they didn't get from Helmstadt. Funds.'

'And you *want* that? You want them to be independently funded?'

'No. Not if that was all there was to it. But I don't intend to let them bargain with me. At the first sign of it I'll threaten to pull out altogether. That would leave them in a worse position than they began, because all the T'ang can offer them is money. They'd lose our contacts, our specialist knowledge, our expertise in battle. And the rest of the Bremen map.'

'I see. And then there's the question of what Wang Sau-leyan wants from this.'

'Exactly. He wouldn't risk contacting the Ping Tiao unless he had some scheme in mind. T'ang or not, if the other members of the Council of Seven heard of his involvement he would be dead.'

Lehmann glanced at the screen. 'It's a thought...'

'Yes. There's always that option. If things get really bad and we need something to divert the Seven.'

'Then what do you intend to do?'

DeVore leaned forward and cleared the screen. At once the lights came up again.

'At present nothing. Mach is meeting Hung Mien-Lo again. In Alexandria in two weeks' time. My man will be there to record it for me. It might be interesting, don't you think? And – who knows? – Mach might even give the T'ang his father's ear back.'

The night was clear and dark, the moon a sharp crescent to the north-east, high above the distant outline of the mountains. It was a warm night. Laughter drifted across the water as the long, high-sided boat made its way out across the lake, the lanterns swinging gently on either side.

Tsu Ma had insisted on taking the oars. He pulled the light craft through the water effortlessly, his handsome mouth formed into a smile, his back held straight, the muscles of his upper arms rippling beneath his silks like the flanks of a running horse. Li Yuan sat behind Tsu Ma in the stern, looking past him at Fei Yen and her cousin, Yin Wu Tsai.

The two girls had their heads together, giggling behind their fans. It had been Fei Yen's idea to have a midnight picnic and Tsu Ma had been delighted when the two girls had come to them with blankets and a basket, interrupting their talk. The two men had smiled and laughed and let themselves be led out on to the lake.

Li Yuan grinned broadly, enjoying himself. In the varicoloured light from the lanterns Fei Yen looked wonderful, like a fairy princess or some mythical creature conjured from the rich legends of his people's past. The flickering patterns of the light made her face seem insubstantial; like something you might glimpse in a dream but which, when you came closer or held a clear light up to see it better, would fade or change back to its true form. He smiled at the fancifulness of the thought, then caught his breath, seeing how her eyes flashed as she laughed at something her cousin had whispered in her ear. And then she looked across at him, her dark eyes smiling, and his blood seemed to catch fire in his veins.

He shuddered, filled by the sight of her. She was his. His.

Fei Yen turned, looking out behind her, then turned back, leaning towards Tsu Ma. 'To the island, Tsu Ma. To the island...'

Tsu Ma bowed his head. 'Whatever you say, my lady.'

The boat began to turn. Beyond the temple on the small hill the lake curved like a swallow's wing. There, near the wing's tip, was a tiny island, reached by a wooden bridge of three spans. Servants had prepared it earlier. As they rounded the point, they could see it clearly, the bridge and the tiny, two-tiered pagoda lit by coloured lanterns.

Li Yuan stared across the water, delighted, then looked back at Fei Yen.

'It's beautiful, you clever thing. When did you plan all this?'

Fei Yen laughed and looked down, clearly pleased by his praise. 'This afternoon. After we'd been riding. I... I did it for our guest, husband.'

Tsu Ma slowed his stroke momentarily and bowed his head to Fei Yen. 'I am touched, my lady. You do me great honour.'

Li Yuan watched the exchange, his breast filled with pride for his wife. She was so clever to have thought of it. It was just the right touch. The perfect end to a perfect day. The kind of thing a man would remember for the rest of his days. Yes, he could imagine it now, forty years from now, he and Tsu Ma, standing on the terrace by the lake, looking back...

She had even been clever enough to provide an escort for the T'ang. A clever, pretty woman who was certain to delight Tsu Ma. Indeed, had Fei Yen not been in the boat, he would have allowed himself to concede that Wu Tsai was herself quite beautiful.

For a moment he studied the two women, comparing them. Wu Tsai was taller than Fei Yen, her face, like her body, longer and somehow grosser, her nose broader, her lips fuller, her cheekbones less refined, her neck stronger, her breasts more prominent beneath the silk of her jacket. Yet it was only by contrast with Fei Yen that these things were noticeable: as if in Fei Yen lay the very archetype of Han beauty, and all else, however fine in itself, was but a flawed copy of that perfection.

The island drew near. Li Yuan leaned forward, instructing Tsu Ma where to land. Then the boat was moored and Tsu Ma was handing the girls up on to the wooden jetty, the soft rustle of their silks as they disembarked seeming, for that brief moment, to merge with the silken darkness of the night and the sweetness of their perfume.

They settled on the terrace, Fei Yen busying herself laying out the table while Wu Tsai sat and made pleasant conversation with Tsu Ma. Li Yuan stood at the rail, looking out across the darkness of the lake, his sense of ease, of inner stillness, lulling him so that for a time he seemed aware only of the dull murmur of the voices behind him and the soft lapping of the water against the wooden posts of the jetty. Then there was the light touch of a hand on his shoulder and he turned to find Fei Yen there, smiling up at him.

'Please, husband. Come sit with us.'

He put his arms about her and lowered his face to meet her lips, then came and sat with them. Fei Yen stood by a tiny table to one side, pouring wine into cups from a porcelain jug; offering first to the T'ang and then to her husband, finally to her cousin. Only then did she give a little bow and, pouring herself some wine, settled, kneeling at her husband's side.

Tsu Ma studied them both a moment, then raised his cup. 'You are a lucky man, Li Yuan, to have such a wife. May your marriage be blessed with many sons!'

Li Yuan bowed his head, inordinately pleased. But it was no more than the truth. He *was* lucky. He looked down at the woman kneeling by his side and felt his chest tighten with his love for her. *His.* It was three days now since the wedding and yet he could not look at her without thinking that. *His.* Of all the men in Chung Kuo, only he was allowed this richness, this lifelong measure of perfection. He shivered and raised his cup, looking back at Tsu Ma.

'To friendship!' he offered, meeting Tsu Ma's eyes. 'To we four, here tonight, and to our eternal friendship!'

Tsu Ma leaned forward, his teeth flashing as he smiled. 'Yes. To friendship!' He clinked his cup against Li Yuan's, then raised it in offering, first to Wu Tsai and finally to Fei Yen.

Fei Yen had been looking up from beneath her lashes, her pose the very image of demure, obedient womanhood. At Tsu Ma's toast, however, she looked down sharply, as if abashed. But it was not bashfulness that made her avert her eyes; it was a deeper, stronger feeling: one that she tried to hide not only from the watchful T'ang, but from herself. She turned her head, looking up at Li Yuan.

'Would my husband like more wine?'

Li Yuan smiled back at her, handsome in his own way, and loving, too – a good man for all his apparent coldness – yet her blood didn't thrill at his touch, neither did her heart race in her chest the way it was racing now in the presence of Tsu Ma.

'In a while, my love,' he answered her. 'But see to our guest first. Tsu Ma's cup is almost empty.'

She bowed her head and, setting down her cup, went to bring the wine jug. Tsu Ma had turned slightly in his seat and now sat there, his booted legs spread, one hand clasping his knee, the other holding out his cup. Turning, seeing him like that, Fei Yen caught her breath. It was so like the way Han Ch'in had used to sit, his strong legs spread arrogantly, his broad hands resting on his knees. She bowed deeply, hiding her sudden confusion, holding out the jug before her.

'Well...?' Li Yuan prompted, making her start and spill some of the wine.

Tsu Ma laughed; a soft, generous laughter that made her look up at him again and meet his eyes. Yes, there was no doubting it; he knew what she was thinking. Knew the effect he'd had upon her.

She poured the wine then backed away, her head bowed, her throat suddenly dry, her heart pounding. Setting the jug down, she settled at her husband's feet again, but now she was barely conscious of Li Yuan. The whole world had suddenly turned about. She knelt there, her head lowered, trying to still the sudden tremor of her hands, the violent beating of her heart, but the sight of his booted feet beneath the table held her eyes. She stared at them, mesmerized, the sound of his voice like a drug on her senses, numbing her.

Wu Tsai was flirting with Tsu Ma, leaning towards him, her words and gestures unmistakable in their message, but Fei Yen could sense how detached the T'ang was from her games. He leaned towards Wu Tsai, laughing, smiling, playing the ancient game with ease and charm, but his attention was focused on herself. She could sense how his body moved towards her subtly; how, with the utmost casualness, he strove at each moment to include her in all that was said. And Li Yuan? He was unaware of this. It was like the poor child was asleep, enmeshed in his dream of perfect love.

She looked away, pained suddenly by all she was thinking. Li Yuan was her husband, and one day he would be T'ang. He deserved her loyalty, in body and soul. And yet...

She rose quietly and went into the pagoda, returning a moment later with a p'i p'a, the ancient four-stringed lute shaped like a giant teardrop.

'What's this?' said Li Yuan, turning to look at her.

She stood there, her head bowed. 'I thought it might be pleasant if we had some music.'

Li Yuan turned and looked across at Tsu Ma, who smiled and gave a tiny nod of his head. But instead of handing the lute to her cousin, as Li Yuan had expected, Fei Yen sat, the lute held upright in her lap, and began to play.

Li Yuan sat there, entranced by the fluency of her playing, the swift certainty of her fingers across the strings, by the passionate tiny movements of her head as she wrought the tune from nothingness. He recognized the song. It was the *Kan Hua Hui*, the 'Flower Fair', a sweet, sprightly tune that took considerable expertise to play. When she finished he gave a short laugh and bowed his head. He was about to speak, to praise her, when she began again – a slower, more thoughtful piece this time.

It was the *Yueh Erh Kao*, 'The Moon on High'.

He shivered, looking out across the blackness of the lake, his heart suddenly in his throat. It was beautiful: as if the notes were tiny silver fishes floating in the darkness. As the playing grew faster, more complex, his gaze was drawn to her face again and he saw how her eyes had almost closed, her whole being suddenly focused on the song, on the movement of her fingers against the strings. It reminded him of that moment years before when she had drawn and aimed the bow. How her whole body had seemed to become part of the bow, and how, when the arrow had been released, it had been as if part of her had flown through the air towards the distant target.

He breathed slowly, his lips parted in wonder. And Han was dead, and she was his. And still the Great Wheel turned...

It ended. For a time no one spoke. Then Wu Tsai leaned forward and took her cup from the table, smiling, looking across at Tsu Ma.

'My cousin is very gifted,' she said. 'It is said in our family that the gods made a mistake the day Fei Yen was born; that they meant Yin Tsu to have another son. But things were mixed up and while she received the soul of a man, she was given the body of a woman.'

Fei Yen had looked up briefly, only to avert her eyes again, but it was clear from her smile that she had heard the story often and was not displeased by it. Tsu Ma, however, turned to face Wu Tsai, coming to Fei Yen's defence.

'From what I've seen, if the gods were mistaken it was in one small respect alone. That Fei Yen is not *quite* perfect...'

Fei Yen met his eyes momentarily, responding to his teasing tone. 'Not quite, *Chieh Hsia?*'

'No...' He held out his empty cup. 'For they should have made you twins. One to fill my cup while the other played.'

There was laughter all round. But when Fei Yen made to get up and pour for him, Tsu Ma took the jug and went round himself, filling their cups.

'There!' he said, sitting back. 'Now I can listen once again.'

Taking his hint, Fei Yen straightened the *p'i p'a* in her lap and, after a moment's concentration, began to play. This time it was a song none of them had heard before. A strange, melancholy tune. And as she played she sang in a high contralto.

> A pretty pair of white geese
> Double, double, far from dusty chaos;
> Wings embracing, they play in bright sunlight,
> Necks caressing roam the blue clouds.
> Trapped by nets or felled by corded arrow
> Hen and cock are parted one dawn.
> Sad echoes drift down river bends,
> Lonesome cries ring out from river banks.
> 'It is not that I don't long for my former mate,
> But because of you I won't reach my flock.'
> Drop by drop she sheds a tear.
> 'A thousand leagues I'll wait for you!'
> How happy to fall in love,
> So sad a lifetime parting.
> Let us cling to our hundred year span,
> Let us pursue every moment of time,
> Like grass on a lonely hill
> Knowing it must wither and die.

Li Yuan, watching her, found himself spellbound by the song, transfixed by the pain in her face as she sang, and astonished that he had never heard her sing before – that he had never guessed she had these talents. When she had finished and the lute had fallen silent, he looked across at Tsu Ma and saw how the T'ang sat there, his head bowed, his hands clasped together tightly as if in grief.

Tsu Ma looked up, tears filming his eyes, his voice soft. 'That was beautiful, Lady Fei. Perhaps the most beautiful thing I have ever heard.'

Fei Yen was looking down, the p'i p'a resting loosely against her breasts, her whole frame bent forward, as if she had emptied herself with the song. She made a tiny motion of her head, acknowledging the T'ang's words; then she stood and, with bows to Tsu Ma and her husband, turned and went back into the pagoda.

'Well...' said Tsu Ma, looking directly at Li Yuan. 'What can I say, my friend? You honour me, tonight. I mean that.'

'I, too, Tsu Ma. This has been an evening to remember.'

Tsu Ma sat back. 'That's true.' He shivered, then seemed to come to himself again and smiled. 'But, come, I am neglecting the Lady Wu.' He turned to Wu Tsai, his smile widening. 'Do you play anything, my lady?'

Li Yuan smiled, recognizing that Tsu Ma was hinting he should go after his wife. With a bow to his guests he went. But Fei Yen was not inside the pagoda. He stood there in the empty room for a moment, frowning, hearing only the laughter from the terrace outside. Then he heard her, calling him softly from the far side of the pagoda.

They strolled back across the bridge, his arm about her neck, her tiny body pressed warm and tight against his side. The night was mild and dark and comforting about them, but the terrace was empty, the pagoda too. Li Yuan looked about him, puzzled, then stiffened, hearing a splash in the water close by.

He crouched, facing the danger. 'Get behind me, Fei Yen!' he said, quietly but urgently, drawing the dagger from his boot.

A peal of laughter rolled out from the darkness in front of them; rich and deep and full of warmth. Li Yuan relaxed. It was Tsu Ma.

'Gods! What are you doing?'

Tsu Ma came closer, into the light of the lanterns. The water was up to his chest and his hair was slicked back wetly from his forehead.

'Swimming,' he answered. 'It's lovely. The water's much warmer than I thought it would be.'

'And the Lady Wu? Has she gone back?'

In answer there was a splashing to their left and a second whoop of laughter.

'You should come in, you two!' she yelled. 'It's marvellous!'

Li Yuan looked about him, puzzled.

Tsu Ma saw and laughed. 'If you're looking for our clothes, they're in the boat. It was the Lady Wu's idea. She told me there were fish in the lake and I wanted to see for myself.'

'And were there?' It was Fei Yen. She had come alongside Li Yuan and was standing there, looking across at Tsu Ma. He stood straighter in the water, his broad chest glistening wetly in the multicoloured light.

'Only an eel,' Wu Tsai answered, coming nearer, her naked shoulders bobbing above the surface of the water. 'A rather stiff little eel...'

'Wu Tsai!' Fei Yen protested, but even Li Yuan was laughing now.

'They say the god Kung-Kung who brought the Great Flood was an eel,' Tsu Ma said, scooping water up over his chest and arms as if he were washing. 'A giant eel. But look, you two, if you're not going to join us, then perhaps you should let us join you. Li Yuan... if you would avert your eyes while the Lady Wu gets out and finds her clothes?'

'Of course...' Li Yuan turned away, hearing the giggling that went on behind his back as Fei Yen went across to help her cousin.

'All right,' Wu Tsai said, after a while. 'You can turn round now, Prince Yuan.'

He turned back. Wu Tsai was kneeling in the boat, fastening her silks. She looked up at him, grinning. 'You really should have joined us.'

He hesitated, conscious of Tsu Ma, naked in the water close by, and of Fei Yen, crouched there beside the boat, watching him.

'It would not have been right...'

Wu Tsai shrugged, and climbed up on to the bank. 'I thought we had made a toast.' Her eyes flashed mischievously. 'You know, eternal friends, and all that...'

Tsu Ma had pushed forward through the water until he was standing just below the deep lip of the bank. Now he spoke, placing his hands flat on the stone flags at the lake's edge. 'Prince Yuan is right, Lady Wu. Forgive me, I wasn't thinking. It would be most... improper.'

Wu Tsai brushed past Li Yuan provocatively, then glanced back at Fei

Yen, smiling. 'I just thought it would have been fun, that's all. Something a little different.'

Li Yuan turned angrily, glaring at her, then, biting back the retort that had come to mind, he turned back, looking at Fei Yen.

She was standing now, her head bowed, her whole stance submissive.

He took a step towards her, one hand raised in appeal. 'You must see how wrong it would have been?'

Her eyes lifted, met his, obedient. 'Of course, my husband.'

He let his breathing calm, then turned back, looking across at the T'ang. 'And you, Tsu Ma? What do you wish? Should we retire to the pagoda while you dress?'

Tsu Ma laughed, his body dark and powerful in the water. 'Gods, no, Yuan. This is much too nice. I think I'll swim back. Float on my back a bit and stare up at the stars.'

Yuan bowed his head. 'Of course. As you will. But what will you do when you get to the far shore?'

But Tsu Ma had turned already and was wading out into the deeper water. He shouted back his answer as he slipped into the blackness. 'Why, I'll get out of the water, Yuan! What else should I do?'

At eleven the next morning, Tolonen was standing at the West Window in the Room of the Five Directions in the East Palace at Tongjiang, looking out across the gardens towards the lake. He had been summoned to this meeting at short notice. That, in itself, was not unusual; but for once he had been told nothing of the reason for the meeting. It was that – that sense of unpreparedness – which made him feel restless standing there; made him turn and pace the room impatiently.

He had paused before the great mirror at the far end of the room, straightening the collar of his uniform jacket, when the door behind him opened. He turned, expecting Li Shai Tung, but it was the Prince, Li Yuan, who entered.

'Prince Yuan,' he said, bowing.

Li Yuan came forward, extending an arm to offer the Marshal a seat. 'Thank you for coming, Knut. My father will join us later.'

Tolonen bowed again, then sat, staring pointedly at the folder in Li Yuan's lap. 'Well, Yuan, what is it?'

Li Yuan smiled. He enjoyed the old man's bluntness – a trait that had grown more pronounced with every year.

'My father has asked me to talk to you on a certain matter. When I've finished, he'll come and speak with you himself. But what I have to say has his full approval. You can direct any questions – or objections – to me, as if you were speaking to my father.'

'Objections?' Tolonen raised his chin. 'If Li Shai Tung has approved it, why should I have objections? He has a job for me, neh?'

'A task, let's say. Something which he feels you should oversee.'

Tolonen nodded. 'I see. And what is this task?'

Li Yuan hesitated. 'Would you like refreshments while we talk?'

Tolonen smiled. 'Thank you, Yuan, but no. Unless your father wishes to detain me, I must be in Nanking three hours from now to meet Major Karr.'

'Of course. Then we'll press on. It would be best, perhaps, if you would let me finish before asking anything. Some of it is quite complex. And, please, record this if you wish.'

Tolonen bowed his head, then turned his right hand palm upward and quickly tapped out the command on the grid of tiny flesh-coloured blisters at his wrist. That done, he settled back, letting the young Prince speak.

Li Yuan watched the Marshal while he talked, barely referring to the folder in his lap, unless it was to take some diagram from it and hand it to Tolonen. He watched attentively, noting every frown, every look of puzzlement, every last betraying blink or twitch in the old man's face, anxious to gauge the depth of his feelings.

Tolonen had not smiled throughout the lengthy exposition. He sat there, grim-faced, his left hand gripping the arm of his chair. But when Yuan finished, he looked down, giving a great heave of a sigh.

'Can I speak now, Yuan?' Tolonen said, his eyes pained, his whole face grave.

'Of course. As I said, you must speak to me as if I were my father. Openly. As you feel.'

Prepared as he was, Li Yuan nonetheless felt a sudden tightening in his stomach. He respected Marshal Tolonen greatly; had grown up in the shadow of the old man. But in this, he knew, they were of a different mind.

Tolonen stared at him a moment, nodding, his lips pressed tightly together, his earnest grey eyes looking out from a face carved like granite.

Then, with a deep sniff that indicated he had considered things long enough, he began.

'You ask me to speak openly. Yet I feel I cannot do that without offending you, Li Yuan. This is, I take it, your idea?'

Li Yuan could sense the great weight of the Marshal's authority bearing down on him, but steeled himself, forcing himself to confront it.

'It is.'

'I see. And yet you command me – speaking with your father's voice – to answer you. Openly. Bluntly.' He sighed. 'Very well then. I'll tell you what I feel. I find this scheme of yours repugnant.'

Li Yuan shivered, but kept his face impassive. 'And I, Marshal Tolonen. And I. This is not something I *want* to do.'

'Then why?'

'Because there is no other way. None that would not result in greater violence, greater bloodshed than that which we are already witnessing.'

Tolonen looked down. Again he sniffed deeply. Then he looked up again, shaking his head. 'No. Even were the worst to come, this is no path for us. To put things in men's heads. To wire them up and treat them like machines. Achh...' He leaned forward, his expression suddenly, unexpectedly, passionate. 'I know what I am, Li Yuan. I know what I have had to do in the service of my T'ang. And sometimes I have difficulty sleeping. But this... this is different in kind. This will rob men of their freedom.'

'Or the illusion of freedom?'

Tolonen waved the words aside impatiently. 'It's no illusion, Prince Yuan. The freedom to choose – bad or good – that's real. And the Mandate of Heaven – those moral criteria by which a T'ang is adjudged a good or bad ruler – that too is real. Take them away and we have nothing. Nothing worth keeping, anyway.'

Li Yuan sat forward. 'I don't agree. If a man is bad, surely it is no bad thing to have a wire in his head – to be able to limit the effects of his badness? And if a man is good—'

Tolonen interrupted him. 'You, I, your father – we are good men. We act because we must – for the good of all. Yet when we have left this earth, what then? How can we guarantee that those who rule Chung Kuo after us will be good? How can we guarantee *their* motives? So, you see, I'd answer you thus, my prince. It does not matter if the man with the wire in his head is good or bad. What matters is the moral standing of the man who holds the wires in his hands, like ten thousand million strings. Will he make the puppets dance? Or will he leave them be?'

Li Yuan sat back slowly, shaking his head. 'You talk of dictatorships, Marshal Tolonen. Yet we are Seven.'

Tolonen turned his head aside, a strange bitterness in his eyes. 'I talk of things to be – whether they come in ten years or ten thousand.' He looked back at Li Yuan, his grey eyes filled with sadness. 'Whatever you or I might wish, history tells us this – that nothing is eternal. Things change.'

'You once thought differently. I have heard you speaking so myself, Knut. Was it not you yourself who said we should build a great dam against the floodwaters of Change?'

Tolonen nodded, suddenly wistful, his lips formed into a sad smile. 'Yes... but *this!*'

He sat there afterwards, when the Prince had gone, staring down at his hands. He would do it. Of course he would. Hadn't his T'ang asked him to take this on? Even so, he felt heavy of heart. Had the dream died, then? The great vision of a world at peace – a world where a man could find his level and raise his family without need or care. And was this the first sign of the nightmare to come? Of the great, engulfing darkness?

He kept thinking of Jelka, and of the grandchildren he would some day have. What kind of a world would it be for them? Could he bear to see them wired – made vulnerable to the least whim of their lords and masters? He gritted his teeth, pained by the thought. Had it changed so much that even he – the cornerstone – began to doubt their course?

'Knut?'

He raised his head, then got to his feet hurriedly. He had been so caught up in his thoughts he not heard the T'ang enter.

'*Chieh Hsia!*' He bowed his head exaggeratedly.

Li Shai Tung sat where his son had been sitting only moments before, silent, studying his Marshal. Then, with a vague nod of his head as if satisfied with what he had seen, he leaned towards Tolonen.

'I heard all that passed between you and my son.'

'Yes, *Chieh Hsia.*'

'And I am grateful for your openness.'

Tolonen met his eyes unflinchingly. 'It was only my duty, Li Shai Tung.'

'Yes. But there was a reason for letting Yuan talk to you first. You see, while my son is, in his way, quite wise, he is also young. Too young, perhaps, to understand the essence of things: the place of li and ch'i in this great world of ours; the fine balance that exists between the shaping force and the passive substance.'

Tolonen frowned, lowering his head slightly. 'I'm afraid I don't follow you, *Chieh Hsia.*'

The T'ang smiled. 'Well, Knut, I'll put it simply, and bind you to keep this secret from my son. I have authorized his scheme, but that is not to say it will ever come about. You understand me?'

'Not fully, my lord. You mean you are only humouring Li Yuan?'

Li Shai Tung hesitated. 'In a way, yes, I suppose you could say I am. But this idea is deep-rooted in Yuan. I have seen it grow from the seed, until now it dominates his thinking. He believes he can shape the world to his conception; that this scheme of his will answer all the questions.'

'And you think he's wrong?'

'Yes.'

'Then why encourage him? Why authorize this madness?'

'Because Yuan will be T'ang one day. If I oppose him now in this, he will only return to it after my death. And that would be disastrous. It would bring him into conflict, not only with his fellow T'ang but with the great mass of the Above. Best, then, to let him purge it from his blood while he is Prince, neh? To discover for himself that he is wrong.'

'Maybe...' Tolonen took a deep breath. 'But if you'll forgive me, *Chieh Hsia,* it still seems something of a gamble. What if this "cure" merely serves to encourage him further? Isn't that possible?'

'Yes. Which is why I summoned you, Knut. Why I wanted you to oversee the Project. To act as brake to my son's ambitions and keep the thing within bounds... And to kill it if you must.'

Tolonen was staring at his T'ang, realization coming slowly to his face. Then he laughed. 'I see, *Chieh Hsia...* I understand!'

Li Shai Tung smiled back at him. 'Good. Then when Tsu Ma returns from riding, I'll tell him you have taken the job, yes?'

Tolonen bowed his head, all heaviness suddenly lifted from his heart. 'I would be honoured, *Chieh Hsia.* Deeply honoured.'

★

Fifteen li north of Tongjiang, at the edge of the T'ang's great estate, were the ruins of an ancient Buddhist monastery that dated from the time of the great Sung dynasty. They stood in the foothills of the Ta Pa Shan, three levels of cinnabar-red buildings climbing the hillside, the once elegant sweep of their grey-tiled roofs smashed like broken mouths, their brickwork crumbling, their doorways cluttered with weed and fallen masonry. They had stood so for more than two hundred and forty years now, victims of the great Ko Ming purges of the 1960s, their ruin becoming, with time, a natural thing – part of the bleak and melancholy landscape that surrounded them.

On the hillside below the buildings stood the ruin of an ancient moss-covered stupa, its squat, heavy base chipped and crumbling, the steps cut into the face cracked, broken in places. It was a great, pot-bellied thing, its slender spire like an afterthought tagged on untidily, the smooth curve of its central surface pocked where the plaster had fallen away in places, exposing the brickwork.

In its shadow, in a square of orange brickwork part hidden by the long grass, stood a circular pool. It had once been a well, serving the monastery, but when the Red Guards had come they had filled it with broken statuary, almost to its rim, and now the water – channelled from the hills above by way of an underground stream – rose to the lip of the well. With the spring thaw, or when the rains fell heavily in the Ta Pa Shan, the well would overflow, making a small marsh of the ground to the south-west of it. Just now, however, the land was dry, the pool a perfect mirror, moss on the statuary below giving it a rich green colour, like a tarnished bronze.

The sky overhead was a cold, metallic blue. To the north, above the mountains, storm clouds were gathering, black and dense, throwing the furthest peaks into an intense shadow.

To the south the land fell away, slowly at first then abruptly. A steep path led down into a narrow, deeply eroded valley through which a clear stream ran, swift yet shallow, to the plains below.

At the southern end of the valley where the sky was brighter, a horseman now appeared, his dark mount reined in, its head pulling to one side as it slowed then came to a halt. A moment later, a second rider came up over the lip of rock and drew up beside the first. They leaned close momentarily then began to come forward again, slowly, looking about them, the first of them pointing up at the ruined monastery.

'What is this place?' Fei Yen asked, looking up to where Tsu Ma was pointing. 'It looks ancient.'

'It is. Li Yuan was telling me about it yesterday. There used to be two hundred monks here.'

'Monks?'

He laughed, turning in his saddle to look at her. 'Yes, monks. But come. Let's go up. I'll explain it when we get there.'

She looked down, smiling, then nudged her horse forward, following him, watching as he began to climb the steep path that cut into the overhang above, his horse straining to make the gradient.

It was difficult. If it had been wet it would have been impossible on horseback, but he managed it. Jumping down from his mount, he came back and stood there at the head of the path, looking down at her.

'Dismount and I'll give you a hand. Or you can leave your mount there, if you like. He'll not stray far.'

In answer she spurred her horse forward, willing it up the path, making Tsu Ma step back sharply as she came on.

'There!' she said, turning the beast sharply, then reaching forward to smooth its neck. 'It wasn't so hard...'

She saw how he was looking at her, his admiration clouded by concern, and looked away quickly. There had been this tension between them all morning; a sense of things unspoken; of gestures not yet made between them. It had lain there beneath the stiff formality of their talk, like fire under ice, surfacing from time to time in a look, a moment's hesitation, a tacit smile.

'You should be more careful,' he said, coming up to her, his fingers reaching up to smooth the horse's flank only a hand's length from her knee. 'You're a good rider, Lady Fei, but that's not a stunt I'd recommend you try a second time.'

She looked down at him, her eyes defiant. 'Because I'm a woman, you mean?'

He smiled back at her, a strange hardness behind his eyes, then shook his head. 'No. Because you're not *that* good a rider. And because I'm responsible for you. What would your husband say if I brought you back in pieces?'

Fei Yen was silent. What *would* he say? She smiled. 'All right. I'll behave myself in future.'

She climbed down, aware suddenly of how close he was to her, closer than he had been all morning, and when she turned, it was to find him looking down at her, a strange expression in his eyes. For a moment she stood there, silent, waiting for him, not knowing what he would do. The moment seemed to stretch out endlessly, his gaze travelling across her face, her neck, her shoulder, returning to her eyes. Then, with a soft laugh, he turned away, letting her breathe again.

'Come!' he said briskly, moving up the slope, away from her. 'Let's explore the place!'

She bent down momentarily, brushing the dust from her clothes, then straightened up, her eyes following him.

'You asked me what monks were,' he said, turning, waiting for her to catch up with him. 'But it's difficult to explain. We've nothing like them now. Not since Tsao Ch'un destroyed them all. There are some similarities to the New Confucian officials, of course – they dressed alike, in saffron robes, and had similar rituals and ceremonies – but in other ways they were completely different.'

'In what way different?'

He smiled and began to climb the slope again, slowly, looking about him all the while, his eyes taking in the ruins, the distant, cloud-wreathed mountains, the two horses grazing just below them. 'Well, let's just say that they had some strange beliefs. And that they let those beliefs shape their lives – as if their lives were of no account.'

They had reached the pool. Tsu Ma went across and stood there, one foot resting lightly on the tiled lip of the well as he looked back across the valley towards the south. Fei Yen hesitated, then came alongside, looking up at him.

'What kind of beliefs?'

'Oh...' He looked down, studying her reflection in the pool; conscious of the vague, moss-covered forms beneath the surface image. 'That each one of us would return after death, in another form. As a butterfly, perhaps, or as a horse.'

'Or as a man?'

'Yes...' He looked up at her, smiling. 'Imagine it! Endless cycles of rebirth. Each newborn form reflecting your behaviour in past lives. If you lived badly you would return as an insect.'

'And if well, as a T'ang?'

He laughed. 'Perhaps... but then again, perhaps not. They held such things as power and government as being of little importance. What they believed in was purity. All that was important to them was that the spirit be purged of all its earthly weaknesses. And because of that – because each new life was a fresh chance to live purely – they believed all life was sacred.'

A path led up from where they stood, its stone flags worn and broken, its progress hidden here and there by moss and weed. They moved on, following it up to the first of the ruined buildings. To either side great chunks of masonry lay in the tall grasses, pieces of fallen statuary among them.

In the doorway she paused, looking up at him. 'I think they sound rather nice. Why did Tsao Ch'un destroy them?'

He sighed, then pushed through, into the deep shadow within. 'That's not an easy question to answer, my lady. To understand, you would have to know how the world was before Tsao Ch'un. How divided it was. How many different forms of religion there were, and every one of them "the truth".'

She stood there, looking in at him. 'I know my history. I've read about the century of rebellions.'

'Yes...' He glanced back at her, then turned away, looking about him at the cluttered floor, the smoke-blackened walls, the broken ceiling of the room he was in. There was a dank, sour smell to everything, a smell of decay and great antiquity. It seemed much colder here than out in the open. He turned back, shaking his head. 'On the surface of things the Buddhists seemed the best of all the religious groups. They were peaceful. They fought no great holy wars in the name of their god. Neither did they persecute anyone who disagreed with them. But ultimately they were every bit as bad as the others.'

'Why? If they threatened no one...'

'Ah, but they did. Their very existence was a threat. This place... it was but one of many thousand such monasteries throughout Chung Kuo. And a small one at that. Some monasteries had ten, twenty thousand monks, many of them living long into their eighties and nineties. Imagine all those men, disdainful of states and princes, taking from the land – eating, drinking, building their temples and their statues, making their books and their prayer flags – *and giving nothing back*. That was what was so threatening about them. It all seemed so harmless, so peaceful, but it was really quite insidious – a debilitating disease that crippled the social body, choking its life from it like a cancer.'

Tsu Ma looked about him, suddenly angry, his eyes taking in the waste of it all. Long centuries of waste. 'They could have done so much. For the sick, the poor, the homeless, but such things were beneath their notice. To purge themselves of earthly desires – that was all they were worried about. Pain and suffering – what did suffering mean to them except as a path to purity?'

'Then you think Tsao Ch'un was right to destroy them?'

'Right?' He came across to her. 'Yes, I think he was right. Not in everything he did. But in this... yes. It's better to feed and clothe and house the masses than to let them rot. Better to give them a good life here than to let them suffer in the vague hope of some better afterlife.'

He placed his right hand against the rounded stone of the upright, leaning over her, staring down fiercely at her as he spoke, more passionate than she had ever seen him. She looked down, her pulse quickening.

'And that's what you believe?' she asked softly. 'That we've only this one life? And nothing after?'

'Don't we all believe that? At core?'

She shivered, then looked up, meeting his eyes. 'One life?'

He hesitated, his eyes narrowing, then reached out and brushed his fingers against her cheek and neck.

'Tsu Ma...'

He drew his hand back sharply. 'Forgive me, I...' He stared at her a moment, his eyes confused, pained. 'I thought...' He looked down, shaking his head, then pushed past her.

Outside the sky was overcast. A wind had blown up, tearing at the grass, rippling the surface of the pool. Tsu Ma knelt at its edge, his chest heaving, his thoughts in turmoil. *One life...* What had she meant if not that? What did she want of him?

He turned, hearing her approach.

'I'm sorry...' she began, but he shook his head.

'It was a mistake, that's all. *We are who we are, neh?*'

She stared at him, pained by the sudden roughness of his words. She had not meant to hurt him.

'If I were free...'

He shook his head, his face suddenly ugly, his eyes bitter. 'But you're not. And the Prince is my friend, neh?'

She turned her face from him, then moved away. The storm was almost upon them now. A dense, rolling mist lay upon the hills behind the ruins and the wind held the faintest suggestion of the downpour to come. The sky was darkening by the moment.

'We'd best get back,' she said, turning to him. But he seemed unaware of the darkness at the back of everything. His eyes held nothing but herself. She shuddered. Was he in love with her? Was that it? And she had thought...

Slowly he stood, his strong, powerful body stretching, as if from sleep. Then, turning his head from her, he strode down the slope towards the horses.

On the flight down to Nanking, Tolonen played back the recording, the words sounding clearly in his head. Listening to his own voice again, he could hear the unease, the bitterness there and wondered what Li Yuan had made of it. Prince Yuan was a clever one, there was no doubting it, so perhaps he understood why the T'ang had appointed him to oversee the Project rather than someone more sympathetic. Maybe that was why he had left things unresolved, their talk at an impasse. But had he guessed the rest of it? Did he know just how deeply his father was opposed to things?

He sighed, then smiled, thinking of the reunion to come. He had not seen Karr in more than three years. Not since he'd seen him off from Nanking back in November 2203. And now Karr was returning, triumphant, his success in tracking down and killing Berdichev a full vindication of their faith in him.

Tolonen leaned forward, looking down out of the porthole. The spaceport was off in the distance ahead, a giant depression in the midst of the great glacial plateau of ice – the City's edge forming a great wall about the outer perimeter. Even from this distance he could see the vast, pitted sprawl of landing pads, twenty li in diameter, its southernmost edge opening out on to Hsuan Wu lake, the curve of the ancient Yangtze forming a natural barrier to the north-east, like a giant moat two li in width. At the very centre of that great sunken circle, like a vast yet slender needle perched on its tip, was the control tower. Seeing it, Tolonen had mixed feelings. The last time he had come to greet someone from Mars it had been DeVore. Before he had known. Before the T'ang's son, Han Ch'in, had died and everything had changed.

But this time it was Karr. And Karr would be the hawk he'd fly against his prey. So maybe it was fitting that it should begin here, at Nanking, where DeVore had first slipped the net.

Ten minutes later he was seated across from a young duty captain as they travelled the fast-link between the City and the spaceport. Things were tight here. Tighter than he remembered them. They had banned all transit flights across the port. Only incoming or outgoing spacecraft were allowed in its airspace. Anything else was destroyed immediately, without warning. So this was the only way in – underneath the port.

Karr's ship was docking even as Tolonen rode the sealed car out to the landing bay. The noise was deafening. He could feel the vibrations in his bones; juddering the cradle into which he was strapped, making him think for a moment that the tiny vehicle was going to shake itself to pieces. Then it eased and the sound dropped down the register. With a hiss, a door irised open up ahead of him and the car slipped through, coming out into a great sunken pit, in the centre of which stood the squatly rounded shape of the interplanetary craft.

He could see the Tientsin clearly through the transparent walls of the car, its underbelly glowing, great wreaths of mist swirling up into the cold air overhead. The track curved sharply, taking his car halfway round the ship before it slowed and stopped. Guards met him, helped him out, standing back, their heads bowed, as he stretched his legs and looked about him.

He smiled, looking back at the craft. It had come all the way from Mars. Like a large black stone slapped down upon the great wei chi board of Chung Kuo. Karr. He could see the big man in his mind's eye even now, lifting Berdichev and breaking him. Ending it quickly, cleanly. Tolonen sniffed. Yes, in that he and Karr were alike. They understood how things worked at this level. It was no good dealing with one's enemies as one dealt with one's friends. Useless to play by rules that the other side constantly broke. In war one had to be utterly ruthless. To concede nothing – unless concession were a path to victory.

As he watched, an r-shaped gantry-lift moved on its rails across to the craft and attached itself to a portal on its uppermost surface. He walked towards it, habit making him look about him, as if, even here, he might expect attack.

Karr was in the first lift, packed in with twenty or thirty others. As the cage descended, Tolonen raised a hand in greeting but stayed where he was, just back from the others waiting there – maintenance crew, customs men and guards. Karr was carrying a small briefcase, the handle chained to his arm. At the barrier he was first in the queue, his Triple-A pass held out for inspection. Even so, it was some three or four minutes before he passed through.

The two men greeted one another warmly, Tolonen hugging the big man to him.

'It's good to see you, Gregor. You did well out there. I'm proud of you!'

'Thank you, sir. But you're looking well yourself.'

Tolonen nodded, then pointed at the briefcase. 'But what's this? Don't we pay you enough that you have to go into the courier business?'

Karr leaned closer, lowering his voice. 'It's my gift for the T'ang. I didn't want to say anything about it until I got back. You know how it is.'

Tolonen sighed. 'I know only too well. But tell me, what is it?'

Karr smiled. 'Berdichev's files. His personal records. Coded, of course, but I'm sure we can crack them. If they're what I think they are, we can polish off the Dispersionists for good.'

'Unless someone's done it already?'

Karr narrowed his eyes. 'The Executive killings?'

'It's one of the theories we're working on. Which is why I wanted you to take over the investigation from young Ebert. You've the nose for it.'

'Hmm...' Karr looked down. 'I've read the files.'

'And?'

'They make no sense. There's no real pattern to it. Good men and bad. It seems almost random. Except for the timing of it all.'

'Yes. But there has to be a connection.'

'Maybe...' Karr's face was clouded a moment, then he brightened. 'But how's that darling daughter of yours? She was a little tiger!'

Tolonen's face lit up. 'Gods, you should see her now, Gregor. Like Mu Lan, she is. A regular little warrior princess. Yes... you must come and train with us some time!'

Karr bowed low. 'I would be greatly honoured.'

'Good, then let's...'

Tolonen stopped. A man was standing just to Karr's right. Karr turned, reacting to the movement in Tolonen's eyes, then relaxed, smiling.

'First Advocate Kung!' Karr gave a small bow and put out his left hand to shake the outstretched hand of the Advocate. 'I hope all goes well for you.'

'Thank you, Major. And your own ventures... I hope they prove successful.'

The Advocate hesitated, looking at Tolonen. Karr saw what his hesitation implied and quickly made the introduction.

'Forgive me. First Advocate Kung, this is Marshal Tolonen, Head of the Council of Generals.'

Tolonen accepted the Advocate's bow with a tight smile. He knew this game too well to be caught in the web of obligation.

'I am delighted to make your acquaintance, Marshal Tolonen,' Kung said, bowing again. Then he turned and clicked his fingers. At once his valet approached, handing him a small case. 'However, it was you, Major Karr, whom I wanted to see. I was most grateful for your hospitality on board ship, and wanted to offer you a small token of my appreciation.'

Tolonen smiled inwardly. He would have to brief Karr afterwards on how to escape from this situation, otherwise First Advocate Kung would be calling upon him for favours from here until doomsday, playing upon the Major's need not to lose face.

'Thank you, Advocate, but—'

Karr saw the case falling away, Kung raising the handgun, both hands clasping the handle, and reacted at once, straight-arming Tolonen so that the old man went down. It was not a moment too soon. The explosion from the big old-fashioned gun was deafening. But he was already swinging the case at the Advocate's head. He felt it connect and followed through with a kick to the stomach. Kung fell and lay still.

There was shouting all about them. The valet had gone down on his knees, his head pressed to the floor, his whole body visibly shaking. It was clear he'd had nothing to do with the assassination attempt. Karr turned, looking for further assassins, then, satisfied there were none, looked down at Tolonen. The Marshal was sitting up, gasping, one hand pressed to his ribs.

Karr went down on one knee. 'Forgive me, Marshal, I...'

Tolonen waved aside his apology, the words coming from him wheezingly. 'You... saved my... life.'

'I wouldn't have believed it. He was Senior Advocate on Mars. A highly respected man.'

'Major!' The call came from behind Karr. He turned. It was one of the spaceport's Security captains.

'What is it?' he answered, standing, looking across to where the captain was kneeling over the fallen man.

'There's no pulse.'

Karr went across and knelt beside Kung, examining the body for himself. It was true. Advocate Kung was dead. Yet the wounds to the head and stomach were minimal. If he had *meant* to kill the man...

'Shit!' he said, turning to look at Tolonen, then frowned. 'What is it, sir?'

Tolonen's eyes were wide, staring at the corpse. As Karr watched him, the old man shuddered. 'Gods...' he said softly. 'It's one of them.'

Karr stared back at him a moment, then his eyes widened, understanding. 'A copy...' He turned and looked across at the valet. The man had been forced to his feet and was being held between two Security men, his head bowed in shame, his hands trembling with fear.

'*You!*' Karr barked at him, getting up and going across to him. 'Tell me, and tell me fast, did you notice anything different about your master? Anything unusual?'

The man shook his head abjectly. 'Nothing, honoured sir. Believe me. I knew nothing of his intentions.'

Karr studied the man a moment longer, then waved the guards away. 'Take him away and interrogate him. Whatever it takes. I want the truth from him.' He turned back. Tolonen was getting to his feet, one of the guards giving him a hand.

Tolonen turned, smiling his thanks, then put out his hand. 'Give me your knife, Sergeant.'

The guard did as he was told, then stood back, watching as Tolonen limped slowly across to the corpse.

He met Karr's eyes. 'If it's like the others...' Karr nodded. They both remembered that day when Han Ch'in had been assassinated. Recalled the team of copy humans who had come in from Mars to kill him. And now here they were again. A second wave, perhaps. Tolonen knelt by the body, setting the knife down at his side.

'Here,' Karr said, coming round to the other side of Kung. 'I'll do it.'

If it was like the others it would have a metal plate set into its chest. The real Kung would have been killed months ago.

Tolonen handed Karr the knife, then sat back on his knees, rubbing at his ribs again, a momentary flicker of pain in his face. 'Okay. Let's see what it is.'

Karr slit the Advocate's tunic open, exposing the flesh, then, leaning right over the body, he dug deeply into the flesh, drawing the blade across the corpse's chest.

Blood welled, flowed freely down the corpse's sides. They had not expected that. But there was something. Not a plate, as they'd both expected, but something much smaller, softer. Karr prised the knife beneath it and lifted it out. It was a wallet. A tiny black wallet no bigger than a child's hand. He frowned, then handed it across.

Tolonen wiped it against his sleeve, then turned it over, studying it. It seemed like an ordinary pouch; the kind one kept tobacco in. For a moment he hesitated. What if it was a bomb? He ought to hand it over to the experts. But he was impatient to know, for the man – and he *was* a man, there was no doubting that now – had almost killed him. He had been that close.

Gently he pressed the two ends of the wallet's rim towards each other. The mouth of the pouch gaped open. He reached in with two fingers, hooking out the thing within.

He stared at it a moment, then handed it across to Karr. He had known. The moment before he had opened it, he had known what would be inside. A stone. A single white *wei chi* stone. Like a calling card. To let the T'ang know who had killed him.

Tolonen met Karr's eyes and smiled bitterly.

'DeVore. This was DeVore's work.'

Karr looked down. 'Yes, and when he hears about it he'll be disappointed. Very disappointed.'

Tolonen was quiet a moment, brooding, then he looked back at Karr. 'Something's wrong, Gregor. My instincts tell me he's up to something. While we're here, distracted by this business. I must get back. At once. Jelka...'

Karr touched his arm. 'We'll go at once.'

★

DeVore turned in his chair and looked across at his lieutenant.

'What is it, Wiegand?'

'I thought you should know, sir. The Han has failed. Marshal Tolonen is still alive.'

'Ah...' He turned, staring out of the long window again, effectively dismissing the man. For a while he sat there, perfectly still, studying the slow movement of cloud above the distant peaks, the thin wisps of cirrus like delicate feathers of snow against the rich blue of the sky. Then he turned back.

He smiled. Like Wiegand, they would all be thinking he had tried to kill Tolonen, but that wasn't what he'd wanted. Killing him would only make him a martyr. Would strengthen the Seven. No, what he wanted was to destroy Tolonen. Day by day. Little by little.

Yes. Tolonen would have found the stone. And he would know it was his doing.

There was a secret lift in his room, behind one of the full-length wall charts. He used it now, descending to the heart of the warren. At the bottom a one-way mirror gave him a view of the corridor outside. He checked it was clear, then stepped out. The room was to the left, fifty ch'i along the corridor, at the end of a cul-de-sac hewn out of the surrounding rock.

At the door he paused and took a small lamp from his pocket, then examined both the locks. They seemed untouched. Satisfied, he tapped in the combinations and placed his eye against the indented pad. The door hissed back.

The girl was asleep. She lay there, face down on her cot, her long, ash-blonde hair spilling out across her naked shoulders.

He had found her in one of the outlying villages. The physical resemblance had struck him at once. Not that she would have fooled anyone as she was, but eighteen months of good food and expert surgery had transformed her, making the thousand yuan he'd paid for her seem the merest trifle. As she was now she was worth a million, maybe ten.

He closed the door and went across, pulling the sheet back slowly, careful not to wake her, exposing the fullness of her rump, the elegance of her back. He studied her a moment, then reached down, shaking her until she woke and turned, looking up at him.

She was so like her. So much so that even her 'father' would have had difficulty telling her from the real thing.

DeVore smiled and reached out to brush her face tenderly with the back of his hand, watching as she pushed up against it gratefully. Yes. She was nearly ready now.

'Who are you?' he asked her gently. 'Tell me what your name is.'

She hesitated then raised her eyes to his again. 'Jelka,' she said. 'My name is Jelka Tolonen.'

Jelka was kicking for Siang's throat when the far wall blew in, sending smoke and debris billowing across the practice arena.

The shock wave threw her backwards, but she rolled and was up at once, facing the direction of the explosion, seeing at a glance that Siang was dead, huge splinters jutting from his back.

They came fast through the smoke: three men in black clingsuits, breathing masks hiding their features, their heads jerking from side to side, their guns searching.

Ping Tiao assassins. She knew it immediately. And acted...

A backflip, then a single-handed grab for the exercise rope, her other hand seeking the wallbars.

The middle assassin fired even as she dropped. Wood splintered next to her. She had only to survive a minute and help would be here.

A minute. It was too long. She would have to attack.

She went low, slid on her belly, then was up, jumping high, higher than she had ever leaped before, her body curled into a tight ball. All three were firing now, but the thick smoke was confusing them; they couldn't see properly through their masks.

She went low again, behind Siang, taking a short breath before turning and kicking upward.

One of the men went down, his leg broken. She heard his scream and felt her blood freeze. The other two turned, firing again. Siang's body jerked and seemed to dance where it lay. But Jelka had moved on, circling them, never stopping, changing direction constantly, dipping low to breathe.

In a moment they would realize what she was doing and keep their fire at floor level. Then she would be dead.

Unless she killed them first.

The fact that there were two hindered them. They couldn't fire continuously for fear of killing each other. As she turned, they had to try to follow her, but the rapidity of her movements, the unpredictability of her changes of direction, kept wrong-footing them. She saw one of them stumble and took her chance, moving in as he staggered up, catching him beneath the chin with stiffened fingers. She felt the bones give and moved away quickly, coughing now, the smoke getting to her at last.

Fifteen seconds. Just fifteen seconds.

Suddenly – from the far end of the arena where the wall had been – there was gunfire. As she collapsed she saw the last of the assassins crumple, his body lifted once, then once again as the shells ripped into him.

And as she passed into unconsciousness she saw her father standing there, the portable cannon at his hip, its fat muzzle smoking.

CHUNG KUO

Chapter 50

SHADOWS

Tolonen sat at his daughter's bedside, his eyes brimming with tears.

'It was all a terrible mistake, my love. They were after me.'

Jelka shook her head, but a huge lump sat in her throat at the thought of what had happened.

She had spent the last ten days in bed, suffering from shock, the after-reaction fierce, frightening. It had felt like she was going mad. Her father had sat with her through the nights, holding her hands, comforting her, robbing himself of sleep to be with her and help her through the worst of it.

Now she felt better, but still it seemed that everything had changed. Suddenly, hideously, the world had become a mask – a paper-thin veil behind which lay another nightmare world. The walls were no longer quite as solid as they'd seemed. Each white-suited attendant seemed to conceal an assassin dressed in black.

It made it no better for her that they had been after her father. No, that simply made things worse. For she'd had vivid dreams – dreams in which he was dead and she had gone to see him in the T'ang's Great Hall, laid out in state, clothed from head to foot in the white cloth of death.

She stared at him a moment, her eyes narrowed slightly, as if she saw through the flesh to the bone itself, and while he met her staring eyes unflinchingly, something in the depths of him squirmed and tried to break away.

They had been *Ping Tiao*. A specially trained cell. But not Security trained, thank the gods.

He looked down at where his hands held those of his daughter. The audacity of the *Ping Tiao* in coming for him had shaken them. They knew now that the danger was far greater than they had estimated. The War had unleashed new currents of dissent: darker, more deadly currents that would be hard to channel.

His own investigations had drawn a blank. He did not know how they would have known his household routines. Siang? It was possible, but now that Siang was dead he would never know. And if not Siang, then who?

It made him feel uneasy – an unease he had communicated to Li Shai Tung when they were alone together. 'You must watch yourself, *Chieh Hsia*,' he had said. 'You must watch those closest to you. For there is a new threat. What it is, I don't exactly know. Not yet. But it exists.'

Bombs and guns. He was reaping the harvest he had sown. They all were. But what other choice had they?

To lie down and die.

Tolonen looked at his daughter, sleeping now, and felt all the fierce warmth of his love for her rise up again. A vast tide of feeling. And with it came an equally fierce pride in her. How magnificent she had been! He had seen the replay from the Security cameras and witnessed the fast, flashing deadliness of her.

He relinquished her hand and stood, stretching the tiredness from his muscles.

They would come again. He knew it for a certainty. They would not rest now until they had snatched his breath from him. Instinct told him so. And though it was not his way to wait passively, in this he found himself help-less, unable to act. They were like shadows. One strove to fight them and they vanished. Or left a corpse, which was no better.

No, there was no centre to them. Nothing substantial for him to act against. Only an idea. A nihilistic concept. Thinking this, he felt his anger rise again, fuelled by a mounting sense of impotence.

He would have crushed them if he could. One by one. Like bugs beneath his heel. But how did one crush shadows?

Fei Yen jumped down from her mount, letting the groom lead it away, then turned to face the messenger.

'Well? Is he home?'

The servant bowed low, offering the sealed note. Fei Yen snatched it from him impatiently, moving past him as if he were not there, making her way towards the East Palace. As she walked she tore at the seal, unfolding the single sheet. As she'd expected, it was from Li Yuan. She slowed, reading what he had written, then stopped, her teeth bared in a smile. He would be back by midday, after four days away on his father's business. She looked about her at the freshness of the morning, then laughed and, pulling her hair out of the tight bun she had secured it in to ride, shook her head. She would prepare herself for him. Would bathe and put on fresh clothes. The new silks he had sent her last week.

She hurried on, the delights of her early morning ride and the joy of his return coursing like twin currents in her blood.

She was about to go into her rooms when she heard noises further down the corridor, in the direction of Li Yuan's private offices. She frowned. That part of the East Palace was supposed to be out of bounds while Li Yuan was away. She took two steps down the corridor, then stopped, relieved. It was only Nan Ho. He was probably preparing the offices for his master's return. She was about to turn away, not wishing to disturb the Master of the Inner Chamber, when she realized what it was she had found strange. There had been voices...

She walked towards him; was halfway down the corridor when he turned.

'Lady Fei...'

She could see at once that he had not expected her. But it was more than that. His surprise in finding her there had not turned to relief as, in normal circumstances, it ought. No. It was almost as if he had something to hide.

'You know Prince Yuan will be here in two hours, Master Nan?'

He bowed his head deeply. 'He sent word, my lady. I was preparing things for him.'

'My husband is fortunate to have such an excellent servant as you, Master Nan. Might I see your preparations?'

He did not lift his head, but she could sense the hesitation in him and knew she had been right.

'You wish to *see*, my lady?'

'If you would, Master Nan. I promise not to disturb anything. I realize my husband has his set ways, and I'd not wish to cause you further work.'

'They are but rooms...'

'But rooms are like clothes. They express the man. Please, Master Nan, indulge my curiosity. I would like to see how Prince Yuan likes his room to be. It would help me as a wife to know such a thing.'

Nan Ho lifted his head and met her eyes. 'My lady, I...'

'Is there some secret, Master Nan? Something I should know?'

He bowed his head, then backed away, clearly upset by her insistence. 'Please, my lady. Follow me. But remember, I am but the Prince's hands.'

She hesitated, her curiosity momentarily tinged with apprehension. What could have flustered the normally imperturbable Nan Ho? Was it some awful thing? Some aspect of Li Yuan he wanted to keep from her? Or was it, instead, a surprise present for her? Something that, in insisting she see it, would spoil Yuan's plans?

For a moment she wondered whether she should withdraw. It was not too late. Li Yuan would hate it if she spoiled his surprise. But curiosity had the better of her. She followed Master Nan, waiting as he unlocked the great double doors again and pushed them open.

She walked through, then stopped dead, her mouth fallen open in surprise.

'You!'

The two girls had risen from the couch at her entrance. Now they stood there, heads bowed, hands folded.

She turned, her face dark with anger. 'What is the meaning of this, Master Nan? What are these creatures doing here?'

Nan Ho had kept his head lowered, bracing himself against her reaction. Even so, the savagery of her words surprised him. He swallowed and, keeping his head low, looked past her at the girls.

'My master said to bring them here this morning. I was to—'

Her shriek cut him off. 'Do you expect me to believe that, Nan Ho? That on the morning of his return my husband would have two such... *low* sorts brought to him?' She shuddered and shook her head, her teeth bared. 'No... I don't know what your plan is, Master Nan, but I know one thing, I can no longer trust you in your present position.'

He jerked his head up, astonished, but before he could utter a word in his defence, Fei Yen had whirled about and stormed across to where the two girls stood.

'And you!' she began. 'I know your sort! Turtles eating barley, that's what you are! Good-for-nothings! You hope to rise on your backs, *neh*?'

The last word was spat out venomously. But Fei Yen was far from finished.

'You! Pearl Heart... that's your name, isn't it?'

Overwhelmed by the viciousness of the attack, Pearl Heart could only manage a slight bob of her head. Her throat was dry and her hands trembled.

'I know why you're here. Don't think I'm blind to it. But the little game's over, my girl. For you and your *pimp* here.' Fei Yen shuddered, pain and an intense anger emphasizing every word. 'I know you've been sleeping with my husband.'

Pearl Heart looked up, dismayed, then bowed her head quickly, frightened by the look in Fei Yen's eyes.

'Well? Admit it!'

'It is true, my lady...' she began, meaning to explain, but Fei Yen's slap sent her sprawling back on to the couch. She sat, looking up at Fei Yen, her eyes wide with shock. Sweet Rose was sobbing now, her whole frame shaking.

Fei Yen's voice hissed at her menacingly. 'Get out... All of you ... *Get out!*'

Pearl Heart struggled up, then stumbled forward, taking her sister's arm as she went, almost dragging her from the room, her own tears flowing freely now, her sense of shame unbearable. Li Yuan ... How her heart ached to see him now; to have him hold her and comfort her. But it was gone. Gone forever. And nothing but darkness lay ahead.

Back in her rooms, Fei Yen stood there, looking about her sightlessly, the blackness lodged in her head. For a while she raged, inarticulate in her grief, rushing about the room uncontrollably, smashing and breaking, the pent-up anger pouring out of her in grunting, shrieking torrents. Then she calmed and sat on the edge of the huge bed, her respiration normalizing, her pulse slowing. Again she looked about her, this time with eyes that moved, surprised, between the broken shapes that lay littered about the room.

She wanted to hurt him. Hurt him badly, just as he had hurt her. But a part of her knew that was not the way. She must be magnanimous. She must swallow her hurt and pay him back with loving kindness. Her revenge would be to enslave him. To make him need her more than he needed anything in the whole of Chung Kuo. More than life itself.

She shuddered then gritted her teeth, forcing down the pain she felt. She would be strong. As she'd been when Han had died. She would deny her feelings and will herself to happiness. For the sake of her sons.

She went to the mirror, studying herself. Her face was blotchy, her eyes puffed from crying. She turned and looked about her, suddenly angered by the mess she had made – by her momentary lapse of control. But it was nothing she could not set right. Quickly she went into the next room, returning a moment later with a small linen basket. Then, on her hands and knees, she worked her way methodically across the floor, picking up every last piece of broken pottery or glass she could find. It took her much longer than she had thought, but it served another purpose. By the time she had finished she had it clearly in her mind what she must do.

She took the basket back into the dressing room and threw a cloth over it, then began to undress, bundling her discarded clothes into the bottom of one of the huge built-in cupboards that lined the walls. Then, naked, she went through and began to fill the huge, sunken bath.

She had decided against the new silks. Had decided to keep it as simple as she could. A single vermilion robe. The robe she had worn that first morning, after they had wed.

While the water steamed from the taps, she busied herself at the long table beneath the bathroom mirror, lifting the lids from the various jars and sniffing at them until she found the one she was searching for. Yes... She would wear nothing but this. His favourite. *Mei hua.* Plum blossom.

She looked at her reflection in the wall-length mirror, lifting her chin. Her eyes were less red than they'd been, her skin less blotchy. She smiled, hesitantly at first then more confidently. It had been foolishness to be so jealous. She was the match of a thousand serving girls.

She nodded to her image, determined, her hands smoothing her flanks, moving slowly upward until they cupped and held her breasts, her nipples rising until they stood out rigidly. She would bewitch him, until he had eyes for nothing but her. She remembered how he had looked at her – awed, his eyes round in his face – and laughed, imagining it. He would be hers. Totally, utterly hers.

Even so, she would have her vengeance on the girls. And on that pimp, Nan Ho. For the hurt they had caused her.

Her smile softened. And after she had made love to him, she would cook for him. A recipe her grandmother had left to her. Yes, while he slept she would prepare it for him. As a wife would.

Li Yuan yawned and stretched as the craft descended, then looked across. His personal secretary, Chang Shih-sen, was gathering his papers together, softly humming to himself.

'We've got through a lot of work in the last four days, Chang,' he said, smiling. 'I don't think I've ever worked so hard.'

Chang smiled back at him, inclining his head slightly. 'It is good to work hard, my lord.'

'Yes...' Li Yuan laughed, feeling the craft touch down beneath him. 'But today we rest, neh? I won't expect to see you until tomorrow morning.'

Chang bowed low, pleased by his master's generosity. 'As the Prince wishes.'

He turned back, looking through the portal at the activity in the hangar. A welcoming committee of four servants, led by Nan Ho, was waiting to one side, while the hangar crew busied themselves about the craft. Chang was right. He felt good despite his tiredness. He had spent more than eighty hours scanning files and interviewing, and now all but two of the places on the Project were filled. If his father agreed, they could go ahead with it within the week.

For one day, however, he would take a break from things. Would set all cares aside and devote himself to Fei Yen.

He looked down, grinning at the thought of her. Life was good. To have important business in one's life and such a woman to return to: that, surely, was all a man could ask for?

And sons...

But that would come. As surely as the seasons.

He heard the hatch hiss open and looked back at Chang Shih-sen. 'Go now, Chang. Put the papers in my study. We'll deal with them tomorrow.'

Chang bowed his head, then turned away. Li Yuan sat there a moment longer, thinking over the satisfactions of the last few days, recollecting the great feeling of *ch'i*, of pure energy, he had experienced in dealing with these matters. Unlike anything he had ever felt before. It made him understand things better. Made him realize why men drove themselves instead of staying at home in the loving arms of their wives. And yet it was good to come home, too. Good to have that to look forward to.

'A balance...' he said softly, then laughed and climbed up out of his seat, making his way down the short gangway, the three servants standing off to one side of him as he passed, their heads bowed low.

Nan Ho came forward as he reached the bottom of the steps, then knelt and touched his head to the ground.

'Welcome home, my lord.'

'Thank you, Master Nan. But tell me, where is Fei Yen?'

Nan Ho lifted his head fractionally. 'She is in her chambers, Prince Yuan. She has given orders for no one to disturb her. Not even her *amah*.'

Li Yuan grinned. 'Ah...'

'My lord...'

But Li Yuan was already moving past. 'Not now, Master Nan.'

Nan Ho turned, his extreme agitation unnoticed by the Prince. 'But, my lord...'

'Later, Nan Ho...'

He ran through the palace, past bowing servants, then threw open the doors to her apartments.

She was waiting for him, sitting on the huge bed, her legs folded under her, the vermilion robe she had worn on their wedding morning pulled about her. Her head was lowered in obedience, but there was a faint smile on her cherry lips.

'My lord?' she said, looking up, her eyes as dark as the night.

'My love...' he said, the words barely a whisper. The scent of plum blossom in the room was intoxicating. Closing the doors behind him, turning the great key, he went across and sat beside her on the bed, drawing her close.

'I've missed you...'

She shrugged the thin silk robe from her shoulders, then drew his head down into the cushion of her breasts, curling her legs about him.

'Make love to me, my lord.'

Afterwards he lay there next to her, staring at her in wonder.

'My love. My darling little swallow...'

She laughed then drew his face close, kissing him gently, tenderly. 'Now you know how much I missed you.'

'And I you...'

She pushed him back and sat up. 'But you're tired, husband. Why don't you sleep a while. And when you wake I'll have a meal ready for you.'

'But, my love, you needn't...'

She put a finger to his lips. 'I want to. Besides, I am your wife.'

He made to protest again, but she shook her head. With a brief laugh he lay back on the bed, closing his eyes. Within a minute he was asleep.

She studied him a moment, laying her hand softly on his chest, feeling the soft rise and fall of his breath, then gently covered the soft fold of his spent manhood. She shivered. He was still such a boy.

She went into the tiny pantry and busied herself, preparing the ingredients she'd had brought from the kitchen only an hour before. It would be two hours before it was ready. Time enough to bathe and change again.

She lay there a long time in the bath, soaking, looking through the open door at his sleeping figure on the bed. He was no bother really. Such a sweet boy. And yet...

As she floated there, she found herself remembering the sight of Tsu Ma in the water, his chest bared, his hair slicked back; the presence of his boots planted so solidly on the earth beneath the table; the deep, warm vibration of his voice.

Tsu Ma...

She opened her eyes again. The boy was still sleeping. Her husband, the boy.

She shivered, then stirred herself in the water. It was time she dressed and saw to his meal.

He woke to find her sat beside him on the bed, watching him. He turned his head, glancing at his timer, then yawned. He had slept more than two hours.

He sat up, breathing in deeply. 'What's that? It smells delicious.'

She smiled and turned away, returning moments later with a bowl and chopsticks. He took it from her, sniffed at it, then tucked in, holding the bowl close to his mouth, smacking his lips in appreciation.

'This is excellent. What is it?'

She was kneeling by the bed, watching him. 'It's a recipe of my grand-mother's. Wolfberry stewed with beef. A tonic for yang energy...' She laughed at his frown. 'An aphrodisiac, my husband. It enhances strength and endurance.'

He nodded enthusiastically. 'It's *good*. Your grandmother was a clever woman, and you, my love, are an excellent cook.'

She looked down, smiling. 'My husband is too kind.'

He was still a moment, watching her, astonished for the hundredth time by the fragile beauty of her, then began to eat again, realizing with a laugh just how hungry he had been.

'Is there anything else, husband? Anything I could get for you?'

He lowered the bowl, smiling at her. 'No. But that reminds me. There is something I must do. One small thing, then the rest of the day is free. We could go riding if you like.'

She looked back at him, her eyes bright. 'I'd like that.'

'Good. Then I'll call Nan Ho—'

Uncharacteristically, she interrupted him. 'Forgive me, husband, but that is not possible.'

'Not possible?' Li Yuan frowned, then gave a short laugh. 'I don't understand.'

She lowered her head, making herself small, submissive. 'I am afraid I had to dismiss Master Nan. He—'

'*Dismiss* him?' Li Yuan set the bowl aside and stood, looking down at her. 'Do I hear you right, Fei Yen? You have dismissed my Master of the Inner Chambers?'

'I had to, my lord...'

He shook his head, then looked away, past her. 'Tell me. Why did you dismiss him? What did he do?'

She glanced up at him, then bowed her head again. 'My lord will be angry with me...'

He looked back at her. 'Have I reason, then, to be angry with you?'

She looked up, meeting his eyes, her own dewed with tears. He hardened himself against the sight; even so, he felt himself moved. He had never seen her as beautiful as at that moment.

'I am your wife, my prince. Did I not have good reason to be angry with the man?'

'Fei Yen... talk sense. I don't follow what you're saying.'

She looked down, swallowing, a sudden bleakness in her face that tore at his heart. 'The girls... Nan Ho had brought girls...' A shudder passed through her. 'Girls for your bed ...'

He took a long breath. So ... She had misunderstood him. 'Forgive me, my love, but you have no reason to be angry with Nan Ho. It was not his doing. I asked him to bring those girls here. That was the thing I had to do.'

'And that makes it *better*?' Her voice was broken, anguished. 'How could you, Yuan? Am I not a good wife to you? Do I deny you anything?' She looked up at him, the hurt in her eyes almost too much for him. When she spoke again, her voice was a mere whisper. 'Or have you tired of me already?'

He was shaking his head. 'No... never. But you mistake me...'

'Mistake you?' Sudden anger flared in her eyes. 'You bring those girls here – girls who have shared your bed – and say I have mistaken you.'

'Fei Yen...'

'Then deny it! Look me in the eyes, husband, and deny that you haven't *had* them?'

'It wasn't like that...'

But his hesitation was enough for her. She tucked her head down bitterly, her hands pulling anxiously at the lap of her dress, then stood angrily.

'Fei Yen! You must believe me...'

'*Believe* you?'

He bristled, suddenly angered that she could think this of him, after all he had done to purify himself for her. Hadn't he cast the maids off? Hadn't he denied himself the pleasures of their company this last year? He shuddered. 'You had no business dismissing Master Nan! Who comes or goes in these rooms is *my* business, not yours!'

She turned away, suddenly very still. Her voice changed, became smaller and yet harder than before. 'Then let a thousand sing-song girls come. Let *them* be wives to you. But not Fei Yen...'

He went to her, taking her shoulders gently, wanting, despite his anger, to make things right between them, but she shrugged him off, turning violently to confront him, the fury in her eyes making him take a step back.

'What kind of a woman do you think I am? Do you think me like them? Do you really think I have no pride?' She drew herself up straighter. 'Am I not the wife of a great prince?'

'You know what you are!'

'No. I only know what you would have me be.'

He went to answer her, but she shook her head dismissively, her eyes boring into him. 'I tried hard, Li Yuan. Tried to dispel my doubts and tell myself it was Nan Ho. I tried to be loving to you. To be a good wife in every way. And how did you repay me? By cheating on me. By bringing in those *whores* behind my back...'

He felt something snap in him. This was too much. To call his girls whores. Even so, he answered her quietly.

'Be careful what you say, Fei Yen. Those girls were my maids. They took good care of me in my childhood. I have a great affection for them.'

She laughed scornfully. 'Whores...'

His bark of anger made her jump. 'Hold your tongue, woman!'

He stood there commandingly, suddenly very different; all childishness, all concession gone from him. He was shouting now. 'It is not your place to criticize *me*. I have done nothing wrong. Understand me? Nothing! But you...' He shivered with indignation. 'To have the audacity to dismiss Master Nan... Who in the God of Hell's name do you think you are?'

She did not answer. But her eyes glared back at him, their look wild and dangerous.

'Nan Ho stays, understand me? And I shall see the girls, as that's my wish.'

He saw a shudder of pure rage ripple through her and felt himself go cold inside. Her face seemed suddenly quite ugly; her lips too thin, her nose too brittle, her perfect brow furrowed with lines of anger. It was as if she were suddenly bewitched, her words spat back at him through a mask of hatred.

'If that's your wish, so be it. But do not expect me in your bed, Prince Yuan. Not tonight. Or any other night.'

His laughter was harsh; a bitter, broken sound; the antithesis of laughter. 'So be it.'

He turned and stormed from the room, slamming the door behind him as he went, his departing footsteps echoing, unrelenting, on the marble tiles.

★

DeVore was pressed up against the wall, Gesell's knife at his throat.

'Give me one good reason why I shouldn't kill you.'

DeVore stared back at Gesell, a vague, almost lazy sense of distaste in his eyes.

'Because I don't know what you're talking about.'

'You lying bastard. You killed those two men. You must have. You were the only one outside the central committee who knew what they were doing. Only you knew how crucial they were to our plans.'

There was a movement behind Gesell.

'Not the only one...'

Gesell turned. Mach had come in silently. He stood there, watching them. Ascher went across, confronting him, her anger, if anything, more pronounced than Gesell's.

'I say we kill him. He's betrayed us. Spat on us.'

Mach shook his head. 'He's done nothing. Let him go.'

'No!' Gesell twisted DeVore's collar tighter. 'Emily's right. We can't trust him after this.'

Mach pushed past the woman. 'For the gods' sakes, let him go, Bent. Don't you understand? I killed them.'

Gesell laughed uncertainly. 'You?'

Mach took the knife from Gesell's hand and sheathed it, then removed his hand from DeVore's collar. Only then did he turn and look at DeVore, inclining his head slightly.

'I apologize, Shih Turner. You must excuse my brother. He was not to know.'

'Of course,' DeVore stretched his neck slightly, loosening the muscles there.

Gesell rounded on Mach. 'Well? What the hell's been happening?'

'I'm sorry, Bent. I had no time to warn you. Besides, I wasn't sure. Not until I'd checked.'

'Sure of what?'

'They were Security. Both of them. They must have been sleepers. Records show they left Security five years back – a year before they joined us.'

A slight tightening about DeVore's eyes was the only sign that he was interested, but none of the others in the room noticed it, or the way he rubbed at his wrist, as if relieving an itch there; they were watching Mach, horrified by this new development.

'Security...' Gesell hissed through his teeth. 'Gods...'

'There are others, too. Three more. In two separate cells.'

'You made checks?'

Mach nodded. 'I'm keeping tags on them. They'll hear what happened. I want to see what they'll do. Whether they'll sit tight or run. If they run I want them. Alive, if possible. I want to find out what they're up to.'

Ascher was shaking her head. 'It doesn't make sense. If they had their men inside our organization, why didn't they act over Helmstadt?'

Mach glanced at DeVore, conscious of how much he was giving away simply by talking in front of him, but he'd had no choice. If Gesell had killed DeVore, they'd have been back to square one. Or worse: they might have found themselves in a tit-for-tat war with DeVore's lieutenants. It was almost certain that the man had given orders to that effect before he'd come here at Gesell's summons.

He turned, facing Ascher. 'I thought of that. But that's how it works sometimes. They're ordered to sit tight until the thing's big enough and ripe enough to be taken. They obviously thought that Helmstadt was worth sacrificing.'

'Or that you wouldn't succeed...' DeVore said.

Mach looked at him. 'Maybe...'

The three men had been an advance squad; trained technicians. Their job had been to locate the communications nerve-centres surrounding Bremen. It was a delicate, sensitive job; one upon which the success or failure of the whole attack depended. The idea was for them to place special devices at these *loci* – devices that the regular maintenance crews would think were innocuous parts of the complex of delicate wiring. Those devices would sit there, unused, for months, until the day when the *Ping Tiao* launched their attack. Then they would be triggered and Bremen would suffer a massive communications blackout.

That had been the plan. But now things were in chaos.

Gesell looked down. 'Do you think they've passed on what they knew?'

Mach shrugged, his expression bitter. Even killing them had not appeased his anger. 'I don't know. I hoped to keep one of them alive for questioning, but they fought hard. It was as if they'd been ordered not to be taken alive.'

'That's so.' Again DeVore entered the conversation. He moved closer. 'You should take one of them now, before they hear of it.'

Ascher nodded. 'I think he's right. What if they take poison or something?'

Mach shivered, then bowed his head. 'Okay. We'll take them now. But if it's like it was with the others, it won't be easy.'

DeVore narrowed his eyes, studying Mach. His respect for the man had grown enormously. Matton and Tucker had been two of his best men; not merely good at their task of infiltrating the Ping Tiao but good fighters, too. He was sorry to lose them. Sorry, too, to have had his network of spies uncovered, his eye amongst the Ping Tiao blinded. Now he would have to depend upon cruder means – on bribery and blackmail. Unsatisfactory means.

'Concentrate on just one of them,' he said, meeting Mach's eyes. 'Take him yourself. Then bind him tightly, so there's no chance of him harming himself. After that you should do things slowly. Time, that's all it needs. Time will break the spirit of any man. Then you'll find out what you want to know.'

Mach stared back at him steadily. 'You've done this?'

DeVore nodded. 'Many times.'

'Then I'll do as you say.'

DeVore smiled. 'Good.' But it would be too late. As soon as Mach had revealed what he had done, DeVore had pressed the tiny panel at his wrist, opening the channel that switched everything he was saying direct into the heads of his three surviving agents. Already his men would have heard his words and taken the appropriate action.

'And if we discover nothing?' Gesell asked, looking directly at DeVore.

'Then we continue. We must assume now that they know about our plan to attack Bremen, but not when or where we will strike. Or *how* precisely. Meanwhile, it would profit us to seem to change our plans. To look for other targets. And let them know…'

Mach looked up again, smiling for the first time since he had entered the room. 'I like that. A diversion…'

DeVore nodded and smiled back at him. 'What does Sun Tzu say? "The crux of military operations lies in the pretence of accommodating one's self to the designs of the enemy." Well, we shall seem to back off, as if discovered, but in reality we shall continue with our scheme. If they know nothing of your plans then no harm has been done today. And even if they do, they'll not expect us to pursue it after this, neh?'

Mach studied him thoughtfully a moment, then nodded. 'Yes. But I must go. Before they hear…'

*

Haavikko closed the door behind him then gave a small shudder, staring at the tiny slip of plastic in his hand. His senior officer had been only too glad to approve his new posting. From Major Erickson's viewpoint it must have seemed a blessing to be rid of him. He had been nothing but trouble. But now he was Karr's man; part of his special services unit. Still a lieutenant, but with a future now. And a friend.

He was meeting Kao Chen in two hours, but first there was one more thing to sort out. His sister, Vesa.

Vesa had been living in a small apartment in the Mids since their aunt had died a year back. Wrapped up in his own debauchery, he had not known of her plight until recently. But now he could do something. The job with Karr brought with it a private living unit in Bremen: four rooms, including the luxury of his own private bathroom. 'But you'll not be there that often,' Karr had warned him. 'Why not move your sister in?'

Vesa had jumped at the idea. She had held on to his neck and wept. Only then had he realized how lonely she had been, how great his neglect, and he had cried and held her tightly. 'It's all right,' he had whispered, kissing her neck. 'Everything will be all right.'

He tucked the transfer document into his tunic, then hurried along the corridors, taking a crowded lift down to the living quarters in the heart of the great multi-stack fortress.

She was waiting for him in the apartment. As he came in, she got up from the couch and came across, embracing him, her eyes bright with excitement.

'This is wonderful, Axel! We'll be happy here. I know we will.'

He smiled and held her to him, looking about the room. The apartment she had been in had been a single room – like his own, spartanly furnished – and she'd had to share washing and night-soil facilities. He gritted his teeth against the shame that welled up at the thought of what he'd let happen to her, then met her eyes again, smiling.

'We'll get a few bits and pieces, neh? Brighten things up a bit. Make it more personal. More us.'

She smiled. 'That would be nice.'

He let her go then stood there, watching her move about the room, disturbed by the thoughts, the memories that insisted on returning to him in her presence. He kept thinking of the girl in Mu Chua's House of the Ninth Ecstasy; the sing-song girl, White Orchid, who had looked so much like Vesa. He looked down. That was all behind him now.

'I thought I might cook you something ...'

He went across. 'Vesa, look... I'm sorry, but there's something I have to do tonight. Something urgent.'

She turned and looked at him, her disappointment sharp. 'But I thought...'

'I know. I'm sorry, I...'

'Is it your new job?'

He swallowed. 'Yes...' He hated lying to her, even over something as innocent as this, but it was important that she didn't get involved. It would be dangerous pinning Ebert down and he didn't want to put her at risk. Not for a single moment.

She came across. 'Never mind. Tomorrow night, neh? I'll cook something special.' She hesitated, watching his face, then smiled, her voice softening. 'You know, Axel, I'm proud of you. I always have been. You were always something more to me than just my big brother. You were like—'

'*Don't...*' he said softly, hurt by her words. Even so, he could not disillusion her; could not tell her the depths to which he had sunk. One day, perhaps, but not now. Maybe when he had nailed Ebert and the truth was out he would tell her everything. But not before.

Her eyes blazed with her fierce sisterly love of him. That look, like purity itself, seared him. He let his eyes fall before it.

'I must go.' He kissed her brow, then turned away, picking up the bag he had packed earlier. He went to the small desk in the corner and took a tiny notebook from the drawer.

'Your new job... is it dangerous?'

'It might be.'

'Then you'd best have this.'

She placed something in his left hand. It was a pendant on a chain. A circle of black and white jade, the two areas meeting in a swirling S shape. A *tai chi*, the symbol of the Absolute – of Yin and Yang in balance. He stared at it a moment, then looked up at her.

'It was Father's,' she said to his unspoken question. 'He left it to me. But now it's yours. It will protect you.'

He set his bag down and slipped the pendant over his neck, holding the jade circle a moment between his fingers, feeling the cool smoothness of its slightly convex surface, then tucked it away beneath his tunic.

He leaned forward and kissed her. 'Thank you... I'll treasure it.'

'And, Axel?'

He had bent down to lift his bag again. 'Yes?'

'Thank you... for all of this.'

He smiled. *Yes, he thought, but I should have done it years ago.*

Klaus Ebert poured two brandies from the big decanter then turned back, offering one to his son.

'Here...'

Hans raised his glass. 'To you, Father.'

Klaus smiled and lifted his glass in acknowledgment. He studied his son a moment, the smile never leaving his face, then nodded.

'There's something I wanted to speak to you about, Hans. Something I didn't want to raise earlier, while Mother was here.'

Hans raised his eyebrows, then took a deep swig of the brandy. 'The Company's all right, isn't it?'

His father laughed. 'Don't you read your reports, Hans? Things have never been healthier. We're twice the size we were five years back. If this continues...'

Hans reached out and touched his father's arm. 'I read the reports, Father. But that isn't what I meant. I've heard rumours about trouble in the mining colonies.'

'Yes...' Klaus eyed his son with new respect. He had only had the reports himself last night. It was good to see that, with all his other duties, Hans kept himself astride such matters. He smiled. 'That's all in hand. But that's not what I wanted to talk to you about. It's something more personal.'

Hans laughed, showing his fine, strong teeth. 'I thought we'd settled that. The Marshal's daughter seems a fine young woman. I'm proud of the way she handled those assassins. She'll make me a good wife, don't you think?'

Klaus nodded, suddenly awkward. 'Yes... Which is why I felt I had to speak to you, Hans. You see, I've been approached by Minister Chuang.'

Hans's look of puzzlement warmed him, reassured him. He had known at once that it was only vicious rumour. For his son to be involved in such an unsavoury business was unthinkable.

'I saw the Minister this morning,' he continued. 'He insisted on coming to see me personally. He was... most distressed. His wife, you see...'

He hesitated, thinking that maybe he should drop the matter. It was clear from Hans's face that he knew nothing about the allegations.

Hans was shaking his head. 'I don't follow you, Father. Is his wife ill?'

'Do you know the woman?'

'Of course. She's quite a popular figure in social circles. I've met her... what?... a dozen, maybe fifteen times.'

'And what do you make of her?'

Hans laughed. 'Why?' Then he frowned, as if suddenly making the connection. He set his glass down, anger flaring in his eyes. 'What is this? Is the Minister alleging something between me and his wife?'

Klaus gave the slightest nod, grateful to his son for articulating it; gratified by the anger he saw in his son's face.

'Well, damn the man!' Hans continued. 'And damn his wife! Is this the way they repay my friendship – with slurs and allegations?'

Klaus reached out and held his son's shoulder. 'I understand your anger, Hans. I too was angry. I told the Minister that I found his allegations incredible. I said that I would not believe a son of mine could behave as he was alleging you had behaved.' He shuddered with indignation. 'Furthermore, I told him either to provide substantive proof of his allegations or be prepared to be sued for defamation of character.'

Hans was staring at his father wide-eyed. 'And what did the Minister say to that?'

Klaus shivered again, then he gave a small laugh. 'He was most put out. He said his wife had insisted it was true.'

'Gods... I wonder why? Do you think...?'

'Think what?'

Hans let out a long breath. 'Perhaps I spurned the woman somehow. I mean, without knowing it... She's always been one to surround herself with young bucks. Perhaps it was simply because I've never fawned over or flattered her. Maybe her pride was hurt by that... Did the Minister say how or why she broke this incredible news to him? It seems... most extraordinary.'

Klaus shook his head. 'I never thought to ask. I was so outraged...'

'Of course. Perhaps the Minister had a row with his wife and to wound him she used my name. After all, you'd not expect the woman to use the name of one of her real lovers, would you?'

Klaus shrugged, out of his depth. 'I guess not...'

'Still... the *nerve* of it! To drag me into her sordid affairs. I've a mind to confront her and her husband and have it out with them.'

Klaus's fingers tightened on his son's shoulder. 'No, Hans. I'd prefer it if you didn't. I think it best if we keep the Minister and his wife at a distance.'

'But, Father...'

'No. I felt I had to mention it to you, but let this be the end of it. All right?'

Hans bowed his head. 'As my father wishes.'

'Good. Then let us talk of more pleasant matters. I hear young Jelka is being sent home tomorrow. Perhaps you should visit her, Hans. You could take her a small gift...'

Klaus nodded to himself, then drained his glass. Yes, it was probably as Hans said: there had been a row and Chuang's wife had used Hans's name to spite her husband. It was not Minister Chuang's fault. He had reacted as any man would. No, the woman was clearly to blame for everything. In the circumstances it would be inadvisable to allow bad feeling to develop from such shadows. Worse still to make an enemy of the Minister. Tomorrow he would send a gift – one of the new range of creatures, perhaps – to smooth things over.

He looked at his son again and smiled, pleased by what he saw. He could not have made a finer creature in his own vats. Though he said it himself, Hans was a masterpiece of genetics – the end product of two centuries of breeding. Like a god, he was. A king among men.

His smile softened. It was as the Seven said, there were levels among men, and Hans, his son, was at the pinnacle. He watched him drain his glass then smile back at him.

'I must get back. You know how it is...' Hans hesitated, then came forward and kissed his father's cheek. 'But thank you.'

Klaus grinned. 'For what? I am your father, Hans. Who, if not I, should defend you against such slanders? Besides, who knows you better than I, neh?'

Hans stepped back, then gave a small bow. 'Even so...'

Klaus lifted his chin, dismissing him. 'Go on, boy. Duty calls.'

Hans grinned, then turned away. When he was gone Klaus Ebert went across to the decanter and poured himself a second brandy. In times like these he was fortunate to have such a son. The kind of son a man could be proud of. A king. He smiled and raised the glass, silently toasting his absent son, then downed the drink in a single, savage gulp. Yes, a king among men.

Haavikko was sitting in Wang Ti's kitchen, Kao Chen's two-year-old daughter, Ch'iang Hsin, snuggled in his lap. Across from him Chen busied himself at his wife's side, preparing the meal. At his feet their five-year-old, Wu, was waging a ferocious battle between two armies of miniature dragons, their tiny power packs making them seem almost alive.

Looking about him, it was hard to imagine anything quite so different from the world he had inhabited these past ten years – a world as divorced from this simple domesticity as death was from life. He shuddered, thinking of it. A world of swirling smoke and smiling wraiths.

Wang Ti turned to him, wiping her hands on a cloth. 'And your sister, Axel? How is she?'

He smiled. 'She's fine, Wang Ti. Never happier.'

She looked at him a moment, as if to read him, then smiled. 'That's good. But you need a woman, Axel Haavikko. A wife.'

Chen laughed and glanced round. 'Leave the poor boy alone, Wang Ti. If he wants a wife he'll find one soon enough. After all, he's a handsome young man. And if an ugly fellow like me can find a wife...'

Wang Ti shook her head. 'Ugly is as ugly does. Never forget that, husband. Besides, if I close my eyes you are the handsomest of men!'

Husband and wife laughed; real warmth – a strong, self-deprecating humour – in their laughter.

'Anyway,' Chen added after a moment, 'marriage isn't always such a good thing. I hear, for instance, that our friend Ebert is to be married to the Marshal's daughter.'

Haavikko looked down, his mood changed utterly by the mention of Ebert.

'Then I pity the girl. The man's a bastard. He cares for nothing except his own self-gratification. Ask anyone who's served with him. They'll all tell you the same...'

Chen exchanged a brief look with Wang Ti as she set the bowls down on the table, then nodded. 'Or would, if they weren't so afraid of crossing him.'

Haavikko nodded. 'That's the truth. I've been watching him these past few weeks – spying on him, you might say – and I've seen how he surrounds himself with cronies. A dozen or more of them at times. He settles all their Mess bills and buys them lavish presents. In return they suck up to him, hanging on to his every word, laughing on cue. You know the kind. It's sickening. They call him "the Hero of Hammerfest", but he's just a shit. A petty little shit.'

Chen wiped his hands, then sat down across from Axel, his blunt face thoughtful. 'I know. I've seen it myself. But I can understand it, can't you? After all, as the world sees it he's a powerful man – a *very* powerful man – and those sucking up to him are only little men, *hsiao jen*. Socially they're nothing without him. But they hope to grow bigger by associating with him. They hope to rise on his coat tails.'

Wang Ti had been watching them, surprised by their change of mood. Gently, careful not to wake the sleeping child, she took Ch'iang Hsin from Haavikko's lap, then turned, facing her husband, the child cradled against her. 'Why so bitter, husband? What has the man ever done to you?'

'Nothing...' Chen said, meeting her eyes only briefly.

Haavikko looked between the two momentarily, noting the strange movement of avoidance in Chen's eyes, knowing it signified something, then leaned towards him again.

'There's one particularly vile specimen who hangs about with him. A man by the name of Fest. He was a cadet with me, and afterwards he served with Ebert and me under Tolonen. He's a captain now, of course. But back then...' Axel shuddered, then continued, 'Well, he was partly to blame for my downfall.'

Chen looked past Axel momentarily, lifting his chin, indicating to Wang Ti that she should wait in the other room, then he looked back at Axel, his face creased with concern, his voice suddenly softer, more sympathetic.

'What happened?'

Haavikko hesitated, then gave a small, bitter laugh. 'It was different then. I can see that now. The world, I mean. It was shaped differently. Not just in my head, but in its externals. You could trust the appearance of things much more. But even then there were some – Ebert among them – who were made... crooked, you might say. *Twisted*. And it's in their nature to shape others in their own distorted form.'

He glanced up, giving a little shiver, the sheer rawness of the hurt in his eyes making Chen catch his breath.

'We'd gone down to the Net, the day it happened. Ebert, Fest and I. We were after the assassins of the T'ang's Minister, Lwo Kang, and had been told to wait for a contact from our Triad connections there. Well, I didn't know that Ebert had arranged for us to stay in a sing-song house. It began there, I guess. He had me drugged and I... well, I woke up in bed with one of the girls. That was the start of it. It doesn't seem much, looking back, but it's... well, it's like I was clean before then; another person, unsullied, untouched by all those darker things that came to dominate me.'

'And that's what happened?'

Haavikko gave a bitter laugh. 'No. But that was where it began. I can see that now. The two things are inseparable. That and what followed. They were part of the same process. Part of the twistedness that emanates from that man.'

'Ebert, you mean?'

Haavikko nodded. 'Anyway... It was later that day. After we'd found the corpses of the assassins. After we'd gone to the Pit and seen Karr defeat and kill the adept, Hwa. Ebert made us go to the dressing rooms after the fight. He wanted to take Karr out to supper and share in his victory. It was something he didn't own, you see, and he wanted to buy it. But Karr was having none of it. And then Tolonen arrived and accepted Karr's services as guide. Oh, it's all linked. I see that clearly now. But back then... well, I thought things just happened – you know the saying, *Mei fa tzu*, it's fate. But there was a design to it. A shape.'

Haavikko paused, taking a deep, shuddering breath, then continued.

'It was as we were coming away from the assassin's apartment. We were in the sedan: Ebert, Fest and I. Ebert was sounding off, first about Karr and then about the General. He said things that he would never have dared say to the General's face. When I called him out for it, Fest came between us. He told me to forget what was said. But I couldn't...'

Haavikko was silent a moment, looking down at his hands. When he looked up again there was a strange sadness in his eyes.

'I don't regret what I did. Even now I don't think I could have acted any other way. It was just... well, let me tell you. When I was alone with the General I asked to be transferred. I felt unclean, you see. Of course, the old man asked me for my reasons. But when I tried to avoid giving them he ordered me to tell him what was up. So I did. I told him what was said in the sedan.'

Chen let out his breath. 'I see...'

'Yes. You can imagine. Tolonen was livid. He called Ebert and Fest back at once. It wasn't what I wanted – even then I didn't feel it was right to get Ebert thrown out of the force for something he'd said in a heated moment. But it was out of my hands at that stage. And then...'

'Fest backed him up?'

Haavikko nodded. 'I couldn't believe it. They were both so convincing. So much so that for months afterwards I kept asking myself whether I'd been wrong. Whether I'd imagined it all. Whether their version of things was really the truth. It was as if I'd had a bad dream. But it was one I couldn't wake from. And it all began back then. On that day ten years ago.'

A voice came from the shadows of the doorway behind them. 'I remember that day well.'

The two men looked round, surprised. There was a figure in the doorway: a giant of a man, his head stooped to clear the lintel, his broad shoulders filling the frame of the door. Karr.

Chen was up out of his chair at once. He went across and embraced the big man, smiling fiercely. 'Gregor! You should have said you were coming!'

Karr held his friend's arms a moment, smiling down into his face, then he looked back at Axel.

'Yes. I remember you well, Axel Haavikko. I remember you coming to watch me fight that day. But I never understood until today why you disappeared from things so suddenly. You have good cause to hate Major Ebert.'

Haavikko looked down, abashed. 'If I spoke out of turn, Major Karr...'

Karr laughed. He had put his arm about Chen's shoulders familiarly, like a father about his son's. 'Here, in Kao Chen's, we have an agreement, and you must be a party to it, Axel. In these rooms there is no rank, no formality, understand? Here we are merely friends. Kao Chen insists on it, and I...' His smile broadened. 'Well, as your senior officer, I insist upon it, too. Here Chen is Chen. And I am Gregor.'

Karr put out a hand. Haavikko stood up slowly, looking at the offered hand, hesitant even now to commit himself so far. But then he looked at

Chen and saw how his friend's eyes urged him to take Karr's hand.

He swallowed drily. 'I'm grateful. But there's one further thing you should know about me before you accept me here.' He looked from one to the other. 'You are good men, and I would have no secrets from you. You must know what I am. What I have done.'

'Go on,' Karr said, his hand still offered.

Haavikko stared back at Karr, meeting his grey eyes unflinchingly. 'You heard me say how it felt as though I were in a bad dream, unable to wake. Well, ten years I inhabited that nightmare, living it day and night. But then, a month or so ago, I woke from it. Again I found myself in bed in a sing-song house, and once again a strange girl was lying there beside me. But this time the girl was dead, and I knew that I had killed her.'

Karr's eyes narrowed. 'You *knew*?'

Haavikko shuddered. 'Yes. I remember it quite vividly.'

Karr and Chen looked at each other, some sign of understanding passing between them, then Karr looked back at Haavikko. His hand had not wavered for a moment. It was still offered.

'We have all done things we are ashamed of, Axel Haavikko. Even this thing you say you did – even that does not make you a bad man. Chen here, for instance. Would you say he was a good man?'

Haavikko looked at Chen. 'I would stake my life on it.'

'Then it would surprise you, perhaps, to learn that Kao Chen was one of the two assassins you were after that day ten years ago.'

Haavikko shook his head. 'No. He can't be. They were dead, both of them. I saw the *kwai*'s body for myself.'

Karr smiled. 'No. That was another man. A man Chen paid to play himself. It's something he's not proud of. Something he'd rather hadn't happened. Even so, it doesn't make him a bad man.'

Haavikko was staring at Chen now with astonishment. 'Of course... the scar.' He moved forward, tracing the scar beneath Chen's left ear with his forefinger. 'I know you now. You were the one on film. With your friend, the small man. In the Main of Level Eleven.'

Chen laughed, surprised. 'You had that on film?'

'Yes...' Haavikko frowned. 'But I still don't understand. If you were one of the killers...'

Karr answered for Chen. 'Li Shai Tung pardoned Kao Chen. He saw what

I saw at once. What you yourself also saw. That Chen is a good man. An honest man, when he's given the chance to be. So men are, unless necessity shapes them otherwise.'

'Or birth...' Haavikko said, thinking again of Ebert.

'So?' Karr said, his hand still offered. 'Will you join us, Axel? Or will you let what's past shape what you will be?'

Haavikko looked from one to the other, then, smiling fiercely at him, tears brimming at the corners of his eyes, he reached out and took Karr's hand.

'Good,' said Wang Ti, appearing in the doorway. She moved past them, smiling at Axel, as if welcoming him for the first time. 'And about time, too. Come, you three. Sit down and eat, before dinner spoils.'

Over the meal Karr outlined what had been happening since his return from Mars. Their one real clue from the Executive killings had led them to a small *Ping Tiao* cell in the Mids fifty li south of Bremen. His men were keeping a watch on the comings and goings of the terrorists. They had strict orders not to let the *Ping Tiao* know they were being observed, but it was not something they could do indefinitely.

'I'm taking a squad in tonight,' Karr said, sitting back from the table and wiping at his mouth with the back of his hand. 'In the small hours. I want to capture as many of the cell members as possible, so we'll need to be on our toes.'

Chen nodded, his mouth full. He chewed for a moment, then swallowed. 'That'll be difficult. They organize tightly and post guards at all hours. And then, when you do confront them, they melt away like shadows. You'll have to corner them somehow. But even if you do, I've heard they'd rather die than be captured.'

'Yes... but, then, so will most men if they're given no other option. Sun Tzu is right: leave but one avenue for a man to escape by and his determination to fight to the death will be totally undermined. He will recognize how sweet life is and cling to it. So it will be tonight. I'll offer them a pathway back to life. If I can capture just one of them, then perhaps we'll get to the bottom of this.'

Haavikko smiled. The man looked, even ate, like a barbarian, but he thought like a general. Tolonen had not been wrong all those years ago when he had recognized this in Karr. Haavikko put his chopsticks down and pushed his bowl away, then reached into his pocket and took the notebook from it.

'What's that?' Karr said, lifting his chin.

Haavikko handed it across the table. 'See for yourself.'

He watched as the big man thumbed through the notebook. At first Karr simply frowned, not understanding, then, slowly, he began to nod, a faint smile forming on his lips. Finally he looked up, meeting Axel's eyes.

'You did this all yourself?'

'Yes.'

Chen pushed his bowl aside then leaned forward, interested. 'What is it?'

Karr met his eyes thoughtfully. 'It's an analysis of the official investigation into Minister Lwo Kang's murder. And if I'm not mistaken, there are a number of things here that were never included in the findings of the T'ang's committee.'

Karr handed the book across to Chen, then looked back at Haavikko. 'May I ask why you did this, Axel?'

'I was ordered to.'

Karr laughed. 'Ordered to?'

'Yes, by General Tolonen, shortly before I was dismissed from his service. He asked me to compile a list of suspects, however improbable. Men who might have been behind the assassins. It was a direct order; one he never rescinded.'

Karr stared back at Haavikko, astonished. 'I see. But, then, surely Marshal Tolonen ought to have it?'

Haavikko hesitated, then looked down, shaking his head.

'I understand,' Karr said after a moment. 'And maybe you're right. After what happened there's no reason why he should trust you, is there? The Marshal would see it only as an attempt to get back at Ebert. He'd think you had invented this to discredit your enemies.'

Haavikko nodded, then looked up again, his eyes burning fiercely now. 'But you two know Ebert. You know what he is. So maybe that,' he indicated the notebook in Chen's hands, 'incomplete as it is, will help us nail the bastard.'

Chen looked up. 'He's right, Gregor. This makes interesting reading.'

'Interesting, yes, but not conclusive.'

Chen nodded thoughtfully, smiling back at Karr. 'Exactly. Even so, it's a beginning.'

'Something to work on.'

'Yes...'

Haavikko saw how the two men smiled knowingly at each other and felt a sudden warmth – a sense of belonging – flood through him. He was alone no longer. Now there were three of them, and together they would break Ebert, expose him for the sham – the hollow shell – he was.

Karr looked back at him. 'Is this the only copy?'

'No. There's a second copy, among some things I've willed to my sister, Vesa.'

'Good.' Karr turned to Chen. 'In that case, you hang on to that copy, Chen. I'm giving you two weeks' paid leave. Starting tomorrow. I want you to follow up some of those leads. Especially those involving men known to be friends or business acquaintances of the Eberts.'

'And if I find anything?'

There was a hammering at the outer door to the apartment. The three men turned, facing it, Kao Chen getting to his feet. There was an exchange of voices, then, a moment later, Wang Ti appeared in the doorway.

'It's a messenger for you, Major Karr,' she said, the use of Karr's rank indicating to them all that the man was within hearing in the next room.

'I'll come,' said Karr, but he was gone only a few moments. When he came back his face was livid with anger.

'I don't believe it. They're dead.'

'Who?' said Chen, alarmed.

'The Ping Tiao cell. All eight of them.' Karr's huge frame shuddered with indignation, then, his eyes looking inward, he nodded to himself. 'Someone knew. Someone's beaten us to it.'

Ebert was standing with his captain, Auden, laughing, his head thrown back, when Karr arrived. Signs of a heavy fire-fight were everywhere. Body bags lay off to one side of the big intersection, while the corridors leading off were strewn with wreckage.

Karr looked about him at the carnage, then turned, facing Ebert. 'Who was it?' he demanded.

'Who was what?' Ebert said tersely, almost belligerently.

'Was it DeVore?'

Ebert laughed coldly. 'What are you talking about, Major Karr? They were *Ping Tiao*. But they're dead now. Eight less of the bastards to worry about.'

Karr went still, suddenly realizing what had happened. 'You killed them?'

Ebert looked at Auden again, a faint smile reappearing. 'Every last one.'

Karr clenched his fists, controlling himself. 'Is there somewhere we can talk?' he said tightly. 'Somewhere private?'

Auden indicated a room off to one side. 'I'll post a guard.'

'No need,' said Karr. 'We'll not be long.'

When the door closed behind them, Karr rounded on Ebert.

'You stupid bastard! Why didn't you report what you were doing? Who gave you permission to go in without notifying me?'

Ebert's eyes flared. 'I don't need *your* permission!'

Karr leaned in on him angrily. 'In this instance you did! Marshal Tolonen put me in charge of this investigation, and while it's still going on, you report to me, understand me, Major Ebert? Your precipitate action has well and truly fucked things up. I had this cell staked out.'

Ebert looked up at the big man defiantly, spitting the words back at him. 'Well, I've simply saved you the trouble, haven't I?'

Karr shook his head. 'You arrogant bastard. Don't you understand? I didn't want them dead. We were going in tonight. I wanted at least one of them alive. Now the whole bloody lot of them will have gone to ground and the gods know when we'll get another chance.'

Ebert was glaring back at him, his hands shaking with anger. 'You're not pinning this on me, Karr. It's you who've fouled up, not me. I was just doing my job. Following up on evidence received. If you can't keep your fellow officers informed...'

Karr raised his hand, the fingers tensed, as if to strike Ebert in the face, then slowly let the tension ease from him. Violence would achieve nothing.

'Did any of our men get hurt?'

There was an ugly movement in Ebert's face. He looked aside, his voice subdued. 'A few...'

'Meaning what?'

Ebert hesitated, then looked back at him again. 'Four dead, six injured.'

'Four dead! *Ai ya!* What the fuck were you up to?' Karr shook his head, then turned away, disgusted. 'You're shit, Ebert, you know that? How could you possibly lose four men? You had only to wait. They'd have had to come at you.'

Ebert glared pure hatred at the big man's back. 'It wasn't as simple as that...'

Karr turned back. 'You fucked up!'

Ebert looked away, then looked back, his whole manner suddenly more threatening. 'I think you've said enough, Karr. Understand? I'm not a man to make an enemy of.'

Karr laughed caustically. 'You repeat yourself, Major Ebert. Or do you forget our first meeting?' He leaned forward and spat between Ebert's feet. 'There! That might jog your memory. You were a shit then and you're a shit now.'

'I'm not afraid of you, Karr.'

'No...' Karr nodded. 'No, you're not a coward, I'll grant you that. But you're still a disgrace to the T'ang's uniform, and if I can, I'll break you.'

Ebert laughed scornfully. 'You'll try.'

'Yes, I'll try. Fucking hard, I'll try. But don't underestimate me, Hans Ebert. Just remember what I did to Master Hwa that time in the Pit. He underestimated me, and he's dead.'

'Is that a threat?'

'Take it as you want. But between men, if you understand me. You go before the Marshal and I'll deny every last word. Like you yourself once did, ten years ago.'

Ebert narrowed his eyes. 'That officer with you... it's Haavikko, isn't it? I thought I recognized the little shit.'

Karr studied Ebert a moment, knowing for certain now that Haavikko had told the truth about him, then he nodded. 'Yes, Haavikko. But don't even think of trying anything against him. If he so much as bruises a finger without good reason, I'll come for you. And a thousand of your cronies won't stop me.'

Tsu Ma stood in the courtyard of the stables at Tongjiang, waiting while the groom brought the Arab from its stall. He looked about him, for once strangely ill at ease, disconcerted to learn that she had ridden off ahead of him.

He had tried to cast her from his mind, to drive from his heart the spell she had cast over him, but it was no use. He was in love with her.

In love. He laughed, surprised at himself. It had never happened to him before. Never, in all his thirty-seven years.

He had only to close his eyes and the image of her would come to him, taking his breath. And then he would remember how it had been, there on the island in the lantern light; how he had watched her lose herself in the tune she had been playing; how her voice had seemed the voice of his spirit singing, freed like a bird into the darkness of the night. And later, when he had been in the water, he had seen how she had stood behind her husband, watching him, her eyes curious, lingering on his naked chest.

One life? she had asked, standing in the doorway of the ruined temple. *One life?* as if it meant something special. As if it invited him to touch her. But then, when he had leaned forward to brush her cheek, her neck, she had moved back as if he had transgressed, and all his knowledge of her had been shattered by her refusal.

Had he been wrong? Had he misjudged her? It seemed so. And yet she had sent word to him. Secretly. A tiny, handwritten note, asking him to forgive her moodiness, to come and ride with her again. Was that merely to be sociable – for her husband's sake – or should he read something more into it?

He could still hear her words. *If I were free...*

Even to contemplate such an affair was madness. It could only make for bad blood between the Li clan and himself and shatter the age-old ties between their families. He knew that. And yet the merest thought of her drove out all consideration of what he *ought* to do. She had bewitched him, robbed him of his senses. That, too, he knew. And yet his knowledge was as nothing beside the compulsion that drove him. To risk everything simply to be with her.

He turned, hearing the groom return, leading the Arab.

'Chieh Hsia.' The boy bowed, offering the reins.

Tsu Ma smiled and took the reins. Then, putting one foot firmly in the stirrup, he swung up on to the Arab's back. She moved skittishly but he steadied her, using his feet. It was Li Yuan's horse; the horse he had ridden the last time he had come. He turned her slowly, getting used to her again, then dug in his heels, spurring her out of the courtyard and north, heading out into the hills.

He knew where he would find her: there at the edge of the temple pool where they had last spoken. She stood there, her face turned from him, her whole stance strangely disconsolate. Her face was pale, far paler than he remembered, as if she had been ill. He frowned, disconcerted, then, with a shock, recognized the clothes she was wearing. Her riding tunic was a pink that was almost white, edged with black, her trousers azure blue. And her hair... her hair was beaded with rubies.

He laughed softly, astonished. They were the same colours – the same jewels – as those he had worn the first time they had met. But what did it mean?

She looked up as he approached, her eyes pained, her lips pressed together, her mouth strangely hard. She had been crying.

'I didn't know if you would come.'

He hesitated, then went to her.

'You shouldn't be riding out so far alone...'

'No?'

The anger in her voice took him aback. He reached into his tunic and took out a silk handkerchief. 'Here... What's wrong?'

He watched her dab her cheeks, then wipe her eyes, his heart torn from him by the tiny shudder she gave. He wanted to reach out and wrap her in his arms, to hold her tight and comfort her, but he had been wrong before.

'I can't bear to see you crying...'

She looked back at him, anger flashing in her eyes again, then looked down, as if relenting. 'No...' She sniffed, then crushed the silk between her hands. 'It's not your fault, Tsu Ma.'

He wet his lips. 'Where is your husband?'

She laughed bitterly, staring down fixedly at her clenched hands. 'Husbands! What is a husband but a tyrant!'

Once more her anger surprised him.

She stared up at him, her eyes wide, her voice bitter. 'He sleeps with his maids. I've *seen* him.'

'Ah...' He looked down into the water, conscious of her image there in front of him. 'Maybe it's because he's a man.'

'A man!' She laughed caustically, her eyes meeting his in the mirror of the pool, challenging him. 'And men are different, are they? Have they different appetites, different needs?' She looked back at the reality of him, forcing him to look back at her and meet her eyes. 'You sound like my brothers. They think the fact of their gender makes them my superior when any fool can see...'

She stopped, then laughed, glancing at him. 'You see, even the language we use betrays me. I would have said, not half the man I am.'

He nodded, for the first time understanding her. 'Yet it is how things are ordered. Without it...'

'I know,' she said impatiently, then repeated it more softly, smiling at him. 'I know.'

He studied her, remembering what her cousin, Yin Wu Tsai, had said: that she had been born with a woman's body and a man's soul. How true that was. She looked so fragile, so easily broken, and yet there was something robust, something hard and uncompromising at the core of her. Maybe it was that – that precarious balance in her nature – that he loved. That sense he had of fire beneath the ice. Of earthiness beneath the superficial glaze.

'You are not like other women.'

He said it softly, admiringly, and saw how it brought a movement in her eyes, a softening of her features.

'And you? Are you like other men?'

Am I? he asked himself. *Or am I simply what they expect me to be?* As he stared back at her he found he had no answer. If to be T'ang meant he could never have his heart's desire, then what use was it being T'ang? Better never to have lived.

'I think I am,' he answered. 'I have the same feelings and desires and thoughts.'

She was watching him intently, as if to solve some riddle she had set herself. Then she looked away, the faintest smile playing on her lips. 'Yes... but it's the balance of those things that makes a man what he is, wouldn't you say?'

'And you think my balance... different?'

She looked up at him challengingly. 'Don't you?' She lifted her chin proudly, her dark eyes wide. 'I don't really know you, Tsu Ma, but I know this much – I know you would defy the world to get what you wanted.'

He felt himself go still. Then she understood him, too. But still he held back, remembering the mistake he had made before. To be rebuffed a second time would be unthinkable, unbearable. He swallowed and looked down.

'I don't know. I...'

She stood abruptly, making him look up at her, surprised.

'All this talking,' she said, looking across to where their horses were grazing. 'It's unhealthy. Unnatural.' She looked back at him. 'Don't you think?'

He stood slowly, fascinated by the twist and turn of her, her ever-changing moods. 'What do you suggest?'

She smiled, suddenly the woman he had met that first time, laughing and self-confident, all depths, all subtleties gone from her.

'I know what,' she said. 'Let's race. To the beacon. You know it?'

He narrowed his eyes. 'We passed it ten li back, no?'

'That's it.' Her smile broadened. 'Well? Are you game?'

'Yes,' he said, laughing. 'Why not? And no quarter, eh? No holding back.'

'Of course,' she answered, her eyes meeting his knowingly. 'No holding back.'

Fei Yen reined in her horse and turned to look back down the steep slope beneath the beacon. Tsu Ma was some fifty ch'i back, his mount straining, its front legs fighting for each ch'i of ground.

Her eyes shone and her chest rose and fell quickly. She felt exhilarated. It had been a race to remember.

Tsu Ma reined in beside her. His mount pulled its head back, over-excited by the chase. He leaned down to smooth it, stroking the broad length of its face. Then he looked up at her, his strong features formed into a smile of pleasure.

'That was good. I haven't enjoyed myself so much in years!'

He laughed, a deep, rich laugh that sent a shiver down her spine. Then he reached out and drew the hair back from where it had fallen across her face, his hand resting against her cheek.

It was the first time he had touched her.

He withdrew his hand and turned from her, standing in his saddle and looking out across the valley. They were at the highest point for twenty li about. To their backs and distant were the foothills of the Ta Pa Shan, but before them was only the plain.

Or what had once been the plain. In his grandfather's time the City had stretched only as far as Ch'ung Ch'ing. Now it covered all the lowlands of Sichuan. From where he looked it glistened whitely in the afternoon sunlight, a crystalline growth come to within a dozen li of where they were. He could not see its full extent from where he stood, but knew that it filled the Ch'ang Chiang basin, eight hundred li south to the mountains, a thousand li east to west. A vast plateau of ice.

He lowered himself in the saddle, then turned, looking back at her. She was watching him, concerned. Such a look as a wife gives her man. Thinking it, he smiled and remembered why he'd come.

He climbed down from his mount and went across to her.

'Come!' he said, offering her his hand to help her down. But this time he did not relinquish her. This time he turned her to face him, enveloping her in his arms.

She looked up at him expectantly, her mouth open, the bottom lip raised, almost brutal in what it implied. Her eyes seared him, so fierce was their demand. And her body, where he gripped it, seemed to force itself into him.

It was as he'd thought.

He kissed her, his mouth crushing hers, answering her need with his own. For a moment they struggled with each other's clothing, tearing at the lacing, freeing themselves, and then he had lifted her on to him and was thrusting deep into her, her legs wrapped about his back, her pelvis pushing down urgently to meet his movements.

'My love,' she said, her dark eyes wide, aroused, her fine, small hands caressing his neck. 'Oh, my love, my lord...'

Chapter 51

THE VEILED LIGHT

Li Yuan stood with his father at the centre of the viewing circle, looking down at the great globe of Chung Kuo, one hundred and sixty thousand li below. Down there it was night. Lit from within, the great, continent-spanning mass of City Europe glowed a soft, almost pearled white, bordered on all sides by an intensity of blackness. To the south, beyond the darkness of Chung Hai, the ancient Mediterranean, glowed City Africa, its broad, elongated shape curving out of view, while to the east – separated from City Europe by the dark barrier of the East European Plantations – City Asia began, a vast glacier, stretching away into the cold heart of the immense land mass.

The room in which they stood was dimly lit; the double doors at the top of the steps leading to the T'ang's private rooms were closed. It was warm in the room, yet, as ever, the illusion of coldness prevailed.

'What have you decided, Father?'

The T'ang turned to his son, studying him thoughtfully, then smiled.

'To wait to hear what the Marshal says. He saw the boy this morning.'

'Ah...' Li Yuan glanced at the slender folder he was carrying beneath his arm. In it were copies of the records Karr had brought back with him from Mars: Berdichev's personal files, taken from the corpse of his private secretary three days before Karr had caught up with Berdichev himself.

It had taken them two weeks to break the complex code, but it had been worth it. Besides giving them access to a number of secret SimFic files

– files that gave them the location of several special projects Berdichev had instigated – they had also contained several items of particular interest.

The first was a detailed breakdown of the events leading up to the assassination of the Edict Minister, Lwo Kang, ten years earlier. It was similar in many respects to the document Tolonen had brought to Li Shai Tung shortly after the event – the papers drawn up by Major DeVore. That document, and the web of inference and connection it had drawn, had been enough to condemn the Dispersionist, Edmund Wyatt, to death for treason. But now they knew it for what it was. Though Wyatt had been against the Seven, he had played no part in the murder of Minister Lwo. He had been set up by his fellow conspirators. But Wyatt's death, almost as surely as the destruction of the starship, *The New Hope*, had brought about the War that followed.

Li Yuan looked back at his father, conscious of how much he had aged in the years between. The War had emptied him; stripped him of all illusions. Five years back he would not have even contemplated the Wiring Project. But times had changed. New solutions were necessary. The second file was confirmation of that.

'About the Aristotle File, Father. Do we know yet if any copies were made?'

Li Shai Tung looked down past his feet at the blue-white circle of Chung Kuo.

'Nothing as yet, Yuan. So maybe we've been lucky. Maybe it wasn't disseminated.'

'Perhaps...' But both knew that the Aristotle File was too important – too potentially damaging to the Seven – for Berdichev to have kept it to himself: for it was no less than the true history of Chung Kuo; the version of events the tyrant Tsao Ch'un had buried beneath his own.

Li Yuan shivered, remembering the day when he had found out the truth about his world; recollecting suddenly the dream he had had – his vision of a vast mountain of bones, filling the plain from horizon to horizon. The foundations of his world.

'You know, Yuan, I was standing here the night you were born. It was late and I was looking down at Chung Kuo, wondering what lay ahead. I had been dreaming...'

He looked up, meeting his son's eyes.

'Dreaming, Father?'

The T'ang hesitated, then gave a small shake of his head. 'No matter... Just that it struck me as strange. The boy and all...'

He knew what his father meant.

The third file concerned a boy Berdichev had taken a personal interest in; a Clayborn child from the Recruitment Project for whom Berdichev had paid the extraordinary sum of ten million *yuan*.

Part of the file was a genotyping – a comparison of the child's genetic material to that of a man alleged to be his father. The result of the genotyping was conclusive. The man *was* the child's father. And the man's name? Edmund Wyatt – the person wrongly executed for orchestrating the assassination of the T'ang's minister, Lwo Kang.

That had been strange enough, but stranger yet was a footnote to the file: a footnote that revealed that far from the Aristotle File being the work of Soren Berdichev, as was claimed on the file itself, it had, in fact, been compiled and authored by the boy.

The fact that had struck them both, however, was the date the genotyping had given for the conception of the boy: a date that coincided with a visit Wyatt, Berdichev and Lehmann had made to a sing-song house in the Clay.

It was the day Li Yuan had been born. The day his mother, Lin Yua, had died giving birth to him, three months premature.

It was as if the gods were playing with them. Taking and giving, and never offering an explanation. But which was the boy – gift or curse? On the evidence of the Aristotle File he seemed – potentially, at least – a curse, yet if the reports on him were to be believed, he might yet prove the greatest asset the Seven possessed. The question that confronted them – the question they had met today to answer – was simple: should they attempt to harness his talents or should they destroy him?

There was a banging on the great doors at the far end of the room.

'Come in!' the T'ang answered, turning to face the newcomer.

It was Tolonen. He strode in purposefully then stopped three paces from the T'ang, clicking his heels together and bowing his head.

'*Chieh Hsia.*'

'Well, Knut? You've seen the boy. What do you think?'

Tolonen lifted his head, surprised by the abruptness with which the T'ang had raised the matter. It was unlike him. He turned briefly to Li Yuan, giving a small bow, then turned back to Li Shai Tung, a smile forming.

'I liked him, *Chieh Hsia*. I liked him very much. But that's not what you asked me, is it? You asked me whether I thought we could trust the boy. Whether we could risk using him in such a delicate area of research.'

'And?'

Tolonen shrugged. 'I'm still not certain, *Chieh Hsia*. My instinct tends to confirm what was in the file. He's loyal. The bond he formed with his tutor, T'ai Cho, for instance, was a strong one. I think that's inbred in his nature. But then there's the fight with the boy Janko to consider and the whole personality reconstruction business subsequent to that. He's not the same person he was before all that. We have to ask ourselves how that has affected him. Has it made him more docile and thus easier to control, or has it destabilized him? I can't answer that, I'm afraid. I really can't.'

The T'ang considered a moment, then nodded, smiling at his Marshal. 'Thank you, Knut. Your fears are the mirror of my own. I have already signed the death warrant. I was merely waiting to hear what you would say...'

'But, Father...' Li Yuan started forward, then stepped back, lowering his head. 'Forgive me, I...'

Li Shai Tung stared at his son a moment, surprised by his interruption. 'Well, Yuan?'

'A thousand apologies, Father. I was forgetting myself.'

'You wished to say something?'

Li Yuan bowed. 'I merely wished to caution against being too hasty in this matter.'

'Hasty?' The old T'ang laughed and looked across at Tolonen. 'I've been told I was many things in my life, but too hasty... What do you mean, Li Yuan?'

'The boy...' Li Yuan looked up, meeting his father's eyes. 'If what is written about the boy is true – if he is but a fraction as talented as is said... well, it would be a great waste to kill him.'

Li Shai Tung studied his son carefully. 'You forget why we fought the War, Li Yuan. To contain Change, not to sponsor it. This boy, Kim. Look at the mischief he has done already with his "talent". Look at the file he made. What is to prevent him making further trouble?'

Li Yuan swallowed, sensing that everything depended on what he said in the next few moments; that his father had not quite made up his mind, even now.

'With respect, Father, things have changed. We all know that. Our enemies are different now; subtler, more devious than ever before. And the means they use have changed, too. While we continue to ignore the possibilities of technology, they are busy harnessing it – against us.' Li Yuan looked down. 'It's as if the gods have given us a gift to use against our enemies. We have only to monitor him closely.'

'It was tried before. You forget just how clever the boy is.'

Li Yuan nodded. 'I realize that, Father. Even so, I think it can be done.'

The T'ang considered a moment, then turned back, facing Tolonen. 'Well, Knut? What do *you* think?'

Tolonen bowed. 'I think it could be done, *Chieh Hsia*. And would it harm to delay a little before a final decision is made?'

The T'ang laughed. 'Then I am outnumbered.'

Tolonen smiled back at him. 'Your one is bigger than our two, *Chieh Hsia*.'

'So it is. But I'm not a stupid man. Or inflexible.' He turned, facing his son again. 'All right, Yuan. For now I'll leave this in your hands. You'll arrange the matter of security with Marshal Tolonen here. But the boy will be your direct responsibility, understand me? He lives because you wish him to. You will keep my warrant with you and use it if you must.'

Li Yuan smiled and bowed his head low. 'As my father wishes.'

'Oh, and one more thing, Yuan. It would be best if you saw the boy yourself.' He smiled. 'You have two places left to fill on the Wiring Project, I understand.'

'I was... keeping them in case.'

'I thought as much. Then go. See the boy at once. And if your view of him confirms the Marshal's, then we'll do as you say. But be careful, Yuan. Knowledge is a two-edged sword.'

When his son was gone, the T'ang turned back, facing his Marshal.

'Keep me closely informed, Knut. Li Yuan is not to know, but I want us to know where Kim is at all times. Maybe he is what Yuan claims. But what can be used by us can just as easily be used by our enemies, and I'm loath to see this one fall back into their hands. You understand me clearly, Knut?'

'I understand, *Chieh Hsia*.'

'Good. Then let us speak of other matters. Your daughter, Jelka. How is she?'

Tolonen's eyes brightened. 'Much better, *Chieh Hsia*. She is back home now.'

Li Shai Tung frowned. 'Was that wise, Knut? I mean... to be back where the attack happened.'

'The doctors thought it best. And I... well, for all that happened, I felt she would be safest there.'

'I see. But she is still not quite as she was, I take it?'

Tolonen looked down, his eyes troubled. 'Not quite, *Chieh Hsia*.'

'I thought as much. Well, listen to me, Knut. Knowing how busy you'll be these next few weeks, I've come up with an idea that might put your mind at ease and allow Jelka to come to terms with her experience.'

'*Chieh Hsia?*'

'You remember the island your family owned? Off the coast of Finland?'

'Near Jakobstad?' Tolonen laughed. 'How could I forget? I spent a month there with Jenny, shortly after we were married.'

'Yes...' The two men were silent a moment, sharing the sweet sadness of the memory. 'Well,' said Li Shai Tung, brightening, 'why not take Jelka there for a few weeks?'

Tolonen beamed. 'Of course!' Then he grew quiet. 'But as you say, I am far too busy, *Chieh Hsia*. Who would look after her? And then there's the question of passes...'

The T'ang reached out and touched his Marshal's arm. It was like Tolonen not to abuse the Pass Laws; not to grant permissions for his family or friends. In all the years he had known him he had not heard of one instance of Tolonen using his position for his own advantage.

'Don't worry, Knut. I've arranged everything already. Passes, supplies, even a special squad to guard her.' He smiled broadly, enjoying the look of surprise on Tolonen's face. 'Your brother Jon and his wife have agreed to stay with her while she's there.'

Tolonen laughed. 'Jon?' Then he shook his head, overcome with emotion. 'I'm deeply grateful, *Chieh Hsia*. It will be perfect. Just the thing she needs. She'll love it, I know she will.'

'Good. Then you'll take her yourself, tomorrow. After you've sorted out this business with the boy. And, Knut?'

'Yes, *Chieh Hsia?*'

'Don't hurry back. Stay with her a night. See her settled in, neh?'

'Is that an order, *Chieh Hsia?*'

The T'ang smiled and nodded. 'Yes, dear friend. It is an order.'

*

After Tolonen had gone Li Shai Tung went through to his private rooms. He bathed and dressed in his evening silks, then settled in the chair beside the carp pond, picking up the *Hung Lou Meng*, the *Dream of Red Mansions*, from where he had discarded it earlier. For a while he tried to read, tried to sink back down into the fortunes of young Pao-yu and his beloved cousin, Tai-yu, but it was no good; his mind kept returning to the question of the Aristotle File and what it might mean for Chung Kuo.

His son, Li Yuan, had seen it all five years before, in those first few days after he had been told the secret of their world – the Great Lie upon which everything was built. He remembered how Yuan had come to him that night, pale and frightened, woken by a terrible dream.

Why do we keep the truth from them? Yuan had demanded. *What are we afraid of? That it might make them think other than we wish them to think? That they might make other choices than the ones we wish them to make?*

Back then he had argued with his son: had denied Yuan's insistence that they were the gaolers of Tsao Ch'un's City, the inheritors of a system that shaped them for ill. *We are our own men,* he had said. But was it so? Were they really in control? Or did unseen forces shape them?

He had always claimed to be acting for the best; not selfishly, but for all men, as the great sage Confucius had said a ruler should act. So he had always believed. But now, as he entered his final years, he had begun to question what had been done in his name.

Was there any real difference between concealing the truth from a man and placing a wire in his head?

Once he might have answered differently – might have said that the two things were different in kind – but now he was not so certain. Five years of war had soured him.

He sighed and looked back down at the page before closing the book.

'You were right, Pao-yu. All streams are sullied. Nothing is *ch'ing...* nothing pure.'

He stood, then cast the book down on to the chair angrily. Where had his certainty gone? Where the clarity of his youth?

He had foreseen it all, sixteen years ago, on that dreadful evening when his darling wife Lin Yua had died giving birth to his second son, Li Yuan.

That night he, too, had woken from an awful dream. A dream of the City sliding down into the maw of chaos; of dear friends and their children dead, and of the darkness to come.

Such dreams had meaning. Were voices from the dark yet knowing part of oneself, voices you ignored only at your peril. And yet they *had* ignored them. Had built a System and a City to deny the power of dreams, filling it with illusions and distractions, as if to kill the inner voices and silence the darkness deep within.

But you could not destroy what was inside a man. So maybe Yuan was right. Maybe it *was* best to control it. Now, before it was too late. For wasn't it better to have peace – even at such a price – than chaos?

He turned, annoyed with himself, exasperated that no clear answer came.

He stared down into the depths of the carp pool, as if seeking the certainty of the past, then shook his head. 'I don't know...' he sighed. 'I just don't know any longer.'

A single carp rose slowly, sluggishly, to the surface, then sank down again. Li Shai Tung watched the ripples spread across the pool, then put his hand up to his plaited beard, stroking it thoughtfully.

And Yuan, his son? Was Yuan as certain as he seemed?

He had heard reports of trouble between Yuan and Fei Yen. Had been told that the Prince, his son, had not visited his new wife's bed for several days, and not through pressure of work. He had been there in the palace at Tongjiang with her, and still he had not visited her bed. That was not right. For a couple to be arguing so early in their relationship did not bode well for the future. He had feared as much – had *known* the match was ill-conceived – but once more he had refused to listen to the voice within. He had let things take their course, like a rider letting go the reins. And if he fell – if his son's unhappiness resulted – who could he blame but himself?

Again the carp rose, swifter this time, as if to bite the air. There was a tiny splash as its mouth lifted above the surface, then it sank down again, merging with the darkness.

Li Shai Tung coiled his fingers through his beard, then nodded. He would let things be. Would watch closely and see how matters developed. But the cusp was fast approaching. He had told Tolonen otherwise, but the truth was that he was not so sure Li Yuan was wrong. Maybe it *was* time to put bit and bridle on the masses – to master events before the whole thing came crashing down on them.

It would not harm, at least, to investigate the matter. And if the boy, Kim, could help them find a way...

The T'ang turned, then bent down and retrieved the book, finding himself strangely reassured by its familiarity. He brushed at the cover, sorry that he had treated it so roughly. It was a book he had read a dozen times in his life; each time with greater understanding and a growing satisfaction. Things changed, he knew that now, after a lifetime of denying it, but certain things – intrinsic things – remained a constant, for all men at all times. And in the interplay of change and certainty each man lived out his life.

It was no different for those who ruled. Yet they had an added burden. To them was ordained the task of shaping the social matrix within which ordinary men had their being. To them was ordained the sacred task of finding balance. For without balance there was nothing.

Nothing but chaos.

It was late afternoon when Li Yuan finally arrived at Bremen. General Nocenzi had offered his office for the young Prince's use, and it was there, at the very top of the vast, three-hundred-level fortress, that he planned to meet the boy.

Kim was waiting down below. He had been there since his early morning session with Tolonen, unaware of how his fate had hung in the balance, but Li Yuan did not summon him at once. Instead he took the opportunity to read the files again and look at extracts from the visual record – films taken over the eight years of Kim's stay within the Recruitment Project.

They had given the boy the surname Ward, not because it was his name – few of the boys emerging from the Clay possessed even the concept of a family name – but because all those who graduated from the Project bore that name. Moreover, it was used in the *Hung Mao* manner – in that curiously inverted way of theirs, where the family name was last and not first.

Li Yuan smiled. Even that minor detail spoke volumes about the differences in cultures. For the Han had always put the family first. Before the individual.

He froze the final image, then shut down the comset and leaned forward to touch the desk's intercom. At once Nocenzi's private secretary appeared at the door.

'Prince Yuan?'

'Have them bring the boy. I understand there's a Project official with him, too. A man by the name of T'ai Cho. Have him come as well.'

'Of course, Excellency.'

He got up from the desk, then went to the window wall and stood there. He was still standing there, his back to them, when they entered.

T'ai Cho cleared his throat. 'Your Excellency... ?'

Li Yuan turned and looked at them. They stood close to the door, the boy a pace behind the official. T'ai Cho was a tall man, more than five ch'i, his height emphasized by the diminutive size of the Clayborn child. Li Yuan studied them a moment, trying to get the key to their relationship – something more than could be gained from the summaries in the file – then returned to the desk and sat, leaving them standing.

There were no chairs on the other side of the desk. He saw how T'ai Cho looked about him, then stepped forward.

'Excellency...' he began, but Li Yuan raised a hand, silencing him. He had noticed how the boy's eyes kept going to the broad window behind him.

'Tell me, Kim. What do you see?'

The boy was so small; more like a child of eight than a boy of fifteen.

Kim shook his head, but still he stared, his large eyes wide, as if afraid.

'Well?' Li Yuan insisted. 'What do you see?'

'Outside,' the boy answered softly. 'I see outside. Those towers. The top of the City. And there,' he pointed out past the Prince, 'the sun.'

He stopped, then shook his head, as if unable to explain. Li Yuan turned to look where he was pointing, as if something wonderful were there. But there were only the familiar guard towers, the blunted edge of the City's walls, the setting sun. Then he understood. Not afraid... *awed*.

Li Yuan turned back, frowning, then, trusting to instinct, came directly to the point.

'I've called you here because you're young, Kim, and flexible of mind. My people tell me you're a genius. That's good. I can use that. But I've chosen you because you're not a part of this infernal scientific set-up. Which means that you're likely to have a much clearer view of things than most, unsullied by ambition and administrative politics – by a reluctance to deal with me and give me what I want.'

He laced his fingers together and sat back.

'I want you to join a scientific team. A team whose aim is to develop and test out a new kind of entertainments system.'

Kim narrowed his eyes, interested but also wary.

'But that's not all I want from you. I want you to do something else for me – something that must be kept secret from the rest of the members of the team, even from Marshal Tolonen.'

The boy hesitated, then nodded.

'Good.' He studied the boy a moment, aware all the time of how closely the tutor was watching him. 'Then let me outline what I want from you. I have a file here of R & D projects undertaken by the late Head of SimFic, the traitor, Berdichev. Some are quite advanced, others are barely more than hypotheses. What I want you to do is look at them and assess – in your considered opinion – whether they can be made to work or not. More than that, I want you to find out what they *could* be used for.'

He saw the boy frown and explained.

'I don't trust the labels Berdichev put on these projects. What he says they were intended for and what their actual use was to be, were, I suspect, quite different.'

Again the boy nodded. Then he spoke.

'But why me? And why keep these things secret from the Marshal?'

Li Yuan smiled. It was as they'd said; the boy had a nimble mind.

'As far as Marshal Tolonen is concerned, these things do not exist. If he knew of them he would have them destroyed at once, and I don't want that to happen.'

'But surely your father would back you in this?'

He hesitated, then, looking at the official sternly, said, 'My father knows nothing of this. He thinks these files have already been destroyed.'

T'ai Cho swallowed and bowed his head. 'Forgive me, Highness, but...'

'Yes?' Li Yuan kept his voice cold, commanding.

'As I say, forgive me, but...' The man swallowed again, knowing how much he risked even in speaking out. 'Well, I am concerned for the safety of my charge.'

'No more than I, *Shih* T'ai. But the job must be done. And to answer Kim's other question, he is, in my estimation, the only one who can do it for me.'

Again T'ai Cho's head went down. 'But, Highness...'

Li Yuan stood angrily. 'You forget yourself, T'ai Cho!' He took a breath, calming himself, then spoke again, softer this time. 'As I said, I too am concerned for Kim's safety. Which is why, this very day, I interceded on the boy's behalf.'

He picked up the warrant and handed it to T'ai Cho, seeing his puzzlement change to bewildered horror. The blood drained from the man's face. T'ai Cho bowed his head low, one trembling hand offering the warrant back. 'And you had this rescinded, Highness?'

'Not rescinded, no. Postponed. Kim lives because I wish him to live. My father has made him my responsibility. But I am a fair man. If Kim does as I wish – if he comes up with the answers I want – then I will tear up this document. You understand, T'ai Cho?'

T'ai Cho kept his head lowered. 'I understand, Highness.'

Fei Yen was sleeping when he came in. He stood above her, in partial darkness, studying her features, then turned away, noting her discarded riding clothes there on the floor beside the bed. He undressed and slipped into the bed beside her, her body warm and naked beneath the silken sheets. He pressed up close, his hand resting on the slope of her thigh.

In the darkness he smiled, content to lie there next to her. He was too awake, too full of things, to sleep; even so he lay there quietly, mulling things over, comforted by her warmth, her presence there beside him.

He understood now. It was only natural for her to be jealous. It was even possible that some strange, feminine instinct of hers had 'known' about his earlier relationship with the girls.

He closed his eyes, listening to her gentle breathing, enjoying the sweet scent of her, the silkiness of her skin beneath his fingers.

After a while he rolled from her and lay there, staring up through layers of darkness at the dim, coiled shape of dragons in the ceiling mosaic, thinking of the boy. Kim was promising – very promising – and he would make sure he got whatever he needed to complete his work. And if, at the end of the year, his results were good, he would reward him handsomely.

That was a lesson he had learned from his father. Such talent as Kim had should be harnessed, such men rewarded well, or destroyed, lest they destroy you. Control was the key. Directed interest.

He stretched and yawned. He had not felt so good in a long time. It was as if everything had suddenly come clear. He laughed softly. It made him feel wonderful – hugely benevolent.

A smile came to his lips as he thought of the thing he had bought Fei Yen that very evening, after he had come from the boy. A thoroughbred; an Arab stallion bred from a line of champions. Its pure white flanks, its fine, strong legs, its proud, aristocratic face; all these combined to form an animal so beautiful he had known at once that she would want it.

He had bought it there and then and had it shipped directly to his stables, here at Tongjiang. He would take her first thing in the morning to see it.

He smiled, imagining the delight in her face. Beside him Fei Yen stirred and turned on to her back.

He sat up, then turned, looking down at her. Slowly, carefully, he drew back the sheet, letting it slip from her body, exposing her nakedness. For a while he simply looked, tracing the subtle curves of her body, his fingers not quite touching the surface of her flesh. So delicate she was. So beautiful.

Wake up, he thought. *Wake up, my love.* But the wish was unrequited. Fei Yen slept on.

He lay there a while longer, unable to relax, then got up and put on his robe. His desire had passed the point where he could lie there and forget it. He went through into the marbled bathroom and stood there in the shower, letting the cold, hard jets of water purge him.

He stood there a while longer, mindlessly enjoying the flow of water over his limbs. It was lukewarm now, but still refreshing, like a fall of rain, clearing his mind. He was standing there, his arms loose at his sides, when she appeared in the doorway.

'Yuan... ?'

He looked up slowly, half-conscious of her, and smiled. 'You're awake?'

She smiled, looking at him. 'Of course. I was waiting for you.'

She slipped off her robe and came to him, stepping into the shower beside him, then gave a small shriek.

'Why, Yuan! It's freezing!' She backed out, laughing.

He laughed, then reached up to cut the flow. Looking across, he saw how her skin was beaded with tiny droplets.

'Like jewels,' he said, stepping out.

She fetched a towel then knelt beside him, towelling him, tending to him obediently, as a wife ought. He looked down, feeling a vague desire for her, but he had doused his earlier fierceness.

She stood to dry his shoulders and his hair, her body brushing against his, her breasts and thighs touching him lightly as she moved about him. Turning from him, she went to the cupboards, returning a moment later with powders and unguents.

'A treat,' she said, standing before him, the fingers of one hand caressing his chest. 'But come, let's go through.'

She laughed, then pushed him through before her. It was a raw, strangely sexual laugh; one he had not heard from her before. It made him turn and look at her, as if to find her transformed, but it was only Fei Yen.

'I've missed you,' she said as she began to rub oils into his shoulders, his neck, the top of his back. 'Missed you a lot.' And as her fingers worked their way down his spine he shivered, the words echoing in his head. 'Like breath itself, my husband. Like breath itself...'

Six hours later and half a world away, in the Mids of Danzig Canton, Marshal Tolonen was standing in the main office of the newly formed Wiring Project. He had seen for himself the progress that had been made in the three days since he had last visited the laboratories. Then there had been nothing – nothing but bare rooms: now there was the semblance of a working facility, even though most of the equipment remained in cases, waiting to be unpacked.

Tolonen turned as Administrator Spatz came hurriedly into the room, bowing low, clearly flustered by the Marshal's unannounced arrival.

'Marshal Tolonen, please forgive me. I was not expecting you.'

Tolonen smiled inwardly. *No*, he thought, *you weren't. And I'll make it my practice in future to call here unannounced.* He drew himself upright. 'I've come to advise you on the last two appointments to your team.'

He saw how Spatz hesitated before nodding and wondered why that was, then, pushing the thought from his mind, he turned and snapped his fingers. At once his equerry handed him two files.

'Here,' Tolonen said, passing them across. 'Please, be seated while you study them.'

Spatz bowed, then returned behind his desk, opening the first of the files, running his finger over the apparently blank page, the warmth of his touch bringing the characters alive briefly on the specially treated paper. After only a minute he looked up, frowning.

'Forgive me, Marshal, but I thought the last two places were to be filled by working scientists.'

'That was the intention.'

Spatz looked aside, then looked back up at the Marshal, choosing his words carefully. 'And yet... well, this man T'ai Cho – he has no scientific background whatsoever. He is a tutor. His qualifications...'

Tolonen nodded. 'I understand your concern, *Shih* Spatz, but if you would look at the other file.'

Spatz nodded, still uncertain, then set the first file aside, opening the second. Again he ran his finger over the page. This time, however, he took his time, working through the file steadily, giving small nods of his head and occasional grunts of surprise or satisfaction. Finished, he looked up, smiling broadly. 'Why, the man's record is extraordinary. I'm surprised I've not heard of him before. Is he from one of the other Cities?'

Tolonen was staring past Spatz, studying the charts on the wall behind him. 'You could say that.'

Spatz nodded to himself. 'And when will he be joining us?'

Tolonen looked back at him. 'Right now, if you like.'

Spatz looked up. 'Really?' He hesitated, then nodded again. 'Good. Then there's just one small thing. A mistake, here on the first page.' He ran his finger over the top of the page again, then looked up, a bland smile on his lips. 'The date of birth...'

Tolonen looked away, snapping his fingers. A moment later his equerry returned. This time he was accompanied. 'There's no mistake,' Tolonen said, turning back.

There was a look of astonishment on Spatz's face. 'You mean, *this* is Ward?'

Tolonen looked across at the boy, trying to see him as Spatz saw him; as he himself had first seen him, before he had seen the films that demonstrated the boy's abilities. Looking at him, it seemed almost impossible that this scrawny, dark-haired creature was the accomplished scientist described in the personnel file, yet it was so. Berdichev had not been alone in believing the boy was something special.

Spatz laughed. 'Is this some kind of joke, Marshal?'

Tolonen felt himself go cold with anger. He glared back at Spatz and saw the man go white beneath the look.

Spatz stood quickly, bowing his head almost to the desktop. 'Forgive me, Marshal, I did not mean...'

'Look after him, Spatz,' Tolonen answered acidly. 'Allocate a man to take care of him for the next few days until his tutor, T'ai Cho, joins him.' He shivered, letting his anger drain from him. 'And you'll ensure he comes to no harm.'

He saw Spatz swallow drily and nodded to himself, satisfied that he had cowed the man sufficiently. 'Good. Then I'll leave him in your custody.'

Spatz watched Tolonen go, then turned his attention to the boy. For a moment he was speechless, still too astonished to take in what it all meant, then he sat heavily and leaned forward, putting his hand down on the summons button. At once his assistant appeared in the doorway.

'Get Hammond in here,' he said, noting the way his assistant's eyes went to the boy. 'At once!'

He sat back, steepling his hands together, staring across at the boy. Then he laughed and shook his head. 'No...'

Now that the first shock was wearing off, he was beginning to feel annoyed, angered by the position he had been put in. Now he would have to return the money he had been given to put names forward for the vacancies. Not only that, but in the place of real scientists he had been lumbered with a no-hoper and a child. What had he done to deserve such a thing? Who had he angered?

He looked down at his desk, sniffing deeply. 'So you're a scientist, are you, Ward?'

When the boy didn't answer, he looked up, anger blazing in his eyes. 'I'll tell you now. I don't know what game people higher up are playing, but I don't believe a word of that file, understand me? And I've no intention of letting you get near anything important. I may have to nursemaid you, but I'll be damned if I'll let you bugger things up for me.'

He stopped. There was someone in the doorway behind the boy.

'You called for me, *Shih* Spatz?'

'Come in, Hammond. I want you to meet our latest recruit, Kim Ward.'

He saw how Hammond glanced at the boy, then looked about the room before finally coming back to him.

'You mean, *you're* Ward?' Hammond asked, unable to hide his surprise. 'Well, the gods save us!' He laughed, then offered a hand. 'I'm Joel Hammond, Senior Technician on the Project.'

Seeing how the boy stared at Hammond's hand a moment before tentatively offering his own, how he studied the meeting of their hands, as if it were something wholly new to him, Spatz understood. The boy had never been out in society before. Had never learned such ways. It made Spatz think. Made him reconsider what was in the file. Or, rather, what wasn't. But he still didn't believe it. Why, the boy looked nine at the very most. He could not have done so much in so brief a time.

'I want you to look after the boy, Hammond. Until his... guardian arrives.'

'His guardian?' Hammond looked at Kim again, narrowing his eyes.

'T'ai Cho,' Kim answered, before Spatz could explain. 'He was my tutor at the Recruitment Project. He was like a father to me.'

Gods, thought Spatz, more convinced than ever that someone up-level was fucking with him; willing him to fail in this. A boy and his 'father', that was all they needed! He leaned forward again, his voice suddenly colder, more businesslike.

'Look, Hammond. Get him settled in. Show him where things are. Then get back here. Within the hour. I want to brief you more fully, right?'

Hammond glanced at the boy again, giving the briefest of smiles, then looked back at Spatz, lowering his head. 'Of course, Director. Whatever you say.'

'Well, Yuan, can I take it off yet?'

He turned her to face him, then untied the silk from her eyes, letting it fall to the ground. She looked up at him, wide-eyed, uncertain, then gave a small, nervous laugh.

'There,' he said, pointing beyond her, smiling broadly now.

She turned, looking about her at the stables. The grooms were standing about idly, their jobs momentarily forgotten, watching the young Prince and his bride, all of them grinning widely, knowing what Li Yuan had arranged.

She frowned, not knowing what it was she was looking for, then turned back, looking at him.

'Go on,' he said, encouraging her. 'Down there, in the end stall.'

Still she hesitated, as if afraid, making him laugh.

'It's a gift, silly.' He lowered his voice slightly. 'My way of saying that I'm sorry.'

'Down there?'

'Yes. Come, I'll show you...'

He took her arm, leading her to the stall.

'There!' he said softly, looking down at her.

She looked. There, in the dimness of the stall, stood the horse he had bought her. As she took first one, then another slow step towards it, the horse turned its long white head, looking back at her, its huge dark eyes assessing her. It made a small noise in its nostrils, then lowered its head slightly, as if bowing to her.

He saw the tiny shudder that went through her and felt himself go still as she went up to the horse and began to stroke its face, its flank. For a moment, that was all. Then she turned and looked back at him, her eyes wet with tears.

'He's beautiful, Yuan. Really beautiful.' She shivered, looking back at the horse, her hand resting in its mane, then lowered her head slightly. 'You shouldn't have, my love. I have a horse already.'

Yuan swallowed, moved by her reaction. 'I know, but I wanted to. As soon as I saw him I knew you'd love him.' He moved closer, into the dimness of the stall itself, and stood there beside her, his hand resting gently on the horse's flank.

She looked up at him, her eyes smiling through the tears. 'Has he a name?'

'He has. But if you want to you can re-name him.'

She looked back at the Arab. 'No. Look at him, Yuan. He is himself, don't you think? A T'ang among horses.'

He smiled. 'That he is, my love. An emperor. And his name is Tai Huo.'

She studied the Arab a moment longer, then turned back, meeting Li Yuan's eyes again. 'Great Fire... Yes, it suits him perfectly.' Her eyes searched Yuan's face, awed, it seemed, by his gift. Then, unexpectedly, she knelt, bowing her head until it touched her knees. 'My husband honours me beyond my worth...'

At once he pulled her up. 'No, Fei Yen. Your husband loves you. I, Yuan, love you. The rest...' he shuddered, 'well, I was mistaken. It was wrong of me...'

'No.' She shook her head, then lifted her eyes to his. 'I spoke out of turn. I realize that now. It was not my place to order your household. Not without your permission...'

'Then you have my permission.'

His words brought her up short. 'Your permission? To run your household?'

He smiled. 'Of course. Many wives do, don't they? And why not mine? After all, I have a clever wife.'

Her smile slowly broadened, then, without warning, she launched herself at him, knocking him on to his back, her kisses overwhelming him.

'Fei Yen!'

There was laughter from the nearby stalls, then a rustling of straw as the watching grooms moved back.

He sat up, looking at her, astonished by her behaviour, then laughed and pulled her close again, kissing her. From the stalls nearby came applause and low whistles of appreciation. He leaned forward, whispering in her ear. 'Shall we finish this indoors?'

In answer she pulled him down on top of her. 'You are a prince, my love,' she said softly, her breath hot in his ear, 'you may do as you wish.'

Joel Hammond stood there in the doorway, watching the boy unpack his things. They had barely spoken yet, but he was already conscious that the boy was different from anyone he had ever met. It was not just the quickness of the child, but something indefinable; something that fool Spatz hadn't even been aware of. It was as if the boy were charged with some powerful yet masked vitality. Hammond smiled and nodded to himself. Yes, it was as if the boy were a compact little battery, filled with the energy of knowing; a veiled light, awaiting its moment to shine out, illuminating the world.

Kim turned, looking back at him, as if conscious suddenly of his watching eyes.

'What did you do before you came here, Shih Hammond?'

'Me?' Hammond moved from the doorway, picking up the map Kim had set down on the table. 'I worked on various things, but the reason I'm here is that I spent five years with SimFic working on artificial intelligence.'

Kim's eyes widened slightly. 'I thought that was illegal? Against the Edict?'

Hammond laughed. 'I believe it was. But I was fortunate. The T'ang is a forgiving man. At least, in my case he was. I was pardoned. And here I am.'

He looked back down at the map again. 'This is the Tun Huang star chart, isn't it? I saw it once, years ago. Back in college. Are you interested in astronomy?'

The boy hesitated. 'I was.' Then he turned, facing Hammond, his dark eyes looking up at him challengingly. 'Spatz says he's going to keep me off the Project. Can he do that?'

Hammond was taken aback. 'I...'

The boy turned away, the fluidity of the sudden movement – so unlike anything he had ever seen before – surprising Hammond. A ripple of fear passed down his spine. It was as if the boy was somehow both more and, at the same time, less human than anyone he had ever come across. For a moment he stood there, his mouth open, astonished, then, like a thunderbolt, it came to him. He shuddered, the words almost a whisper.

'You're Clayborn, aren't you?'

Kim took a number of books from the bottom of his bag and added them to the pile on the desk, then looked up again. 'I lived there until I was six.'

Hammond shuddered, seeing the boy in a totally new light. 'I'm sorry. It must have been awful.'

Kim shrugged. 'I don't know. I can't remember. But I'm here now. This is my home.'

Hammond looked about him at the bare white walls, then nodded. 'I suppose it is.' He put the chart down and picked up one of the books. It was Liu Hui's *Chiu Chang Suan Shu*, his 'Nine Chapters on the Mathematical Art', the famous third-century treatise from which all Han science began. He smiled and opened it, surprised to find it in the original Mandarin. Flicking through, he noticed the notations in the margin, the tiny, beautifully drawn pictograms in red and black and green.

'You speak *Kuo-yu*, Kim?'

Kim straightened the books, then turned, looking back at Hammond. He studied him a moment, intently, almost fiercely, then pointed up at the overhead camera. 'Does that thing work?'

Hammond looked up. 'Not yet. It'll be two or three days before they've installed the system.'

'And Spatz? Does he speak *Kuo-yu*... Mandarin?'

Hammond considered a moment, then shook his head. 'I'm not sure. I don't think so, but I can check easily enough. Why?'

Kim was staring back at him, the openness of his face disarming Hammond. 'I'm not naive, *Shih* Hammond. I understand your position here. You're here on sufferance. We're alike in that. We do what we're told or we're nothing. *Nothing.*'

Hammond shivered. He had never thought of it in quite those terms, but it was true. He set the book down. 'I still don't follow you. What is all this leading to?'

Kim picked the book up and opened it at random, then handed it back to Hammond. 'Read the first paragraph.'

Hammond read it, pronouncing the Mandarin with a slight southern accent, then looked back at Kim. 'Well?'

'I thought so. I saw how you looked at it. I knew at once that you'd recognized the title.'

Hammond smiled. 'So?'

Kim took the book back, then set it beside the others on the shelf.

'How good is your memory?'

'Pretty good, I'd say.'

'Good enough to hold a code?'

'A code?'

'When you go back, Spatz will order you not to speak to me about anything to do with the Project. He'll instruct you to keep me away from all but the most harmless piece of equipment.'

'You know this?'

Kim looked round. 'It's what he threatened, shortly before you arrived. But I know his type. I've met them before. He'll do all he can to discredit me.'

Hammond laughed and began to shake his head, then stopped, seeing how Kim was looking at him. He looked down. 'What if I don't play his game? What if I refuse to shut you out?'

'Then he'll discredit you. You're vulnerable. He knows you'll have to do what he says. Besides, he'll set a man to watch you. Someone you think of as a friend.'

'Then what *can* I do?'

'You can keep a diary. On your personal comset. Something that, when Spatz checks on it, will seem completely innocent.'

'I see. But how will you get access?'

'Leave that to me.' Kim turned away, taking the last of the objects from the bag and setting it down on the bedside table.

'And the code?'

Kim laughed. 'That's the part you'll enjoy. You're going to become a poet, *Shih* Hammond. A regular Wang Wei.'

DeVore sat at his desk in the tiny room at the heart of the mountain. The door was locked, the room unlit but for the faint glow of a small screen to one side of the desk. It was late, almost two in the morning, yet he felt no trace of tiredness. He slept little – two, three hours at most a night – but just now there was too much to do to even think of sleep.

He had spent the afternoon teaching Sun Tzu to his senior officers: the final chapter on the employment of secret agents. It was the section of Sun Tzu's work that most soldiers found unpalatable. On the whole they were creatures of directness, like Tolonen. They viewed such methods as a necessary evil, unavoidable yet somehow beneath their dignity. But they were wrong. Sun Tzu had placed the subject at the end of his thirteen-chapter work with good reason. It was the key to all. As Sun Tzu himself had said, the reason why an enlightened prince or a wise general triumphed over their enemies whenever they moved – why their achievements surpassed those of ordinary men – was foreknowledge. And as Chia Lin had commented many centuries later, 'An army without secret agents is like a man without eyes or ears.'

So it was. And the more one knew, the more control one could wield over circumstance.

He smiled. Today had been a good day. Months of hard work had paid off. Things had connected, falling into a new shape – a shape that boded well for the future.

The loss of his agents amongst the *Ping Tiao* had been a serious setback, and the men he had bought from amongst their ranks had proved unsatisfactory in almost every respect. He'd had barely a glimpse of what the *Ping*

Tiao hierarchy were up to for almost a week now. Until today, that was, when suddenly two very different pieces of information had come to hand.

The first was simply a codeword one of his paid agents had stumbled upon: a single Mandarin character, the indentation of which had been left on a notepad Jan Mach had discarded. A character that looked like a house running on four legs. The character *yu*, the Han word for fish, the symbol of the *Ping Tiao*. It had meant nothing at first, but then he had thought to try it as an entry code to some of the secret *Ping Tiao* computer networks he had discovered weeks before but had failed to penetrate.

At the third attempt he found himself in. *Yu* was a new recruitment campaign; a rallying call; a word passed from lip to ear; a look, perhaps, between two sympathetic to the cause. DeVore had scrolled through quickly, astonished by what he read. If this were true...

But of course it was true. It made sense. Mach was unhappy with what was happening in the *Ping Tiao*. He felt unclean dealing with the likes of T'angs and renegade majors. What better reason, then, to start up a new movement? A splinter movement that would, in time, prove greater and more effective than the *Ping Tiao*. A movement that made no deals, no compromises. That movement was *Yu*.

Yu. The very word was rich with ambivalence, for *yu* was phonetically identical with the Han word meaning 'abundance'. It was the very symbol of wealth, and yet tradition had it that when the fish swam upriver in great numbers it was a harbinger of social unrest. *Yu* was thus the very symbol of civil disorder.

And if the file was to be trusted, *Yu* was already a force to be reckoned with. Not as powerful yet as the *Ping Tiao*, or as rich in its resources, yet significant enough to make him change his plans. He would have to deal with Mach. And soon.

The second item had come from Fischer in Alexandria. The message had been brief – a mere minute and three quarters of scrambled signal – yet it was potentially enough, in its decoded form, to shake the very foundations of the Seven.

He leaned forward and ran the film again.

The first thirty seconds were fairly inconclusive. They showed Wang Sau-leyan with his Chancellor, Hung Mien-lo. As Fischer entered, the T'ang turned slightly, disappearing from camera view as the Captain bowed.

'Are they here?' Wang asked, his face returning to view as Fischer came out of his bow.

'Four of them, *Chieh Hsia*. They've been searched and scanned, together with their gift.'

'Good,' the T'ang said, turning away, looking excitedly at his Chancellor. 'Then bring them in.'

'*Chieh Hsia...*'

DeVore touched the pad, pausing at that moment. Wang Sau-leyan was still in full view of Fischer's secreted camera, his well-fleshed face split by a grin that revealed unexpectedly fine teeth. He was a gross character, but interesting. For all his sybaritic tendencies, Wang Sau-leyan was sharp; sharper, perhaps, than any amongst the Seven, barring the young Prince, Li Shai Tung's son, Yuan.

He sat back, studying the two men for a time, unhappy that he had not been privy to their conversations before and after this important meeting. It would have been invaluable to know what it was they really wanted from their association with the *Ping Tiao*. But Fischer's quick thinking had at least given him an insight into their apparent reasons.

He let the film run again, watching as it cut to a later moment when Fischer had interrupted the meeting to tell the T'ang about the fire.

The camera caught the six men squarely in its lens: Wang Sau-leyan to the left, Hung Mien-lo just behind him, Gesell, Mach and their two companions to the right. It was an important moment to capture – one that, if need be, could be used against the T'ang of Africa. But equally important was the moment just before Fischer had knocked then thrown the doors wide; a moment when Wang's voice had boomed out clearly.

'Then you understand, *ch'un tzu*, that I cannot provide such backing without some sign of your good intentions. The smell of burning wheat, perhaps, or news of a whole crop ruined through the accidental pollution of a water source. I'm sure I don't have to spell it out for you.'

DeVore smiled. No, there was no need for Wang Sau-leyan to say anything more. It was clear what he intended. In exchange for funds he would get the *Ping Tiao* to do his dirty work – to burn the East European Plantations and create havoc with City Europe's food supplies, thus destabilizing Li Shai Tung's City. But would the *Ping Tiao* take such a radical action? After all, it was their people who would suffer most from the subsequent food shortages. Would they dare risk alienating public opinion so soon after they had regained it?

He knew the answer. They would. Because Mach was quite prepared to see the *Ping Tiao* discredited. He would be happy to see the *Yu* step into the gap left by the demise of the *Ping Tiao*. He was tired of deferring to Gesell. Tired of seeing his advice passed over.

Well, thought DeVore, pausing the film again, *perhaps we can use all these tensions – redirect them and control them. But not yet. Not quite yet.*

They had broken their meeting temporarily while the fire was dealt with, but when Fischer returned the *Ping Tiao* had already gone. Even so, the final forty seconds of the film provided a fascinating little coda on all that had happened.

Wang Sau-leyan was sitting in the far corner of the room, turning the gift the *Ping Tiao* had given him in his hands, studying it. It was the tiny jade sculpture of Kuan Yin that DeVore had given Gesell only the week before.

'It's astonishing,' Wang was saying. 'Where do you think they stole it?'

Hung Mien-lo, standing several paces away, looked up. 'I'm sorry, *Chieh Hsia*?'

'This.' He held the tiny statue up so that it was in clear view of the camera. 'It's genuine, I'd say. T'ang dynasty. Where in hell's name do you think they got their hands on it?'

Hung Mien-lo shrugged, then moved closer to his T'ang, lowering his voice marginally. 'More to the point, *Chieh Hsia*, how do you know that they'll do as you ask?'

Wang Sau-leyan studied the piece a moment longer, then looked back at his Chancellor, smiling. 'Because I ask them to do only what is in their own interest.' He nodded, then looked across, directly into camera. 'Well, Captain Fischer, is it out?'

The film ended there, as Fischer bowed, but it was enough. It gave DeVore plenty to consider. Plenty to use.

And that was not all. The day had been rich with surprises. A sealed package had arrived from Mars: a copy of the files Karr had taken from Berdichev's private secretary.

DeVore smiled. He had been telling his senior officers the story only that afternoon – the tale of T'sao and the Tanguts. The Tanguts were northern

enemies of the Han, and T'sao, the Han Chief of Staff, had pardoned a condemned man on the understanding that he would swallow a ball of wax,
dress up as a monk and enter the kingdom of the Tanguts. The man did so
and was eventually captured and imprisoned by the Tanguts. Under inter-
rogation he told them about the ball of wax and, when he finally shat it out,
they cut it open and found a letter. The letter was from T'sao to their own
Chief Strategist. The Tangut King was enraged and ordered the execution
both of the false monk and his own Chief Strategist. Thus did T'sao rid
himself of the most able man in his enemies' camp for no greater price than
the life of a condemned man.

So it was with the boy. He would be the means through which the Seven
would be destroyed; not, as Berdichev had imagined, from without but
from within. The Seven would be the agents of their own destruction. For
the boy carried within him not a ball of wax but an idea. One single, all-
transforming idea.

DeVore sat back. Yes, and Li Yuan would fight to preserve the boy, for he
honestly believed that he could control him. But Li Yuan had not the slightest conception of what the boy represented. No, not even the boy himself
understood that yet. But he had seen it at once, when Berdichev had first
shown him the Aristotle File. The file was a remarkable achievement, yet
it was as nothing beside what the boy was capable of. His potential was
astonishing. Li Yuan might as well try to harness Change itself as try to force
the boy's talents to conform to the needs of State.

Li Shai Tung had been right to sign the boy's death warrant. The old
man's gut instincts had always been good. It was fortunate that the War had
undermined his certainty. The old Li Shai Tung would have acted without
hesitation. But the old T'ang was effectively dead – murdered along with his
son, Han Ch'in, eight years ago.

DeVore nodded to himself, then cleared his mind of it, coming to the
final matter. The report was brief, no more than a single line of coded
message, yet it was significant. It was what he had been waiting for.

He took the tiny piece of crumpled paper from his top pocket and
unfolded it. It had been passed from hand to hand along a chain of trusted
men until it came into his own, its message comprehensible only to his
eyes. 'The tiger is restless,' it read. He smiled. The tiger was his codeword
for Hans Ebert, the handwriting on the paper that of his man, Auden.

He had recruited Auden long ago – years before he'd had the man appointed sergeant under Ebert – but Hammerfest had been a heaven-sent opportunity. Auden had saved Ebert's life that day, eight years ago, and Ebert had never forgotten it. Hans Ebert was a selfish young man but curiously loyal to those about him. At least, to those he felt deserved his loyalty, and Auden was one such. But it did not do to use all one's pieces at once. Life was like *wei chi* in that respect; the master chose to play a waiting game, to plan ahead. So he with Auden. But now he was capitalizing upon his long and patient preparation. It had been easy, for instance, for Auden to persuade Ebert into launching the premature attack on the *Ping Tiao* cell; an attack that had prevented Karr from discovering the links between the terrorists and himself. But that had been only the start: a test of the young man's potential. Now he would take things much further and see whether he could translate Ebert's restlessness into something more useful. Something more constructive.

Yes, but not through Auden. He would keep Auden dark, his true nature masked from Ebert. There were other ways of getting to Ebert; other men he trusted, if not as much. His uncle, Lutz, for instance.

DeVore folded the paper and tucked it back into the pocket. No. Auden was part of a much longer game: part of a shape that, as yet, existed in his head alone.

He smiled, then stood, stretching, his sense of well-being brimming over, making him laugh softly. Then he checked himself. *Have a care, Howard DeVore*, he thought. *And don't relax. It's only a shape you've glimpsed. It isn't real. Not yet. Not until you make it real.*

'But I will,' he said softly, allowing himself the smallest of smiles. 'Just see if I don't.'

The pimp was sleeping, one of his girls either side of him. The room was in semi-darkness, a wall-mounted flatlamp beside the door casting a faint green shadow across the sleeping forms. It was after fourth bell and the last of the evening's guests had left an hour back. Now only the snores of the sleepers broke the silence of the house.

Chen slid the door back quietly and slipped into the room. At once he seemed to merge with the green-black forms of the room. He hesitated a moment, his eyes growing accustomed to the subtle change in lighting, then crossed the room, quickly, silently, and stood beside the bed.

The pimp was lying on his back, his head tipped to one side, his mouth open. A strong scent of wine and onions wafted up from him: a tart, sickly smell that mixed with the heavy mustiness of the room.

Yes, thought Chen. *It's him all right. I'd know that ugly face anywhere.*

He took the strip of plaster from the pouch at his belt and peeled off two short lengths, taping them loosely to his upper arm. He threw the strip down then drew his gun. Leaning across the girl he placed it firmly against the pimp's right temple.

'Liu Chang...' he said softly, as the pimp stirred. 'Liu Chang, listen to me very carefully. Do exactly as I say or I'll cover the mattress with your brains!'

Liu Chang had gone very still. His eyes flicked open, straining to see the gun then focusing on the masked figure above him. He swallowed, then gave a tiny, fearful nod.

'What do you want?' he began, his voice a whisper, then fell silent as Chen increased the pressure of the gun against the side of his head.

Chen scowled at him. 'Shut up, Liu Chang,' he said, quietly but firmly. 'I'll tell you when to speak.'

The pimp nodded again, his eyes wide now, his whole body tensed, cowering before the gunman.

'Good. This is what you'll do. You'll sit up very slowly. *Very* slowly, understand? Make a sudden move and you're dead.' Chen smiled cruelly. 'I'm not playing games, Liu Chang. I'd as soon see you dead as let you go. But my people want answers. Understand?'

Liu Chang's mouth opened as if to form a question, then clicked shut. He swallowed deeply, sweat running down his neck, and nodded.

'Good. Now up.'

The pimp raised himself slowly on his elbows, Chen's gun pressed all the while against his right temple.

Chen nodded, satisfied, then thrust his right arm closer to the pimp. 'Take one of the strips of plaster from my arm and put it over the girl here's mouth. Then do the same with the other. And get no ideas about wrestling with me, Liu Chang. Your only chance of living is if you do what I say.'

Again there was that slight movement in the pimp's face – the sign of a question unasked – before he nodded.

As he leaned forward, Chen pushed slightly with the gun, reminding the pimp of its presence, but it was only a precaution – if the file was correct, he should have little bother with the man. Liu Chang had been an actor in the Han opera before he had become a pimp, more noted for his prowess in bed than his ability with a knife. Even so, it was wise to take care.

Liu Chang moved back from Chen, then leaned forward again, placing the strip across the sleeping girl's mouth. It woke her and for a moment she struggled, her hands coming up as if to tear it away. Then she saw Chen and the gun and grew still, her eyes wide with fear.

'Now the other.'

He noted the slight hesitation in Liu Chang and pressed harder with the gun.

'Do it!'

The pimp took the strip and placed it over the other girl's mouth. She too woke and, after a moment's struggle, lay still.

Good, Chen thought. *Now to business.*

'You're wondering what I want, aren't you, Liu Chang?'

Liu Chang nodded, twice.

'Yes. Well, it's simple. A girl of yours was killed here, a month or two ago. I'm sure you remember it. There was a young officer here when it happened. He thinks he did it. But you know better than that, don't you, Liu Chang? You know what really happened.'

Liu Chang looked down, then away; anything but meet Chen's gaze. He began to shake his head in denial, but Chen jabbed the gun hard against his head, drawing blood.

'This is no fake I'm holding here, Liu Chang. You'll discover that if you try to lie to me. I *know* you set Lieutenant Haavikko up. I even know how. But I want to know the precise details. And I want to know who gave the orders.'

Liu Chang looked down miserably. His heart was beating wildly now and the sweat was running from him. For a moment longer he hesitated, then he looked up again, meeting Chen's eyes.

'Okay, Liu Chang. Speak. Tell me what happened.'

The pimp swallowed, then found his voice. 'And if I tell you?'

'Then you live. But only if you tell me everything.'

Liu Chang shuddered. 'All right.' But from the way he glanced at the girls, Chen knew what he was thinking. If he lived, the girls would have to die. Because they had heard. And because Liu Chang could not risk them saying anything to anyone. In case it got back.

Only it doesn't matter, Chen thought, listening as the pimp began his tale; *because you're dead already, Liu Chang. For what you did. And for what you would do, if I let you live.*

Herrick's was forty *li* east of Liu Chang's, a tiny, crowded place at the very bottom of the City, below the Net.

It was less than an hour since Chen had come from the sing-song house; not time enough for anyone to have discovered Liu Chang's body, or for the girls to have undone their bonds. Nevertheless he moved quickly down the corridors – shabby, ill-lit alleyways that, even at this early hour, were busy – knowing that every minute brought closer the chance of Herrick being warned.

It had been two years since he had last been below the Net, but his early discomfort quickly passed, older habits taking over, changing the way he moved, the way he held himself. Down here he was *kwai* again, trusting to his instincts as *kwai*, and, as if sensing this, men moved back from him as he passed.

It was a maze, the regular patterning of the levels above broken up long ago. Makeshift barriers closed off corridors, marking out the territory of rival gangs, while elsewhere emergency doors had been removed and new corridors created through what had once been living quarters. To another it might have seemed utter confusion, but Chen had been born here. He knew it was a question of keeping a direction in your head, like a compass needle.

Even so, he felt appalled. The very smell of the place – the same wherever one went below the Net – brought back the nightmare of living here. He looked about him as he made his way through, horrified by the squalor, the ugliness of everything he saw, and wondered how he had stood it.

At the next intersection he drew in against the left-hand wall, peering round the corner into the corridor to his left. It was as Liu Chang had said. There, a little way along, a dragon had been painted on the wall in green. But it was not just any dragon: this dragon had a man's face; the thin, sallow face of a *Hung Mao*, the eyes intensely blue, the mouth thin-lipped and almost sneering.

If Liu Chang was right, Herrick would be there now, working. Like many below the Net, he was a night bird, keeping hours that the great City overhead thought unsociable. Here there were no curfews, no periods of darkness. Here it was always twilight, the corridors lit or unlit according to whether or not the local gang bosses had made deals with those Above who controlled the basic facilities like lighting, sanitation and water.

Such thoughts made him feel uneasy, working for the Seven, for it was they, his masters, who permitted the existence of this place. They who, through the accident of his birth here, had made him what he was – *kwai*, a hired knife, a killer. They had the wealth, the power, to change this place and make it habitable for those who wished it so, and yet they did nothing. Why? He took a deep breath, knowing the answer. Because without this at the bottom, nothing else worked. There had to be this place – this lawless pit – beneath it all. To keep those above in check. To curb their excesses. Or so they argued.

He set the thoughts aside. This now was not for the Seven. This was for Axel. And for himself. Karr's hunch had been right. If Ebert had been paying for Axel's debauchery, the chances were that he was behind the death of the girl. There were ways, Karr had said, of making a man think he'd done something he hadn't: ways of implanting false memories in the mind.

And there were places where one could buy such technology. Places like Herrick's.

Chen smiled. He was almost certain now that Karr was right. Liu Chang had said as much, but he had to be sure. Had to have evidence to convince Axel that he was innocent of the girl's murder.

Quickly, silently, he moved round the corner and down the corridor, stopping outside the door beside the dragon. At once a camera above the door turned, focusing on him.

There was a faint buzzing, then a voice – tinny and distorted – came from a speaker beside the camera.

'What do you want?'

Chen looked up at the camera and made the hand sign Liu Chang had taught him. This, he knew, was the crucial moment. If Liu Chang had lied to him, or had given him a signal that would tip Herrick off...

There was a pause, then, 'Who sent you?'

'The pimp,' he said. 'Liu Chang.'

Most of Herrick's business was with the Above. Illicit stuff. There were a thousand uses for Herrick's implants, but most would be used as they had on Haavikko – to leave a man vulnerable by making him believe he had done something he hadn't. In these days of response-testing and truth drugs it was the perfect way of setting a man up. The perfect tool for blackmail. Chen looked down, masking his inner anger, wondering how many innocent men had died or lost all they had because of Herrick's wizardry.

'What's your name?'

'Tong Chou,' he said, using the pseudonym he had used in the Plantation that time; knowing that if they checked the records they would find an entry there under that name and a face to match his face. Apparently they did, for there was a long pause before the door hissed open.

A small man – a Han – stood there in the hallway beyond the door. 'Come in, Shih Tong. I'm sorry, but we have to be very careful who we deal with here. I am Ling Hen, Shih Herrick's assistant.' He smiled and gave a tiny bow. 'Forgive me, but I must ask you to leave any weapons here, in the outer office.'

'Of course,' Chen said, taking the big handgun from inside his jacket and handing it across. 'You want to search me?'

Ling Hen hesitated a moment, then shook his head. 'That will not be necessary. However, there is one other thing.'

Chen understood. Again, Karr had prepared him for this. He took out the three ten thousand yuan 'chips' and offered them to the man.

Ling smiled, but shook his head. 'No, Shih Tong. You hold on to those for the moment. I just wanted to be sure you understood our house rules. Liu Chang's briefed you fully, I see. We don't deal in credit. Payment's up front, but then delivery's fast. We guarantee a tailored implant – to your specifications – within three days.'

'Three days?' Chen said. 'I'd hoped...'

Ling lowered his head slightly. 'Well... Come. Let's talk of such matters within. I'm sure we can come to some kind of accommodation, neh, Shih Tong?'

Chen returned the man's bow, then followed him down the hallway to another door. A guard moved back, letting them pass, the door hissing open at their approach.

It was all very sophisticated. Herrick had taken great pains to make sure he was protected. But that was to be expected down here. It was a cut-throat world. He would have had to make deals with numerous petty bosses to get where he was today, and still there was no guarantee against the greed of the Triads. It paid to be paranoid below the Net.

They stepped through, into the cool semi-darkness of the inner sanctum. Here the only sound was the faint hum of the air-filters overhead. After the stench of the corridors, the clean, cool air was welcome. Chen took a deep breath, then looked about him at the banks of monitors that filled every wall of the huge, hexagonal room, impressed despite himself. The screens glowed with soft colours, displaying a thousand different images. He stared at those closest to him, trying to make some sense of the complex chains of symbols, then shrugged; it was an alien language, all this, yet he had a sense that these shapes – the spirals and branching trees, the clusters and irregular pyramids – had something to do with the complex chemistry of the human body.

He looked across at the central desk. A tall, angular-looking man was hunched over one of the control panels, perfectly still, attentive, a bulky wraparound making his head seem grotesquely huge.

Ling turned to him, his voice hushed. 'Wait but a moment, *Shih* Tong. My master is just finishing something. Please, take a chair, he'll be with you in a while.'

Chen smiled, but made no move to sit, watching as Ling Hen went across to the figure at the control desk. If Karr was right, Herrick would have kept copies of all his jobs – as a precaution. But where? And where was the guardroom? Or had Herrick himself let them in?

He looked down momentarily, considering things. There were too many variables for his liking, but he had committed himself now. He would have to be audacious.

He looked up again and saw that Herrick had removed the wraparound and was staring across at him. In the light of the screens his face seemed gaunter, far more skeletal than in the dragon portrait on the wall outside.

'*Shih* Tong...' Herrick said, coming across, his voice strong and rich, surprising Chen. He had expected something thin and high and spiderish. Likewise his handshake. Chen looked down at the hand that had grasped his own so firmly. It was a long, clever hand, like a larger version of his dead companion, Jyan's. He looked up and met Herrick's eyes, smiling at the recollection.

'What is it?' Herrick asked, his hawk-like eyes amused.

'Your hand,' Chen said. 'It reminded me of a friend's hand.'

Herrick gave the slightest shrug. 'I see.' He turned away, looking round him at the great nest of screens and machinery. 'Well... you have a job for me, I understand. You know what I charge?'

'Yes... A friend of mine came to you a few months back. It was a rather simple thing, I understand. I want something similar.'

Herrick looked back at him, then looked down. 'A simple thing?' He laughed. 'Nothing I do is simple, Shih Tong. That's why I charge so much. What I do is an art form. Few others can do it. They haven't the talent, or the technical ability. That's why people come here. People like you, Shih Tong.' He looked up again, meeting Chen's eyes, his own hard and cold. 'So don't insult me, my friend.'

'Forgive me,' Chen said hastily, bowing his head. 'I didn't mean to infer... Well, it's just that I'd heard...'

'Heard what?' Herrick was staring away again, as if bored.

'That you were capable of marvels.'

Herrick smiled. 'That's so, Shih Tong. But even your "simple things" are beyond most men.' He sniffed, then nodded. 'All right, then, tell me what it was this friend of yours had me do for him, and I'll tell you whether I can do "something similar".'

Chen smiled inwardly. Yes, he had Herrick's measure now. Knew his weak spot. Herrick was vain, over-proud of his abilities. Well, he could use that. Could play on it and make him talk.

'As I understand it, my friend was having trouble with a soldier. A young lieutenant. He had been causing my friend a great deal of trouble, so, to shut him up, he had you make an implant of the man committing a murder. A young Hung Mao girl.'

Herrick was nodding. 'Yes... Of course. I remember it. In a brothel, wasn't it? Yes, now I see the connection. Liu Chang. He made the introduction, didn't he?'

Chen felt himself go very still. So it wasn't Liu Chang who had come here in that instance. He had merely made the introduction. Then why hadn't he said?

'So Captain Auden is a good friend of yours, Shih Tong?' Herrick said, looking at him again.

Auden...? Chen hesitated, then nodded. 'Ten years now.'

Herrick's smile tightened into an expression of distaste. 'How odd. I had the feeling he disliked Han. Still...'

'Do you think I could see the earlier implant? He told me about it, but... well, I wanted to see whether it really was the kind of thing I wanted.'

Herrick screwed up his face. 'It's very unusual, Shih Tong. I like to keep my customers' affairs discrete, you understand? It would be most upsetting if Captain Auden were to hear I had shown you the implant I designed for him.'

'Of course.' Chen saw at once what he wanted and took one of the chips from his pocket. 'Would this be guarantee enough of my silence, Shih Herrick?'

Herrick took the chip, examining it a moment beneath a nearby desk light, then turned back to Chen, smiling. 'I think that should do, Shih Tong. I'll just find my copy of the implant.'

Herrick returned to the central desk and was busy a moment at the keyboard, then he returned, a thin film of transparent card held delicately between the fingers of his left hand.

'Is that it?'

Herrick nodded. 'This is just the analog copy. The visual element of it, anyway. The real thing is much more complex. An implant is far more than the simple visual component.' He laughed coldly, then moved past Chen, slipping the card into a slot beneath one of the empty screens. 'If it were simply that it would hardly be convincing, would it?'

Chen shrugged, then turned in time to see the screen light up.

'No,' Herrick continued. 'That's the art of it, you see. To create the whole experience. To give the victim the *feeling* of having committed the act, whatever it is. The smell and taste and touch of it – the fear and the hatred and the sheer delight of doing something illicit.'

He laughed again, turning to glance at Chen, an unhealthy gleam in his eyes. 'That's what fascinates me, really. What keeps me going. Not the money, but the challenge of tailoring the experience to the man. Take this Haavikko, for instance. From what I was given on him it was very easy to construct something from his guilt, his sense of self-degradation. It was easy to convince him of his worthlessness – to make him believe he was capable of such an act. That, too, is part of my art, you see – to make such abnormal behaviour seem a coherent part of the victim's reality.'

Chen shuddered. Herrick spoke as if he had no conception of what he was doing. To him it was merely a challenge – a focus for his twisted genius. He lacked all feeling for the men whose lives he destroyed. The misery and pain he caused were, for him, merely a measure of his success. It was evil. Truly evil. Chen wanted to reach out and choke him to death, but first he had to get hold of the copy and get out with it.

An image began to form on the screen. The frozen image of a naked girl, sprawled on a bed, backing away, her face distorted with fear.

'There's one thing I don't understand, *Shih* Herrick. My friend told me that Haavikko took a drink of some kind. A drug. But how was the implant put into his head? He's only a junior officer, so he isn't wired. How, then, was it done?'

Herrick laughed. 'You think in such crude terms, *Shih* Tong. The implant isn't a physical thing – not in the sense that you mean. It's not like the card. That's only storage – a permanent record. No, the implant *was* the drug. A highly complex drug made up of a whole series of chemicals with different reaction times, designed to fire particular synapses in the brain itself – to create, if you like, a false landscape of experience. An animated landscape, complete with a predetermined sequence of events.'

Chen shook his head. 'I don't see how.'

Herrick looked away past him, his eyes staring off into some imaginary distance. 'That's because you don't understand the function of the brain. It's all chemicals and electrics, in essence. The whole of experience. It comes in at the nerve-ends and is translated into chemical and electrical reactions. I merely bypass those nerve-ends. What I create is a dream. But a dream more real, more vivid, than reality!'

Chen stared at him, momentarily frightened by the power of the man, then looked back at the screen. He didn't want to see the girl get killed. Instinctively, he reached across, ejecting the card, and slipped it into his pocket.

Herrick started forward. 'What the fuck...?'

Chen grabbed Herrick by the neck, then drew the knife from his boot and held it against his throat.

'I've heard enough, *Shih* Herrick. More than enough, if you must know.

But now I've got what I came for, so I'll be going.'

Herrick swallowed uncomfortably. 'You won't get out of here. I've a dozen guards...'

Chen pulled the knife towards him sharply, scoring the flesh beneath Herrick's chin. Herrick cried out and began to struggle, but Chen tightened his grip.

'You'd better do as I say, *Shih* Herrick, and get me out of here. Or you're dead. And not pretend dead. Really dead. One more shit comment from you and I'll implant this knife in the back of your throat.'

Herrick's eyes searched the room, then looked back at Chen. 'All right. But you'll have to let me give instructions to my men.'

Chen laughed. 'Just tell them to open the doors and get out of the way.' He raised his voice, looking up at one of the security cameras. 'You hear me, *Shih* Ling? If you want to see your boss again, do as I say. Any tricks and he's dead, and where will you be then? Runner to some gang boss, dead in a year.'

He waited a moment, searching the walls for signs of some technological trickery. Then there was a hiss and a door on the far side of the room slid open.

He pressed harder with the knife. 'Tell them I want to go out the way I came in, *Shih* Herrick. Tell them quickly, or you're dead.'

Herrick swallowed, then made a tiny movement of his head. 'Do as he says.'

They moved out slowly into the corridor, Chen looking about him, prepared at any moment to thrust the knife deep into Herrick's throat.

'Who are you working for?'

'Why should I be working for anyone?'

'Then I don't understand...'

No, thought Chen. *You wouldn't, would you?*

They came to the second door. It hissed open. Beyond it stood four guards, their knives drawn.

'No further,' said Ling, coming from behind them.

Chen met Ling's eyes, tightening his grip on Herrick's throat. 'Didn't you hear me, Ling? You want your master to die?'

Ling smiled. 'You won't kill him, Tong. You can't. Because you can't get out without him.'

Chen answered Ling's smile with his own, then pulled Herrick closer to him, his knife hand tensed.

'This is for my friend, Axel. And for all those others whose lives you have destroyed.'

He heard the cry and looked back, seeing how the blood had drained from Ling's face, then let the body fall from him.

'Now,' he said, crouching, holding the knife out before him. 'Come, Shih Ling. Let's see what you can do against a *kwai*.'

Chapter 52

ISLANDS

Jelka leaned out over the side of the boat, straining against the safety harness as she watched the rise and fall of the waves through which they ploughed, the old thirty-footer rolling, shuddering beneath her, the wind tugging at her hair, taking her breath, the salt spray bitingly cold against her face.

The water was a turmoil of glassy green threaded with white strands of spume. She let her hand trail in the chill water then put her fingers to her mouth, the flesh strangely cold and hard, her lips almost numb. She sucked at them, the salt taste strong in her mouth, envigorating. A savage, ancient taste.

She turned, looking back at the mainland. Tall fingers of ash-grey rock thrust up from the water, like the sunken bones of giants. Beyond them lay the City, its high, smooth, cliff-like walls dazzling in the morning light – a ribbon of whiteness stretching from north to south. She turned back, conscious suddenly of the swaying of the boat, the creak and groan of the wood, the high-pitched howl of the wind contesting with the noise of the engine – a dull, repetitive churring that sounded in her bones – and the constant slap and spray of water against the boat's side.

She looked up. The open sky was vast. Great fists of cloud sailed overhead, their whiteness laced with sunlight and shadow, while up ahead the sea stretched away, endless it seemed, its rutted surface shimmering with light.

Sea birds followed in their wake, wheeling and calling, like souls in torment. She laughed, the first laughter she had enjoyed in weeks, and squinted forward, looking out across the sun-dazzled water, trying to make out the island.

At first she could see nothing. Ahead, the sea seemed relatively flat, unbroken. And then she saw it, tiny at first, a vague shape of green and grey, melding and merging with the surrounding sea, as if overrun. Then, slowly, it grew, rising out of the sea to meet her, growing more definite by the moment, its basalt cliffs looming up, waves swelling, washing against their base.

Jelka looked across at her father. He sat there stiffly, one hand clenched and covered by the other, his neck muscles tensed; yet there was a vague, almost dreamy expression in his eyes. He was facing the island, but his eyes looked inward. Jelka watched him a moment, then looked away, knowing he was thinking of her mother.

As the boat slowed, drifting in towards the jetty, she looked past the harbour at the land beyond. A scattering of old stone houses surrounded the quayside, low, grey-green buildings with slate roofs of a dull orange. To the far right of the jetty a white crescent of shingle ended in rocks. But her eyes were drawn upward, beyond the beach and the strange shapes of the houses, to the hillside beyond. Pines crowded the steep slope, broken here and there by huge, iron-grey outcrops of rock. She shivered, looking up at it. It was all so raw, so primitive. Like nothing she had ever imagined.

She felt something wake deep within her and raised her head, sniffing the air, the strong scent of pine merging with the smell of brine and leather and engine oil, filling her senses, forming a single distinctive odour. The smell of the island.

Her father helped her up on to the stone jetty. She turned, looking back across the water at the mainland. It was hazed in a light mist, its walls of ice still visible yet somehow less impressive from this distance. It was all another world from this.

Sea birds called overhead, their cries an echoing, melancholy sound. She looked up, her eyes following their wheeling forms, then looked down again as a wave broke heavily against the beach, drawing the shingle with it as it ebbed.

'Well...' her father said softly. 'Here we are. What do you think?'

She shivered. It was like coming home.

Jelka looked across at the houses, her eyes moving from one to another, searching for signs of life.

'Which one?' she asked, looking back at him.

Her father laughed. 'Oh, none of those.' He turned, giving orders to the men in the boat, then looked back at her. 'Come on, I'll show you.'

Where the cobbles of the jetty ended they turned left, on to an old dirt track. It led up through the trees, away from the houses and the waterfront.

The track led up on to a broad ledge of smooth, grey rock. There was a gap in the screen of trees and a view across the water.

'Careful,' he said, his grip on her hand tightening as she moved closer to the edge. 'It can be slippery.' Then she saw it.

Below her was a tiny bay, enclosed on three sides by the dense growth of pines. But at one point the tree cover was broken. Directly across from her a great spur of rock rose abruptly from the water, and on its summit – so like the rock in colour and texture that at first she had not recognized it – was the house.

It was astonishing. Huge walls of solid stone rose sheer from the rock, ending in narrow turrets and castellated battlements. A steep roof, grey and lichen-stained, ran almost the length of the house. Only at its far end, where the sea surrounded it on three sides, was its steep pitch broken. There a tower rose, two storeys higher than the rest of the house, capped with a spire that shone darkly in the sunlight.

She stared at it open-mouthed, then looked back at her father.

'I thought it was a house.'

He laughed. 'It is. It was my great-grandfather's house. And his grand-father's before that. It has been in our family nine generations.'

She narrowed her eyes, not understanding. 'You mean, it's ours?'

'It was. I guess it still is. But it is for Li Shai Tung to say whether or not we might use it.'

'It seems so unfair.'

He stared at her, surprised, then answered her. 'No. It has to be like this. The peasants must work the land. They must be outside. And the Seven, they carry a heavy burden, they need their estates. But there is not land enough for all those who wish to live outside. There would be much resentment if we had this and others didn't.'

'But, surely, if it's ours...'

He shook his head firmly. 'No. The world has grown too small for such luxuries. It's a small price to pay for peace and stability.'

They walked on, still climbing. Then he turned back, pointing downward. 'We have to go down here. There are some steps, cut into the rock. They're tricky, so you'd better take my hand again.'

She let him help her down. It was cooler, more shaded beneath the ridge, the ground rockier, the long, straight trunks of the pines more spaced.

'There,' he said, pointing between the trees.

She looked. About fifty *ch'i* distant was a grey stone wall. It was hard to tell how high it was from where she stood, but it seemed massive – twice her father's height at least. To the left it turned back on itself, hugging the cliff's edge, to the right it vanished among the trees. Partway along was a huge gate, flanked by pillars, and beyond that – still, silent in the late morning sunlight – the tower.

She turned to find him looking past her at the house, a distant smile on his face. Then he looked down at her.

'Kalevala,' he said softly. 'We're home, Jelka. Home.'

'Do you know the thing I miss most?'

T'ai Cho looked up. Kim was standing in the doorway, looking past him. T'ai Cho smiled. 'What's that?'

'The pool. I used to do all my best thinking in the pool.'

He laughed. 'Well, can't we do something about that?'

Kim made a small movement of his head, indicating the overhead camera. 'Only if *Shih* Spatz wills it.'

T'ai Cho stared at Kim a moment longer, then returned to his unpacking.

'I'll put in a request,' he said, taking the last few things from the bag, then stowed it beneath the pull-down bed. 'He can only say no, after all.' He looked up again, meeting Kim's eyes with a smile. 'Anyway, how have things been? Is the work interesting?'

Kim looked away. 'No,' he answered quietly.

T'ai Cho straightened up, surprised. 'Really? But I thought you said the research would be challenging?'

'It is. But Spatz is not letting me get anywhere near it.'

T'ai Cho stiffened. 'But he can't do that! I won't let him do that to you, Kim. I'll contact the Prince.'

'No. I don't want to go running to Prince Yuan every time I've a problem.'

T'ai Cho turned angrily. 'But you must. The Prince will have Spatz removed. He'll—'

'You don't see it, do you, T'ai Cho? You think this is just a piece of pure science research, but it's not. I saw that at once. This is political. And very sensitive. Practically all of the men they've recruited for it are vulnerable. They were on the wrong side in the War and now they've no choice but to work on this. All except for Spatz, and he's no scientist. At least, not a good enough scientist to be on a project of this nature. He's here to keep a lid on things.'

'But that's outrageous.'

'Not at all. You see, someone wants this project to fail. That's why Spatz was made Administrator. Why Tolonen was appointed overall Head.'

'And you'll allow that to happen?'

'It's not up to me, T'ai Cho. I've no choice in the matter. I do as I'm told. As I've always done. But that's all right. There are plenty of things we can do. All that's asked of us is that we don't rock the boat.'

T'ai Cho was staring at him, his eyes narrowed. 'That's not like you, Kim. To lie down and do nothing.'

Kim looked down. 'Maybe it wasn't, in the past. But where did it ever get me?' He looked up again, his dark eyes searing T'ai Cho. 'Five years of Socialization. Of brutal reconditioning. That was my reward for standing up for myself. But next time they won't bother. They'll just write me off.' He laughed bitterly. 'I'm not even a citizen. I exist only because Li Yuan wills my existence. You heard him yourself, T'ai Cho. That's the fact of the matter. So don't lecture me about doing something. Things are easy here. Why make trouble for ourselves?'

T'ai Cho stared back at him, open-mouthed, hardly believing what he was hearing. 'Well, you'd better go,' he said abruptly. 'I've things to do.'

'I'm sorry, T'ai Cho. I...'

But T'ai Cho was busying himself, putting clothes into a drawer.

'I'll see you later, then?' Kim asked, but T'ai Cho made no sign that he had even heard.

Back in his room Kim went to the desk and sat there, the first of the poems Hammond had written on the screen in front of him.

It had not been easy, making T'ai Cho believe he had given up. It had hurt to disillusion his old tutor, but it was necessary. If he was to function at all in this set-up, he had to allay Spatz's suspicions. Had to make Spatz believe he was behaving himself. And what better way of convincing Spatz than by manipulating the reactions of the man supposedly closest to him? T'ai Cho's indignation – his angry disappointment in Kim – would throw Spatz off the scent. Would give Kim that tiny bit of room he needed.

Even so, it hurt. And that surprised Kim, because he had begun to question whether he had any feelings left after what they had done to him in Socialization. He recalled all the times he had met T'ai Cho since then, knowing what the man had once been to him, yet feeling nothing. Nothing at all. He had lain awake at nights, worried about that absence in himself, fearing that the ability to love had been taken from him, perhaps for good. So this – this hurt he felt at hurting another – was a sign of hope. Of a change in him.

He looked down at the poem on the desk, then sighed. What made it worse was that there was an element of truth in what he'd said. Remove Spatz and another Spatz would be appointed in his place. So it was in this life. Moreover, it was true what he had said about himself. Truer, perhaps, than he had intended.

All his life he had been owned. Possessed, not for himself, but for the thing within him – his 'talent'. They used him, as they would a machine. And, like a machine, if he malfunctioned he was to be repaired, or junked.

He laughed softly, suddenly amused. *Yes*, he asked, *but what makes me different from the machines? What qualities distinguish me from them? And are those qualities imperfections – weaknesses – or are they strengths? Should I be more like them or less?*

They had conditioned him; walled off his past, taught him to mistrust his darker self; yet it was the very part of him from which it all emanated – the wellspring of his being.

The thinking part... they overvalued it. It was only the processor. The insights came from a deeper well than that. The upper mind merely refined it.

He smiled, knowing they were watching him, listening to his words. Well, let them watch and listen. He was better at this game than they. Much better.

He leaned forward, studying the poem.

To the watching eyes it would mean nothing. To them it seemed a meaningless string of chemical formulae; the mathematical expression of a complex chain of molecules. But Kim could see through the surface of the page and glimpse the Mandarin characters each formula represented. He smiled to himself, wondering what Spatz would make of it. Beyond the simple one-for-one code Kim had devised to print out the information taken from Hammond's personal files was a second code he had agreed upon with Hammond. That, too, was quite simple – providing you had the key to how it worked and a fluent understanding of Mandarin.

The poem itself was clumsy, its images awkward, clichéd – but that was understandable. Hammond was a scientist, not a poet. And whilst the examination system insisted upon the study of ancient poetry, it was something that most men of a scientific bias put behind them as quickly as possible. What was important, however, was the information contained within the central images. Three white swans represented how Spatz had divided the research into three teams. Then, in each of the next three lines, Hammond detailed – by use of other images – the area of study each team was undertaking.

It was a crude beginning – no more than a foundation – yet it showed it could be done. As Hammond gained confidence he would develop subtlety: a necessity in the days to come, for the information would be of a degree of complexity that would tax their inventiveness to the limit.

That said, the most difficult part was already resolved. Kim had devised a means by which he could respond to Hammond. His co-conspirator had only to touch a certain key on his computer keyboard and Kim's input would automatically load into his personal files. That same instruction would effectively shut down Hammond's keyboard – render it useless, its individual keys unconnected to its regular program. Whichever key Hammond subsequently pressed would bring up one character of Kim's reply, until his message was complete.

It was a trick he had learned in Socialization. A game he'd played, haunting the files of others with his cryptic messages. And no one had dreamed it was possible.

He typed his queries out quickly, keeping this first response simple, modelling his poem on one by the fourth-century poet, T'ao Ch'ien. It printed up on the screen as further chains of molecules. Then, happy with what he had done, he punched the code to send it to Hammond's file.

He switched off the set and sat back, stretching, suddenly tired. Then, unexpectedly, the comset came alive again, the printer at the side of the desk beginning to chatter. He caught his breath, watching the printout slowly emerge. A moment later it fell silent. He leaned forward and tore the printout off, then sat back, reading it through.

It was from Spatz, informing him that he had been given permission to use the recreational facilities of the local Security forces.

He studied it a moment and then laughed. A pool! Spatz had given him a pool!

Her Uncle Jon had set and lit a fire in the huge hearth. Its flickering light filled the big, tall-ceilinged room, making it seem mysterious and half-formed, as if, at any moment, the walls would melt and run. Her father was sitting in a big, upright armchair by the window, staring out at the sea. Standing in the doorway, she looked across at him then back at the fire, entranced. It was something she had never seen before. Something she had never thought to see. Outside, beyond the latticed windows, evening was falling, dark clouds gathering over the sea, but here, inside, the firelight filled the room with warmth.

She knelt beside the fire, putting her hands out to it, shivering suddenly, not from the cold but from a feeling of familiarity; from a strange sense of having made the gesture before, in another life than this.

'Careful,' her father said, almost lazily. 'It's hot. Much hotter than you'd think.'

She knelt there in the half-shadow, mesmerized by the flickering pattern of the firelight, its fierce heat, its ever-changing dance of forms, then looked back at her father. His face was changed by the fire's light; had become a mask of black and gold, his eyes living, liquid jewels. For some reason it moved her deeply. At that moment her love for him was like something solid: she could touch it and smell it; could feel its very texture.

She looked about her. There were shelves on the walls, and books. Real books, like those she had seen in the museum once – leather-bound. She turned, hearing the door creak open, and looked up, smiling, at her uncle. Behind him came her aunt, carrying a tray of drinks.

'What are all the books?'

She saw how her uncle looked to her father before he answered her; as if seeking his permission.

'They're old things. History books and myth.'

'Myth?'

Her Aunt Helga looked up, a strange expression in her eyes, then looked down again, busying herself with the drinks.

Again her Uncle Jon looked to his brother uncertainly. 'They're stories, Jelka. Old legends. Things from before the City.'

He was about to say more, but her father interrupted him. 'There are things that belong here only. You must not take them back with you, understand me, child? You must not even mention them. Not to anyone.'

She looked down. 'Why?'

'Content yourself that they are.'

She looked across at him again. His voice had been harsh, almost angry, but his eyes seemed troubled. He looked away, then back at her, relenting. 'While you're here you may look at them, if that's what you want. But remember, these things are forbidden back in the City. If anyone knew...'

She frowned. Forbidden? Why forbidden?

'Jelka?'

She looked up, then quickly took the glass her Aunt Helga was holding out to her. 'Thanks...'

She was silent a moment, then looked across at her uncle. 'Daddy said this place had a name. Kalevala. Why is it called that?'

Jon laughed, then took a glass from his wife and came across, sitting in the chair nearest Jelka.

'You want to know why this house is called Kalevala? Well' – he looked across at her father then back at Jelka – 'it's like this...'

She listened, entranced, as her uncle talked of a distant past and a land of heroes, and of a people – her people – who had lived in that land. Of a time before the Han and their great City, when vast forests filled the land and the people were few. Her mind opened up to the freedom of such a past – to a world so much bigger than the world she knew. A vast, limitless world, bounded by mist and built upon nothingness. Kalevala, the land of heroes.

When he was finished, she sat there, astonished, her drink untouched.

'Well?' her father said over the crackle of the fire, his voice strangely heavy. 'Do you understand now why we are forbidden this? Can't you see what restlessness there would be if this were known to all?'

She stared at him, not recognizing him for a moment, the vision filling her mind, consuming her. Then she lowered her eyes and nodded. 'I think so. And yet...'

He smiled sadly. 'I know. I feel it too, my love. It calls us strongly. But this is now, not then. We cannot go back. This is a new age and the heroes are dead. The land of Kalevala is gone. We cannot bring it back.'

She shivered. *No*, she wanted to say; *it's still alive, inside us – in that part of us that dreams and seeks fulfilment.* And yet he was right. There was only this left. This faint, sad echo of a greater, more heroic age. This only. And when it too was gone?

She closed her eyes, overwhelmed by a sudden sense of loss. The loss of something she had never known. And yet not so, for it was still a part of her. She could feel it – there in the sinew and bone and blood of her.

'Jelka?'

She looked up. Her uncle was standing by the shelves, watching her, concerned, the pain in his eyes the reflection of her own.

'The Kalevala... Would you like to read it?'

He stretched out his hand, offering one of the thick, leather-bound volumes. Jelka stared back at him a moment, then went across to him, taking the book. For a moment she simply stared at it, astonished, tracing the embossed lettering of the cover with her finger, then she turned, looking at her father.

'Can I?'

'Of course. But remember what I said. It belongs here. Nowhere else.'

Jelka nodded, then looked back at the book. She opened the cover and read the title page.

'I didn't think...' she began, then laughed.

'Didn't think what?' said her uncle, standing beside her.

'This,' she said, looking up into his face. 'I never dreamed there would be a book of it.'

'It wasn't a book. Not at first. It was all songs, thousands of songs, sung by peasants in the homelands of Karelia. One man collected them and made them into a single tale. But now there's only this. This last copy. The rest of it has gone – singers and songs, the people and the land – as if it had never been.'

She looked back at him, then stared at the book in her hands, awed. The last copy. It frightened her somehow.

'Then I'll take good care of it,' she said. 'As if it were a sister to me.'

Chen raised himself uneasily in the bed, then pulled the cover up, getting comfortable again. His chest was strapped, his arm in bandages, but he had been lucky. The knife had glanced against a rib, missing anything vital. He had lost a lot of blood, but he would heal. As for the arm wound, that was superficial – the kind of thing one got in a hard training session.

Karr was sitting across from him, scowling, his huge frame far too big for the hospital chair. He leaned forward angrily, giving vent to what he'd had to hold in earlier while the nurse had been in the room.

'You were stupid, Chen. You should have waited for me.'

Chen gritted his teeth against a sudden wash of pain, then answered his friend.

'I'm sorry, Gregor. There wasn't time.'

'You could have contacted me. From Liu Chang's. You could have let me know what you planned. As it was I didn't even know you'd gone to see the pimp until half an hour back. I thought we were waiting for the Security report on Liu Chang.'

'I got it back before I went in. It confirmed what we'd thought. He was an actor, in opera, before he became a pimp. And there was one unproven charge of murder against him. That was the reason he was demoted to the Net.'

Karr huffed impatiently. 'Even so, you should have waited. You could have been killed.'

It was true. He *should* have waited. But he hadn't. Why? Perhaps because he had wanted to do it himself. It was mixed up with Pavel somehow – the boy on the Plantation who had been killed by DeVore's henchman. He still felt guilty about that. So perhaps he had put himself at risk to punish himself. Or maybe it was more complex than that. Maybe it had to do with the risks involved. He had enjoyed it, after all. Had liked the way the odds were stacked against him.

Five to one. And he had come out of it alive. Had fought them hand to hand and beaten them. *Kwai* he was. He knew it now, clearer than he had ever known it before. *Kwai.*

'I'm sorry,' he said again. 'It was wrong of me.'

Karr sat back a little, then laughed, meeting Chen's eyes, his anger dissipating. 'Still, you're alive.'

There was a knock, then a head poked round the door.

'Axel!' Chen tried to sit up, then eased back, groaning softly.

Haavikko came into the room. Giving a small nod of acknowledgment to Karr, he went across and took Chen's hand, concerned.

'What happened? Gregor told me you'd been hurt, but not how.'

Chen took a painful breath, then grinned up at Haavikko, squeezing his hand. 'It was only a scrape...'

Karr laughed. 'Only a scrape! You know what our friend here has been doing, Axel?'

Haavikko looked, shaking his head.

'Shall I tell him, Chen, or do you want to?'

'Go ahead,' said Chen, the pain from his ribs momentarily robbing him of breath.

Karr pointed beyond Haavikko, indicating a chair in the corner. 'Those are Chen's clothes. Look in the top pocket of the tunic. You'll find something there that will interest you.'

Haavikko turned and looked. The tunic was ripped and bloodstained, but the pocket was intact. He reached inside and drew out a thin piece of transparent card.

'This?'

Karr nodded and watched as Haavikko studied it a moment then looked back at him, his expression blank. 'So? What is it?'

Karr went across, taking the card. 'I'll show you exactly how it works later on. For now take my word on it. This is what they call an implant. Or, at least, the record of one. On this card is stored all the information you'd need to make a special chemical. One that could create a false memory in someone's head.'

Haavikko looked up. 'So?'

'So the information on this particular card was designed for one specific person. You.'

'Me?' Haavikko laughed. 'What do you mean?'

'Just this. Chen here did some digging into your friend Liu Chang's past. And then he paid the man a visit. From that he got confirmation of something he and I had suspected from the start. That and an address below the Net. At that address he found a man named Herrick who makes these things. And from Herrick he got this card – which is a copy of a false memory that was implanted in your head. The memory of killing a young sing-song girl.'

Haavikko had blanched. 'No... It's not possible. I remember...' His voice faltered and he looked down, wetting his lips with his tongue. 'It can't have been false. It was too real. Too...'

Karr reached out, touching his shoulder. 'And yet it's true, Axel Haavikko. You didn't kill her. Someone else did. Probably Liu Chang. Your only mistake was to take the drug that was mixed in with your wine. It was that which made you think you'd killed her.'

'No...'

'It's true,' said Chen. 'Wait until you see the copy. You never touched her. You couldn't have done, don't you see? You're not that kind of man.'

They watched him. Watched his chest rise and fall. Then saw how he looked at them again, disbelief warring with a new hope in him.

'Then I *really* didn't do it? I didn't kill that poor girl?'

'No,' said Karr fiercely, taking his arm. 'No, my friend. But we know who did. We can't prove it yet but we will. And when we do we'll nail the bastard. For all the lives he's ruined.'

Jelka cried out, then sat up in the darkness, the terror of the dream still gripping her. She could see the three men vividly: tall, thin men, standing there at the lake's edge, staring across at her, their eyes like black stones in their unnaturally white faces, their long, almost skeletal hands dripping with blood. And herself, there at the centre of the lake, the great slab of stone sinking slowly beneath her feet, drawing her down into the icy depths.

She heard footsteps on the flags of the corridor outside, then the creaking of her door as it opened. Her heart leaped to her mouth, certain they had come for her again, but as the lamplight spilled into the room she saw it was only her father.

'What is it, my love?'

He came across and, setting the lamp down on the bedside table, sat beside her on the bed, holding her to him. She closed her eyes a moment, shuddering, letting him comfort her, then moved back slightly, looking up into his face.

'It was the dream again. But worse. This time I was in Kalevala... in the land of heroes. All about me was a wilderness of tree and rock and shallow pools. And still they came for me, following me through the trees. As if they had travelled back across the years to find me...'

His face creased in sympathetic pain. He drew her close, comforting her. 'There, my love. It's all right. I'm here now. No one will harm you. I promise you.'

His arms encircled her, strong, powerful arms that were like great walls of stone, protecting her, but still she could see the three assassins; see how they smiled, toothless, their mouths black like coals, as she sank into the ice-cold water.

He moved back, looking down at her. 'Shall I ask Helga to come?'

She hesitated, then nodded.

He went to the door, then turned, looking back at her. 'And don't worry. No one will harm you here. No one.'

She was up early the next morning, watching her father pack. Later she sat there at the harbour's edge, watching the boat slowly disappear from sight. For a while she just stared at the nothingness, aching for him to return, then, with a start, she realized that the nothingness was filled with living things: was a universe of form and colour.

She walked back slowly to the house, looking about her, Erkki, the young guard her father had insisted on, trailing some twenty ch'i behind. There was a whole world here to explore, different in kind from the soft and sun-baked islands of Sumatra she had known during her father's exile. No, even the light was different here; was somehow familiar. Already the island seemed not strange but merely something she had forgotten.

In the days that followed she explored the island. Day by day she added to her knowledge of its ways; its dark pools and tiny waterfalls, its narrow inlets and silent places, its caves and meadows. And slowly, very slowly, she fell in love with it.

Above all there was one special place...

It was the afternoon of her fourth day and she was making her way down from the island's summit, Erkki following. Usually he stayed close, calling her back when he felt she was taking too great a risk, but the path down from the crest was familiar now, and he relaxed, letting her go ahead.

She made her way across the grassy hilltop to a place where the land fell away. There, at the cliff's edge, stood a ruined chapel, its roof open to the sky, the doorway empty, gaping. It was a tiny building, the floor inside cracked and overgrown with weeds, one of the side walls collapsed, the heavy stones spilled out across the grass. Yet you could still read the lettering carved into the stone lintel and see the symbols of fish, lamb and cross cut into the stone inside.

She had asked her uncle about the words – words that seemed familiar despite their strangeness; which shared the same letters as her own tongue, yet were alien in their form – but he had not known their meaning, only that they were Latin, the ancient language of the *Ta Ts'in*. As for the symbols, he knew but he would not say.

For a moment she stood there, staring out at the sea beyond the ruin, then went on, finding the path down.

It was an old path, worn by many feet, and near the bottom, where the way grew steep, steps had been cut into the rock. She picked her way nimbly between the rocks and out beneath the overhang. There, on the far side of the broad shelf of rock, was the cave.

This was her special place; the place of voices. Here the island spoke to her in a thousand ancient tongues.

She went halfway across the ledge then stopped, crouching, looking down through the crack in the great grey slab. There, below her, the incoming tide was channelled into a fissure in the rock. For a moment she watched the rush and foam of the water through the narrow channel, then looked across at the young guard, noting how he was watching her, smiling, amused by what she was doing.

'Can't you hear it, Erkki? It's talking to me.'

He laughed. 'It's just a noise.'

She looked down at it again, then lifted her head, listening for the other voices – for the sound of the wind, the branches singing overhead, the cry of sea birds calling out to sea. 'No,' she said finally. 'They're voices. But you have to listen carefully.'

Again he laughed. 'If you say so, *Nu shi* Tolonen. But it's just noise to me. I haven't the ear for it, I guess.'

She looked at him a moment, then smiled and turned away. No, he hadn't the ear for it but, then, few had these days. A constant diet of trivee shows and holodramas had immunized them against it; had dulled their senses and filled their heads with illusions. But she could hear it – the inner voice of things. Could feel it in her blood. The pulse of the great world – more real, more alive, than anything within the levels.

She paused, wiping her hands against her thighs, then went across and stood there at the edge of the rock, looking out across the rutted surface of the sea. She could feel the wind like a hand against her face, roughly caress-ing her; could taste the salt tang on her lips. For a moment she stood there, her eyes closed, imagining herself at the helm of a great ship, crossing the vast ocean, on her way to discover new lands. Then, smiling, she turned and went across to the cave, ducking beneath the low shelf of rock into the darkness beyond.

For a moment she paused, letting her eyes grow accustomed to the darkness, sniffing at the air. Then she frowned. Maybe it was only her imag-ination, but today it seemed different, less dank and musty than usual, but maybe that had to do with the weather. Her uncle had said a storm was on its way. Had warned her to be indoors when it came.

She smiled and turned, looking about her. There, on the wall behind her, were the ancient letters, a hand's length in height, scored into the rock and dyed a burned ochre against the pale cream of the rock. Their stick-like, angular shapes brought to mind a game she had played as a child with her *amah's* yarrow stalks. Further in, where the ceiling sloped down to meet the floor of the cave, she had found a pile of tiny bones and the charred remains of an ancient fire. She bent down, squinting into the deep shadows, then frowned. They had been disturbed.

A tiny ripple of fear went up her back. And then she heard it. A strange, rustling noise at the back of the cave.

'Erkki!' she called, in a low, urgent whisper.

He was there in a moment, crouched in the cave's entrance, his gun searching the dark interior.

'What is it?' he said quietly.

She held her breath. Maybe she had imagined it. But then it came again, closer now. She shivered, then caught her breath as a pair of eyes looked back at her from the darkness. Dark, feral eyes that held her own, unblinking.

'It's an animal,' she said softly, fear giving way to astonishment in her. 'A wild animal.'

She heard the click as Erkki took the safety off his gun and put her hand out, signalling him to hold still.

She took a slow step backward, then another, until she was beside him. 'It won't harm us. It's more afraid of us than we are of it. It must have been sleeping at the back of the cave, and I disturbed it.'

Beside her Erkki shivered. 'I thought all the animals were dead.'

Yes, she thought. *So did I. But there's one – and probably more than one – here on the island.* She could make out more of it now – could see how dark its fur was, how small, yet powerful its limbs. She had seen its like in her school textbooks. It was a fox. A real live fox.

Erkki touched her arm gently. 'Shall I bring a cage? There's one in the house. We could catch it and take it back with us.'

She shook her head. 'No. Let it go free. It belongs here. Look at it – it wasn't meant to be caged.'

Nor we, she thought, wondering how long ago the trap had been set on her own kind, the bars secured on every side. But she could do this much: could leave this tiny fragment of wildness here where it belonged. To make a pet of it... She shuddered. It would die if they put it in a cage.

'Come,' she said, 'let's get back. The storm is coming.'

At the summit she stopped again, looking about her. Gulls circled overhead, their cries shrill, bad-tempered. She pulled her jacket close about her. The wind was growing stronger, more blustery. To the north-east storm clouds were gathering, dark and threatening, massing above the City. A storm was coming, just as her uncle had said. She laughed. Let it come! Let the heavens open! She would greet it here, if need be. Then she turned and saw Erkki watching her.

'Okay. I'm coming. Just a little longer...'

He nodded and started down. For a moment longer she stood there, looking about her, imagining herself mistress of all she saw. Then, with a sigh, she followed Erkki down towards the lights of the house.

★

Director Spatz sat back in his chair, pointing directly at the screen.

'Well, Ellis? What in the gods' names is that?'

'We're not sure as yet, Director, but we're working on it. At first we thought it might be some kind of star chart, considering the boy's interest in astronomy, but we've run it through the computer for a possible match and there's nothing.'

For a moment both men were silent, staring at the screen. There were forty-six points in all, most of them linked by straight lines to three or four other lines. They formed a tight cat's cradle on the screen, elliptical in structure, like the upper half of a skull.

Spatz huffed loudly. 'You're absolutely certain it has nothing to do with what we're working on?'

'Absolutely. Apart from the fact that we've barely begun work on the actual positioning of the wires, those points simply don't correspond to the areas of the brain we'd be looking to use. In my opinion it's only coincidence that it has that shape.'

'Hmm.' Spatz leaned forward and blanked the screen, then turned, looking up at his assistant. 'I know what you think, Ellis, but you're wrong. He's up to something. I'm sure of it. So keep looking. I don't want your team to relax until you've found out what he's doing.'

Ellis bowed. Once outside the room he drew a long breath, then shook his head. The Director's obsession with the boy was bordering upon the insane. He was convinced that the boy had been introduced for one of two reasons – either to spy upon him or to ensure that the Project failed. Either way he felt threatened. But the truth was far simpler.

He had been studying the boy for ten days now and was convinced that he was genuine. He had watched Kim working on several of his own projects and had seen how he applied himself to problems. There was no faking that; no way of counterfeiting that quickness of mind. But Spatz would not hear of it. Second-rate himself, he would not have it that a mere boy – and a Clayborn boy at that – could be his intellectual superior.

But Spatz wasn't to have it all his own way. Ellis had seen the directive that had come down only moments before he had gone in to see the Director. And there was nothing Spatz could do about it.

He laughed, then walked on. No, not even Project Director Spatz would have the nerve to countermand Prince Yuan's direct command.

*

Kim was lying on his back in the pool, his eyes closed. It was late and the pool was empty, but from the gym nearby came the harsh hiss and grunt of the men working out on the exercise machines.

For a time he simply floated there, relaxing, then, rolling over, he kicked out for the side, glancing up at the cameras overhead.

Did they watch him even here? He smiled and ducked his face under, then lifted it, throwing the water out from him in a spray. Almost certainly. Even when he was pissing they'd have a camera on him. Spatz was like that. But he wasn't atypical. There were many like Spatz. The City bred them in their hundred thousands.

He pulled himself up and sat there on the side, moving his legs lazily in the water. He had always been watched – it was almost the condition of his existence – but he had never come to like it. At best he used it, as he did now, as a goad, challenging himself to defeat its constrictions.

In that the reports on him were accurate. In this one respect the Clay had shaped him – for he was cunning. And not just cunning, but inventive in his cunning, as if the very directness of his mind – that aspect of him which could grasp the essence of a thing at once and use it – needed this other 'twisted' part to permit its function. He smiled and looked down, wondering, as ever, what they made of his smiles – what they thought when they saw him smile so, or so.

He looked up; looked directly into camera. What do you see, *Shih* Spatz? Does the image you have of me bear any relationship to the being that I truly am?

No, he answered, looking away. *No relationship at all.* But, then, Spatz had no idea what Chung Kuo would be like if the Project succeeded. All that concerned him was his own position on the social ladder, whether he rose or fell. All else was irrelevant.

Kim stretched his neck, then yawned. He had slept little these past few nights, trying to see through the mesh of details to the heart of the problem.

What *would* Chung Kuo be like if everyone were wired?

He had run various scenarios through his head. For instance, the Seven might limit the use of wiring to known criminals and political dissidents. Or, at the other extreme, they might wire everyone, even their wives and cousins. Not only that, but there was the nature of the wiring to consider. Was it to be a simple tracing mechanism, or would it be more complex? Would they be content to use it as a method of policing Chung Kuo's vast population, or would they seek to change behaviour by its use?

This last caused him much concern, for the wire held a far greater potential for manipulation than Li Yuan probably envisaged. When one began to tinker with the human mind there was no limit to the subtle changes one might make. It was possible – even quite simple – to create attractions and aversions, to mould a thousand million personalities to a single mental template and make the species docile, timid, uncreative. But was that worse than what was happening anyway? It could be argued that Chung Kuo – the great utopian City of Tsao Ch'un – had been created for that very purpose: to geld Mankind and keep the curious beast within his bars. In such a light this latest step – this plan to 'wire' each individual – was merely a perfection of that scheme. Restraint alone had failed. The bars were not enough. Now they must put the bars – the walls – within, or see the whole vast edifice come crashing down.

It was an unsettling thought.

Against this he set three things: his 'duty' to Li Yuan; his certainty that, with him or without, this thing would be; and, last, the simple challenge of the thing.

He had tried to convince himself that he owed nothing to any man, but the truth was otherwise. His fate had always been in the hands of others. And wasn't that so for all men? Wasn't even the most basic thing – a man's existence – dependent upon a consensus amongst those he lived with: on the agreement to let him be? Hadn't he learned that much in the Clay? No man was truly free. No man had any rights but those granted him by his fellows. In Li Yuan's favour, the Prince at least had recognized his worth and given him this chance. Surely that deserved repayment of some kind?

As to the second matter, he was certain now that only total catastrophe could prevent Li Yuan's scheme from becoming a reality. Indeed, catastrophe now seemed the sole alternative to the Wiring Project. The fuse had been lit long ago, in the Seven's refusal to confront the problem of massive population increases. Their reluctance to tackle that fundamental – a decision shaped by their veneration of the family and of the right of every man to have sons – had hamstrung any attempt to balance the slow increase in resources against the overwhelming increase in demand and to make of Chung Kuo the utopia it was meant to be. But that was nothing new; it was an age-old problem – a problem that the emperors of Chung Kuo had been forced to face for more than two thousand years. Famine and plague and revolution were the price of such imbalance, and such would come again – unless the tide were turned, the great generative force harnessed. But that would not happen without an evolutionary change in the species. In the meantime, this – this artificial means – would have to do. The Seven had no option. They would have to wire or go under.

And the challenge? That, too, he saw in moral terms. As he conceived it now, the scheme presented mainly technical problems – problems that required not the kind of inventiveness he was good at but the perfecting of existing systems. In many ways it was a matter of pure organizational complexity: of breaking down the Wiring Project into its constituent parts and then rebuilding it. The end, however, was not unachievable. Far from it. Most of the technology required already existed. He could have said as much to Prince Yuan at their first meeting, but the challenge – the real challenge – lay in directing the research: in determining not the *quality* of the eventual wire, but its *kind*.

And there, perhaps, he overstepped the brief Li Yuan had given him, for he had not been asked to consider what the wire should be capable of; he had been asked only to determine whether the scheme would work. Again he was to be simply the tool – the vehicle – for another's needs; the instrument by which their dreams might become realities. As ever, he was supposed to have no say in the matter. Yet he *would* have his say.

Kim stilled the movement of his legs in the water and looked up.

'Joel!'

Hammond stood there on the far side of the pool. 'Kim... I thought I'd find you here.'

Kim clambered up and went round the pool to greet him.

'How long have you been there?'

'I've just got here. You looked deep in thought. Troubles?'

They were both conscious of the watching cameras. Kim shrugged and, smiling, moved past the older man, taking his towel from the rail, then turned, looking back at him. 'What brings you here?'

Hammond held out a wafer-thin piece of printout paper. 'This came.'

Kim took it. A moment later he looked up, his dark eyes wide with surprise. 'This is for real?'

'Absolutely. Director Spatz confirmed it with Prince Yuan's secretary. I'm to accompany you. To keep you out of trouble.'

Kim laughed, then handed the paper back, pulling the towel up about his shoulders. 'But that's amazing. An observatory. Does that mean we'll be going into space?'

Hammond shook his head. 'No. Quite the opposite. The observatory at Heilbronn is situated at the bottom of a mineshaft, more than three li underground.'

Kim looked away, then laughed. 'Of course. It makes sense.' He looked back. 'When do we go?'

'Tomorrow. First thing.'

Kim smiled, then drew closer, whispering. 'Was Spatz angry?'

Hammond bent down, giving his answer to Kim's ear. 'Angry? He was furious!'

Jelka woke. Outside the storm was raging, hurling gusts of rain against the window pane. Throwing on her nightgown, she went out into the passageway. The night growled and roared beyond the thick stone walls of the house. She stood there a moment, listening, then started as the window at the far end of the passage lit up brilliantly. Seconds later a huge thunderclap shook the house.

She shivered, then laughed, her fear replaced by a surge of excitement. The storm was upon them!

She hurried down the great stairway, then stood there in the darkness of the hallway, the tiles cold beneath her naked feet. Again there was a flash, filling the huge, stained-glass window at the far end of the hallway with brilliant colour. And then darkness, intense and menacing, filled by the tremendous power of the thunderclap that followed.

She went on, finding her way blindly to the door at the far end of the passageway. Usually it was locked, but for once she found it open. She stood there a moment, trembling. Here, behind the thick stone of the outer wall, it was still, almost silent, only the muted rumble of distant thunder disturbing the darkness. When the next flash came, she pulled the door open and went up, into the tower.

At once the sound of the storm grew louder. She went up the narrow, twisting steps in darkness, her left arm extended, steadying herself against the wall, coming out into a room she had not seen before. Blindly, she began to edge towards the centre of the room, away from the hole in the floor, then froze as a blaze of light filled the room from the narrow window to her left. The accompanying thunderclap exploded in the tiny space and, in the momentary brilliance, she glimpsed the sparse contents of the room.

Jelka saw herself briefly in the mirror opposite – a tiny figure in an almost empty room, her body framed in searing light, her face in intense shadow, one arm raised as if to fend off the thunder, the dark square of the stair-hole just behind her.

She went across, finding the steps in the darkness, then went up as a sudden flash filled the stairwell with light.

She went to the window. The glass was cold against her face, beaded with brilliant drops. The wooden boards were smooth and cool beneath her feet. Wind and rain rattled the glass. And then a vast hand seemed to shake the building. The tower seemed alive. As alive as she. She pressed her hands against the wood of the window's frame and stared out, waiting for each vivid stroke, each growl of elemental anger.

As the window lit up again she turned, looking behind her. On the far side of the room a metal ladder had been set into the wall. Above it, set square and solid in the ceiling, was a hatch. For a moment she stared at it, then pushed away from the window.

In the sudden dark she stumbled and fell, then clambered up again, her hands held out before her until they met the cold stone surface. For a moment she searched the wall blindly, cursing softly to herself, then found the metal rung and, pulling herself across, began to climb.

She was pushing upward when the next flash filled the room. Above her the great hatch shuddered against her hands as the thunderclap shook the tower. She shivered, momentarily frightened by the power of the storm, then pushed her head and shoulder up against the hatch until it gave.

Suddenly she was outside, the rain pouring down, the wind whipping cruelly at her hair, soaking the thin nightgown she was wearing.

She pulled herself up and, in the half-light, went to the parapet, steeling herself against the sudden cold, the insane fury of the wind, her hands gripping the metal rail tightly. As the sky lit up she looked down. Below her the sea seemed to writhe and boil, then throw a huge, clear fist of water against the rocks at the base of the tower. Spray splintered all about her and, as if on cue, the air about her filled with a ferocious, elemental roar that juddered the tower and shook her to the bone. And then darkness. An intense, brooding darkness, filled with the fury of the storm.

She was breathing deeply now, erratically. It felt as though the storm were part of her. Each time the lightning flashed and forked in the sky she felt a tremor go through her from head to toe, as sharp as splintered ice. And when the thunder growled it sounded in her bones, exploding with a suddenness that made her shudder with a fierce delight.

She shivered, her teeth clenched tight, her eyes wide, her limbs trembling with a strange, unexpected joy. Water ran freely down her face and neck, cleansing her, while below her the sea raged and churned, boiling against the rocks, its voice a scream of unarticulated pain, indistinguishable from the wind.

'Jelka!'

She heard the call from far below, the cry almost lost in the roar of the storm, and turned, looking across at the open hatch. For one brief moment she failed to recognize what it was, then she came to herself. Her Uncle Jon...

The call came again, closer this time, as if just below.

'Jelka? Are you up there?'

She turned, yelling back at him, her voice barely audible over the grumble of the storm. 'It's all right! I'm here!'

She looked out across the sea again, trembling, her whole body quivering, awaiting the next flash, the next sudden, thrilling detonation. And as it came she turned and saw him, his head poking up from the hatch, his eyes wide with fear.

'What in Heaven's name are you doing? Come down! It isn't safe!'

She laughed, exhilarated. 'But it's wonderful!'

She saw how he shuddered, his eyes pleading with her. 'Come down! Please, Jelka! It's dangerous!'

The wind howled, tearing at her breath, hurling great sheets of rain against the tower. And then with a mighty crash of thunder – louder than anything that had preceded it – the hillside to her right exploded in flame.

For a moment the after-image of the lightning bolt lingered before her eyes, then she shuddered, awed by the sight that met her eyes.

Seven pines were on fire, great wings of flame gusting up into the darkness, hissing, steaming where they met and fought the downpour. She gritted her teeth, chilled by what she saw. And still the fire raged, as if the rain had no power to control it.

She turned, staring at her uncle, then, staggering, she ran across to him and let him help her down. For a moment he held her to him, trembling against her, his arms gripping her tightly. Then, bending down, he picked up the gown he'd brought and wrapped it about her shoulders.

'You're soaked,' he said, his voice pained. 'Gods, Jelka, what do you think you were doing? Didn't you know how dangerous it was?'

The sight of the burning trees had sobered her. 'No,' she said quietly, shivering now, realizing just how cold she was. 'It was so...'

She fell quiet, letting him lead her down, his pained remonstrances washing over her.

He let her move past him, out into the passageway. The passage light was on. At the far end, at the bottom of the great staircase, stood her aunt, her look of concern mirroring her husband's.

'It's all right,' Jelka said. 'I couldn't sleep. The storm. I wanted to see.'

Jon nodded, a look passing between him and his wife. Then he placed his arm about Jelka's shoulder.

'I can see that, my love, but it really wasn't safe. What if you'd fallen?'

But Jelka could think only of the power of the storm; of the way it had seemed a part of her, each sudden, brilliant flash, each brutal detonation bringing her alive, vividly alive. She could see it yet, the sea foaming wildly below, the huge sky spread out like a bruise above, the air alive with voices.

'There are fresh clothes in the bathroom,' her uncle said gently, squeezing her shoulder, bringing her back from her reverie. 'Get changed, then come through into the kitchen. I'll make some toast and ch'a. We can sit and talk.'

He looked up, waving his wife away, then looked back at Jelka, smiling. 'Go on now. I can see you won't sleep until this has blown over.'

She did as she was told, then went through, standing by the kitchen window, staring out through the glass at the storm-tossed waters of the harbour while he brewed the *ch'a*.

'Here,' he said after a while, handing her an old earthenware mug filled with steaming *ch'a*. He stood beside her, staring outward, then gave a soft laugh.

'I've done this before, you know, when I was much younger than I am now. Your mother was like you, Jelka. Knut could never understand it. If there was a storm he would tuck his head beneath the blankets and try to sleep through it – as if it were all a damned nuisance sent to rob him of his sleep and no more than that. But she was like you. She wanted to see. Wanted to be out there in the thick of it. I think she would have thrown herself in the water if she'd not had the sense to know she'd drown.'

He laughed again and looked down at her. Jelka was staring up at him, fascinated.

'What was she like? I mean, what was she *really* like?'

He nodded towards the broad pine table. They sat, he in the huge farm-house chair, she on the bench beside him, a heavy dressing gown draped about her shoulders.

'That's better. It gets in my bones, you know. The damp. The changes in pressure.' He smiled and sipped at his mug. 'But that's not what you want to know, is it? You want to know about your mother...'

He shook his head slowly. 'Where to start, eh? What to say first?' He looked at her, his eyes grown sad. 'Oh, she was like you, Jelka. So very much like you.' He let out a long breath, then leaned forward, folding his big broad hands together on the tabletop. 'Let me start with the first moment I ever saw her, there on the rocks at the harbour's mouth...'

She sat there, listening, her mouth open, her breathing shallow. The *ch'a* in her mug grew cold and still she listened, as if gazing through a door into the past.

Through into another world. Into a time before her time. A place at once familiar and utterly alien. That pre-existent world a child can only ever imagine, never be part of. And yet how she ached to see the things he spoke of; how she longed to go back and see what he had seen.

She could *almost* see it. Her mother, turning slowly in the firelight, danc-ing to a song that was in her head alone, up on her toes, her arms extended, dreaming... Or, later, her mother, heavily pregnant with herself, standing in the doorway of the kitchen where she now sat, smiling...

She turned and looked but there was nothing; nothing but the empty doorway. She closed her eyes and listened, but again there was nothing; nothing but the storm outside. She could not see it – not as it really was. Even with her eyes closed she couldn't see it.

Ghosts. The past was filled with ghosts. Images from the dark side of vision.

Hours passed. The storm died. And then a faint dawn light showed at the sea's far edge, beyond the harbour and the hills. She watched it grow, feeling tired now, ready for sleep.

Her uncle stood, gently touching her shoulder. 'Bed, my child,' he said softly. 'Your father will be here tomorrow.'

The deep-level telescope at Heilbronn was more than one hundred and fifty years old. The big satellite observatories at the edge of the Solar System had made it almost an irrelevancy, yet it was still popular with many astronomers, perhaps because the idea of going deep into the earth to see the stars held some curious, paradoxical appeal.

'It feels strange,' Kim said, turning to face Hammond as they rode the lift down into the earth. 'Like going back.'

Hammond nodded. 'But not uncomfortable, I hope?'

'No...' Kim looked away thoughtfully, then smiled. 'Just odd, that's all. Like being lowered down a well.'

The lift slowed then juddered to a halt. The safety doors hissed open and they stepped out, two suited guards greeting them.

'In there,' said one of the guards, pointing to their right. They went in. It was a decontamination room. Ten minutes later they emerged, their skin tingling, the special clothing clinging uncomfortably to them. An official greeted them and led them along a narrow, brightly lit corridor and into the complex of labs and viewing-rooms.

There were four telescopes in Heilbronn's shaft, but only one of them could be used at any one time, a vast roundabout, set into the rock, holding the four huge lenses. One of the research scientists – a young man in his early twenties – acted as their guide, showing them around, talking excitedly of the most recent discoveries. Few of them were made at Heilbronn now

– the edge observatories were the pioneers of new research – but Heilbronn did good work nonetheless, checking and amassing detail, verifying what the edge observatories hadn't time to process.

Hammond listened politely, amused by the young man's enthusiasm, but for Kim it was different: he shared that sense of excitement. For him the young man's words were alive, vivid with burgeoning life. Listening, Kim found he wanted to know much more than he already did. Wanted to grasp it whole.

Finally, their guide took them into one of the hemispherical viewing-rooms, settled them into chairs and demonstrated how they could use the enquiry facility.

His explanation over, he bowed, leaving them to it.

Kim looked to Hammond.

'No, Kim. You're the one Prince Yuan arranged this for.'

Kim smiled and leaned forward, drawing the control panel into his lap, then dimmed the lights.

It was like being out in the open, floating high above the world, the night sky all about them. But that was only the beginning. Computer graphics transformed the viewing-room into an armchair spaceship. From where they sat they could travel anywhere they liked among the stars: to distant galaxies far across the universe, or to nearer, better-charted stars, circling them, moving among their planetary systems. Here distance was of little consequence and the relativistic laws of physics held no sway. In an instant you had crossed the heavens. It was exhilarating to see the stars rush by at such incredible speeds, flickering in the corners of the eyes like agitated dust particles. For a while they rushed here and there, laughing, enjoying the giddy vistas of the room. Then they came back to Earth – to a night sky that ought to have been familiar to them, but wasn't.

'There are losses, living as we do.'

Hammond grunted his assent. 'It makes me feel... insignificant. I mean, just look at it. It's so big. There's so much power there. So many worlds. And all so old. So unimaginably old.' He laughed awkwardly, his hand falling back to the arm of the chair. 'It makes me feel so small.'

'Why? They're only stars.'

'Only stars!' Hammond laughed, amused by the understatement. 'How can you say that?'

Kim turned in his chair, his face, his tiny figure indistinct in the darkness, only the curved, wet surfaces of his eyes lit by reflected starlight. 'It's only matter, reacting in predictable ways. Physical things, bound on all sides by things physical. But look at you, Joel Hammond. You're a man. *Homo sapiens*. A beast that thinks, that has feelings.'

'Four pails of water and a bag of salts.'

Kim shook his head. 'No. We're more than mere chemicals. Even the meanest of us.'

Hammond looked down. 'I don't know, Kim. I don't really see it like that. I've never been able to see myself that way.'

'But we have to. We're more than earth, Joel. More than mere clay to be moulded.'

There was a hint of bitterness in the last that made the man look up and meet the boy's eyes.

'What is it?'

'Nothing. Just the memory of something.'

It was strange. They had not really spoken before now. Oh, there had been the poems – the transfer of matters scientific – but nothing personal. They were like two machines, passing information one to the other. But nothing real.

Hammond hesitated, sensing the boy's reluctance, then spoke, watching to see how his words were taken. 'Do you want to talk about it?'

Kim looked back at him. 'This feels like home.'

'Home?'

'Down deep. Under the earth.'

'Ah... the Clay.'

Kim smiled sadly. 'You should have seen me, Joel. Eight years back. Such a tiny, skulking thing I was. And thin. So thin. Like something dead.' He sighed, tilting his head back, remembering. 'A bony little thing with wide, staring eyes. That's how T'ai Cho first saw me.'

He laughed; a tighter, smaller sound than before. More like surprise than laughter. 'I wonder what it was he saw in me. Why he didn't just gas me and dispose of me. I was just...' he shrugged, and his eyes came up to meet the older man's; dark eyes, filled with sudden, half-remembered pain '... just a growth. A clod of earth. A scrap of the darkness from beneath.'

Hammond was breathing shallowly, intent on every word.

'Twice I was lucky. If it wasn't for T'ai Cho I'd be dead. He saved me. When I reverted he made a bargain for me. Because of what he saw in me. Five years I spent in Socialization. Doing penance. Being retrained, restructured. Taming me.'

Hammond looked up, suddenly understanding. So that was why Kim's life was forfeit. 'What did you do?'

Kim looked away. The question went unanswered. Then, after a while, he began to speak again. Slower this time. Hammond's question had been too close, perhaps, for what Kim said next seemed less personal, as if he were talking of a stranger, describing the days in Socialization, the humiliations and degradations, the death of friends who hadn't made it. And other, darker things. How had he survived all that? How emerged as he was?

Kim turned away, leaning across to activate the viewer. Slowly the hemisphere of stars revolved about them.

'We were talking about stars, Joel. About vastness and significance.' He stood, then walked to the edge, placing his hand against the upward curving wall. 'They seem so isolated – tiny islands in the great ocean of space, separated by billions of lì of nothingness. Bright points of heat in all that endless cold. But look at them again.' He drew a line between two stars, and then another two. 'See how they're all connected. Each one linked to a billion billion others. A vast web of light, weaving the galaxy together.'

He came across, standing close to Hammond, looking down at him. 'That's what's significant, Joel. Not the vastness or the power of it all, but how it's connected.' He smiled and reached down to take Hammond's hand, clasping it firmly. 'Apart or a-part. There are always two ways of seeing it.'

'A web,' said Hammond, frowning, then shook his head and laughed, squeezing the hand that held his own. 'A bloody web. You're mad, you know that, Kim Ward? Mad!'

'Not mad, Joel. Touched, perhaps, but not mad.'

It was her last day on the island. She had slept late and had woken hungry. Now she walked the wooded slopes beside the house, Erkki shadowing her. It was a cool, fresh day. The storm had washed the air clean and the sky, glimpsed through the tall, black bars of pine, was a perfect, unblemished blue.

At the edge of the clearing she turned and looked back at the young guard. He was walking along distractedly, looking down at the ground, his gun hung loosely about his left shoulder.

'Did you hear it?'

He looked up, smiling. 'Hear what?'

'The storm...'

He shrugged. 'I must have slept through it.'

She studied him a moment, then turned back. In front of her the fire had burned a great circle amidst the stand of trees. Charred branches lay all about her. No more than a pace from where she stood, the ground was black. She looked up. The trees on all sides of the blackened circle had been seared by the heat of the blaze, their branches withered. She looked down, then stepped forward, into the circle.

The dark layer of incinerated wood cracked and powdered beneath her tread. She took a second step, feeling the darkness give slightly beneath her weight, then stopped, looking about her. If she closed her eyes she could still see it, the flames leaping up into the darkness, their brightness searing the night sky, steaming, hissing where they met the violent downpour.

Now there was only ash. Ash and the fire-blackened stumps of seven trees, forming a staggered H in the centre of the circle. She went across to the nearest and touched it with the toe of her boot. It crumbled and fell away, leaving nothing.

She turned full circle, looking about her, then shivered, awed by the stillness, the desolation of the place. She had seen the violent flash and roar of the gods' touch; now she stood in its imprint, reminded of her smallness by the destructive power of the storm. And yet for the briefest moment last night she had seemed part of it, her thinking self lost, consumed by the elemental anger raging all about her.

She crouched and reached out, putting her fingers to the dark, soft-crumbling surface, then lifted one to her mouth, tasting the darkness. It was sour, unappetizing. Wiping her fingers against her knee, she stood and moved further in, until she stood at the very centre of the circle.

'Kuan Yin! What happened here?'

She turned and looked back at Erkki. He stood at the circle's edge, his eyes wide with wonder.

'It was the lightning,' she said, but saw at once that he didn't understand.

Of course, she thought; *you slept through it, didn't you? In that you're like my father – like all of them – you carry the City within you, wherever you are.*

She turned back, looking down. This evening, after supper, her father was coming to take her back. She sighed. It would be nice to see him again, and yet the thought of returning to the City was suddenly anathema. She looked about her, desperate to see it all one last time, to hold it fast in memory, in case...

She shuddered, then finished the thought. In case she never came again.

The nightmares no longer haunted her, the three gaunt men no longer came to the edge of the lake, their mocking eyes staring across at her. Even so, the threat remained. She was the Marshal's daughter, and while he remained important to the T'ang so her life would be in danger.

She understood it now: saw it vividly, as if her mind had been washed as clear as the sky. They had not been after her father. They had been after her. For her death would have left her father drained, emotionally incapacitated, a dead man filling the uniform of the Marshal.

She saw it clearly now. Saw how her death would have brought about her father's fall. And if the keystone fell, how could the arch itself hold up?

She knew her father's weaknesses; knew that he had four of the five qualities Sun Tzu had considered dangerous in the character of a general: his courage too often bordered on recklessness; he was impulsive and quick-tempered and would, if provoked, charge in without considering the difficulties; his sense of honour was delicate and left him open to false accusations; and, lastly, he was deeply compassionate. Against these she set his strengths, chief of which was the loyalty he engendered in those who served under him. As Sun Tzu had said in the tenth book of the *Art Of War*, 'Because such a general regards his men as infants they will march with him into the deepest valleys. He treats them as his own beloved sons and they will die with him.'

She nodded to herself. Yes, and weaknesses sometimes were strengths and strengths weaknesses. Take Hans Ebert, for instance. A fine, brave soldier he might be, handsome too and well mannered, yet her father's eyes saw a different man from the one she had seen that day in the Ebert Mansion. To her father he was the son he had never had and was thus born to be his daughter's life companion. But that was to forget her own existence – to leave out her own feelings on the matter.

She turned, chilled by the thought, then looked across at the young guard. 'Come, Erkki. Let's get back. I ought to pack.'

She looked about her as she walked, seeing it all as if it had already passed. Yet she would never wholly lose it now. She had found herself here – had discovered in this harsh and forbidding landscape the reflection of her inner self, her true self, and once awakened to it she was sure she would never feel the same. The scent of pine and earth, the salt tang of the sea; these things were part of her now, inseparable, like the voices of the island. Before she had been but a shadow of her self, entranced by the dream that was the City, unaware of her inner emptiness. But now she was awake; herself – fully herself.

The Mess orderly set the glasses down on the table between the two men, then, with a smart bow, left the room.

'Kan pei!' said Tolonen, lifting his glass to his future son-in-law.

'Kan pei!' Ebert answered, raising his glass. Then, looking about him, he smiled. 'This is nice, sir. Very nice.'

'Yes...' Tolonen laughed. 'A Marshal's privileges. But one day you'll be Marshal, Hans, and this room will be yours.'

'Maybe so,' Ebert answered, setting his glass down. 'But not for many years, I hope.'

Tolonen smiled. He liked young Ebert hugely, and it was reassuring to know that Jelka would be in such good hands when she was married. Just now, however, there was work to be done – other matters to preoccupy them.

'I've come from the T'ang,' he said, sitting back. 'I had to deliver the interim report on the Executive killings.' He paused and sniffed, his features re-forming themselves into a frown. 'Li Shai Tung wasn't pleased, Hans. He felt we ought to have got somewhere by now, and perhaps he's right. But the very fact that we've drawn so many blanks convinces me that DeVore's behind this somehow.'

'Do you think so, sir?' Ebert looked away, as if considering the matter, then looked back, meeting Tolonen's eyes. 'But surely we'd have found something to connect him. It would be rather too clever of him, don't you think, not to have left some trace somewhere? So many people were involved, after all.'

'Hmm...' Tolonen sipped at his drink – a fruit cordial – then set his glass down again. 'Maybe. But there's another matter, Hans. Something I didn't know about until the T'ang told me of it today. It seems that more was taken in the raid on Helmstadt than the garrison expenses. Jewellery for the main part, but also several special items. They were in the safe the *Ping Tiao* took. Three items of T'ang pottery. Items worth the gods know how much on the collectors' market.'

Tolonen reached into his tunic pocket and pulled out three thick squares of black ice. They were 'flats', hologramic stills.

'Here,' he said, handing them across.

Ebert held them up, looking at them a moment, then placed one on the table beside his drink and pressed the indented strip that ran along one edge. At once a hologram formed in the air above the 'flat'.

He studied each in turn, then handed them back to the Marshal. 'They're beautiful. And as you say, they'd fetch astronomical prices, even on the black market.' He hesitated, looking down. 'I realize it's awkward but... might I ask what they were doing in the safe at Helmstadt?'

Tolonen tucked the flats away and picked up his glass again. 'I have the T'ang's permission to discuss this with you, Hans. But remember, this is mouth-to-ear stuff.'

Ebert nodded.

'Good. Well, it seems Li Shai Tung was planning an experiment. The statuettes were to be sold to finance that experiment.'

'An experiment?'

'Yes. There have been talks – highly secretive talks, you understand – between the T'ang's private staff and several of the Net's biggest Triad bosses.'

Ebert sat back, surprised. 'I see. But what for?'

Tolonen sniffed. 'Li Shai Tung wants to try to reclaim parts of the Net. To bring them back into the fold. He'll guarantee basic services and limited travel in the lower levels, as well as huge cash injections to bring facilities up to standard. In return the Triad bosses will guarantee to keep the peace, within the framework of existing law.'

Ebert looked down. 'Forgive me for being candid, sir, but I'd say it was highly optimistic, wouldn't you?'

Tolonen lowered his voice. 'Just between us, Hans, I fully agree. But ours is not to question policy, ours is to carry that policy out. We are our master's hands, neh?'

There was a moment's silence between the men, then Tolonen continued. 'Anyway, it seems that the loss of the three statues has thrown things into flux. The T'ang is reluctant to part with any more of his treasures until we learn what happened to these three. If the Triads *were* involved – if they *are* trying to have their cake and eat it – Li Shai Tung wants to know that. It may answer other questions, too. We've had our suspicions for some while that the *Ping Tiao* were working with another group in their raid on Helmstadt. If they were acting in conjunction with one or other of the larger Triad bosses, it would explain a lot. Maybe it would even give us a handle on these murders.'

'I see. And you want me to investigate?'

'That's right. Some of the jewellery has already shown up on the black market. I want you to find out who's been trading the stuff. Then I want you to trace it back and get some answers.'

Ebert was silent a moment, considering, then he looked up again, meeting the Marshal's eyes. 'Why not Karr?'

'Major Karr has quite enough on his hands already.' Tolonen leaned forward and covered Ebert's hand with his own. 'No, Hans, you look after this for me, neh? Get me some answers that'll please the T'ang. It'll do you no harm, I guarantee. The murders, they're one thing. But this... Well, it could prove far more important in the long run.'

Ebert smiled. 'Of course. When do you want me to report?'

'The T'ang has given me three days.'

'Then three days it is. Whatever it takes. I'll find out who's behind all this.'

'Good.' Tolonen beamed. 'I knew I could count on you, Hans.'

It was thirty minutes later and he was in the corridor outside his apartment when the woman approached him, grabbing his arm and shrieking into his face.

'You bastard! You *bought* her, didn't you? To humiliate me!'

Ebert turned and shook her off. 'I don't know what you mean, Madam Chuang. Bought whom?'

'You know fucking well *whom!*' Her face was pale, her eyes dark with sleeplessness, while her clothes...

'Gods, woman, look at you! You're a mess! And such language! You forget yourself, Madam Chuang. A Minister's wife!'

He gave her a look of disgust and made to turn away, but she grabbed at him again. He turned back angrily, taking her hand from his arm and squeezing it painfully. 'If you don't desist...' he said quietly, but threateningly.

She tore her hand away, then leaned towards him, spitting full in his face.

He swore, rubbing at his face, then, glaring at her, turned away. But as he did so, she pulled a knife from among her clothes and struck out at him, catching him glancingly on the arm.

'Shit!'

He was turning as she struck the second blow, lifting his wounded arm to try to fend her off. She grunted as she delivered the blow, her full weight behind it, her face distorted with a mad lust of hatred as she thrust at him. This time the knife caught him squarely on the back of the head, knocking him forward on to his hands and knees. But the knife had gone scattering away.

Madam Chuang looked in horror. Where the knife had caught him the hair had ripped away, revealing a shining metal plate. He half turned his head, looking up at her, stunned by the force of the blow, yet still alive. She shrieked and made to leap on him, but strong hands pulled her back, then threw her down roughly. A moment later she felt something hard press down brutally against her temple and knew it was a gun. She closed her eyes.

'No! Leave her!' The voice was Ebert's. He got to his knees, trying to steady himself. 'Leave her...'

Auden looked across at his Major, then, with a small shudder, pulled the gun back from the woman's temple and returned it to the holster. 'She would have killed you, Hans.'

Ebert looked up, smiling through his pain. 'I know. She's got spirit, that one! Real spirit. Wouldn't you like to fuck her?'

Auden looked away.

Ebert laughed. 'No. Maybe not. But perhaps we should frighten her off, neh? After all, I can't always be watching my back, can I? There are times...' He laughed again, then reached up and touched the back of his head tenderly.

'What do you suggest?' Auden asked, looking back at him.

'Her breasts,' Ebert said, wincing. 'She was always proud of them. Cut her breasts.'

Auden turned, pushing the woman down, and tore her silks open roughly, exposing her breasts. Then he knelt over her, pinning down her arms.

She looked up at him, horrified, her voice a mere breath. 'You can't...'

He hit her savagely with the back of his hand, splitting her lip, then drew his knife from his belt. There was a moment's hesitation, then, pinning her neck down with his left hand, he drew the knife across her breasts, once, twice, a third time, ignoring her screams of pain, the razor-sharp blade ripping open the skin.

He stood, sheathing his knife, looking down at the distraught woman, then turned back, seeing at once how Ebert had been watching; how his eyes were wide with excitement; how his chest rose and fell.

'Thanks,' Ebert said quietly. 'You'll see to her?'

Auden nodded, then bent down, recovering the package he had dropped in coming to Ebert's aid. 'Here,' he said, handing it to Ebert. 'It came this morning.'

Ebert glanced at it, then looked across at the woman again. 'Who would have believed it, eh? Who'd have thought the old girl had it in her?' He laughed, then got unsteadily to his feet, swaying, closing his eyes momentarily. Auden went to him and put his arm about him, supporting him.

'Are you sure you're all right? Should I get a medic?'

Ebert shook his head, slowly, smiling through the pain he clearly felt. 'No. I'll rest a while. It'll be all right.'

Auden turned, looking across at the Minister's wife. She had turned on to her side now, huddled into herself, whimpering, her bloodied silks pulled about her torn and ruined breasts. 'I'll see to her. Don't you worry about that. I'll say she was attacked in the corridors by a gang. Fest will back me up.'

Ebert swallowed, then put his hand on Auden's arm. 'Good. Then get moving. I'll go inside and lie down for a while. There's help there if I need it.'

He watched Auden go over to the woman and crouch down, speaking into his wrist-set, summoning assistance, then turned away. It would be all right. Auden would sort things out. He touched his arm. It was only a superficial wound, but the blow to his head... Well, perhaps Auden was right. Perhaps he should have the medics in. She had caught him a cracking blow, after all. He could easily be concussed.

He turned to face the door. 'Fancy that...' he said softly, placing his hand against the lock and lifting his face to look directly into the overhead camera. At once the door hissed open. 'She could have killed me,' he said, going inside. 'The fucking woman could have killed me!'

The great hall of the Jakobstad Terminal was uncharacteristically silent, the departure lounge emptied of its normal crowds, the doors barred and guarded by soldiers. As the tiny party came through, their footsteps echoed across the massive space. It was almost a li from landing pad to platform, but Tolonen had waved away the sedan and had led his party on by foot, marching quickly, his daughter just behind him, the twelve-man elite corps squad fanned out about them, prepared for anything.

The Marshal had taken extraordinary steps to bring his daughter home. Things were in flux again and if their enemies were to strike anywhere, they would strike here, at one of the terminals. Which was why he was taking no chances.

The 'bolt' was waiting for them, its normal crew of eighty pared down to ten trusted men, its usual complement of fifteen hundred passengers reduced to fourteen for this one journey. It was a fast-track monorail, cutting directly through the City, south to Turku, then east to Helsinki Terminal. From there they would commission another transporter and fly across the Baltic direct to Danzig.

Tolonen looked about him, tense despite his strict arrangements. For once he had chosen to trust no one; only he knew what he had planned. Even so, it would not be difficult for his enemies to second-guess him. If they could get into his home, what could they not do?

As they boarded the bolt he hesitated, scanning the platform both ways, then went inside. Jelka was already seated, her long legs stretched out in front of her. He smiled, studying her a moment, noticing how she had got a colour from being outside, how her hair seemed even blonder than usual. He sat, facing her, leaning forward, his hands clasped together between his knees.

'Well?'

It was the first time they had relaxed together. On the flight across from the island he had been busy, taking reports and giving orders, but now he could take time to talk; to ask her how she had enjoyed her stay.

She looked back at him and smiled, her eyes sparkling. 'It was beautiful, Daddy. Just beautiful.'

'So you enjoyed it?' He laughed. 'That's good...'

She looked away. For a moment there was a strange wistfulness in her eyes; a wistfulness he shared and understood.

For a moment he just looked at her, realizing how precious she was to him. She was so like her mother now. So like the woman he had loved.

'You look tired,' she said, concerned for him.

'Do I?' He laughed again, then nodded. 'Well, perhaps I am.' He smiled and leaned forward again, reaching out to take her hands in his. 'Listen, we've got one stop-off to make, but then I've got the evening free. How do you fancy coming to the opera? I've booked a box. It's the T'ang's own company. They're doing The South Branch.'

She laughed, delighted, for a moment forgetting her heaviness of heart. She had always liked the opera, and if The South Branch wasn't the lightest of subjects, it was still opera.

'Where are we going first?'

He sat back, relinquishing her hands. 'It's just business. It won't take long. A half-hour at most. Then we can get back and get changed, neh?'

They felt the bolt judder then begin to move, picking up speed very quickly. Jelka looked away, watching the dragon pattern on the wall beyond the window flicker and then blur, until it was just seven lines of red and green and gold.

'Did Uncle Jon tell you about the storm?'

'No...' He laughed. 'There was a storm, was there?'

'Yes.' She turned, looking back at him. 'It was so powerful. So...'

He looked down, as if disturbed. 'Yes,' he said quietly. 'I'd forgotten.'

She stared at him a moment, surprised by his sudden change of mood. 'What is it?'

He looked up at her again, forcing a smile. 'Nothing... Just that it suddenly reminded me of your mother.'

'Ah...' She nodded. Then it was as her uncle had said. Yes, she could see it now; how different her father and mother had been, and yet how much in love.

She turned her head, seeing their reflections in the glass of the window, and smiled sadly. It must have been hard for him; harder even than his exile.

She pushed the thought away, trying to cheer herself with the prospect of the evening ahead, but then, raising her hand to touch her cheek, she caught the unexpected scent of burnt pine on her fingers and felt herself go still.

'What is it?' her father asked, his eyes never leaving her.

'Nothing,' she answered, turning, smiling at him again. 'Nothing at all.'

'Who's that?'

Tolonen came back to the one-way mirror and stood beside his daughter. 'That? Why that's Ward. Kim Ward. He's a strange one. Quite brilliant. They say his mind is quicker than a machine.'

She laughed, surprised. 'You mean he's one of the team?'

'Yes, and probably the best, by all accounts. It's astonishing, considering...'

Jelka looked up at him. 'Considering what?'

Her father looked away, as if the matter were distasteful. 'He's Clayborn. Can't you see it in him? That darkness behind the eyes. He's been conditioned, but even so, it's never quite the same, is it? There's always that little bit of savagery left in them.' He looked back at her, smiling. 'Still... let's get on, eh? I've done here now and Hans is waiting back home.'

She nodded vaguely, looking back at the boy, pressing her face close up against the glass to stare at him. She could see what her father meant. When he turned to face the glass it was as though something else – something other than the boy – looked back at her. Some wild and uncaged thing that owed nothing to this world of levels. She shivered, not from fear but from a sense of recognition. She laughed softly, surprised to find him here, when she had thought him left behind her on the island. Then, as if coming to herself, she pushed back slightly from the glass, afraid.

And yet it was true. She could see it, there, in his eyes. Clayborn, her father had said. But he was more than that.

'Come, Jelka. Let's get on.'

For a moment longer she hesitated, watching the boy, then turned, following her father, only then realizing what he had said earlier.

'The gods preserve us...' she said almost inaudibly. 'Hans Ebert! That's all I need!'

Kim turned, looking across the table at Hammond.

'Who was that?'

'Who?'

'The girl. The one with Marshal Tolonen.'

Hammond laughed. 'Oh, her... That was his daughter, didn't you know?'

'Ah...' For a while he had thought it might have been his wife. It was the habit of such men, after all, to take young girls for wives. Or so he had heard. But he was strangely pleased that he'd been mistaken.

'Did you hear the rumours?' one of the other men said, keeping his voice low. 'They say the *Ping Tiao* tried to assassinate her.'

Kim frowned. 'It wasn't on the news.'

'No,' one of the others said conspiratorially. 'It wouldn't be. Just now they want everyone to believe that things are quiet and that they're in control. But I've heard... well, they say a whole squad of them attacked the Marshal's apartment. She killed six of them before her father intervened.'

Kim felt a strange ripple of excitement – or was it fear? – move down his spine. He looked at Hammond again.

'What's her name?'

Hammond frowned. 'I'm not sure. Jukka, or something.'

'Jelka,' one of them corrected him. 'Jelka Tolonen.'

Jelka. He shivered, then looked down. Yes, the name fitted her perfectly. Like something out of myth...

'What's going on here?'

Kim looked up, meeting Spatz's eyes. 'Nothing,' he said. 'Nothing at all.'

'Good. Then you can go now, Ward. I've no further use for you.'

He bowed slightly, keeping all expression from his face, but inwardly he felt elated. Spatz had had no choice other than to bring him into the laboratories for the duration of the Marshal's visit and Kim had made the most of it, calling up files and asking questions until he was as fully briefed of developments as the best of them. Yet as he walked back down the corridor to his room he found himself thinking not of the Project but of the girl. Who was she? What was she like? What did she sound like when she spoke? How did her face change when she laughed?

He paused at his doorway, thinking of how she had stood there at her father's side, her deeply blue eyes taking in everything. And then, briefly, her eyes had met his own and she had frowned. As if...

He shook his head, then palmed the lock and stepped inside as the door irised open. It wasn't possible. It was only his imagination. And yet... well, for the briefest moment it had seemed that she had *seen* him. Not just the outward form of him, but his deeper self.

He smiled, dismissing the thought, then sat down on his bed, looking about him. *What would you make of this, Jelka Tolonen?* he wondered. It would be too alien, I'm sure. Too dull. Too esoteric.

Yes, for she was not of his kind. She was First Level; powerful, sophisticated, rich. No doubt she was in love with fine clothes and dances, opera and gallant young officers. It was ridiculous even to think...

And yet he *was* thinking it.

For a moment he closed his eyes, seeing her again: so straight and tall and perfectly proportioned, her skin so pure and white, her hair like gold and silver blended, her eyes...

He caught his breath, remembering her eyes. *Like something out of myth.*

Chapter 53

KING OF THE WORLD

Tsu Ma stood on the grassy slope, looking south, the ruined monastery above him, at his back. He could see her in the distance, a tiny figure beneath the huge, cloudless sky, spurring her horse on along the narrow track between the rocks. For a brief moment he lost sight of her behind the great tor at the valley's head, then she reappeared, closer now, her dark hair loose, streaming behind her as she leaned forward in the saddle, climbing the long slope.

He looked down, sighing. They had met here several times these last few weeks, and every time they had ended by making love, despite his resolve to cast her off and mend his ways. But this time it was different. This time he had to end it. To break off with her, before they were discovered.

He was still in love with her; there was no denying that. But love was not enough, he knew that now; for this love – a love that had begun in passion and bewilderment – had now become a torment, keeping him from sleep, distracting him at every moment, until he felt he had to halt it or go mad. He could not now meet with Li Yuan or his father without wanting to throw himself at their feet and beg forgiveness for the wrong he had done them both.

So now an end to it. While it was yet within his power to end it.

He watched her come on, hearing her voice now, encouraging the horse; saw how she sat up in the saddle, looking for him, then raised a hand in greeting. He returned the gesture uncertainly, steeling himself against the thoughts that came. Last time they had climbed the hill together, hand in hand, then gone inside, into the ruined temple, and lain there on his cloak three hours, naked, their eyes, their hands and lips, feasting upon each other's bodies. The sweetness of the memory ate at him now, like sugar on a tooth. He groaned and clenched his fists against it. Even so, his sex stirred and his heart began to hammer in his chest.

He had never known how dreadful love could be; had never imagined how the heart could grieve and yet exult at the same time. But so his did.

She drew nearer, her horse labouring under her, snorting, straining to make the steep gradient. Seeing her thus reminded him of that first time, when she had ridden past him, ignoring his offer of help. Back then he had been thrilled by her defiance, for all he'd said to her of taking care, but now that recklessness in her seemed less attractive. Was the very thing, perhaps, that forged his determination to bring things to a head.

'Tsu Ma!'

She jumped down and ran to him, throwing her arms about him, her lips seeking his, but he held still against her, as if made of stone. She drew back, astonished, her eyes wide, looking up into his face.

'What is it, my love? What's happened?'

He looked down at her, his hands trembling now, her beauty, the warmth of her hands where they touched him, almost robbing him of his senses. Her perfume was intoxicating, her eyes like oceans in which a man could drown.

'I love you,' he began, the full depth of what he felt for her concentrated in those few words.

'I know,' she interrupted him, pressing closer, relief flooding her face. 'And I've news...'

'Hear me out!' he said harshly, then relented, his hand brushing against her face, his voice softening. 'Please, my love, hear me out. This is difficult enough...'

Her face changed again. She tried to smile, then frowned. 'Difficult?'

'Yes. I...' He swallowed. Never had anything been so difficult as this. Not even the death of his father and the ritual killing of the 'copy' had prepared him for the hardship of this moment.

He fell silent. Even now it was not said. Even now he could take her in his arms and carry her up into the temple rooms and lay her on his cloak. Even now he could have that sweetness one last time.

But no. If this once then he would want her for ever. And that could not be. Not while there were Seven. Chung Kuo itself would have to fall before he could have Fei Yen.

He looked down, the pain of what he felt almost overwhelming him.

'You want to end it? Is that it?'

Her voice was strangely soft, surprisingly sympathetic. He looked up and saw how she was looking at him, saw how his own hurt was reflected in her face. And even as he watched he saw the first tears begin to gather in the corners of her eyes and fall, slowly, ever so slowly, down the porcelain perfection of her cheek.

'Fei Yen...' he said, his voice a whisper. 'You know I love you.'

'And I you.' She shuddered, then stepped back from him. 'I had a dream. A dream that I was free to become your wife.'

He shivered, horrified by the words. 'It cannot be.'

Her eyes were pleading with him now. 'Why not? I was his brother's wife. You know our laws.'

'And yet you married him. The Seven put their seals to the special Edict. It was done. It cannot be undone.'

'Why not? You willed the law changed once, now will it back.'

He shook his head. It was as he said; it could not be undone. Though all the seven T'ang agreed the match was ill-chosen, they would not change this thing. Not now. For one day Li Yuan would be T'ang, and to do this would be to wound him deeply. Only catastrophe could come of that. Only the end of everything they were.

He spoke clearly now, articulating each word separately. 'I would we both were free, Fei Yen. I would give up all I have for that. But only ill – great ill – would come of it. And this, this *play* between us... it too must end. We must not meet like this again. Not ever.'

She winced at his finality. 'Not *ever*?'

The sweetness of the words, their pain and pleading, seemed to tear his soul from him, and yet he stood firm against her, knowing that to soften now would undo everything. 'Not ever. Understand me, Li Yuan's wife? From now on we are but... acquaintances, who meet at functions and the like. All other thoughts must now be put aside.'

'Would you forget...?' she began, then fell silent, dropping her head, for he was glaring at her.

'Enough! Would you have me die before you've done with me?'

'Never...' she answered, the word a mere breath, a whisper.

'Then go. At once.'

She bowed, obedient, for a moment so like a wife to him that he caught his breath, pained, beyond all curing pained by the sight of her, broken, defeated by his own determination not to have her.

And then she was gone and he was alone again. He sat down heavily, feeling suddenly empty, hollowed of everything but grief, and wept.

Fei Yen jumped down and, without waiting for her groom to come and take the horse, made towards the palace. As she ran through the stable yards, grooms and servants bowed low then straightened up, watching her back, astonished. No one dared say a word, but their exchanged glances spoke eloquently. They had seen her ruined face and understood, for they, at least, knew what had been happening between the Princess and the handsome young T'ang.

And now, it seemed, it was over.

In the corridor Nan Ho made to greet her, but she ran past him as if he was not there. He turned, frowning, deciding not to pursue her but to go out to the stables and investigate the matter. It was his duty, after all, to serve his Prince. And how better than to understand and gauge the volatile moods of the woman closest to him?

Fei Yen herself went into her rooms and slammed the doors behind her, locking them, then threw herself down on to the bed, letting the enormity of what had happened wash over her at last, her tiny body shaken by great shuddering sobs.

For a while she slept, then woke an hour later, all of the anger and hurt washed from her. She stood and looked about her, studying the hangings, the rich furnishings of her room, frowning at their strangeness, finding no connection between herself and these things. It was as if she had died and come to life again, for she felt nothing. Only an overpowering numbness where feeling ought to be.

She turned, catching her own reflection in the glass on the far side of the room. She took a step towards it then stopped, looking down sharply.

Her news... She had never had a chance to tell him her news.

She stood there a moment, trembling, a single tear running down her cheek, then lifted her head defiantly, taking control of herself again, knowing what she must do.

She bathed, then summoned her maids and had them put her hair up and dress her in a simple *chi pao*, the silk a pale lavender trimmed with blue. Then, to perfect the look, she removed all of her bangles and her rings, bar his, wearing nothing about her neck. That done, she stood before the mirror, examining herself minutely.

Yes. That was the look she wanted. Not sumptuous and sophisticated but plain and almost earthy – like a peasant girl. She had kept even her make-up simple.

Smiling, she turned from the mirror and went out, into the corridor.

'Master Nan!' she called, glimpsing the Master of the Inner Chambers at the far end of the corridor.

Nan Ho turned, acknowledging her, then, giving a small bow to the man he had been talking to, hastened to her, stopping four paces from Fei Yen and bowing low, his eyes averted.

'Master Nan, is my husband back yet?'

Nan Ho kept his head lowered. 'He is, my lady. Twenty minutes past.'

'Good.' She turned, looking away from him. 'Then go to him, Master Nan, and tell him his wife would welcome a few moments of his time.'

Nan Ho looked up, surprised, then looked down quickly. 'Forgive me, my lady, but the Prince asked not to be disturbed. He has important work to finish.'

'He is in his study, then?'

Nan Ho bowed his head slightly. 'That is so, my lady. With his personal secretary, Chang Shih-Sen.'

'Then you need worry yourself no longer, Nan Ho. I'll go to him myself.'

'But, my lady...'

'You are dismissed, Nan Ho.'

He bowed very low. 'As my lady wishes.'

She watched him go, then turned away, walking quickly towards her husband's study.

In front of the door she hesitated, composing herself, then knocked.

There was a moment's silence, then footsteps. A second later the door opened slightly and Secretary Chang looked out at her.

'My lady...' He bowed, then opened the door wider, stepping back, at the same time looking across at Li Yuan.

'It is your wife, my lord, the Princess Fei.'

Li Yuan stood up behind his desk as Fei Yen entered, his face lighting at the sight of her.

'Fei Yen... I thought you were out riding.'

'I...' She hesitated, then crossed the room until only the desk was between them. 'The truth is, husband, I could not settle until I had seen you. Master Nan said you had returned...'

Li Yuan looked past her at his secretary. 'Go now, Shih-sen. We'll finish this later.' Then, smiling, he came round the desk and embraced her, lifting her face to kiss her lips. 'Your eagerness to see me warms me, my love. I've missed you too.'

She let her head rest against his chest a moment, then looked up at him again. 'I've missed you, yes, but that isn't why I've interrupted you...'

He laughed gently. 'You need no reason to interrupt me. You are reason enough in yourself.'

She smiled and looked down. 'Even so, it wasn't only my eagerness to see you. I have some news.'

'News?' He moved her slightly back from him, taking her upper arms gently in his hands, studying her. Then he smiled again. 'Well, let us go outside, into the garden. We'll sit on the bench seat, side by side, like doves on a perch, and you can tell me your news.'

Returning his smile, she let herself be led out into the sunlit warmth of the garden. From somewhere near at hand a songbird called, then called again. They sat, facing each other on the sun-warmed bench.

'You look beautiful, my love,' he said, admiring her. 'I don't know what you've done, but it suits you.' He reached out, his fingers brushing against her cheek, caressing the bare, unadorned flesh of her neck. 'But come, my love, what news is this you have?'

For a second or two her eyes searched his, as if for prior knowledge of what she was about to say; but he, poor boy, suspected nothing.

'What would you say if I told you I had fallen?'

He laughed, then shook his head, puzzled. 'Fallen?'

She smiled, then reached out, taking his hands in her own. 'Yes, my wise and yet foolish husband. *Fallen*. The doctors confirmed it this very morning.'

She saw how his eyes widened with sudden comprehension and laughed, nodding her head. 'Yes, my love. That's right. We're going to have a child.'

It was late afternoon and the Officers' Club at Bremen was almost empty. A few men stood between the pillars on the far side of the vast, hexagonal lounge, talking idly, but only one of the tables was occupied.

A Han servant, his shaven head bowed, made his way across the huge expanse of green-blue carpet to the table, a heavily laden tray carried effortlessly in one hand. And as he moved between the men, scrupulously avoiding touching or even brushing against them as he set down their drinks, he affected not to hear their mocking laughter, or the substance of their talk.

One of them, a tall, moustachioed man named Scott, leaned forward, laughing, then stubbed out his cigar in one of the empty glasses.

'It's the talk of the Above,' he said, leaning back and looking about him at his fellow officers. Then, more drily, 'What's more, they're already placing bets on who'll succeed the old bugger as Minister.'

Their laughter spilled out across the empty space, making the Han working behind the bar look up before they averted their eyes again.

They were talking of Minister Chuang's marriage earlier that day. The old man had cast off his first wife and taken a new one – a young girl of only fourteen. It was this last that Scott had been rather salaciously referring to.

'Well, good luck to the man, I say,' another of them, Panshin, said, raising his glass in a toast. Again there was laughter. Only when it had died down did Hans Ebert sit forward slightly and begin to talk. He had been quieter than usual, preferring for once to sit and listen rather than be the focus of their talk, but now all eyes looked to him.

'It's a sad story,' he began, looking down. 'And if I'd had an inkling of how it would turn out I would never have got involved.'

There was a murmur of sympathy at that – an exchange of glances and a nodding of heads.

'Yes, well... there's a lesson to us all, neh?' he continued, looking about him, meeting their eyes candidly. 'The woman was clearly deranged long before I came across her.'

For once there was no attempt to derive a second meaning from his words. All there realized the significance of what had happened. An affair was one thing, but this was different. Events had got out of hand and the woman had overstepped the mark when she had attacked Ebert.

'No,' Ebert went on. 'It saddens me to say so, but I do believe Madam Chuang would have ended in the sanatorium whether I'd crossed her path or not. As for her husband, I'm sure he's much better off with his *tian-fang*,' he smiled, looking at Scott, 'even if the girl kills him from sheer pleasure.'

There were smiles at that but no laughter. Even so, their mood was suddenly lighter. The matter had been there, unstated, behind all their earlier talk, dampening their spirits. But now it was said and all felt easier for it.

'No one blames you, Hans,' Panshin said, leaning forward to touch his arm. 'As you say, it would have happened anyway. It was just bad luck that you got involved.'

'That's so,' Ebert said, lifting his shot-glass to his lips and downing its contents in one sharp, savage gulp. 'And there are consolations. The *mui tsai* for one.'

Fest leaned forward, leering, his speech slurred. 'Does that mean you've cooled towards the other one, Hans?' He laughed suggestively. 'You know. The young chink whore... Golden Heart.'

Fest was not known for his discretion at the best of times, but this once his words had clearly offended Ebert. He sat there, glaring at Fest. 'That's my business,' he said coldly. 'Don't you agree?'

Fest's smile faded. He sat back, shaking his head, suddenly more sober. 'Forgive me, Hans, I didn't mean...' He fell silent, bowing his head.

Ebert stared at Fest a moment longer, then looked about him, smiling. 'Excuse my friend, *ch'un tzu*. I think he's had enough.' He looked back at Fest. 'I think you'd best go home, Fest. Auden here will take you if you want.'

Fest swallowed, then shook his head. 'No. I'll be all right. It's not far.' He sought Ebert's eyes again. 'Really, Hans, I didn't mean anything by it.'

Ebert smiled tightly. 'It's all right. I understand. You drank too much, that's all.'

'Yes...' Fest set his glass down and got unsteadily to his feet. He moved out from his seat almost exaggeratedly, then turned, bowing to each of them in turn. 'Friends...'

When he was gone, Ebert looked about him, lowering his voice slightly.

'Forgive me for being so sharp with him, but sometimes he forgets his place. It's a question of breeding, I suppose. His father climbed the levels, and sometimes his manners...' He spread his arms. 'Well, you know how it is.'

'We understand,' Panshin said, touching his arm again. 'But duty calls me too, I'm afraid, much as I'd like to sit here all afternoon. Perhaps you'd care to call on me some time, Hans? For dinner?'

Ebert smiled broadly. 'I'd like that, Anton. Arrange something with my equerry. I'm busy this week, but next?'

Slowly it broke up, the other officers going their own ways, until only Auden was there with him at the table.

'Well?' Auden asked, after a moment, noticing how deep in thought Ebert was.

Ebert looked up, chewing on a nail.

'You're annoyed, aren't you?'

'Too fucking right I am. The bastard doesn't know when to hold his tongue. It was bad enough the Minister committing his wife to the asylum, but I don't want to be made a total laughing stock.'

Auden hesitated, then nodded. 'So what do you want me to do?'

Ebert sat back, staring away across the sea of empty tables towards the bar, then looked back at him, shuddering with anger.

'I want him taught a lesson, that's what I want. I want something that'll remind him to keep his fucking mouth shut and drink a little less.'

'A warning, you mean?'

Ebert nodded. 'Yes. But nothing too drastic. A little roughing up, perhaps.'

'Okay. I'll go there now, if you like.' He hesitated, then added, 'And the pictures?'

Ebert stared back at him a moment. Auden was referring to the package he had left with him the day he had been attacked by the madwoman. He took a breath, then laughed. 'They were interesting, Will. Very interesting. Where did you get them?'

Auden smiled. 'From a friend, let's say. One of my contacts in the Net.'

Ebert nodded. It had been quite a coincidence. There he'd been, only half an hour before, talking to Marshal Tolonen about the missing sculptures, and there was Auden, handing him the package containing holograms of the selfsame items he had been instructed to find.

'So what do you want to do?' Auden prompted.

'Nothing,' Ebert answered, smiling enigmatically. 'Unless your friend has something else for me.'

Auden met his eyes a moment, then looked away. So he understood at last. But would he bite? 'I've a letter for you,' he said, taking the envelope from his tunic pocket. 'From your Uncle Lutz.'

Ebert took it from him, then laughed. 'You know what's in this?'

Auden shook his head. 'I'm only the messenger, Hans. It wouldn't do for me to know what's going on.'

Ebert studied his friend a while, then nodded slowly. 'No, it wouldn't, would it?' He looked down at the envelope and smiled. 'And this? Is this your friend's work, too?'

Auden frowned. 'I don't know what you mean, Hans. As I said...'

Ebert raised a hand. 'It doesn't matter.' He leaned forward, taking Auden's hand, his face suddenly earnest. 'I trust you, Will. Alone of all this crowd of shits and hangers-on, you're the only one I can count on absolutely. You know that, don't you?'

Auden nodded. 'I know. That's why I'd never let you down.'

'No,' Ebert smiled back at him fiercely, then sat back, releasing his hand. 'Then get going, Will. Before that loud-mouthed bastard falls asleep. Meanwhile, I'll find out what my uncle wants.'

Auden rose, then bowed. 'Take care, Hans.'

'And you, Will. And you.'

Fest leaned against the wall pad, locking the door behind him, then threw his tunic down on to the floor. Ebert had been right. He *had* had too much to drink. But what the hell? Ebert was no saint when it came to drinking. Many was the night *he'd* fallen from his chair incapable. And that business about the girl, the chink whore, Golden Heart. Fest laughed.

'I touched a sore spot there, didn't I, Hans, old pal? Too fucking sore for your liking, neh?'

He shivered, then laughed again. Ebert would be mad for a day or two, but that was all. If he kept his distance for a bit it would all blow over. Hans would forget, and then...

He belched, then put his arm out to steady himself against the wall. 'Time to piss...'

He stood there, over the sink, unbuttoning himself. It was illegal to urinate in the wash basins, but what the shit? Everyone did it. It was too much to expect a man to walk down the corridor to the urinals every time he wanted a piss.

He was partway through, thinking of the young sing-song girl, Golden Heart, and what he'd like to do to her when the door chime sounded. He half turned, pissing on his boots and trouser leg, then looked down, cursing.

'Who the hell...?'

He tucked himself in and, not bothering to button up, staggered back out into the room.

'Who is it?' he called out, then realized he didn't have his hand on the intercom.

What the fuck? he thought, *it's probably Scott, come to tell me what happened after I'd gone.* He went across and banged his hand against the lock to open it, then turned away, bending down to pick his tunic up off the floor.

He was straightening up when a boot against his buttocks sent him sprawling head first. Then his arms were being pulled up sharply behind his back and his wrists fastened together with a restraining brace.

'What in hell's name?' he gasped, trying to turn his head and see who it was, but a blow against the side of the head stunned him and he lay there a moment, tasting blood, the weight of the man on his back preventing him from getting up.

He groaned, then felt a movement in his throat. 'Oh, fuck... I'm going to be sick...'

The weight lifted from him, letting him bring his knees up slightly and hunch over, his forehead pressed against the floor as he heaved and heaved. Then he was done. For a moment, he rested there, his eyes closed, sweat beading his forehead, the stench of sickness filling the room.

'Gods, but you disgust me, Fest.'

He looked sideways, finding it hard to focus, then swallowed awkwardly. 'And who the fuck are you?'

The man laughed coldly. 'Don't you recognize me, Fest? Was it so long ago that your feeble little mind has discarded the memory?'

Fest swallowed again. 'Haavikko. You're Haavikko, aren't you?'

The man nodded. 'And this here is my friend, Kao Chen.'

A second face, that of a Han, appeared beside Haavikko's, then moved away. It was a strangely familiar face, though Fest couldn't recall why. And that name...

Fest closed his eyes, the throbbing in his head momentarily painful, then slowly opened them again. The bastard had hit him hard. Very hard. He'd get him for that.

'What do you want?' he asked, his cut lip stinging now.

Haavikko crouched next to him, pulling his head back by the hair. 'Justice, I'd have said, once upon a time, but that's no longer enough – not after what I've been through. No. I want to hurt you and humiliate you, Fest, as much as I've been hurt and humiliated.'

Fest shook his head slowly, restrained by the other's grip on him. 'I don't understand. I've done nothing to you, Haavikko. Nothing.'

'Nothing?' Haavikko's laugh of disbelief was sour. He tugged Fest's head back sharply, making him cry out. 'You call backing Ebert up and having me dishonoured before the General nothing?' He snorted, then let go, pushing Fest's head away roughly. He stood. 'You shit. You call that *nothing*?'

Fest grimaced. 'I warned you. I told you to leave it, but you wouldn't. If only you'd kept your mouth shut...'

Haavikko's boot caught Fest on the shoulder. He fell on to his side, groaning, then lay there, the pain lancing through him. For a time he was still, silent, then he turned his head again, trying to look back at Haavikko.

'You think you'll get away with this?'

It was the Han who answered him, his face pressed close to Fest's, his breath sour on Fest's cheek. 'See this?' He brought a knife into the range of Fest's vision – a big, vicious-looking knife, longer and broader than the regulation issue, the edge honed razor-sharp.

'I see it,' Fest said, fighting down the fear he suddenly felt.

'Good. Then you'll be polite, my friend, and not tell us what we can or cannot do.'

There was something coldly fanatical about the Han. Something odd. As if all his hatred were detached from him. It made him much more dangerous than Haavikko, for all Haavikko's threats. Fest looked away, a cold thrill of fear rippling through him.

'What are you going to do?'

The Han laughed. Again it was cold, impersonal. 'Not us, Fest. You.

What are *you* going to do? Are you going to help us nail that bastard, Ebert, or are you going to be difficult?'

Fest went very still. So that was it. Ebert. They wanted to get at Ebert. He turned back, meeting the Han's eyes again. 'And if I don't help you?'

The Han smiled. A killer's smile. 'If you don't, then you go down with him. Because we'll get him, be assured of that. And when we do, we'll nail you at the same time, Captain Fest. For all the shit *you've* done at his behest.'

Fest swallowed. It was true. His hands were far from clean. But he also sensed the unstated threat in the Han's words. If he *didn't* help... He looked away, certain that the Han would kill him if he said no. And then, suddenly, something broke in him and he was sobbing, his face pressed against the floor, the smell of his own vomit foul in his nostrils.

'I hate him. Don't you understand that? *Hate* him.'

Haavikko snorted his disgust. 'I don't believe you, Fest. You're his creature. You do his bidding. You forget, old friend, I've seen you at your work.'

But Fest was shaking his head. He looked up at Haavikko, his face pained, his voice broken now. 'I *had* to. Don't you understand that, Haavikko? That time before Tolonen – I *had* to lie. Because if I hadn't...'

The Han looked to Haavikko, something passing between them, then he looked back at Fest. 'Go on,' he said, his voice harder than before. 'Tell us. What *could* he have done? You only had to tell the truth.'

Fest closed his eyes, shuddering. 'Gods, how I wished I had. But I was scared.'

'You're a disgrace—' Haavikko began, but Fest interrupted him.

'No. You still don't understand. I *couldn't*. I...' He looked down hopelessly, then shook his head again. 'You see, I killed a girl...'

Haavikko started forward angrily. 'You lying bastard!'

Fest stared back at him, wide-eyed, astonished by his reaction; not understanding what he meant by it. 'But it's true! I killed a girl. It was an accident... in a sing-song house – and Ebert found out about it...'

Haavikko turned, outraged. 'He's lying, Chen! Mocking me!'

'No!' Chen put his hand on Haavikko's arm, restraining him. 'Hear him out. And think, Axel. Think. Ebert's not that imaginative a man. What he did to you – where would he have got that idea if not from Fest here? And what better guarantee that it would work than having seen it done once before?'

Haavikko stared back at him open-mouthed, then nodded. He turned, looking back at Fest, sobered. 'Go on,' he said, almost gently this time. 'Tell us, Fest. Tell us what happened.'

Fest shivered, looking from man to man, then, lowering his eyes, he began.

The doorman bowed low, then stepped back, his fingers nimbly tucking the folded note into his back pocket as he did so.

'If the gentleman would care to wait, I'll let *Shih* Ebert know he's here.'

DeVore went inside and took a seat, looking about him. The lobby of the Abacus Club was a big, high-ceilinged room, dimly lit and furnished with low, heavy-looking armchairs. In the centre of the room a tiny pool was set into a raised platform, a fountain playing musically in its midst, while here and there huge bronze urns stood like pot-bellied wrestlers, their arms transformed to ornately curved handles, their heads to bluntly flattened lids.

Across from him the wall space was taken up by a single huge tapestry. It depicted an ancient trading hall, the space beneath its rafters overflowing with human life, busy with frenetic activity, each trader's table piled high with coins and notes and scrolled documents. In the foreground a clearly prosperous merchant haggled with a customer while his harried clerk sat at the table behind him, his fingers nimbly working the beads of his abacus. The whole thing was no doubt meant to illustrate the principles of honest trade and sturdy self-reliance, but to the eye of an impartial observer the impression was merely one of greed.

DeVore smiled to himself, then looked up as Lutz Ebert appeared at the far end of the lobby. He went across, meeting Ebert halfway.

Lutz Ebert was very different from his brother, Klaus. Ten years his brother's junior, he had inherited little of his father's vast fortune and even less, it seemed, of his distinctive personal traits. Lutz was a tall, slim, dark-haired man, more suave in his manner than his brother – the product of his father's second marriage to an opera star. Years before DeVore had heard someone describe Lutz as honey-tongued, and it was true. Unlike his brother he'd had to make his own way in the world and the experience had marked him. He was wont to look away when he talked to you or press one's hand overzealously, as if to emphasize his friendship. The blunt, no-nonsense aloofness that was his brother's way was not allowed him, and he knew it. He was not his brother, neither in power nor personality, though he was not averse to using the connection, letting others make what they would of his relationship with – and his possible influence over – one of Chung Kuo's most powerful men. He had swung many deals that way: deals which the force of his own personality and limited circumstances might have put outside his grasp. Here, in the Abacus Club, however, he was in his element – among his own kind.

Lutz smiled warmly, greeting him, then gave a small, respectful bow.

'What an unexpected pleasure, *Shih* Loehr. You'll dine with me, I hope. My private rooms are at the back. We can talk there undisturbed.'

'Of course.'

The rooms were small but sumptuously furnished in the latest First Level fashion. DeVore unbuttoned his tunic, looking about him, noting the bedroom off to one side. No doubt much of Lutz Ebert's business was trans-acted thus, in shared debauchery with others of his kind. DeVore smiled to himself again, then raised a hand, politely refusing the drink Ebert had poured for him.

'I won't, thanks. I've had a tiring journey and I've a few other visits to make before the day's over. But if you've a fruit juice or something...'

'Of course.' Ebert turned away and busied himself at the drinks cabinet again.

'This is very nice, my friend. Very nice indeed. Might I ask what kind of rental you pay on these rooms?'

Ebert laughed, then turned, offering DeVore the glass. 'Nominally it's only twenty thousand a year, but in reality it works out to three or four times that.'

DeVore nodded, raising his glass in a silent toast. He understood. There were two prices for everything in this world. One was the official, regulated price: the price you'd pay if things were fair and there were no officials to pay squeeze to, no queues to jump. The other was the actual price – the cost of oiling palms and getting what a thousand others wanted.

Ebert sat, facing him. 'However, I'm sure that's not why you came to see me.'

'No. I came about your nephew.'

'I thought as much.'

'You've written to him?'

'In the terms you suggested, proposing that he calls on me tomorrow evening for supper.'

'And will he come?'

Ebert smiled, then took an envelope from his top pocket and handed it to DeVore. Inside was a brief handwritten note from Hans, saying he would be delighted to dine with his uncle.

DeVore handed the letter back. 'You know what to say?'

'Don't worry, Howard. I know how to draw a man. You say you've gauged his mood already – well, fair enough – but I know my nephew. He's a proud one. What if he doesn't want this meeting?'

DeVore sat back. 'He'll want it, Lutz, I guarantee it. But you must make it clear that there's no pressure on him, no obligation. I'd like to meet him, that's all – to have the opportunity of talking with him.'

He saw Ebert's hesitation and smiled inwardly. Ebert knew what risks he was taking simply in being here, but really he'd had no option. His last business venture had failed miserably, leaving him heavily indebted. To clear those debts Ebert had to work with him, whether he wished it or not. In any case, he was being paid very well for his services as go-between – a quarter of a million *yuan* – with the promise, if things worked out, of further payments.

There was a knock at the door. It was the steward, come to take their orders for dinner. Ebert dealt with him, then turned back to DeVore, smiling, more relaxed now the matter had been raised and dealt with.

'Are you sure there's nothing else I can do for you, Howard? Nothing I can arrange?'

DeVore sat back, then nodded. 'Now you mention it, Lutz, there is one small thing you can do for me. There's something I want to find a buyer for. A statuette...'

In the transporter returning to the Wilds, DeVore lay back, his eyes closed, thinking over his day's work. He had started early, going down beneath the Net to meet with Gesell and Mach. It had been a hard session, but he had emerged triumphant. As he'd suspected, Wang Sau-leyan had convinced them – Gesell particularly – that they ought to attack Li Shai Tung's Plantations in Eastern Europe. Once implanted, this notion had been hard to dislodge, but eventually he had succeeded, persuading Mach that an attack on Bremen would strike a far more damaging blow against the T'ang while damaging his own people less. His agreement to hand over the remaining maps and to fund and train the special Ping Tiao squads had further clinched it. He could still see how they had looked at each other at the end of the meeting, as if they'd pulled a stroke on him, when it had been he who had called the tune.

From there he had gone on to dine with Ebert's uncle, and then to his final meeting of the day. He smiled. If life were a great game of wei chi, then what he had done today could be summarized thus. In his negotiations with the Ping Tiao he had extended his line and turned a defensive shape into an offensive one. In making advances to Hans Ebert through his uncle he sought to surround and thus remove one of his opponent's potentially strongest groups. These two were perfections of plays he had begun long ago, but the last was a brand-new play – the first stone set down on a different part of the board; the first shadowing of a wholly new shape.

The scientist had been easy to deal with. It was as his informer had said: the man was discontented and corrupt. The first made it possible to deal with him, the second to buy him. And bought him he had, spelling out precisely what he wanted for his money.

'Do this for me,' he'd said, 'and I'll make you rich beyond your dreams.' And in token of that promise he had given the man a chip for twenty thousand yuan. 'Fail me, however, and you had better have eyes in your back and a friend to guard your sleep. Likewise if you breathe but a single word of what I've asked you to do today.' He had leaned forward threateningly. 'I'm a generous man, Shih Barycz, but I'm also deadly if I'm crossed.'

He had seen the effect his words had had on the scientist and was satisfied it would be enough. But just to make sure he had bought a second man to watch the first. Because it never hurt to make sure.

And so he had laid his stone down, there where his opponents least expected it, at the heart of their own formation – the Wiring Project. For the boy, Kim, was to be his own, when he was ready for him. Meanwhile he would keep an eye on him and ensure he came to no harm. Barycz would be his eyes and ears and report back.

When the time came he would take the boy off planet. To Mars. And there he would begin a new campaign against the Seven. A campaign of such imaginative scope as would make their defensive measures seem like the ignorant posturings of cavemen.

He laughed and sat up, glimpsing the mountains through the portal to his left as the craft banked, circling the base.

But first he would undermine them. First he would smash their confidence – would break the *Ywe Lung*, the great wheel of dragons, and make them question every act they undertook. Would set them one against another, until...

Again he laughed. Until the final dragon ate its own tail. And then there would be nothing. Nothing but himself.

Hans Ebert smiled and placed his arm about Fest's shoulders. 'Don't worry, Edgar. The matter's closed. Now, what will you drink? I've a bottle of the T'ang's own finest *Shen*, if you'd like. It would be good to renew our friendship over such a good wine, don't you think?'

Fest lowered his head slightly, still ill at ease despite Ebert's apparent friendliness. He had thought of running when he'd first received Ebert's note summoning him to his apartment, but where would he run? In any case, it was only a bout of paranoia brought on by the visit of Haavikko and the Han to his rooms – there was no real reason why he should fear Ebert. And as for the other matter – the business with Golden Heart – not only had Ebert forgiven him, he had astonished him by offering him use of the girl.

'I've tired of her,' Ebert had said, standing there in the doorway next to him, looking in at the sleeping girl. 'I've trained her far too well, I suspect. She's far too docile. No, my preference is for a woman with more spirit. Like the *mui tsai*.'

Fest had looked about for her, but Ebert had quickly explained that he'd sent the *mui tsai* away. For a day or two.

Ebert had laughed again. 'It doesn't do to jade the appetite. A few days' abstinence sharpens the hunger, don't you find?'

Fest had nodded. It had been six days since he'd had a woman and his own hunger was sharp as a razor. From where he stood he could see the girl's naked breasts, the curve of her stomach where she had pushed down the sheet in her sleep, and swallowed. How often he'd imagined it. Ever since that first time in Mu Chua's.

Ebert had turned his face, meeting Fest's eyes. 'Well, Edgar? Wouldn't you like to have her?'

Slowly, reluctantly, he had nodded, and Ebert, as if satisfied, had smiled and drawn him back, pulling the door to.

'Well, maybe you will, eh? Maybe I'll let you use her.'

Now they stood there in the lounge, toasting their friendship, and Fest, having feared the very worst, began to relax.

Ebert turned, looking about him, then sat, smiling across at Fest.

'That's a nasty bruise you've got on the side of your face, Edgar. How did that come about?'

The question seemed innocuous – a mere pleasantry – yet Fest felt himself stiffen defensively. But Ebert seemed unconcerned. He looked down, sipping his drink, as if the answer were of no importance.

'I fell,' Fest began. 'Truth was, I was pissing in the sink and slipped. Caught myself a real crack on the cheek and almost knocked myself out.'

Ebert looked up at him. 'And your friends... how are they?'

Fest frowned. 'My friends? Scott, you mean? Panshin?'

Ebert shook his head slowly. 'No. Your other friends.'

'I don't know what you mean. What other friends?'

'Your new friends. The friends you made yesterday.'

Fest swallowed. So he knew. Or did he? And if he did, then why the earlier show of friendship? Why the offer of the girl? Unless it was all a game to draw him and make him commit himself.

He decided to brazen it out. 'I still don't follow you, Hans. I've no new friends.'

The speed with which Ebert came up out of his chair surprised him. Fest took a step backwards, spilling his drink.

'You fucking liar. You loud-mouthed, cheating liar. And to think I trusted you.'

Fest shivered. The change in Ebert was frightening. His smile had become a snarl. His eyes were wide with anger.

'It's all lies, Hans. Someone's been telling lies...'

Again Ebert shook his head, his contempt for Fest revealed at last in his eyes. He spat the words out venomously. 'You want to fuck the girl, eh? Well, I'd sooner see you dead first. And as for liars, there's only one here, and that's you, you fucking creep! Here, look at this.'

He picked up the picture Auden had taken from outside Fest's apartment and handed it across. It showed Fest standing in his doorway, saying goodbye to Haavikko and the Han. All three of them were smiling.

'Well? What have you got to say for yourself? Give me one good reason why I shouldn't kick your arse from here to Pei Ching!'

Fest stood there a moment longer, staring down at the photo, then let it fall from his fingers. He looked back at Ebert and smiled, for the first time in a long while feeling free, unbeholden to the man.

'Go fuck yourself, Hans Ebert.'

It was what he had wanted to say for more than fifteen years but had never had the courage to say until now. He saw how Ebert's eyes flared at his words and laughed.

'You little shit...'

He reacted slowly. Ebert's hand caught him a stinging blow to the ear, making him stagger back, knocking his glass from his hand. Then he was crouched, facing Ebert, knife in hand.

'Try that again, Ebert, and I'll cut you open.'

Ebert faced him, circling slowly, sneering now. 'You were always a windy little sod, Fest, but you were never any good with a knife. Why, if I'd not kept you for my amusement you'd have never made sergeant, let alone captain.'

Fest lunged, but again he was too slow. Ebert had moved. Fest's knife cut nothing but air. But Ebert caught his arm and held it in a vice-like grip, bringing it down savagely on to his knee.

Fest screamed, but his scream was cut short as Ebert smashed his face down on to his knee. Then, drawing his own knife, he thrust it once, twice, a third time into Fest's stomach, grunting with the effort, heaving it up through the mass of soft tissues until it glanced against the bone.

He thrust Fest away from him, then threw his knife down. For a moment Fest's eyes stared up at him, horrified, then he spasmed and his eyes glazed over. He had been disembowelled.

Ebert stood there a moment, looking down at what he had done, then turned and walked across, looking into the room where Golden Heart lay. She lay on her side now, her back to him, but he could see at once that she was sleeping. He shivered, then closed the door, locking it from his side.

He turned back. Blood was still welling from the corpse, bubbling like a tiny fountain from a severed artery, pooling on the floor beside the body. He stared at it a moment, fascinated, then went across to the comset and tapped in Auden's code.

In a moment Auden's face appeared. 'What is it, Hans?'

Ebert hesitated, then smiled. 'I had a little bother with our friend, I'm afraid. It... got out of hand. If you could come?'

'Of course. I'll be there directly. And, Hans?'

'What?'

'Don't forget. You've supper with your uncle tonight. Get washed and ready. I'll deal with the rest.'

Golden Heart lay there, hardly daring to breathe, still trembling from what she had witnessed through the narrow gap in the door. She had seen Ebert draw his knife and stab the other man, not once, to disable him, but three times...

She had heard him come to the doorway and look in, then had tensed as she heard the doorlock click, not daring to look and see if he were inside the room with her or not – expecting her own turn to be next. But then she had heard his voice, speaking on the comset outside, and had almost wept with relief.

Yet when she closed her eyes she could still see him, his face distorted with a mad fury, grunting as he pulled his knife up through the other man's flesh, tearing him open. *Murdering* him.

She shuddered and pulled the sheet tight about her. Yes, Ebert had murdered Fest, there was no other word for it. Fest had drawn his knife first, but Ebert had disarmed him before he'd drawn his own. And what followed had been nothing less than vicious, brutal murder.

And if he knew. If for a single moment he suspected she had seen...

She lay there a moment longer, listening to him moving about in the next room, getting ready for his supper date, then got up and went into the tiny washroom, closing the door quietly behind her before she knelt over the basin, sluicing the cold, clear water up into her face again and again, as if to wash the awful image from her eyes.

★

On the western terrace at Tongjiang it was early evening. Long shadows lay across the sunlit gardens below the balcony, while from the meadows by the lake a peacock cried, breaking the silence.

On the terrace itself tables had been laid with food and drink. At one end, against the wall of the Palace, a golden canopy had been erected, its platform slightly raised. There, enthroned in the dragon chair, sat the T'ang, Li Shai Tung, Prince Yuan and the Lady Fei standing to one side of him beneath the bright red awning.

The T'ang had summoned all of the household servants who could be spared out on to the terrace. They stood there, crowded into the space in front of the canopy, more than six hundred in all, silent, wine tumblers in hand, waiting for the T'ang to speak.

To one side of this gathering the Master of the Inner Chamber, Nan Ho, stood among the grooms. He had spent the whole day looking into what had disturbed the Lady Fei that morning; interviewing staff and rooting through the tangle of rumour and counter-rumour to sort fact from fancy. And now he knew.

He looked across at her, seeing how sweetly she smiled up at her husband, how warmly he returned her gaze, and shivered, his sense of fore-boding strong. In the warm glow of the late afternoon sunlight she seemed particularly beautiful, the simplicity of her attire setting her off, as the shell sets off the oyster. Yet that beauty was badly flawed. In time the mask she wore would slip and all would see her as he saw her now, with knowing eyes. He saw the Prince reach out and take her hand and looked down, knowing where his duty lay.

One thing was paramount; one thing alone – his master's happiness. And if the Prince's happiness depended on this weak and foolish woman, then so it had to be, for it was not his place to change his master's heart, merely to guard it against the worst the world could do. For that reason he had given special instructions to all he had discussed the matter with, warn-ing them that from henceforth the smallest mention of the subject – even the most idle speculation – would be punished with instant dismissal. Or worse. For he was determined that no word of the matter would ever reach the ears of Li Yuan or his father. No. He would let nothing come between the Prince and his happiness.

He sighed and looked back, even as the great T'ang stood and began to speak, his joy like winter sunlight in his wizened face. But for Nan Ho that joy was hollow. Like the thin light, it only seemed to cast its warmth. Beneath the flesh his bones were cold, his feelings in suspense. A son! All about him his fellow servants raised their voices, excited by the news, and he raised his; but he could hear – could *feel* – the falseness in his voice.

Strangely, his thoughts turned to Pearl Heart. Yes, he thought, Pearl Heart would have made a better, finer wife than this false creature. Truer to you. She would have made you strong when you were T'ang. Would have made of you a paragon among rulers.

Yes, but Pearl Heart was only a serving maid – a beast to warm your bed and teach you bedroom manners. What lineage she had was the lineage of unknown parenthood. She could not match the breeding of this whore.

Nan Ho looked up again, seeing once more his Prince's joy. That, at least, was no counterfeit. And that was why he would hold his tongue and keep this fragile boat afloat. Not for her, for what was she now but a painted thing – a mask to hide corruption – but for Li Yuan.

And then who knew what change a child might bring?

He lifted his head, listening. There was the faint growl of engines in the distance, coming nearer. He turned, looking into the setting sun and saw them – two craft, coming in low from the west. For a moment he was afraid, but then, looking across at his T'ang, he saw how Li Shai Tung looked then nodded to himself, as if he were expecting two such craft to come.

'Let us drink to the health of my son and his wife,' Li Shai Tung said, smiling, raising his glass. 'And to my grandson. *Kan pei!*'

The blessing echoed across the terrace as the craft came on.

Li Shai Tung paused in the coolness of the anteroom and looked about him. He had not been certain they would come, but here they were in answer to his request. Surely that meant something in itself? Surely that meant they were willing to take the first step?

Damn them! he thought, suddenly angry. *Damn them that I should have to make such deals with their like!* Then he looked down, realizing where his thoughts had led him, for both men, after all, were T'ang, whatever their personal faults.

T'ang! He shivered, wondering what his grandfather would have made of Wang Sau-leyan. Then, clearing his head of such thoughts, he went into his study, taking a seat behind his desk, composing himself, waiting for his Chancellor, Chung Hu-yan, to bring them through.

After long thought, he had decided to pre-empt matters; to make peace before the division in Council grew into enmity. And if that meant swallowing his pride and meeting Wang Sau-leyan and Hou Tung-po halfway, then he would do that. For balance. And to buy time, so that the Seven might be strong again.

Hou Tung-po was not the problem. The young T'ang of South America had merely fallen under his friend's charismatic spell. No, his only fault was to be weak-minded and impressionable. The real cause of dissent was Wang Hsien's fourth son, Sau-leyan, the present T'ang of Africa.

He laughed despairingly. How cruelly the times mocked them to make such a man a T'ang – a man who was fit only to be sent below the Net! For two whole cycles they had been strong, their purpose clear, their unity unquestioned, and now...

He shook his head, then let his fingers brush against the two documents he had had prepared. If all went well they would be shreds within the hour, their only significance having lain in the gesture of their destruction.

But would that be enough? Would that satisfy the T'ang of Africa?

Outside, in the corridors, two bells sounded, one low, one high. A moment later Chung Hu-yan appeared in the great doorway, his head lowered.

'Your guests are here, *Chieh Hsia*.'

'Good.' He stood and came round the desk. 'Show them in, Chung. Then bring us wines and sweetmeats. We may be here some while.'

The Chancellor bowed and backed away, his face registering an understanding of how difficult the task was that lay before his master. A moment later he returned, still bowed, leading the two T'ang into the room.

'Good cousins,' Li Shai Tung said, taking their hands briefly. 'I thank you for sparing the time from busy schedules to come and see me at such short notice.'

He saw how Hou Tung-po looked at once to his friend for his lead; how his welcoming smile faded as he noted the blank expression on Wang Sau-leyan's face.

'I would not have come had I not felt it was important to see you, Li Shai Tung,' Wang answered, staring past him.

Li Shai Tung stiffened, angered not merely by the hostility he sensed emanating from the young T'ang but also by the inference that a T'ang might even consider not coming at his cousin's urgent wish. Even so, he curbed his anger. This time young Wang would not draw him.

'And so it is,' he answered, smiling pleasantly. 'A matter of the utmost importance.'

Wang Sau-leyan looked about him with the air of a man considering buying something, then looked back at Li Shai Tung. 'Well? I'm listening.'

It was so rude, so wholly unexpected, that Li Shai Tung found himself momentarily lost for words. Then he laughed. *Is that really the way you want it?* he thought, *or is that too a pose – designed to throw me from my purpose and win yourself advantage?*

He put his hand to his beard thoughtfully. 'You're like your father, Sau-leyan. He too could be blunt when it was called for.'

'My father was a foolish old man!'

Li Shai Tung stiffened, shocked by the young man's utterance. He looked across at Hou Tung-po and saw how he looked away, embarrassed, then shook his head. He took a breath and began again.

'The other day, in Council...'

'You seek to lecture me, Li Shai Tung?'

Li Shai Tung felt himself go cold. Would the young fool not even let him finish a sentence?

He bowed his head slightly, softening his voice. 'You mistake me, good cousin. I seek nothing but an understanding between us. It seems we've started badly, you and I. I sought only to mend that. To find some way of redressing your grievances.'

He saw how Wang Sau-leyan straightened slightly at that, as if sensing concession on his part. Again it angered him, for his instinct was not to accommodate but to crush the arrogance he saw displayed before him, but he kept all sign of anger from his face.

Wang Sau-leyan turned, meeting his eyes directly. 'A deal, you mean?'

He stared back at the young T'ang a moment, then looked aside. 'I realize that we want different things, Wang Sau-leyan, but is there not a way of satisfying us both?'

The young man turned, looking across at Hou Tung-po. 'Is it not as I said, Hou?' He raised a hand dismissively, indicating Li Shai Tung. 'The *lao jen* wants to buy my silence. To bridle me in Council.'

Li Shai Tung looked down, coldly furious. *Lao jen* – old man – was a term of respect, but not in the way Wang Sau-leyan had used it. The scornful intonation he had given the word had made of it an insult – an insult that could not be ignored.

'An offered hand should not be spat upon...'

Wang Sau-leyan looked back at him, his expression openly hostile. 'What could you offer me that I might possibly want, *lao jen*?'

Li Shai Tung had clenched his hands. Now he relaxed them, letting his breath escape him in a sigh. 'Why in the gods' names are you so inflexible, Wang Sau-leyan? What do you want of us?'

Wang Sau-leyan took a step closer. 'Inflexible? Was I not "flexible" when your son married his brother's wife? Or by flexible do you really mean unprincipled – willing to do as you and not others wish?'

Li Shai Tung turned sharply, facing him, openly angry now. 'You go too far! Hell's teeth, boy!'

Wang Sau-leyan smiled sourly. 'Boy... That's how you see me, isn't it? A boy, to be chastised or humoured. Or locked away, perhaps...'

'This is not right...' Li Shai Tung began, but again the young T'ang interrupted him, his voice soft yet threatening.

'This is a new age, old man. New things are happening in the world. The Seven must change with the times or go under. And if I must break your power in Council to bring about that change, then break it I shall. But do not think to buy or silence me, for I'll not be bought or silenced.'

Li Shai Tung stood there, astonished, his lips parted. *Break it? Break his power?* But before he could speak there was a knocking at the door.

'Come in!' he said, only half-aware of what he said, his eyes still resting on the figure of the young T'ang.

It was Chung Hu-yan. Behind him came four servants, carrying trays. '*Chieh Hsia?*' he began, then stepped back hurriedly as Wang Sau-leyan stormed past him, pushing angrily through the servants, their trays clattering to the tiled floor as they hastened to move back, out of the T'ang's way.

Hou Tung-po hung back a moment, clearly dismayed by what had happened. Taking a step towards Li Shai Tung, he bowed, then turned away, hurrying to catch up with his friend.

Li Shai Tung stood there a moment longer, then, waving his Chancellor away, went to the desk and picked up one of the documents. He stared at it a moment, his hands trembling with anger, then, one by one, he began to pick off the unmarked seals with his fingernails, dropping them on to the floor beside his feet, until only his own remained at the foot of the page.

He would have offered this today. Would have gladly torn this document to shreds to forge a peaceful understanding. But what had transpired just now convinced him that such a thing was impossible. Wang Sau-leyan would not permit it. Well, then, he would act alone in this.

He turned his hand, placing the dark, dull metal of the ring into the depression at the desk's edge, letting it grow warm, then lifted his hand and pressed the seal into the wax.

There. It was done. He had sanctioned his son's scheme. Had given it life.

For a moment longer he stood there, staring down at the document – at the six blank spaces where the seals had been – then turned away, his anger unassuaged, speaking softly to himself, his words an echo of what the young T'ang had said to him.

'This is a new age, old man. New things are happening in the world.'

He laughed bitterly. 'So it is, Wang Sau-leyan. So it is. But you'll not break me. Not while I have breath.'

Karr stood there on the mountainside, shielding his eyes, looking about him at the empty slopes. It was cold, much colder than he'd imagined. He pulled the collar of his jacket up around his ears and shivered, still searching the broken landscape for some sign, some clue as to where to look.

The trouble was, it was just too big a place, too vast. One could hide a hundred armies here and never find them.

He looked down, blowing on his hands to warm them. How easy, then, to hide a single army here?

It had begun two days ago, after he had been to see Tolonen. His report on the Executive killings had taken almost an hour to deliver. Even so, they were still no closer to finding out who had been behind the spate of murders.

Officially, that was. For himself he was certain who was behind it all, and he knew the T'ang and Tolonen agreed. DeVore. It had to be. The whole thing was too neat, too well orchestrated, to be the work of anyone else.

But if DeVore, then why was there no trace of him within the City? Why was there no sign of his face somewhere in the levels? After all, every Security camera, every single guard and official in the whole vast City, was on the lookout for that face.

That absence had nagged at him for weeks, until, coming away from his meeting with Tolonen, he had realized its significance. If DeVore couldn't be found inside, then maybe he wasn't inside – maybe he was outside? Karr had gone back to his office and stood there before the map of City Europe, staring at it, his eyes drawn time and again to the long, irregular space at the centre of the City – the Wilds – until he knew for a certainty that was where he'd find DeVore. *There*, somewhere in that tiny space.

But what had seemed small on the map was gigantic in reality. The mountains were overpowering, both in their size and number. They filled the sky from one horizon to the other, and when he turned, there they were again, marching away into the distance, until the whole world seemed but one long mountain range and the City nothing.

So, where to start? Where, in all this vastness of rock and ice, to start? How search this godsforsaken place?

He was pondering that when he saw the second craft come up over the ridge and descend, landing beside his own, in the valley far below. A moment later a figure spilled from the craft and began to make its way towards him, climbing the slope. It was Chen.

'Gregor!' Chen greeted him. 'I've been looking all over for you.'

'What is it?' Karr answered, trudging down through the snow to meet him.

Chen stopped, then lifted his snow-goggles, looking up at him. 'I've brought new orders. From the T'ang.'

Karr stared at him, then took the sealed package and tore it open.

'What does it say?'

'That we're to close the files on the murders. Not only that, but we're to stop our search for DeVore – temporarily, at least – and concentrate on penetrating the *Ping Tiao* organization. It seems they're planning something big.'

Chen watched the big man nod to himself, as if taking in this new information, then look about him and laugh.

'What is it?' he asked, surprised by Karr's laughter.

'Just this,' Karr answered, holding the T'ang's orders up. 'And this,' he added, indicating the mountains all about them. 'I was thinking... two paths, but the goal's the same. *DeVore.*'

'DeVore?'

'Yes. The T'ang wants us to investigate the Ping Tiao, and so we shall, but when we lift that stone, you can lay odds on which insect will come scuttling out from under it.'

'DeVore,' said Chen, smiling.

Hans Ebert stood on the wooden veranda of the lodge, staring up the steep, snowcovered slope, his breath pluming in the crisp air. As he watched, the dark spot high up the slope descended slowly, coming closer, growing, until it was discernibly a human figure. It was coming on apace, in a zigzag path that would bring it to the lodge.

Ebert clapped his gloved hands together and turned to look back inside the lodge. There were three other men with him; his comrades in arms. Men he could trust.

'He's here!' he shouted in to them. 'Quick now! You know your orders!'

They got up from the table at once, taking their weapons from the rack near the door before going to their posts.

When the skier drew up beneath the veranda, the lodge seemed empty except for the figure leaning out over the balcony. The skier thrust his sticks into the snow, then lifted his goggles and peeled off his gloves.

'I'm pleased to see you, Hans. I didn't know if you would come.'

Ebert straightened up then started down the steps. 'My uncle is a persuasive man, Shih DeVore. I hadn't realized he was an old friend of yours.'

DeVore laughed, stooping to unfasten his boots. He snapped the clips and stepped off the skis. 'He isn't. Not officially. Nor will you be. Officially.'

He met the younger man at the bottom of the steps and shook both his hands firmly, warmly, flesh to gloves.

'I understand it now.'

'Understand what? Come, Hans, let's go inside. The air is too keen for such talk.'

Hans let himself be led back up into the lodge. When they were sitting, drinks in hand, he continued. 'What I meant is, I understand now how you've managed to avoid us all these years. More old friends, eh?'

'One or two,' said DeVore cryptically, and laughed.

'Yes,' Ebert said thoughtfully, 'you're a regular member of the family, aren't you?' He had been studying DeVore, trying to gauge whether he was armed or not.

'You forget how useful I once was to your father.'

'No...' Ebert chose the next few words more carefully. 'I simply remember how harmful you were subsequently. How dangerous. Even to meet you like this, it's...'

'Fraught with danger?' DeVore laughed again, a hearty, sincere laughter that strangely irritated the younger man.

DeVore looked across the room. In one corner a *wei chi* board had been set up, seven black stones forming an H on the otherwise empty grid.

'I see you've thought of everything,' he said, smiling again. 'Do you want to play while we talk?'

Ebert hesitated, then gave a nod. DeVore seemed somehow too bright, too at ease, for his liking.

The two men went to the table in the corner.

'Where shall I sit? *Here?*'

Ebert smiled. 'If you like.' It was exactly where he wanted DeVore. At that point he was covered by all three of the marksmen concealed overhead. If he tried *anything*...

DeVore sat, perfectly at ease, lifting the lid from the pot, then placed the first of his stones in *tsu*, the north. Ebert sat, facing him, studying him a moment, then lifted the lid from his pot and took one of the black stones between his fingers. He had prepared his men beforehand. If he played in one particular place – in the middle of the board, on the edge of *shang*, the south, on the intersection beside his own central stone – then they were to open fire, killing DeVore. Otherwise they were to fire only if Ebert's life was endangered.

Ebert reached across, playing at the top of *shang*, two places out from his own corner stone, two lines down from the edge.

'Well?' he said, looking at DeVore across the board. 'You're not here to ask after my health. What do you want?'

DeVore was studying the board as if he could see the game to come – the patterns of black stones and white, their shape and interaction. 'Me? I don't want anything. At least, nothing from you, Hans. That's not why I'm here.'

He set down a white stone, close by Ebert's last, then looked up, smiling again. 'I'm here because there's something *you* might want.'

Ebert stared at him, astonished, then laughed. 'What could I possibly want from you?' He slapped a stone down almost carelessly, three spaces out from the first.

DeVore studied the move, then shook his head. He took a stone from his pot and set it down midway between the corner and the centre, as if to divide some future formation of Ebert's stones.

'You have everything you need, then, Hans?'

Ebert narrowed his eyes, then slapped down another stone irritably. It was two spaces out from the centre, between DeVore's and his own, so that the five stones now formed a broken diagonal line from the corner to the centre, two black, one white, then two more black.

DeVore smiled broadly. 'That's an interesting shape, don't you think? But it's weak, like the Seven. Black might outnumber white, but white isn't surrounded.'

Ebert sat back. 'Meaning what?'

DeVore set down another stone, pushing out towards *ch'u*, the west. A triangle of three white stones now sat to the right of a triangle of black stones. Ebert stared at the position a moment, then looked up into DeVore's face again.

DeVore was watching him closely, his eyes suddenly sharp, alert, the smile gone from his lips.

'Meaning that you serve a master you despise. Accordingly, you play badly. Winning or losing has no meaning for you. No *interest*.'

Ebert touched his upper teeth with his tongue, then took another stone and placed it, eight down, six out in *shang*. It was a necessary move; a strengthening move. It prevented DeVore from breaking his line while expanding the territory he now surrounded. The game was going well for him.

'You read my mind, then, *Shih* DeVore? You know how I think?'

'I know that you're a man of considerable talent, Hans. And I know that you're bored. I can see it in the things you do, the decisions you make. I can see how you hold the greater part of yourself back constantly. Am I wrong, then? Is what I see really the best you can do?'

DeVore set down another stone. Unexpectedly it cut across the shape Ebert had just made, pushing into the territory he had mapped out. It seemed an absurd move, a weak move, but Ebert knew that DeVore was a master at this game. He would not make such a move without good reason.

'It seems you want me to cut you. But if I do, it means you infiltrate this area here.' He sketched it out.

'And if you don't?'

'Well, it's obvious. You cut me. You separate my groups.'

DeVore smiled. 'So. A dilemma. What to choose?'

Ebert looked up again, meeting his eyes. He knew that DeVore was saying something to him through the game. But what? Was DeVore asking him to make a choice? The Seven or himself? Was he asking him to come out in the open and declare himself?

He set down his stone, cutting DeVore, keeping his own lines open.

'You say the Seven are weak, but you, are you any stronger?'

'At present, no. Look at me, I'm like these five white stones here on the board. I'm cut and scattered and outnumbered. But I'm a good player and the odds are better than when I started. Then they were seven to one. Now...' he placed his sixth stone, six down, four out in *shang*, threatening the corner '... it's only two to one. And every move improves my chances. I'll win. Eventually.'

Ebert placed another black stone in the diagonal line, preventing DeVore from linking with his other stones, but again it allowed DeVore space within his own territory and he sensed that DeVore would make a living group there.

'You know, I've always admired you, Howard. You would have been Marshal eventually. You would have run things for the Seven.'

'That's so... But it was never enough for me to serve another. Nor you. We find it hard to bow to lesser men.'

Ebert laughed, then realized how far DeVore had brought him. Only it was true. Everything he said was true. He watched DeVore set another stone down, shadowing his own line, sketching out territory inside his own, robbing him of what he'd thought was safely his.

'I see...' he said, meaning two things. For a time, then, they simply played. Forty moves later he could see that it was lost. DeVore had taken five of his stones from the board and had formed a living group of half of *shang*. Worse, he had pushed out towards *ch'u* and down into *p'ing*. Now a small group of four of his stones were threatened at the centre and there was only one way to save it, to play in the space in *shang* beside the central stone – the signal for his men to open fire on DeVore. Ebert sat back, holding the black stone between his fingers, then laughed.

'It seems you've forced me to a decision.'

DeVore smiled back at him. 'I was wondering what you would do.'

Ebert eyed him sharply. 'Wondering?'

'Yes. I wasn't sure at first. But now I know. You won't play that space. You'll play here instead.' He leaned across and touched the intersection with his fingertip. It was the move that gave only temporary respite. It did not save the group.

'Why should I do that?'

'Because you don't want to kill me. And because you're seriously interested in my proposition.'

Ebert laughed, astonished. 'You *knew*?'

'Oh, I know you've three of your best stormtroopers here, Hans. I've been conscious of the risks *I've* been taking. But how about you?'

'I *think* I know,' Ebert said, even more cautiously. Then, with a small laugh of admiration he set the stone down where DeVore had indicated.

'Good.' DeVore leaned across and set a white stone in the special space, on the edge of *shang*, beside Ebert's central stone, then leaned back again. 'I'm certain you'll have assessed the potential rewards, too.' He smiled, looking down at his hands. 'King of the world, Hans. That's what you could be. T'ang of all Chung Kuo.'

Ebert stared back at him, his mouth open but set.

'But not without me.' DeVore looked up at him, his eyes piercing him through. 'Not without me. You understand that?'

'I could have you killed. Right now. And be hailed as a hero.'

DeVore nodded. 'Of course. I knew what I was doing. But I assumed you knew why you were here. That you knew how much you had to gain.'

It was Ebert's turn to laugh. 'This is insane.'

DeVore was watching him calmly, as if he knew now how things would turn out between them. 'Insane? No. It's no more insane than the rule of the Seven. And how long can that last? In ten years, maybe less, the whole pack of cards is going to come tumbling down, whatever happens. The more astute of the Above realize that and want to do something about it. They want to control the process. But they need a figurehead. Someone they admire. Someone from amongst their number. Someone capable and in a position of power.'

'I don't fit your description.'

DeVore laughed. 'Not now, perhaps. But you will. In a year from now you will.'

Ebert looked down. He knew it was a moment for decisiveness, not prevarication. 'And when I'm T'ang?'

DeVore smiled and looked down at the board. 'Then the stars will be ours. A world for each of us.'

A world for each of us. Ebert thought about it a moment. This, then, was what it was really all about. Expansion. Taking the lid off City Earth and getting away. But what would that leave him?

'However,' DeVore went on. 'You didn't mean that, did you?' He stood and went across to the drinks cabinet, pouring himself a second glass of brandy. Turning, he looked directly at the younger man. 'What you meant was, what's in it for me?'

Ebert met his look unflinchingly. 'Of course. What other motive could there be?'

DeVore smiled blandly. Ebert was a shallow, selfish young man, but he was useful. He would never be T'ang, of course – it would be a mistake to give such a man *real* power – but it served for now to let him think he would.

'Your brandy is excellent, Hans.' DeVore walked to the window and looked out. The mountains looked beautiful. He could see the Matterhorn from where he stood, its peak like a broken blade. Winter was coming.

Ebert was silent, waiting for him.

'What's in it for you, you ask? This world. To do with as you wish. What more could you want?' He turned to face the younger man, noting at once the calculation in his face.

'You failed,' Ebert said after a moment. 'There were many of you. Now there's just you. Why should you succeed this time?'

DeVore tilted his head, then laughed, 'Ah, yes...'

Ebert frowned and set his glass down. 'And they're strong.'

DeVore interrupted him. 'No. You're wrong, Hans. They're weak. Weaker than they've been since they began. *We almost won...*'

Ebert hesitated, then nodded. It was so. He recognized how thin the

Families were spread now; how much they depended on the goodwill of those in the Above who had remained faithful. Men like his father.

And when his father was dead?

He looked up sharply, his decision made.

'Well?' DeVore prompted. 'Will you be T'ang?'

Ebert stood, offering his hand.

DeVore smiled and set his drink down. Then he stepped forward and, ignoring the hand, embraced the young man.

Part 13   Artifice and Innocence

Spring 2207

'The more abstract the truth you want to teach the
  more you must seduce the senses to it.'
—Friedrich Nietzsche, *Beyond Good And Evil*

'Reach me a gentian, give me a torch!
let me guide myself with the blue, forked touch of
  this flower down the dark and darker steps, where
  blue is darkened on blueness
even where Persephone goes, just now, from the
  frosted September
to the sightless realm where darkness is awake upon
  the dark
and Persephone herself is but a voice
of a darkness invisible enfolded in the deeper dark
of the arms Plutonic, and pierced with the passion of
  dense gloom,
among the splendour of torches of darkness,
  shedding darkness on the lost bride and her
  groom.'
—D. H. Lawrence, *Bavarian Gentians*

Chapter 54

THE FEAST OF THE DEAD

A bank of eight screens, four long, two deep, glowed dimly on the far side of the darkened room. In each lay the outline image of a hollowed skull. There were other shapes in the room, vague forms only partly lit by the glow. A squat and bulky mechanism studded with controls was wedged beneath the screens. Beside it was a metallic frame, like a tiny four-poster stretched with wires. In the left-hand corner rested a narrow trolley containing racks of tapes, their wafer-thin top edges glistening in the half-light. Next to that was a vaguely human form, slumped against a bed, its facial features missing. Finally, in the very centre of the room was a graphics artboard, the thin screen blank and dull, the light from the eight monitors focused in its concave surface.

It was late – after three in the morning – and Ben Shepherd was tired, but there was this one last thing to be done before he slept. He squatted by the trolley and flicked through the tapes until he found what he wanted, then went to the artboard and fed in the tape. The image of a bird formed instantly. He froze it, using the controls to turn it, studying it from every angle, as if searching for some flaw in its conception, then, satisfied, he let it run, watching as the bird stretched its wings and launched into the air. Again he froze the image. The bird's wings were stretched back now, thrusting it forward powerfully.

It was a simple image in many ways. An idealized image of a bird, formed in a vacuum.

He sorted through the tapes again and pulled out three, then returned to the artboard and rewound the first tape. That done he fed the new tapes into the slot and synchronized all four to a preset signal. Then he pressed to play.

This time the bird was resting on a perch inside a pagoda-like cage. As he watched, the cage door sprang open and the bird flew free, launching itself out through the narrow opening.

He froze the image, then rotated it. This time the bird seemed trapped, its beak and part of its sleek, proud head jutting from the cage, the rest contained within the bars. In the background could be seen the familiar environment of The Square. As the complex image turned, the tables of the Café Burgundy came into view. He could see himself at one of the nearer tables, the girl beside him. He was facing directly into the shot, his hand raised, pointing, as if to indicate the sudden springing of the bird, but her head was turned, facing him, her flame-red hair a sharp contrast to the rich, overhanging greenery.

He smiled uncertainly and let the tape run on a moment at one-fifth speed, watching her head come slowly round to face the escaping bird. In that moment, as she faced it fully, the bird's wing came up, eclipsing the watchers at the table. There it ended.

It was a brief segment, no more than nine seconds in all, but it had taken him weeks of hard work to get it right. Now, however, he was thinking of abandoning it completely.

This was his favourite piece in the whole composition – the key image with which it had begun – yet as the work had grown this tiny fragment had proved ever more problematic.

For the rest of the work the viewpoint was established in the viewer's head – behind the eyes – yet for this brief moment he had broken away entirely. In another art form this would have caused no problems – might, indeed, have been a strength – but here it created all kinds of unwanted difficulties. Experienced from within the Shell, it was as if, for the brief nine seconds that the segment lasted, one went outside one's skull. It was a strange, disorienting experience, and no tampering with the surround-ing images could mute that effect, or repair the damage it did to the work as a whole.

In all the Shells he had experienced before, such abrupt switches of view-point had been made to serve the purpose of the story: used for their sudden shock value. But, then, all forms of the Shell before his own had insisted only upon a cartoon version of the real, whereas what he wanted was reality itself. Or a close approximation. Such abrupt changes destroyed the balance he was seeking – shattered every attempt of his to create that illusion of the really real.

Only now was he beginning to understand the cost – in artistic terms – of such realism: the limiting factors and the disciplines involved. It was not enough to create the perfect illusion; it was also necessary to maintain a sequential integrity in the experiencing mind. The illusion depended on him staying within his own skull, behind his own eyes, the story developing in real time.

There was, of course, a simple answer: one abandoned all breaches of sequential integrity. But that limited the kind of story one could tell. It was a straitjacket of the worst kind, limiting fiction to the vignette, briefly told. He had recognized this at once and agonized over it, but weeks of wrestling with the problem had left him without an answer.

Perhaps this was why all previous practitioners of the form had kept to the quasi-realism of a cartoon, leaving the experiencing imagination to suspend disbelief and form a bridge between what was presented and the reality. Maybe some of them had even tried what he was attempting now – had experimented with 'perfected', realistic images and had faced the same constricting factors. Maybe so, but he had to make a choice: to pursue his ideal of a perfect art form or compromise that vision in favour of a patently synthetic form – a mere embellishment of the old. It was no real choice at all, yet still he prevaricated.

He wound the tapes back and replayed, this time at one-tenth speed – five frames a second – watching the bird thrust slowly outward from the cage in an explosion of sudden, golden, living fire; seeing beyond it the girl's face, its whiteness framed in flames of red as it turned to face the screen.

He closed his eyes and froze the image. It was the best thing he had done. Something real and beautiful – a tiny, perfect work of art. And yet... He shivered, then pressed ERASE. In an instant it was done, the tapes blanked. He stood there for a long time afterwards, leaning against the machine, perfectly still, his eyes closed. Then, with a tiny shudder, he turned away. There was that much anyway – it was there – it would *always* be there, in his head.

He went over to the bed and sat, not knowing what he felt, staring intently, almost obsessively at the narrow ridge of flesh that circled his left wrist. Then he got up again and went out into the other room.

For a while he stood there in the centre of the room, his mind still working at the problem; but just now he could not see past his tiredness. He was stretched thin by the demands he had placed on himself these last few weeks. All he could see were problems, not solutions.

He took a long, shuddering breath.

'Small steps,' he told himself, his voice soft, small in the darkness. 'There is an answer,' he added after a moment, as if to reassure himself. Yet he was far from certain.

He turned away, rubbing at his eyes, too tired to pursue the thought, for once wanting nothing but the purging oblivion of sleep. And in the morning?

In the morning he would begin anew.

The Square was a huge, airy space at the top of Oxford Canton; the uppermost level of a complex warren of colleges that extended deep into the stack below. To the eternal delight of each new generation of students, however, The Square was not square at all, but hexagonal: a whole deck opened up for leisure. Long, open balconies overlooked the vastness of The Green, leaning back in five great tiered layers on every side, while overhead the great dome of the stars turned slowly, in perfect imitation of the sky beyond the ice.

Here, some seventeen years ago, so rumour had it, Berdichev, Lehmann and Wyatt had met and formed the Dispersionist party, determined to bring change to this world of levels, but whether the rumour was true or not, it was a place to which the young intelligentsia of all seven Cities were drawn. If the world of thought were a wheel, this was its hub, The Green its focus.

A line of oaks bordered The Green, hybrid evergreens produced in the vats of SynFlor, while at its centre was an aviary: a tall, pagoda-like cage of thirteen tiers, modelled upon the Liu he t'a, the Pagoda of the Six Harmonies at Hang Chou. As ever, young men and women strolled arm in arm on the vast lawn or gathered about the lowest tier, looking in at the brightly coloured birds.

The Square was the pride of Oxford Canton and the haunt of its ten thousand students. The elite of the Above sent their children to Oxford, just as the elite of a small nation-state had done centuries before. It was a place of culture and, for the children of First Level families, a guarantee of continuity.

No big MedFac screens cluttered The Green itself, but in the cool walkways beneath the overhang, small Vidscreens showed the local cable channels to a clientele whose interests and tastes differed considerably from the rest of the Above.

The overhang was a place of coffee shops and restaurants, CulVid boutiques and Syn-Parlours. It was a curious mixture of new and old, of timelessness and state of the art, of purity and decadence; its schizophrenic face a reflection of its devotees.

At the Café Burgundy business was brisk. It was a favourite haunt of the Arts Faculty students who, at this hour, crowded every available table, talking, drinking, gesturing wildly with all the passion and flamboyance of youth. The tables themselves – more than two hundred in all – spread out from beneath the overhang towards the edge of The Green. Overhead, a network of webbing, draped between strong poles, supported a luxuriant growth of flowering creepers. The plants were a lush, almost luminous green, decorated with blooms of vivid purples, yellows, reds and oranges – huge, gaping flowers with tongues of contrasting hues, like the silent heads of monsters. Beneath them the tables and chairs were all antiques, the wood stained and polished. They were a special feature of the Café, a talking point, though in an earlier century they would have seemed quite unexceptional.

Han waiters made their way between the packed tables, carrying trays and taking orders. They were dressed in the plain, round-collared robes of the Tang dynasty, the sleeves narrow, the long er-silks a dark vermilion with an orange band below the knee: the clothes of an earlier, simpler age.

At a table near the edge sat four students. Their table was clear but for three glasses and a bottle. They had eaten and were on their third bottle of the excellent Burgundy from which the Café took its name. A vacant chair rested between the two males of the party, as if they were expecting another to join them. But it was not so. All spaces at the table had to be paid for, and they had paid to keep it vacant.

There was laughter at the table. A dark-haired, olive-skinned young man was holding sway, leaning well back in his chair, a wine glass canted in his hand. The sing-song tones of his voice were rather pleasant, well modulated. He was a handsome, aristocratic man with a pronounced aquiline profile, a finely formed mouth, and dark, almost gypsy eyes. Strong limbed and broad shouldered, he looked more a sportsman than an artist, though a fastidiousness about his clothes somewhat redressed that impression. As he talked, his free hand carved forms from the air, the movements deft, rehearsed. He was older than the others by some four or five years, a factor that made them defer to him in most things, and often – as now – he monopolized their talk, leading it where he would.

His name was Sergey Novacek and he was a Master's student and a sculptor. His father, Lubos, was a well-to-do merchant who, at his wife's behest, indulged his only son, buying him a place at Oxford. Not that Sergey was unintelligent. He could easily have won a scholarship. It was simply a matter of prestige. Of status. At the level on which Lubos Novacek had his interests, it was not done to accept State charity.

Just now Sergey was telling them of the ceremony he had attended the previous day; a ceremony at which six of his sculptures had been on display. He had not long been fulfilling such commissions, yet he spoke as if he had great experience in the matter. But that was his way, and his friends admired him for it, even if others found it somewhat arrogant.

'It all went very well, at first,' he said, his handsome features serious a moment. 'Everyone was most respectful. They fed me and watered me and tried their best to be polite and hide from themselves the fact that I was neither family nor Han.' He laughed. 'None too successfully, I'm afraid. But, anyway... The tomb was magnificent. It stood in its own walled gardens next to the house. A massive thing, two storeys high, clad all over in white marble, and with a gate you could have driven a team of four horses through.' Sergey sipped at his drink, then laughed. 'In fact, the tomb was a damn sight bigger than the house!'

There was laughter.

'That's so typical of them,' said the second young man, Wolf, lifting his glass to his lips. He was taller and more heavily built than his friend, his perfect North European features topped by a close-cropped growth of ash-blond hair. 'They're so into death.'

Sergey raised his glass. 'And a good job too, neh?'

'For you,' one of the girls, Lotte, said teasingly, her blue eyes flashing. It was true. Most of Sergey's commissions were funerary – tomb statues for the Minor Families.

Lotte was a pale-skinned, large-breasted girl, who wore her blonde hair unfashionably long and plaited, in defiance of fashion. These things aside she looked exactly what she was – the twin of her brother, Wolf. Beside her, silent, sat the fourth of their small group, Catherine. She was smaller than her friends, more delicately built; a slender redhead with Slavic features and green eyes.

Sergey smiled. 'Anyway. As I was saying. It was all going well and then the ceremony proper began. You know how it is; a lot of New Confucian priests chanting for the souls of the departed. And then the eldest son comes to the front and lights a candle for the ancestors. Well... it had just got to that stage when, would you believe it, eldest son trips over his *pau*, stumbles forward and falls against the lines of paper charms.'

'No!' All three sat forward, Wolf amused, the two girls horrified.

'Unfortunate, you might think, and embarrassing, but not disastrous. And so it might have been, except that in falling he dropped the lighted candle amongst the charms.' Sergey laughed shortly and nodded to himself. 'You should have seen it. There must have been two or three thousand charms hanging up on those lines, dry as bone, just waiting to go up in one great sheet of flame. And that's exactly what they did. Eldest son was all right, of course. The servants pulled him away at once. But before anyone could do a thing, the flames set off the overhead sprinklers. Worse than that, no one knew the combination sequence to the cut-out and the key to the manual override was missing. It just poured and poured. We were all soaked. But the worst was to come. Because the garden was enclosed, the water couldn't drain away. Much of it sank into the thin soil layer, but soon that became waterlogged, and when that happened the water began to pour down the steps into the tomb. Within minutes the water was up to the top step. That's when it happened.'

He leaned forward and filled his glass, then looked about him, enjoying himself, knowing he had their full attention. 'Well? What do you think?'

Wolf shook his head. 'I don't know. The eldest son fell in, perhaps?'

Sergey narrowed his eyes. 'Ah, yes, that would have been good, wouldn't it? But this was better. Much better. Imagine it. There we all are, still waiting for someone to switch the damn sprinklers off, our expensive clothes ruined, the ground a total bog beneath our feet, no one willing to show disrespect by leaving the gardens before the ceremony's over, when what should happen but the unthinkable. Out floats the coffin!'

'Kuan Yin preserve us!' Wolf said, his eyes round as coins.

'Poor man,' murmured Catherine, looking down.

Sergey laughed. 'Poor man, my arse! He was dead. No, but you should have seen the faces on those Han. It was as if they'd had hot irons poked up their backsides! There was a muttering and a spluttering and then – damn me if they didn't try to shove the coffin back into the tomb against the current! You should have seen the eldest son, slipping about in the mud like a lunatic!'

'Gods preserve us!' Wolf said. 'And did they manage it?'

'Third time they did. But by then the sprinklers were off and the servants were carrying the water away in anything they could find.'

The two men laughed, sitting back in their chairs and baring their teeth. Across from Wolf, Lotte smiled broadly, enjoying her brother's laughter. Only Catherine seemed detached from their enjoyment, as if preoccupied. Sergey noticed this and leaned towards her slightly. 'What is it?'

She looked up. 'It's nothing...'

He raised an eyebrow, making her laugh.

'Okay,' she said, relenting. 'I was just thinking about the painting I'm working on.'

'You're having trouble?'

She nodded.

Wolf leaned across to nudge Sergey. 'I shouldn't worry. She's not a real artist.'

Catherine glared at him, then looked away. Wolf was always mocking her for working on an oilboard, when, as he said, any artist worth their ricebowl worked in watercolours. But she discounted his opinion. She had seen his work. It was technically perfect, yet somehow lifeless. He could copy but he couldn't create.

She looked back at Sergey. 'I was thinking I might go to the lecture this afternoon.'

He lifted his chin slightly. 'Lecture?'

She smiled. 'Oh... I forgot. You weren't here when the College officials came round, were you?' She searched in her bag for something, then set a small, hexagonal pad down on the table. She placed her palm against it momentarily, warming the surface, then moved her hand away. At once a tiny, three-dimensional image formed in the air and began to speak.

'That's Fan Liang-wei, isn't it?' said Wolf, leaning across to refill his glass.

'Shhhh,' Sergey said, touching his arm. 'Let's hear what the old bugger has to say.'

Fan Liang-wei was one of the most respected *shanshui* artists in City Europe. His paintings hung in the homes of most of the Minor Families. The Great Man's long white hair and triple-braided beard were familiar sights to those who tuned in to the ArtVid channel, and even to those whose tastes were less refined, Fan Liang-wei was the very personification of the *wen ren*, the scholar-artist.

It was standard practice for professors of the College to advertise their lectures in this way, since their fees were paid according to attendance figures. Indeed, it was the practice for some of the less charismatic of them to bribe students to attend – filling the first few rows of the hall with sleepers. For the Great Man, however, such advertising was not strictly necessary. His fee was guaranteed whatever the attendance. Nonetheless, it was a matter of ego – a question of proving his supreme status to his fellow academicians.

The tiny figure bowed to its unseen audience and began to talk of the lecture it was to give that afternoon, its internal timer updating its speech so that when it referred to the lecture it reminded the listeners that it was 'less than two hours from now'. The lecture was to be on the two *shanshui* artists, Tung Ch'i-ch'ang and Cheng Ro, and was entitled 'Spontaneity and Meticulousness'. Sergey watched it a moment longer, then smiled and reached out to put his hand over the pad, killing the image.

'It could be amusing. I've heard the old man's worth hearing.'

'And Heng Chian-ye?' Wolf asked. 'You've not forgotten the card game?'

Sergey looked across and saw how Catherine had looked away angrily. He knew how strongly she disapproved of this side of him – the gambling and the late-night drinking sessions – but it only spurred him on to greater excesses, as if to test her love.

He smiled, then turned back to Wolf. 'That's all right. I told him I'd see him at four, but it'll do the little yellow bastard good to wait a bit. It'll make him more eager.'

Wolf laughed. 'Do you still intend to challenge him? They say he's a good player.'

Sergey lifted his chin and looked away thoughtfully. 'Yes. But Heng's an arrogant young fool. He's inflexible. Worse, he's rash when put under pressure. Like all these Han, he's more concerned with saving face than saving a fortune. And that will be his undoing, I promise you. So, yes, I'll challenge him. It's about time someone raised the stakes on young Heng.'

Sergey leaned forward, looking across at Lotte. 'And you, Lotte? Are you coming along?'

Again his words, his action in leaning towards Lotte, were designed to upset the other girl. They all knew how much Lotte was besotted with the handsome young sculptor. It was a joke which even she, on occasions, shared. But that didn't lessen the pangs of jealousy that affected Catherine.

As ever, Lotte looked at her brother before she answered, a faint colour at her cheeks. 'Well, I ought, I know, but...'

'You must,' Sergey said, reaching out to cover her hand with his own. 'I insist. You'd never forgive yourself if you didn't see the Great Man.'

Wolf answered for her. 'We were going to do some shopping. But I'm sure...'

Wolf looked at Lotte, smiling encouragement, and she nodded. Wolf still had hopes that his sister might marry Novacek. Not that it affected his relationship with Catherine. Not significantly.

'Good,' said Sergey, leaning back and looking about the circle of his friends. 'And afterwards I'll treat you all to a meal.'

The tiers of the lecture hall were packed to overflowing. Stewards scurried up and down the gangways, trying to find seats for the crowds pressing into the hall, clearly put out by the size of the attendance. Normally the hall seemed vast and echoing, but today it was like a hive, buzzing with expectation.

At three precisely the lights dimmed and the hall fell silent. On a raised platform at the front of the hall a single spotlight picked out a lectern. For a while there was no movement on stage, then a figure stepped out of the darkness. A murmur of surprise rose from the watching tiers. It was Chu Ta Yun, the Minister of Education. He stood to one side of the lectern, his head slightly bowed, his hands folded at his waist.

'*Ch'un tzu*,' he began, his tone humble, 'I have been given the great pleasure and honour of introducing one of the outstanding figures of our time; a man whose distinctions are too numerous to be listed here and whose accomplishments place him in the very first rank of painters. A man who, when the history of our culture is set down by future generations, will be seen as the epitome – the touchstone – of our art. *Ch'un tzu*, I ask you to welcome to our college the Honourable Fan Liang-wei, Painter to the court of His Most Serene Highness, Li Shai Tung.'

As the Minister withdrew, head bowed, into the darkness, Fan Liang-wei came into the spotlight, resting his hands lightly on the edge of the lectern then bowing his head to his audience. There was a faint shuffling noise as, in unison, the packed tiers lowered their heads in respect to the Great Man.

'*Ch'un tzu*,' he began, in the same vein as the Minister, then, smiling, added, 'Friends...'

There was a small ripple of laughter from the tiers. The ice had been broken. But at once his face grew serious again, his chin lifting in an extravagant yet thoughtful gesture, his voice taking on an immediate tone of authority.

'I have come here today to talk of art, and, in particular, of the art of *shanshui* painting, something of which I have, or so I delude myself, some small knowledge.'

Again there was the faintest ripple of amusement, but, as before, it was tinged with the deepest respect. There was not one there who did not consider Fan Liang-wei Chung Kuo's foremost expert on the ancient art of *shanshui*.

The Great Man looked about the tiers, as if noting friends there amongst the crowd, then spoke again. 'As you may know, I have called today's talk "Spontaneity and Meticulousness", and it is upon these two extremes of expression that I wish to dwell, taking as my examples the works of two great exponents of the art of *shanshui*, the Ming painter Tung Ch'i-ch'ang and the Song painter Cheng Ro. But before I come to them and to specific examples of their work, I would like to take this opportunity of reminding you of the critic Hsieh Ho's Six Principles, for it is to these that we shall, time and again, return during this lecture.'

Fan Liang-wei paused, looking about him. He had just opened his mouth to speak when the door to his right swung open and a young man strode into the hall, ignoring the hushed remonstrances of a steward. The steward followed him two or three paces into the hall, then backed away, head bowed, glancing up at the platform apologetically before drawing the door closed behind him. The young man, meanwhile, moved unselfconsciously along the gangway in front of the platform and began to climb the stairs. He was halfway up when the Great Man cleared his throat.

'Forgive me, young Master, but am I interrupting something?'

The young man half turned, looking back at the speaker, then, without a word, climbed the rest of the steps and sat down at their head.

There was a murmur of astonishment from the surrounding tiers and even a few harshly whispered words of criticism, but the young man seemed oblivious. He sat there, staring down at the platform, a strange intensity in his manner making him seem brooding, almost malicious in intent.

'Are we comfortable?' the Great Man asked, a faint trace of annoyance in his voice.

The young man gave the barest nod.

'Good. Then perhaps we might continue. As I was saying... Hsieh Ho, in his classic fifth-century work, the Ku Hua-p'in-lu, set down for all time the Six Principles by which the great artist might be recognized. In reiterating these, we might remember that, while Hsieh Ho intended that all six should be present in a great work of art, they do, nonetheless, form a kind of hierarchy, the First Principle, that of spirit-consonance, of harmony of spirit to the motion of life – that sense we have of the painting coming alive through the harmonizing of the vital force, the ch'i, of the painter with the ch'i of his subject matter – forming the first rank, the First Level, if you like.'

There was a mild ripple of laughter at the Great Man's play of words. He continued quickly, his anger at the rudeness of the young man's interruption set aside momentarily.

'Bearing this in mind, we see how the Second Principle, the bone-structure of the brushwork – and its strength in conveying the ch'i or vital energy – stems from the First and is, indeed, dependent upon it, as a Minister is dependent upon the favour of his T'ang. Likewise, the Third Principle, the fidelity or faithfulness of the artistic representation to the subject, is dependent upon these first two. And so forth...'

He hesitated, then looked directly at the young man seated at the head of the stairs. 'You understand me, young Master?'

Again the young man nodded.

'Good. Then let me move on quickly. Fourth of the Six great Principles is likeness in colour. Fifth is the proper placing of the various elements within the scheme of the painting. And Sixth, and last in our great hierarchy, is the preservation of the experience of the past through making pictorial reference to the great classical paintings.'

Fan Liang-wei smiled, looking about him, then moved to one side, half turning as the screen behind him lit up, showing an ancient painting.

'There is, of course, one further quality that Hsieh Ho demanded from the great artist – a quality which, because it is intrinsic to art, is enshrined in each of those six great Principles – that of *ching*. Of precision or minuteness of detail.'

He indicated the painting. 'This, as you may recognize, is Tung Ch'i-ch'ang's *Shaded Dwelling among Streams and Mountains*, one of the great works of Ming art. This hanging scroll...'

The Great Man had turned, looking back at his audience, but now he stopped, his mouth open, for the young man had stood and was making his way slowly down the steps again.

'Forgive me,' he said tartly, his patience snapping, 'but have I to suffer more of your interruptions?'

The young man stopped, a faint smile playing on his lips. 'No. I've heard enough.'

'Heard enough...' For the briefest moment Fan's face was contorted with anger. Then, controlling himself, he came to the edge of the platform, confronting the young man. 'What do you mean, *heard enough?*'

The young man stared back at Fan Liang-wei, unperturbed, it seemed, by the hardness in his voice, undaunted by his reputation.

'I mean what I said. I've heard enough. I don't have to wait to hear what you have to say – you've said it all already.'

Fan laughed, astonished. 'I see...'

The young man lifted his arm, pointing beyond Fan at the screen. 'That, for instance. It's crap.'

There was a gasp of astonishment from the tiers, followed by a low murmur of voices. Fan Liang-wei, however, was smiling now.

'Crap, eh? That's your considered opinion, is it, Shih...?'

The young man ignored the request for his name, just as he ignored the ripple of laughter that issued from the benches on all sides. 'Yes,' he answered, taking two slow steps closer to the platform. 'It's dead. Anyone with a pair of eyes can see it. But you...' He shook his head. 'Well, to call this lifeless piece of junk one of the great works of Ming art is an insult to the intelligence.'

Fan straightened, bristling, then gave a short laugh. 'You're a student of painting, then, young Master?'

The young man shook his head.

'Ah, I see. Then what are you precisely? You *are* a member of the college, I assume?'

There was more laughter from the tiers; a harder, crueller laughter as the students warmed to the exchange. The young man had stepped out of line. Now the Great Man would humiliate him.

'I'm a scientist...'

'A scientist? Ah, *I see*.'

The laughter was like a great wave this time, rolling from end to end of the great lecture hall. Fan Liang-wei smiled, looking about him, sensing victory.

'Then you know about things like *painting*?'

The young man stood there, the laughter in the hall washing over him, waiting for it to subside. When it did he answered the Great Man.

'Enough to know that Tung Ch'i-ch'ang was the dead-end of a process of slow emasculation of a once-vital art form.'

The Great Man nodded. 'I see. And Cheng Ro... I suppose he *was* a great painter... in your estimation?'

There was more laughter, but it was tenser now. The atmosphere had changed, become electric with anticipation. They sensed blood.

The young man looked down. Then, unexpectedly, he laughed. 'You know your trouble, Fan Liang-wei?' He looked up at the older man challengingly. 'You're a slave to convention. To an art that's not a real art at all, just an unimaginative and imitative *craft*.'

There was a low murmur of disapproval from the tiers at that. As for

Fan himself, he was still smiling, but it was a tight, tense mask of a smile, behind which he seethed.

'But to answer your question,' the young man continued. 'Yes, Cheng Ro was a great painter. He had *lueh*, that invaluable quality of being able to produce something casually, almost uncaringly. His ink drawing of dragons...'

'*Enough!*' Fan roared, shivering with indignation. 'How *dare* you lecture me about art, you know-nothing! How *dare* you stand there and insult me with your garbled nonsense!'

The young man stared back defiantly at Fan. 'I dare because I'm right. Because I know when I'm listening to a fool.'

The hall had gone deathly silent. Fan, standing there at the edge of the platform, was very still. The smile had drained from his face.

'*A fool?*' he said finally, his voice chill. 'And you think you can do better?'

For a moment the young man hesitated. Then, astonishingly, he nodded and, his eyes never leaving Fan Liang-wei's face, began to make his way down to the platform.

The Café Burgundy was alive with news of what had happened.

At a table near the edge of The Green, the four friends leaned in close, talking. Wolf had missed the lecture, but Sergey had been there with Lotte and had seen the young man mount the platform.

'You should have seen him,' Sergey said, his eyes glinting. 'As cool as anything, he got up there and stood at the lectern, as if he'd been meaning to speak all along.'

Wolf shook his head. 'And what did Fan say?'

'What *could* he say? For a moment he was so dumbfounded that he stood there with his mouth hanging open, like a fish. Then he went a brilliant red and began to shout at Shepherd to sit down. Oh, it was marvellous. "It's *my* lecture," the old boy kept saying, over and over. And Shepherd, bold as brass, turns to him and says, "Then you could do us all the courtesy of talking sense."'

They all roared at that; all but Catherine, who looked down. 'I've seen him, I think,' she said, 'in here.'

Sergey nodded. 'You can't really miss him. He's an ostentatious little sod. Do you know what he does?' He looked about the table, then leaned back, lifting his glass. 'He comes in at the busiest time of day and has a table to himself. He actually pays for all five places. And then he sits there, drinking coffee, not touching a bite of food, a pocket comset on the table in front of him.' Sergey lifted his nose in a gesture of disdain, then drained his glass.

Wolf leaned forward. 'Yes, but what happened? What did Fan say?'

Sergey gave a sharp little laugh. 'Well, it was strange. It was as if Shepherd had challenged him. I don't know. I suppose it had become a matter of face... Anyway, instead of just sending for the stewards and having him thrown out, Fan told him to go ahead.'

'I bet that shut him up!'

'No. And that's the most amazing part of it. You see, Shepherd actually began to lecture us.'

'No!' Wolf said, his eyes wide with astonishment. Beside him, Catherine stared down into her glass.

'Yes... he droned on for ages. A lot of nonsense about the artist and the object, and about there being two kinds of vision. Oh, a lot of high-sounding mumbo-jumbo.'

'He didn't drone, Sergey. And he was good. Very good.'

Sergey laughed and leaned across the table, smiling at the red-haired girl who had been his lover for almost two years. 'Who told you that? Lotte here?' He laughed. 'Well, whoever it was, they were wrong. It's a pity you missed it, Catherine. Shepherd was quite impressive, in a bullshitting sort of way, but...' He shrugged, lifting his free hand, the fingers wide open. 'Well, that's all it was, really. Bullshit.'

Catherine glanced up at him, as ever slightly intimidated by his manner. She picked up her glass and cradled it against her cheek, the chill red wine casting a roseate shadow across her face. 'I didn't just *hear* about it. I was there. At the back of the hall. I got there late, that's all.'

'Then you know it was crap.'

She hesitated, embarrassed. She didn't like to contradict him, but in this he was wrong. 'I... I don't agree...'

He laughed. 'You *don't* agree?'

She wanted to leave it at that, but he insisted.

'What do you mean?'

She took a breath. 'I mean that he was right. There *is* more to it than

Fan Liang-wei claims. The Six Principles... they strangle art. Because it isn't simply a matter of selection and interpretation. As Shepherd said, it has to do with other factors – with things unseen.'

Sergey snorted.

She shivered, irritated by his manner. 'I knew you'd do that. You're just like Fan Liang-wei, sneering at anything you disagree with. And both of you... well, you see only the material aspect of the art – its structure and its plastic elements, you don't see—'

Sergey had been shaking his head, a patient, condescending smile fixed on his lips, but now he interrupted her.

'What else is there? There's only light and shadow, texture and colour. That's all you can put on a canvas. It's a two-dimensional thing. And all this business about things unseen, it's...' He waved it away lightly with his hand.

She shook her head violently, for once really angry with him. 'No! What you're talking about is great design, not great art. Shepherd was right. That painting, for instance – the Tung Ch'i-ch'ang – it was crap.'

Sergey snorted again. 'So you say. But it has nothing to do with art, really, has it?' He smiled, sitting back in his chair. 'You fancy the fellow, don't you?'

She set her glass down angrily. Wine splashed and spilled across the dark green cloth. 'Now you're talking bullshit!'

He shook his head, talking over her protestations. 'My friend, Amand-sun, tells me that the man's not even a member of the Arts Faculty. He really is a scientist of some kind. A technician.'

He emphasized each syllable of the final word, giving it a distinctly unwholesome flavour.

Catherine glared at him a moment, then turned away, facing the aviary and its colourful occupants. On one of the higher perches a great golden bird fluffed out its wings as if to stretch into flight. The long, silken under-feathers were as black as night. It opened its beak, then settled again, making no sound.

Sergey watched the girl a moment, his eyes half-lidded, then, sensing victory, pushed home with his taunts.

'Yes, I bet our dear Catherine wouldn't mind him tinkering with her things unseen.'

That did it. She turned and took her glass, then threw its contents into his face. He swore and started to get up, wiping at his eyes, but Wolf leaned across, holding his arm firmly. 'Too far, Sergey. Just a bit too far...' he said, looking across at Catherine as he spoke.

Catherine stood there a moment longer, her head held back, fierce, proud, her face lit with anger; then she took five coins from her purse and threw them down on to the table. 'For the meal,' she said. Then she was gone; was walking out into the Mainway, ignoring the turned heads at other tables.

Sergey was wiping the wine from his eyes with the edge of the tablecloth. 'It stings! It fucking well stings!'

'It serves you right,' said Lotte, watching her friend go, her eyes uncharacteristically thoughtful. 'You always have to push it beyond the limits, don't you?'

Sergey glared at her, then relented. The front of his hair was slick with wine, his collar stained. After a moment he laughed. 'But I was right, wasn't I? It hit home. Dead centre!'

Beside him Wolf laughed, looking across at his sister and meeting her eyes. 'Yes...' he said, smiling, seeing his smile mirrored back. 'I've never seen her so angry. But who is this Shepherd? I mean, what's his background?'

Sergey shrugged. 'No one seems to know. He's not from one of the known families. And he doesn't make friends, that's for sure.'

'An upstart, do you think?' Lotte leaned across, collecting up the coins and stacking them in a neat pile.

'I guess so.' Sergey wiped at his fringe with his fingers, then licked them. 'Hmm. It might be interesting to find out, don't you think? To try to unearth something about him?'

Wolf laughed. 'Unearth... I like that. Do you think... ?'

Sergey wrinkled his nose, then shook his head. 'No. He's too big to have come from the Clay. You can spot those runts from ten li off. No, Mid-Levels, I'd say.'

Lotte looked up, smiling. 'Well, wherever he comes from, he has nerve, I'll say that for him.'

Sergey considered, then grudgingly agreed. 'Yes. He's impressive in a sort of gauche, unpolished way. No manners, though. I mean, poor old Fan was completely at a loss. You can be sure *he* won't rest until he's found a way of getting even with our friend.'

Wolf nodded. 'That's the trouble with the lower levels,' he said, watching his sister's hands as they stacked and unstacked the coins. 'They've no sense of what's right. No sense of li. Of propriety.'

'Or of art...' Sergey added.

'No...' And their laughter carried across the tables.

Ben drew back, into the shadows, watching. The two old men had gone down on to their knees before the makeshift shrine, the paper offerings and the bowls of food laid out in front of them. As he watched they bowed in unison, mumbling a prayer to the spirits of the departed. Then, while one of them stood and stepped back, his head still bowed, the other took a small brush from his inside jacket pocket and, lifting the bowls one at a time, swept the space before the tablets.

The two men were no more than ten or fifteen paces from Ben, yet it seemed as if a vast gulf separated them from him – an abyss of comprehension. He noted the paper money they had laid down for the dead, the sprigs of plastic 'willow' each wore hanging from their hair knots, and frowned, not understanding.

When they were gone he went across and stood there, looking at the wall and at the offerings laid out before it. It was a simple square of wall, the end of one of the many cul-de-sacs that led from Main, yet it had been transformed. Where one expected blankness, one came upon a hundred tiny tablets, each inscribed with the names and dates of the deceased. He looked, reading several of them, then bent down, picking up one of the paper notes of money. It was beautifully made, like the other presents here, but none of it was real. These were things for the dead.

For the last hour he had simply walked, here in the lowest levels of Oxford stack, trying to understand the events in the lecture hall. Had drifted through the corridors like a ghost, purposeless.

Or so he'd thought.

Their laughter had not touched him. It had been an empty, meaningless noise; a braying to fill the void within. No, but that emptiness itself – that unease he had seen behind every eye as he was speaking – that worried him. It had been like speaking to the dead. To the hordes of hungry ghosts who, so the Han believed, had no roots to tie them to this world – no living descendants to fulfil their all-too-human needs. They were lost and they looked lost. Even their guide, the Great Man. He more than any of them.

These thoughts had filled him, darkening his mood. And then, to come upon this...

Ben turned, hearing a noise behind him, but it was only an old man, two pots slung from the yoke that rested on his shoulders, the one balancing the other. As the old man came on he noticed Ben and stopped, his ancient face wrinkling, as if suspicious of Ben's motives.

Ben stood. 'Forgive me. I didn't mean to startle you. I was just looking...' He smiled. 'Are you a *ch'a* seller?'

'*Ch'a*?' The old man stared back at Ben, puzzled, then looked down at one of the pots he was carrying and gave a cackle of laughter. 'No, Master. You have it wrong. This...' He laughed again, showing his broken teeth. 'This isn't *ch'a*, Master. This here is ash.'

'Ash?'

The old man grinned back at him fiercely. 'Of course. I'm *Lu Nan Jen* for this stack.'

The oven man! Of course! So the ash... Ben laughed, surprised. 'And all this?' he asked, half turning to indicate the shrine, the paper offerings, the bowls of food.

The old man laughed uneasily. 'You're a strange one, Master. Don't you know what day it is? It's *Sao Mu*, the Feast of the Dead.'

Ben's eyes widened. Of course! The fifteenth day of the third month of the old calendar. *Ch'ing Ming*, it was, the festival of brightness and purity, when the graves were swept and offerings made to the deceased.

'Forgive me,' he offered quickly. 'I'm a student. My studies... they've kept me very busy recently.'

'Ah, a *student*...' The old man bowed respectfully, the yoke about his neck bobbing up and down with the movement. Then he looked up, his old eyes twinkling. 'I'm afraid I can't offer you any of this ash, Master, but the *ch'a* kettle is on inside if you'd honour me with your presence.'

Ben hesitated a moment, then returned the old man's bow. 'I would be honoured, *Lu Nan Jen*.'

The old man grinned back at him, delighted, his head bobbing, then made his way across to a door on the far side of the corridor. Ben followed him in, looking about the tiny room while the old man set down his pots and freed himself from the yoke.

'I must apologize for the state of things, Master. I have few visitors. Few *live* visitors, if you understand me?'

Ben nodded. There was a second door at the other end of the room with a sign in Mandarin that forbade unauthorized entry. On the wall beside it was a narrow shelf, on which were a meagre dozen or so tape-books – the kind that were touch-operated. Apart from that there was only a bed, a small stool and a low table on which were a ch'a kettle and a single bowl. He watched while the old man poured the ch'a then turned to him, offering the bowl.

'You will share with me, I hope?' he said, meeting the old man's eyes.

'I...' The old man hesitated, then gave a small bow. It was clear he had not expected such a kindness.

Ben sipped at the ch'a, then offered the bowl to the old man. Again he hesitated, then, encouraged by Ben's warm smile, he took the bowl and drank noisily from it.

'It must be strange, this life of yours, *Lu Nan Jen*.'

The oven man laughed and looked about him, as if considering it for the first time. 'No stranger than any man's.'

'Maybe so. But what kind of life is it?'

The old man sat, then leaned forward on the stool, the ch'a bowl held loosely in one hand. 'You want the job?' he asked, amused by Ben's query.

Ben laughed. 'No. I have enough to do, *lao jen*. But your work... it fascinates me.'

The old man narrowed his eyes slightly. 'Do you mean my work, or what I work with?'

'You can separate the two things that easily?'

The oven man looked down, a strange smile on his lips, then he looked up again, offering the ch'a bowl to Ben. 'You seem to know a lot, young Master. What is it that you're a student of?'

'Of life,' Ben answered. 'At least, so my father says.'

The old man held his eyes a moment, then nodded, impressed by the seriousness he saw in the younger man's face.

'This is a solitary life, young Master.' He gave a small chuckle, then rubbed at his lightly bearded chin. 'Oh... I see many people, but few who are either able or inclined to talk.'

'You've always been alone?'

'Always?' The old man sniffed, his dark eyes suddenly intense. 'Always is a long time, Master, as any of my clients would tell you if they could. But to answer you... No, there were women – one or two – in the early years.' He looked up, suddenly more serious. 'Oh, don't mistake me, Master, I am like other men in that. Age does not diminish need and a good fuck is a good fuck, neh?'

When Ben didn't answer, the old man shrugged.

'Anyway... there were one or two. But they didn't stay long. Not after they discovered what was in the back room.'

Ben turned, looking at the door, his eyebrows lifted.

'You want to see?'

'May I?'

He set the *ch'a* down and followed the old man, not knowing what he would find. A private oven? A room piled high with skulls? Fresh corpses, part dissected? Or something even more gruesome? He felt a small shiver of anticipation run through him. But the reality of what met his eyes was wholly unexpected.

He moved closer, then laughed, delighted. 'But it's... beautiful!'

'*Beautiful?*' The old man came and stood beside him, trying to see it as Ben saw it, with new eyes.

'Yes...' Ben said, reaching out to touch one of the tiny figures by the tree. Then he drew his finger back and touched it to his tongue. The taste was strange and yet familiar. 'What did you use?'

The old man pointed to one side. There, on a small table, were his brushes and paints and beside the paint pots a bowl like the two he had been carrying when Ben had first met him. A bowl filled with ashes.

'I see,' said Ben. 'And you mix the ash with dyes?'

The old man nodded.

Ben looked back at the mural. It almost filled the end wall, only a few white spaces here and there, at the edges and the top left of the painting, revealing where the composition was unfinished. Ben stared and stared, then remembered suddenly what the old man had said.

'How long did you say you've been working at this?'

The old man crouched down, inspecting something at the bottom of the painting. 'I didn't.'

'But...' Ben turned slightly, looking at him, seeing things there in his face that he had failed to notice earlier. 'I mean, what you said about the women, when you were younger. Was this here then?'

'This?' The old man laughed. 'No, not this. At least, not all of it. Just a small part. This here...' He sketched out a tiny portion of the composition, at the bottom centre of the wall.

'Yes. Of course.' Ben could see it now. The figures there were much cruder than the others. Now that his attention had been drawn to it, he could see how the composition had grown, from the centre out. The Oven Man had learned his art slowly, patiently, year by year adding to it, extending the range of his expression. Until...

Ben stood back, taking in the whole of the composition for the first time.

It was the dance of death. To the far left, a giant figure – huge, that was, compared to the other, much smaller figures – led the dance. It was a tall, emaciated figure, its skin glass-pale, its body like that of an ill-fed fighter, the bare arms lithely muscled, the long legs stretched taut like a runner's. Its body was facing to the left – to the west and the darkness beyond – but its horse-like, shaven head was turned unnaturally on its long neck, staring back dispassionately at the naked host that followed, hand in hand, down the path through the trees.

In its long, thin hands Death held a flute, the reed placed to its lipless mouth. From the tapered mouth of the flute spilled a flock of tiny birds, dark like ravens, yet cruel, their round eyes like tiny beads of milky white as they fell on to the host below, pecking at eye and limb.

The trees were to the right. Willow and ash and mulberry. Beneath them and to their left, in the centre of the mural, a stream fell between rocks, heavy with the yellow earth of northern China. These were the Yellow Springs, beneath which, it was said, the dead had their domain, ti yu, the 'earth prison'. He saw how several among that host – Han and Hung Mao alike – looked up at that golden spill of water as they passed, despairing, seeing nothing of its shining beauty.

It was a scene of torment, yet there was compassion there, too. Beneath one of the trees the two figures he had first noticed embraced one final time before they joined the dance. It was a mother and her child, the mother conquering her fear to comfort her tearful daughter. And, further on, beneath the biggest of the willows, two lovers pressed their faces close in one last, desperate kiss, knowing they must part for ever.

He looked and looked, drinking it in, then nodded, recognizing the style. It was *shanshui* – mountains and water. But this was nothing like the lifeless perfection Tung Ch'i-ch'ang had painted. These mountains were alive, in motion, the flow of water turbulent, disturbed by the fall of rock from above.

It was a vision of last things. Of the death not of a single man, but of a world. Of Chung Kuo itself.

He stood back, shivering. It was some while since he had been moved so profoundly by anything. The oven man was not a great painter – at least, not technically – yet what he lacked in skill he more than made up for in vision. For this was real. This had *ch'i* – vitality. Had it in excess.

'I can see why they left you, *Lu Nan Jen*. Was this a dream?'

The old man turned, looking at Ben, his whole manner changed. There was no mistaking him now for a simple *ch'a* seller.

'You understand, then?'

Ben met his eyes. 'When did it come?'

'When I was ten. My life...' He shrugged, then looked away. 'I guess there was nothing I could be after that but *Lu Nan Jen*. There was no other school for me.'

'Yes...' Ben turned, looking at it again, awed by its simple power. 'All this... your work ... it must keep you busy.'

'Busy?' The old man laughed. 'There is no busier person in the Seven Cities than the oven man, unless it is the Midwife. They say eight hundred million die each year. Eight hundred million, and more each year. Always more. There is no room for such numbers in the earth. And so they come to my ovens.' He laughed, a strangely thoughtful expression on his face. 'Does that disturb you, young Master?'

'No,' Ben answered honestly, yet it made him think of his father. How long would it be before Hal too was dead – alive in memory alone? Yet he, at least, would lie at rest in the earth. Ben frowned. 'Your vision is marvellous, *Lu Nan Jen*. And yet, when you talk, you make it all sound so... so prosaic. So meaningless.'

'From nothing they come. To nothing they return.'

'Is that what you believe?'

The old man shrugged, his eyes going to the darkness at the far left of the mural, beyond the figure of Death. 'To believe in nothing, is that a belief? If so, I believe.'

Ben smiled. There was more sense, more wisdom, in this old man than in a thousand Fan Liang-weis. And himself? What did he believe? Did he believe in nothing? Was the darkness simply darkness? Or was there something there, within it? Just as there seemed to be a force behind the light, was there not also a force behind the dark? Maybe even the same force?

The old man sighed. 'Forgive me, young Master, but I must leave you now. I have my ovens to attend. But, please, if you wish to stay here...'

Ben lowered his head. 'I thank you, *Lu Nan Jen*. And I am honoured that you showed me your work. It is not every day that I come across something so real.'

The oven man bowed, then met Ben's eyes again. 'I am glad you came, young Master. It is not every day that I meet someone who understands such things. The dream uses us, does it not?'

Ben nodded, moved by the old man's humility. To create *this* and yet to know how little *he* had to do with its creating. That was true knowledge.

He bowed again and made to go, then stopped. 'One last thing,' he said, turning back. 'Do you believe in ghosts?'

The oven man laughed and looked about him at the air. 'Ghosts? Why, there's nothing here but ghosts.'

'Catherine? Are you in there?'

She closed her eyes and let her forehead rest against the smooth, cool surface of the door, willing him to go and leave her in peace, but his voice returned, stronger, more insistent.

'Catherine? You are there, aren't you? Let me in.'

'Go away,' she said, hearing the tiredness in her voice. 'You've a date with young Heng, haven't you? Why don't you just go to that and leave me be.'

'Let me in,' he said, ignoring her comment. 'Come on. We need to talk.'

She sighed then stepped back, reaching across to touch the lock. At once the door slid back.

Sergey had changed. He was wearing his gambling clothes – dark silks that lent him a hard, almost sinister air. She had never liked them, least of all now, when she was angry with him.

'Still sulking?' he asked, making his way past her into the room.

She had thrown a sheet over the oilboard to conceal what she had been working on, but he went straight to it, throwing back the sheet.

'Is this what's been causing all the difficulties?'

She punched the touch-pad irritably, closing the door, then turned to face him.

'What do you want?'

He laughed, then came across to her. 'Is that how you greet me?'

He made to embrace her, but she pushed him away.

'You forget,' she said, moving past him and throwing the sheet back over the oilboard.

'It was a joke...' he began, but she rounded on him angrily.

'You're a child! Do you know that?'

He shrugged. 'I thought that's what you liked about me? Besides, it wasn't you who had wine thrown in your face. That hurt.'

'Good.'

She turned away, but he caught her arm and pulled her back.

'Let go of me,' she said coldly, looking down at where he held her.

'Not until you apologize.'

She laughed, astonished by him. '*Me* apologize? After what you said? You can go rot in hell before I apologize to you!'

He tightened his grip until she cried out, tearing her arm away from his grasp.

'You bastard... You've no right...'

'No *right*?' He came closer, his face leaning into hers threateningly. 'After what we've been to each other these last two years, you have the nerve to say I've no right?' His voice was hard, harder than she had ever heard it before, and she found herself suddenly frightened by this aspect of him. Had it always been there, just below the surface of his charm? Yes. She'd always known it about him. Perhaps that was even what had first attracted her. But she was tired of it now. Tired of his thoughtless domination of her. Let him drink himself to death, or take his whores, or gamble away all his money – she would have no more of it.

'Just go, Sergey. Now, before you make even more of a fool of yourself.'

She saw his eyes widen with anger and knew she had said the wrong thing. He reached out and grabbed her neck roughly, pulling her closer to him. 'A fool?'

Through her fear she recognized the strange parallel of the words with those Fan Liang-wei had used to Shepherd. Then she was fighting to get away from him, hitting his arms and back as he pulled her chin round forcibly and pressed his mouth against her own. Only then did he release her, pushing her back away from him, as if he had done with her.

'And *now* I'll go see Heng.'

She shivered, one hand wiping at her mouth unconsciously. 'You bastard...' she said, her voice small. 'You obnoxious bastard...' She was close to tears now, her anger displaced suddenly by the hurt she felt. How *dare* he do that to her? How *dare* he treat her like his thing?

But he only shook his head. 'Grow up, Catherine. For the gods' sake, grow up.'

'Me... ?' But her indignation was wasted on him. He had turned away. Slamming his fist against the lock, he pushed out through the door, barely waiting for it to open. Then he was gone.

She stood there a while, staring at the open doorway, fear and hurt and anger coursing through her. Then, as the automatic lock came on and the door hissed closed, she turned and went out into the kitchen. She reached up and pulled down the bottle of peach brandy and poured herself a large glass, her hands trembling. Then, using both hands to steady the glass, she took a long, deep swig of it, closing her eyes, the rich, dark liquid burning her throat.

She shuddered. The bastard! How *dare* he?

Back in the other room, she set the glass down on the floor, then threw the sheet back from the oilboard, looking at the painting. It was meant to be a joint portrait. Of her and Sergey. Something she had meant to give him for their second anniversary, two weeks away. But now...

She looked at it, seeing it with new eyes. It was shit. Lifeless shit. As bad as the Tung Ch'i-ch'ang landscape. She pressed to erase then stood back, watching as the faces faded and the coloured, contoured screen became a simple, silk smooth rectangle of uncreated whiteness.

For a moment she felt nothing, then, kneeling, she picked up her glass, cradling it against her cheek momentarily before she put it to her lips and drank.

She looked up again, suddenly determined. Fuck him! If that was what he thought of her – if that was how he was prepared to treat her – then she would have no more of it. Let it be an end between them.

She swallowed, the warmth in her throat deceptive, the tears threatening to come despite her determination not to cry. She sniffed, then raised her glass, offering a toast to the silent doorway.

'Go fuck yourself, Sergey Novacek! May you rot in hell!'

Sergey stood there at the top of the steps, looking down into the huge, dimly lit gaming room of The Jade Peony. Lights above the tables picked out where games were in progress, while at the far end a bar ran from left to right, backlit and curved like a crescent moon. The floor below was busy. Crowds gathered about several of the tables, the excited murmur of their voices carrying to where he stood.

There was a sweet, almost peppery scent in the air, like cinnamon mixed with plum and jasmine, strangely feminine, yet much too strong to be pleasant. It was the smell of them – of the sons of the Minor Families and their friends. The distinguishing mark of this Han elite; like a pheromonal dye. Sergey smiled. In theory The Jade Peony was a mixed club, membership determined not by race but by recommendation and election, but in practice the only *Hung Mao* here were guests, like himself.

Yang kuei tzu, they called his kind. 'Ocean devils'. *Barbarians*.

Even the Han at the door had looked down on him. He had seen the contempt that lay behind that superficial mask of politeness. Had heard him turn, after he had gone, and mutter a word or two of his own tongue to the other doorman. Had heard them laugh and knew it was about himself.

Well, he'd wipe a few smiles from their faces tonight. And Heng? His smile broadened momentarily. He would make sure Heng would not be smiling for some time.

He went down the plushly carpeted stairway, past the great dragon-head sculpture that stood to one side, making his way to the bar.

As he passed they stared at him openly, their hostility unmasked.

Heng Chian-ye was where he said he would be, at a table on the far left, close to the bar. A big, hexagonal table covered in a bright red silk. Representations of the *wu fu*, the five gods of good luck, formed a patterned border around its edge, the tiny silhouettes picked out in green.

He smiled and bowed. 'Heng Chian-ye... You received my message, I hope.'

Heng Chian-ye was seated on the far side of the table, a glass and a wine bottle in front of him. To either side of him sat his friends, four in all, young, fresh-faced Han in their early twenties, their long fingernails and elaborately embroidered silks the calling card of their kind. They stared back at Sergey coldly, as if at a stranger, while Heng leaned forward, a faint smile playing on his lips.

'Welcome, *Shih* Novacek. I got your message. Even so, I did wonder whether you would make an appearance tonight.' His smile broadened momentarily, as if to emphasize the jest. 'Anyway, you're here now, neh? So... please, take a seat. I'll ask the waiter to bring you a drink.'

'Just wine,' he said, answering the unspoken query, then sat, smiling a greeting at the others at the table; inwardly contemptuous.

He smiled, then, taking the silken pouch from his jacket pocket, threw it across the table so that it landed just in front of Heng Chian-ye. It was deliberately done; not so much an insult as an act of gaucheness. In the circles in which Heng mixed it was not necessary to provide proof of means before you began to play. It was assumed that if you sat at a gaming table you could meet your debts. So it was among the *ch'un tzu*. Only *hsiao jen* – little men – acted as Sergey was acting now.

Sergey saw the looks that passed amongst Heng and his friends and smiled inwardly. Their arrogance, their ready assumption of superiority – these were weaknesses. And the more he could feed that arrogance, the weaker they would become. The weaker they, the stronger he.

'What's this?' Heng said, fingering the string of the pouch as if it were unclean.

'My stake,' Sergey said, sitting forward slightly, as if discomfited. 'Look and see. I think you'll find it's enough.'

Heng laughed and shook his head. 'Really, *Shih* Novacek. That's not how we do things here.'

Sergey raised his eyebrows, as if puzzled. 'You do not wish to play, then? But I thought...'

Heng was smiling tightly. His English was tightly clipped, polite. 'It isn't what I meant.' He lifted the pouch with two fingers and threw it back across the table. 'You would not be here if I... doubted your ability to pay.'

Sergey smiled. 'Forgive me,' he said, looking about him as he picked up the pouch and returned it to his pocket. 'I did not mean to offend.'

'Of course,' Heng answered, smiling, yet the way he glanced at his friends revealed what he was really thinking. 'I understand, *Shih* Novacek. Our ways differ. But the game...'

Sergey lowered his head slightly, as if acknowledging the wisdom of what Heng Chian-ye had said. 'The game is itself. The same for Han and *Hung Mao* alike.'

Heng gave the barest nod. 'So it is. Well... shall we play?'

'Just you and I, Heng Chian-ye? Or will the *ch'un tzu* join us?'

Heng looked to either side of him. 'Chan Wen-fu? Tsang Yi? Will you play?'

Two of the Han nodded; the other two – as if on cue – stood, letting the others spread out round the table.

'You will be West, *Shih* Novacek, I East. My friends here will be North and South.'

Sergey sat back, taking the wine from the waiter who had appeared at his side. 'That's fine with me. You have new cards?'

Heng lifted his chin, as if in signal to the waiter. A moment later the man returned with a sealed pack, offering them to Sergey. He took them and hefted them a moment, then set them down on the table.

'Bring another.'

Heng smiled tightly. 'Is there something wrong with them, *Shih* Novacek?'

'Not at all, Heng Chian-ye. Please, bear with me. It is a foible of mine. A... *superstition*.' He spoke the last word quietly, as if ashamed of such a weakness, and saw the movement in Heng's eyes; the way he looked to North and South, as if to reinforce the point to his two friends.

'You have many superstitions, *Shih* Novacek?'

'Not many. But this...' He shrugged, then turned, taking the new pack from the waiter and setting it down beside the other. Then, to Heng's surprise, he picked up the first and broke the seal.

'But I thought...'

Sergey looked down, ignoring Heng's query, fanning the huge cards out on the table in front of him. There were one hundred and sixty cards in a pack of *Chou*, or 'State', arranged into nine levels, or groupings. At the head of all was the Emperor, enthroned in golden robes. Beneath him were his seven Ministers, these greybeards plainly dressed, as if in contrast. At the third level were the Family Heads – the twenty-nine cards richly decorated, each one quite different from the others. At the next level down the four Generals seemed at first glance quite uniform; yet the staunch Hung Mao faces of the old men differed considerably. Beneath them came the four wives of the Emperor, ranked in their household order, and beneath them – at the sixth level – came the two concubines, their scantily dressed figures making them the most attractive of the cards. Next were the eight sons, their resemblance to their respective mothers suggested by their facial features and cleverly underlined by use of colour and decoration. Then, at the eighth level of this complex hierarchy came the eighty-one officials, ranked in nine levels of nine, their great chi ling patches displayed on the chests of their powder-blue gowns. And finally, at the ninth level – last in the great pecking order of State – were the twenty-four Company Heads, their corporate symbols – some long forgotten, some just as familiar now as when the game was first played one hundred and twenty years before – emblazoned on the copy of the Edict scroll each held.

He turned one of the cards a moment, studying the reverse carefully for special markings, then compared it with a second. The backs of the cards were a bright, silken red, broken in the centre by a pattern of three concentric circles, three rings of dragons: twenty-nine black dragons in the outer circle, seven larger dragons in the second, and, at the very centre, a single golden dragon, larger than all the others, its great jaws closing on its tail.

Sergey smiled and looked up. 'These are beautiful cards, Heng Chian-ye. The faces... they look almost as if they were drawn from life.'

Heng laughed. 'So they were, my friend. These are copies of the very first Chou pack, hand drawn by Tung Men-tiao.'

Sergey looked down at the cards with a new respect. Then these were tiny portraits of the actual people who had filled those roles. Men and women whom the great artist and satirist Tung Men-tiao had known in life. He smiled. Somehow it gave the game an added bite.

'Shall we start?' Heng asked. 'If you'll stack the cards, we'll cut to see who deals.'

For the first few hours he had tried to keep things fairly even, attributing his victories to good fortune, his defeats to his own stupidity. And all the while he had studied their play – had seen how the other two played to Heng, even while making it seem that they had only their own interests at heart. It was clever but transparent, and he could see how it would have fooled another, but he was not just any player. At *Chou* he excelled. He had mastered this as a child, playing his father and uncles for his pocket money.

In the last game he had drawn the Emperor and, despite a strong hand, had proceeded to ensure he lost: rather than consolidating power, he played into the hands of Heng's three Minister cards. Heng's rebellion had succeeded and Sergey had ended by losing a thousand *yuan*. He had seen the gleam in Heng's eyes as he noted down his winnings on the tab and knew that the time was ripe. Heng had won the last two games. He must feel he was on a winning streak. What better time, then, to up the stakes?

Sergey looked down, pretending not to see how Heng looked to his left at Tsang Yi, knowing what was to come.

'Forgive me, *ch'un tzu*,' the Han began, getting to his feet and bowing, first to his friends, and then – his head barely inclined – to Sergey, 'but I must go. My father…'

'Of course,' Heng said smoothly, before Sergey could object. 'We understand, don't we, *Shih* Novacek?'

We do, he thought, smiling inwardly, then watching as another of Heng's circle took Tsang's place at table.

'I'll buy Tsang out,' the Han said, his eyes meeting Sergey's briefly, challengingly. Then, turning to Heng, he added, 'But look, Chian-ye, why don't we make the game more… *exciting*?'

Heng laughed, acting as though he didn't understand his friend. 'How so, Yi Shan-ch'i? Was that last game not exciting enough for you?'

Yi inclined his head slightly. 'Forgive me, honourable cousin, but that is not what I meant. The game itself was good. As enjoyable to watch as I'm sure it was to play. But such a game needs an added bite, don't you think? If the stake were to be raised to ten thousand *yuan* a game…'

Heng laughed, then looked across at Sergey. 'Maybe so. But let's ask our friend here. Well, *Shih* Novacek? What do you say? Would you like to raise the stakes, or are you happy as it is?'

It was delicately put. Almost too delicately, for it was phrased as if to let him back off without losing face. But things were not so simple. He was not one of them, even though he sat at their table. He was *Yang kuei tzu*. A foreign devil. A *barbarian*. He looked down, wrinkling up his face as if considering the matter, then looked up again.

'Ten thousand *yuan*...' He laughed nervously. 'It's more than I've lost in a whole evening before now. Still... Yi Shan-ch'i is right. It *would* make the game more interesting.'

Heng looked to his two friends, then back at Sergey. 'I would not like to pressure you...'

'No.' Sergey shook his head firmly, as if he had made up his mind and was now determined on it. 'Ten thousand *yuan* it is. For good or ill.'

He sat back, watching Yi deal. As ever Heng picked up each card as it was dealt, his face an eloquent map of his fortunes. For his own part, Sergey waited until all seventeen cards were lain face down before him, watching the other two sort their cards before he picked up his own.

As he sorted his hand he thought back to the last time he had played Heng. The object of *Chou* was straightforward and could be expressed quite simply: it was to hold the most points in one's hand at the end of the final play. To do so, however, one had not only to strengthen one's own hand but to weaken one's opponents. The game's complex system of discards and exchanges, blind draws and open challenges was designed to simulate this aspect of political life; to counterfeit the sticky web of intrigue that underpinned it all. Heng played, however, as if he barely understood this aspect of the game. As if only the relative levels of the cards – their positive attributes – mattered to him. He sought to cram his hand full of high-scoring cards and bonus combinations – Ministers and Family Heads and Generals – failing, like so many of his kind, to understand the other side of things: the powerfully destructive potential of Concubines and Sons.

In *Chou* the value of a card did not always express its significance in the scheme of things. So it was with Concubines. At the end of the game they were worth only eight points – fifty-six points less than a Family Head and one hundred and twenty points less than a Minister. Unless...

Unless the Emperor were without a Wife. In which case, the Concubine took on its negative aspect, cancelling out not only its own value but the two hundred and fifty-six points that the Emperor would otherwise score.

Likewise with the Sons. While they scored only four a piece at the final count, in the company of their respective mothers they became a liability, cancelling out not merely their own value but that of any Minister held.

The skilful player sought, therefore, to pair Wives with Sons and hold back Wives from those who held the Emperor and then, at the last throw, to offload their pairings and Concubines in an exchange of hostages. To win by undermining their opponents.

Sergey smiled, noting that he had both Concubines in his hand. Well, good. This time he would keep them. Would make it seem he had drawn them late in the play, before he could offload them on another.

A half-hour later he had lost.

'Another game, *ch'un tzu?*' Heng asked, jotting down Yi's victory on the tab. Sergey glanced across. He was eleven thousand down, Chan nine, Heng eight. Yi, who had taken on Tsang's deficit of two thousand, was now twenty-eight thousand up.

Heng dealt this time. 'Has anyone the Emperor?' he asked, having sorted out his own hand.

Sergey laid it down before him, then reached across to take another card from the pile. Having the Emperor made one strong. But it also made one vulnerable – to Concubines and the scheming Sons of Wives.

Again he smiled. He had a good hand – no, an excellent hand. Three Wives and Three Ministers and there, at the far left of his hand, one of the Concubines. The tiny, doe-eyed one.

He looked down, momentarily abstracted from the game, thinking back to earlier that evening and to the row with Catherine. He had shut it out before, but now it came back to him. It had been his fault. He could see that now. But why did she always have to provoke him so? Why couldn't she be more like the other women he knew? He felt a mild irritation at her behaviour. Why did she always have to be so stubborn? Didn't she know what it did to him? And all that business with the 'technician'. Shepherd. Why had she done that, if not to spite him? She knew how jealous he was. Why couldn't she be a bit more compliant? Then again, he liked her spirit. So different from Lotte and her kind.

He laughed softly, conscious of the contradiction.

'You have a good hand, *Shih* Novacek?' Heng asked, smiling tightly at him, misunderstanding the cause of his laughter.

'I think so, Heng Chian-ye,' he answered, leaning forward to place two of the Ministers face down on to the discard pile. 'I think so.'

Two hours later he was sixty-one thousand down. He wasn't the only one down, of course. Chan had a deficit of nineteen thousand marked against his name. But Yi was eighteen thousand up, and Heng, who had won three of the last four games, was sixty-two thousand in credit.

It had gone perfectly. Exactly as he'd planned. He looked across. Heng Chian-ye was smiling broadly. In the last hour Heng had begun to drink quite heavily, as if to buoy up his nerves. He had drunk so much, in fact, that he had almost made a simple mistake, discarding the wrong card. An error that could have lost him everything. Only Yi's quick action had prevented it – an intercession Sergey had pretended not to see.

Now, then, was the time. While Heng was at the height of his pride. But it must come from Heng. In such company as this it must seem that it was not he, but Heng, who raised the stakes a second time.

In the last hour a small crowd had gathered about the table, intrigued by the sight of a *Hung Mao* playing *Chou* in The Jade Peony. Sergey had noted how a ripple of satisfaction had gone through the watchers on each occasion he had lost and had felt something harden deep inside him. Well, now he would show them.

He leaned back in his seat, pretending to stifle a yawn. 'I'm tired,' he said. 'Too many late nights, I guess.' He smiled across at Heng. 'Maybe I should stop now, while I've any of my fortune left.'

Heng glanced across at his friends, then looked back at him. 'You mean to leave us soon, *Shih* Novacek?'

He straightened up and took a deep breath, as if trying to sober up. 'Fairly soon...'

'Your luck must change...'

'Must it?' He laughed harshly, then seemed to relent. 'Well, maybe...'

'In which case...' Heng looked about him, then leaned towards Sergey again. 'Maybe you'd like the chance to win your money back, eh, my friend? One game. Just you and I. For sixty-one thousand.'

Sergey looked down. Then, surprisingly, he shook his head. 'I wouldn't hear of it. Even if I won, well, it would be as if we hadn't played.' He looked up, meeting Heng's eyes. 'No, my friend. There must be winners and losers in this world of ours, neh? If we are to play, let it be for... seventy-five thousand. That way I at least have a small chance of coming out ahead.'

Heng smiled and his eyes travelled quickly to his friends again. There was an expectant hush now about the table.

'Make it a hundred...'

He made a mime of considering the matter, then shrugged. 'All right. So be it.' He turned, summoning a waiter. 'Bring me a coffee. Black, two sugars. I might need my wits about me this time.'

It took him twenty minutes.

'It seems my luck has changed,' he said, meeting Heng's eyes; seeing at once how angry the other man was with himself, for he had made it seem as though victory were the Han's, only to snatch it away at the last moment. 'I was fortunate to draw that last card.'

He saw what it cost Heng to keep back the words that almost came to his lips and knew he had him.

'Anyway...' he added quickly, 'I really should go now. I thank you for your hospitality, Heng Chian-ye. Settle with me when you will. You know where to find me.' He pushed his chair back from the table and got to his feet.

'Wait!'

Heng was leaning forward, his hand extended towards Sergey.

'Surely you won't go now, *Shih* Novacek? As you yourself said... your luck has changed. Why, then, do you hurry from your fortune? Surely you aren't afraid, my friend?'

Sergey stared back at him. *'Afraid?'*

Heng leaned back, a faint smile coming to his lips. 'Yes. Afraid.' He hesitated, then, 'I'll play you again, *Shih* Novacek. One final game. But this time we'll make the stakes worth playing for. Two hundred thousand. No. *Two fifty* thousand.'

Sergey looked about him at the watching Han, seeing the tension in every face. This was no longer about the money; for Heng it was now a matter of pride – of *face*.

He sat, placing his hands firmly on the edge of the table, looking back at Heng, fixing him in his gaze, his manner suddenly different – harder, almost brutal in its challenge.

'All right. But not for two fifty. Let's have no half-measures between us, Heng Chian-ye. If I play you, I play you for a million. Understand me?'

There were low gasps from all round the table, then a furious murmur of voices. But Heng seemed unaware of the hubbub that surrounded him. He sat there, staring back fixedly at Sergey, his eyes wide, as if in shock. His hands were trembling now, his brow beaded with sweat.

'Well?'

Unable to find his voice, Heng nodded.

'Good.' Sergey leaned forward and took the cards, then, surprising them all, handed them to Yi. 'You deal, Yi Shan-ch'i. I want no one to say that this was not a fair game.'

He saw Heng's eyes widen at that. Saw realization dawn in Heng's frightened face.

So now you know.

He kept his face a mask, yet inwardly he was exulting. *I've got you now, you bastard. Got you precisely where I wanted you.* A million. Yes, it was more than Heng Chian-ye had. More than he could possibly borrow from his friends. He would have no alternative. If he lost he would have to go to his uncle.

Heng Yu turned in his seat, dismissing the servant, then went outside into the anteroom. Heng Chian-ye knelt there, on the far side of the room, his head bowed low, his forehead touched almost to the tiled floor. He crossed the room, then stood over the young man, looking down at him.

'What is it, cousin?'

Heng Chian-ye stayed as he was. 'Forgive me, Uncle Yu, but I have the most grave request to make of you.'

Heng Yu, Minister of Transportation for Li Shai Tung and Head of the Heng family, pulled at his beard, astonished. Chian-ye was fourteen years his junior, the youngest son of his uncle, the former Minister, Heng Chi-po, who had passed away eleven years ago. Several times over the past five years he had been forced to bail the boy out when he had been in trouble, but all that had changed six months back, when Chian-ye had come into his inheritance. Now that he had his own income, Chian-ye had been a much rarer visitor at his Uncle Yu's house.

'A grave request? At this hour, Chian-ye? Do you *know* what time it is? Can it not wait until the morning?'

Heng Chian-ye made a small, miserable movement of his head. 'I would not have come, Uncle, were it not a matter of the utmost urgency.'

Heng Yu frowned, confused, his head still full of figures from the report he had been studying.

'What is it, Chian-ye? Is someone ill?'

But he knew, even as he said it, that it was not that. Fu Hen would have come with such news, not Chian-ye. Unless... He felt himself go cold.

'It isn't Fu Hen, is it?'

Heng Chian-ye raised his head the tiniest bit. 'No, Honoured Uncle. No one is ill.'

Heng Yu sighed with relief, then leaned closer. 'Have you been drinking, Chian-ye?'

'I...' Then, astonishingly, Chian-ye burst into tears. Chian-ye, who had never so much as expressed one word of remorse over his own wasteful lifestyle, in tears! Heng Yu looked down at where Chian-ye's hand gripped the hem of his *pau* and shook his head. His voice was suddenly forceful; the voice of a Minister commanding an underling.

'Heng Chian-ye! Remember who you are! Look at you! Crying like a four-year-old! Aren't you ashamed of yourself?'

'Forgive me, Uncle! I cannot help it! I have disgraced our noble family. I have lost a million *yuan*!'

Heng Yu fell silent. Then he gave a small laugh of disbelief.

'Surely I heard you wrong, Chian-ye? A million *yuan*?'

But a tiny nod of Chian-ye's bowed head confirmed it. A million *yuan* had been lost. Probably at the gaming table.

Heng Yu looked about him at the cold formality of the anteroom, at its mock pillars and the tiny bronze statues of gods that rested in the alcoves to either side, the unreality of it all striking him forcibly. Then he shook his head. 'It isn't possible, Chian-ye. Even *you* cannot have lost that much, surely?'

But he knew that it was. Nothing less would have brought Chian-ye here. Nothing less would have reduced him to such a state.

Heng Yu sighed, his irritation mixed with a sudden despair. Was he never to be free of his uncle's failings? First that business with Lwo Kang, and now this. As if the father were reborn in his wastrel son – to blight the family's fortunes with his carelessness and selfishness.

For now he would have to borrow to carry out his schemes. Would have to take that high-interest loan *Shih* Saxton had offered him. A million *yuan*! He cursed silently, then drew away, irritably freeing his *pau* from his cousin's grasp.

'Come into the study, Chian-ye, and tell me what has happened.'

He sat behind his great ministerial desk, his face stern, listening to Chian-ye's story. When his cousin finished, he sat there silently, considering. Finally he looked back at Chian-ye, shaking his head.

'You have been a foolish young man, Chian-ye. First you overstretched yourself. That was bad enough. But then... well, to promise something that was not yours to promise, that was... insufferable.'

He saw how Chian-ye blushed and hung his head at that. *So there is some sense of rightness in you,* he thought. *Some sense of shame.*

'However,' he continued, heartened by the clear sign of his cousin's shame, 'you are family, Chian-ye. You are *Heng*.' He pronounced the word with a pride that made his cousin look up and meet his eyes, surprised.

'Yes. Heng. And the word of a Heng must be honoured, whether given mistakenly or otherwise.'

'You mean...?'

Heng Yu's voice hardened. 'I mean, cousin, that you will be silent and listen to me!'

Heng Chian-ye lowered his head again, chastened; his whole manner subservient now.

'As I was saying. The word of a Heng must be honoured. So, yes, Chian-ye, I shall meet *Shih* Novacek's conditions. He shall have the *Ko Ming* bronze in settlement for your debt. As for the information he wanted, you can do that for yourself, right now. The terminal is over there, in the corner. However... there are two things you will do for me.'

Chian-ye raised his head slightly, suddenly attentive.

'First you will sign over half of your annual income, to be placed in a trust that will mature only when you are thirty.'

Chian-ye hesitated, then gave a reluctant nod.

'Good. And, second, you will resign your membership to The Jade Peony.'

Heng Chian-ye looked up, astonished. 'But, Uncle...?' Then, seeing the angry determination in Heng Yu's face, he lowered his eyes. 'As you say, Uncle Yu.'

'Good,' Heng Yu said, more kindly now that it was settled. 'Then go to the terminal. You know how to operate it. The codes are marked to the right. But ask me if you must. I shall be here a few hours yet, finishing my reports.'

He watched Chian-ye go to the terminal, then sat back, smoothing at his beard with his left hand, his right hand resting on the desk. A million *yuan*! That, truly, would have been disastrous. But this... this deal. He smiled. Yes, it was a gods-given opportunity to put a bit and brace on his reckless cousin – to school him to self-discipline. And the price? One ugly bronze worth, at most, two hundred thousand, and a small snippet of information on a fellow student!

He nodded, strangely pleased with the way things had turned out, then picked up the report again. He was about to push it into the slot behind his ear when Chian-ye turned, looking across at him.

'Uncle Yu?'

'Yes, Chian-ye?'

'There seems to be no file.'

Heng Yu laughed, then stood, coming round his desk. 'Of course there's a file, Chian-ye. There's a file on everyone in Chung Kuo. You must have keyed the code incorrectly.'

He stared at the screen. INFORMATION NOT AVAILABLE, it read.

'Here,' he said, taking the scrap of paper from his cousin's hand. 'Let me see those details.'

He stopped dead, staring at the name that was written on the paper, then laughed uncomfortably.

'Is something wrong, Uncle Yu?'

'No... nothing. I...' He smiled reassuringly, then repeated what Chian-ye had tried before, getting the same response. 'Hmm...' he said. 'There must be something wrong with this terminal. I'll call one of my men to come and see to it.'

Heng Chian-ye was watching him strangely. 'Shall I wait, Uncle?'

For a moment he didn't answer, his head filled with questions. Then he shook his head absently. 'No, Chian-ye...' Then, remembering what day it was, he turned, facing him.

'You realize what day it is, Chian-ye?'

The young man shook his head.

'You mean, you have been wasting your time gambling, when your father's grave remains unswept?'

Chian-ye swallowed and looked down, abashed. '*Sao Mu*,' he said quietly.

'Yes, *Sao Mu*... Or so it is for another three-quarters of an hour. Now go,

Chian-ye, and do your duty. I'll have these details for you by the morning, I promise you.'

When Chian-ye was gone he locked the door, then came back to the terminal.

Ben Shepherd... Now, what would *Shih* Novacek be doing wanting to know about the Shepherd boy? One thing was certain – it wasn't a harmless enquiry. For no one, Han or *Hung Mao*, threw a million *yuan* away on such a small thing. Unless it wasn't small.

He turned, looking across at the tiny chip of the report where it lay on his desk, then turned back, his decision made. The report could wait. This was much more important. Whatever it was.

CHUNG KUO

Chapter 55

CATHERINE

'Would you mind if I sat with you?'

He looked up at her, smiling, seeming to see her, to *create* her, for the very first time. She felt unnerved by that gaze. Its intensity was unexpected, unnatural. And yet he was smiling.

'With me?'

She was suddenly uncertain. There was only one chair at his table. The waiters had removed the others, isolating him. So that no one would approach him.

She felt herself colouring. Her neck and her cheeks felt hot, and, after that first, startling contact, her eyes avoided his.

'Well?' he said, leaning back, his fingers resting lightly on the casing of the comset on the table in front of him.

He seemed unreachable, and yet he was smiling.

'I... I wanted...' Her eyes reached out, making contact with his. So unfathomably deep they were. They held hers, drawing her out from herself. '... to sit with you.'

But she was suddenly afraid; her body tensed against him.

'Sit where?' His hand lifted, the fingers opening in a gesture of emptiness. The smile grew broader. Then he relented. 'All right. Get a chair.'

She brought a chair and set it down across from him.

'No. Closer.' He indicated the space beside him. 'I can't talk across tables.'

She nodded, setting the chair down where he indicated.

'Better.'

He was still watching her. His eyes had not left her face from the moment she had first spoken to him.

Again she felt a flash of fear, pure fear, pass through her. He was like no one she had ever met. So... She shook her head, the merest suggestion of movement, and felt a shiver run along her spine. No, she had never felt like this before – so... helpless.

'What do you do?'

Not 'Who are you?' Nothing as formal as an introduction. Instead, this. Direct and unabashed. *What do you do?* Peeling away all surfaces.

For the first time she smiled at him. 'I... paint.'

He nodded, his lips pinched together momentarily. Then he reached out and took her hands in his own, studying them, turning them over in his own.

So firm and warm and fine, those hands. Her own lay caged in his, her fingers thinner, paler than those that held them.

'Good hands,' he said, but did not relinquish them. 'Now, tell me what you wanted to talk to me about.'

About hands, perhaps. Or a million other things. But the warmth, the simple warmth of his hands curled about her own, had robbed her of her voice.

He looked down again, following her eyes. 'What is it, Catherine?'

She looked up sharply, searching his face, wondering how he knew her name.

He watched her a moment longer, then gave a soft laugh. 'There's little you don't pick up, sitting here. Voices carry.'

'And you hear it all? Remember it?'

'Yes.'

His eyes were less fierce now, less predatory in their gaze, yet it still seemed as if he was staring at her; as if his wide-eyed look was drug-induced. But it no longer frightened her; no longer picked her up and held her there, suspended, soul-naked and vulnerable before it.

Her fear of him subsided. The warmth of his hands...

'What do you paint?'

Until a moment ago it had seemed important. All-important. But now? She tilted her head, looking past him, aware of the shape of his head, the way he sat there, so easy, so comfortable in his body. Again, so unexpected.

He laughed. Fine, open laughter. Enjoying the moment. She had not thought him capable of such laughter.

'You're a regular chatterbox, aren't you? So *eloquent...*'

He lifted his head as he uttered the last word, giving it a clipped, sophisticated sound that was designed to make her laugh.

She laughed, enjoying his gentle mockery.

'You had a reason for approaching me, I'm sure. But now you merely sit there, mute, glorious... and quite beautiful.'

His voice had softened. His eyes were half-lidded now, like dark, occluded suns.

He turned her hands within his own and held them, his fingers laid upon her wrists, tracing the blood's quickening pulse.

She looked up, surprised, then looked down at his left hand again, feeling the ridge there. A clear, defined line of skin, circling the wrist.

'Your hand...?'

'Is a hand,' he said, lifting it to her face so that she could see it better. 'An accident. When I was a child.'

'Oh...' Her fingers traced the line of flesh, a shiver passing through her. It was a fine, strong hand. She closed her hand on his, her fingers laced into his fingers, and looked at him.

'Can I paint you?'

His eyes widened, seeming to search her own for meanings. Then he smiled at her; the smile like a flower unfolding slowly to the sun. 'Yes,' he said. 'I'd like that.'

It was not the best she had ever done, but it was good, the composition sound, the seated figure lifelike. She looked from the canvas to the reality, sat there on her bed, and smiled.

'I've finished.'

He looked up distractedly. 'Finished?'

She laughed. 'The portrait, Ben. I've finished it.'

'Ah...' He stood up, stretching, then looked across at her again. 'That was quick.'

'Hardly quick. You've been sitting for me the best part of three hours.'

'Three hours?' He laughed strangely. 'I'm sorry. I was miles away.'

'Miles?'

He smiled. 'It's nothing. Just an old word, that's all...'

She moved aside, letting him stand before the canvas, anxious to know what he thought of it. For a moment she looked at it anew, trying to see it for the first time, as he was seeing it. Then she looked back at him.

He was frowning.

'What is it?' she asked, feeling a pulse start in her throat.

He put one hand out vaguely, indicating the canvas. 'Where am I?'

She gave a small laugh. 'What do you mean?'

'This...' He lifted the picture from its mechanical easel and threw it down. 'It's shit, Catherine. Lifeless shit!'

She stood there a moment, too shocked to say anything, unable to believe that he could act so badly, so... *boorishly*. She glared at him, furious at what he'd done, then bent down and picked the painting up. Where he had thrown it down the frame had snapped, damaging the bottom of the picture. It would be impossible to repair.

She clutched the painting to her, her deep sense of hurt fuelling the anger she felt towards him.

'Get out!' she screamed at him. 'Go on, get out of here, right now!'

He turned away, seemingly unaffected by her outburst, then leaned over the bed, picking up the folder he had brought with him. She watched him, expecting him to leave, to go without a further word, but he turned back, facing her, offering the folder.

'Here,' he said, meeting her eyes calmly. 'This is what I mean. This is the kind of thing you should be doing, not that crap you mistake for art.'

She gave a laugh of astonishment. He was unbelievable.

'You arrogant bastard.'

She felt like slapping his face. Like smashing the canvas over his smug, self-complacent head.

'Take it,' he said, suddenly more forceful, his voice assuming an air of command. Then, strangely, he relented, his voice softening. 'Just look. That's all. And afterwards, if you can't see what I mean, I'll go. It's just that I thought you were different from the rest. I thought...'

He shrugged, then looked down at the folder again. It was a simple art folder – the kind you carried holo flats in – its jet-black cover unmarked.

She hesitated, her eyes searching his face, looking for some further insult, but if anything he seemed subdued, disappointed in her. She frowned, then set the painting down.

'Here,' she said, taking the folder from him angrily. 'You've got nerve, I'll give you that.'

He said nothing. He was watching her now, expectantly, those dark eyes of his seeming to catch and hold every last atom of her being, their gaze disconcerting her.

She sat down on the edge of the bed, the folder in her lap, looking up at him through half-lidded eyes.

'What is this?'

'Open it and see.'

For a long time she was silent, her head down, her fingers tracing the shapes and forms that stared up at her from the sheaf of papers that had been inside the folder. Then she looked up at him, wide-eyed, all anger gone from her.

'Who painted these?'

He sat down beside her, taking the folder and flicking through to the first of the reproductions.

'This here is by Caravaggio. His *Supper At Emmaus*, painted more than six hundred years ago. And this... this is Vermeer, painted almost sixty years later. He called it *The Artist's Studio*. And this is by Rembrandt, his *Aristotle Contemplating a Bust of Homer*, painted ten years earlier. And this is *Laocoon* by El Greco...'

She put her hand on his, stopping him from turning the print over, staring at the stretched white forms that lay there on the page.

'I've... I've never seen anything like these. They're...'

She shivered, then looked up at him, suddenly afraid.

'Why have I never seen them? I mean, they're beautiful. They're *real* somehow...'

She stopped, suddenly embarrassed, realizing now what he had meant. She had painted him in the traditional way – the only way she knew – but he had known something better.

'What does it mean?' she asked, her fingers tracing the pale, elongated forms. 'Who are they?'

He gave a small laugh, then shook his head. 'The old man lying down in the centre, he's Laocoon. He was the priest who warned the Trojans not to allow the wooden horse into Troy.'

She gave a little shake of her head, then laughed. 'Troy? Where was Troy? And what do you mean by wooden horse...?'

He laughed, once again that openness, that strange naturalness of his surfacing unexpectedly. 'It was an ancient tale. About a war that happened three thousand years ago between two small nation-states. A war that was fought over a woman.'

'A woman?'

'Yes...' He looked away, a faint smile on his lips.

'How strange. To fight a war over a woman.' She turned the page. 'And this?'

Ben was silent for a time, simply staring at the painting, then he looked up at her again. 'What do you make of it?'

She gave a little shrug. 'I don't know. It's different from the others. They're all so... so dark and intense and brooding. But this... there's such serenity there, such knowledge in those eyes.'

'Yes...' He laughed softly, surprised by her. 'It's beautiful, isn't it? The painter was a man called Modigliani, and it was painted some three hundred years after those others. It's called *Last Love*. The girl was his lover, a woman called Jeanne Hebuterne. When he died she threw herself from a fifth-floor window.'

She looked up at him sharply, then looked back down at the painting. 'Poor woman. I ...' She hesitated, then turned, facing him. 'But why, Ben? Why haven't I heard of any of these painters? Why don't they teach them in college?'

He looked back at her. 'Because they don't exist. Not officially.'

'What do you mean?'

He paused, then shook his head. 'No. It's dangerous. I shouldn't have shown you. Even to know about these...'

He made to close the folder but she stopped him, flicking through the remaining paintings until she came to one near the end.

'This,' she said. 'Why have I never seen this before?'

Ben hesitated, staring at the print she was holding out to him. He had no need to look at it, it was imprinted so firmly in his memory, but he looked at it anyway, trying to see it fresh – free of its context – as she was seeing it.

'That's Da Vinci,' he said softly. 'Leonardo Da Vinci. It's called *The Virgin and Child with Saint Anne and John the Baptist* and it was painted exactly seven hundred and eight years ago.'

She was silent a moment, studying the print, then she looked up at him again, her eyes pained now, demanding.

'Yes, Ben, but why? And what do you mean, they don't exist? These paintings exist, don't they? And the men who painted them – they existed, didn't they? Or is this all some kind of joke?'

He shook his head, suddenly weary of it all. Was he to blame that these things had gone from the world? Was it his fault that the truth was kept from them? No. And yet he felt a dreadful burden of guilt, just knowing this. Or was it guilt? Wasn't it something to do with the feeling he'd had ever since he'd come here, into the City? That feeling that only *he* was real? That awful feeling of distance from everything and everyone – as if, when he reached out to touch it all, it would dissolve, leaving him there in the midst of nothingness, falling back towards the earth.

He heard the old man's voice echo in his head. *Ghosts? Why there's nothing here but ghosts!* and shivered.

Was that why he had shown her these? To make some kind of connection? To reassure himself that he wasn't the only living, breathing creature in this vast mirage – this house of cards?

Maybe. But now he realized what he had done. He had committed her. Seduced her with these glimpses of another world. So what now? Should he back off and tell her to forget all that she'd seen, or should he take her one step further?

He looked at her again, taking her hand, for that one brief moment balanced between the two courses that lay open to him. Then he smiled and squeezed her hand.

'Have you ever read *Wuthering Heights*?'

She hesitated, then nodded.

'Good. Then I want you to read it again. But this time in the original version. As it was first written, three hundred and sixty years ago.'

'But that's...' She laughed then looked down, disturbed by all of this. 'What are you doing, Ben? Why are you showing me these things?'

'To wake you up. To make you see all of this as I see it.' He looked away from her, his eyes moving back to the broken painting on the easel.

'I met someone yesterday. A *Lu Nan Jen*. You know, what they call an oven man. He painted, too. Not like you. He didn't have your skill with a brush, your eye for classical composition. But he did have something you haven't – something the whole of Han art hasn't – and that's vision. He could see clear through the forms of things. Through to the bone. He understood what made it all tick and set it down – clearly, powerfully. For himself. So that he could understand it all. When you came up to me in the Café Burgundy I had been sitting there thinking about him – thinking about what he'd done; how he'd spent his life trying to set down that vision, that *dream* of his. And I wondered suddenly what it would be like to wake that in someone. To make it blossom in the soul of someone who had the talent to set it down as it really ought to be set down. And then... there you were, and I thought...'

She was watching him closely now, her head pushed forward, her lips parted in expectation.

'You thought what?'

He turned back, looking at her. 'What are you doing this afternoon?'

She sat back, disappointed. 'Nothing. Why?'

'Would you like to come with me somewhere? Somewhere you've never been before?'

She narrowed her eyes. 'Where?'

'Somewhere no one ever goes. Beneath here. Into the Clay.'

Ben had hired a man to walk ten paces in front of them, his arc lamp held high, its fierce white light revealing the facades of old greystone buildings, their stark shapes edged in deepest shadow.

Ben held a second, smaller lamp: a lightweight affair on a long, slender handle. Its light was gentler, casting a small, pearled pool of brightness about the walking couple.

Catherine held his hand tightly, fascinated and afraid. She hadn't known. She had thought it all destroyed. But here it was, preserved, deserted, left to the darkness; isolated from the savage wilderness surrounding it.

As they walked, Ben's voice filled the hollow darkness, speaking from memory, telling her the history of the place.

'Unlike all previous architects, the man who designed City Earth made no accommodation for the old. The new was everything to him. Even that most simple of concessions – the destruction of the old – was, as far as possible, bypassed. The tallest buildings were destroyed, of course, but the rest was simply built over, as if they really had no further use for the past.' He turned, looking back at her. 'What we have now is not so much a new form of architecture as a new geological age. With City Earth we entered the Technozoic. All else was left behind us, in the Clay.'

He paused, pointing across at a rounded dome the guide's lamp had revealed. 'Have you ever noticed how there are no domes in our City, even in the mansions of First Level? No. There are copies of Han architecture, of course, but of the old West there's nothing. All that elegance of line has been replaced by harder shapes – hexagons, octagons, an interlacing of complex crystalline structures, as if the world had frozen over.'

'But that...' She pointed up at the curved roof of the dome. 'That's beautiful.'

'It is, isn't it?'

'But why?'

'The desire for conformity, I guess. Things like that dome induce a sense of individuality in us. And they didn't want that.'

'I don't follow you.'

Ben looked about him. The circle of light extended only so far. Beyond, it was as if the great stone buildings faded into uncreated nothingness. As if they had no existence other than that which the light gave them in its passage through their realm. Ben smiled at the thought, realizing that this was a clue to what he himself was doing. For he – as artist – was the light, creating that tiny circle of mock-reality about him as he passed.

He turned back, looking at the girl, answering her.

'When it all fell apart, shortly before City Earth was built, there was an age of great excess – of individual expression unmatched in the history of our species. The architects of City Earth – Tsao Ch'un, his Ministers and their servants – identified the symptom as the cause. They saw the excesses and the extravagance, the beauty and the expression as cultural viruses and sought to destroy them. But there was too much to destroy. They would have found it easier to destroy the species. It was too deeply ingrained. So, instead, they tried to mask it – to bury it beneath new forms. City Earth was to be a place where no one wanted for anything. Where everything the physical self could need would be provided for. It was to be Utopia – the world beyond Peach-Blossom River.'

She frowned at him, not recognizing the term, but he seemed almost unaware of her now. Slowly he led her on through the labyrinth of streets, the doubled lights, like sun and moon, reflected in the ceiling high above.

'But the City was a cage. It catered only for the grounded, physical being. It did not cater for the higher soul – the winged soul that wants to fly.'

She laughed, surprised by him. But of course one caged birds. Who had ever heard of a bird flying free?

The walls closed about them on either side. They were walking now through a narrow back alley, the guide only paces in front of them, his lamp filling the darkness with its strong white light. For a moment they could almost have been walking in the City.

Unless you looked up. Unless you stopped and listened to the silence; sensing the darkness all around.

Ben had been silent, looking away. Now he turned, looking back at her.

'It was to be a landscape devoid of all meaning. A landscape of unrelated form.'

He had paused and she had been obliged to stop with him. But all she wanted now was to get out, for all the strange beauty of this place. She felt uncomfortable here. Afraid, and vulnerable.

'We are creatures of the earth, Catherine,' he said, his eyes sharing something of the darkness beyond the lamp's fierce circle. 'Creatures of the earth... and yet...' he hesitated, as if in pain, 'and yet we want to fly. Don't you find that strange?'

She looked past him, at the old brickwork, itself a geometric pattern. 'I don't know,' she said. 'Perhaps we were always looking to create something like the City. Perhaps it's only the perfection of something we always had in us.'

He looked at her fiercely, shaking his head in denial. 'No! It's death, that's what it is! Death!'

He shuddered. She felt it through her hand. A shudder of revulsion. She hadn't understood before, but now she saw. Why he had isolated himself. Why he always seemed so hostile.

'You talk as if you're not from the City,' she said. 'As if...' But she left her question unasked. He would tell her if he wanted.

'We keep the names,' he said, 'but they mean nothing any more. They're cut off. Like most of us, they're cut off.'

'But not you,' she said after a moment.

He laughed but said nothing.

It irritated her for once, that enigmatic side of him. She freed her hand from his and walked on. He followed, the light from his lamp throwing faint shadows off to one side.

She was angry. Hurt that he made no concessions to her. As if she meant nothing to him.

She stopped, then turned to face him.

He stood there, the lamp held high, the light throwing his face into strange lines; the shadows making it seem wrong: a face half in brightness, half in dark.

'Shall we go on?' he asked. But she could make out no expression on his face. His features were a rigid mask of shadow and light.

'I hate it here.'

He turned, looking about him once again, the light wavering with the movement, throwing ghostly shards of brilliance against the windows of the buildings to either side. Dead, black eyes of glass, reflecting nothing.

She reached out and touched his arm. 'Let's go back, Ben. Please. Back to Oxford.'

He smiled bitterly, then nodded. Back to Oxford, then. The name meant nothing to her, after all. But it was where they had been these last two hours. A place, unlike the bright unreality that had been built over it. A real place. For all its darkness.

In her dream she saw herself, walking beside him, the lamp held up above their heads, the shadowed, ancient town surrounding them, the floor of the City lost in the darkness overhead.

She saw the labyrinth again; saw its dark and secret rivers, the Isis and the Cherwell, flow silently, like blood in the veins of the earth. His words. His image for them. In her dream she stood there with him on the old stone bridge, her flesh connected to his at the palm. And when he lifted his lamp the water shone. Wine red it shone, the water black as ink beneath the surface.

She woke, feeling hot, feverish, and switched on the bedside lamp. It was four in the morning. She sat up, rubbing her palms together, looking at them in amazement and relief. It had been so real. She had felt where her flesh sank into his and shared a pulse, seen the wine-dark flow where it passed beneath the stone arch of the bridge...

So real that waking seemed a step down.

For a while she sat there, shivering, not from cold but from a surreal sense of her other self. Of her sleeping, dreaming self who, like the figure in the dream, walked on in darkness, understanding nothing.

She closed her eyes, trying to recapture it, but the image was fading fast, the feeling of it slipping from her. Then the pulse of it faltered, died.

She got up and went across to the canvas, then sat on the stool in front of it, the seat cold against her naked buttocks, her toes curled about the rounded bar. Her body was curved, lithe, like a cat's, while her fine, flame-like hair fell straight, fanning halfway down her back, her flesh like ivory between its livid strands.

She stared at the painting, studying it minutely.

It was dark. Reds and greens dominated the visual textures, sharply contrasted, framed in shapes of black that bled from the edge of the painting. Harsh, angular shapes, the paint laid thick on the canvas, ridged and shadowed like a landscape.

His face stared out at her, flecks of red and green like broken glass forming his flesh, the green of his eyes so intense it seemed to flare and set all else in darkness.

She had shown him seated in her chair, his shoulders slightly forward, his arms tensed, as if he were in the act of rising. His long, spatulate fingers gripped the arms firmly, almost lovingly.

There was a hard-edged abstract quality to the composition that none of her friends would have recognized as hers, yet something softer showed through: a secondary presence that began to dominate once that first, strong sense of angularity and darkness diminished.

The painting lived. She smiled, knowing that in this she had transcended herself. It was a breakthrough. A new kind of art. Not the mimicry she had long accepted as her art, but a new thing, different in kind to anything she had ever done before.

Behind the firmness of the forms there was an aura. A light behind the darkness. A tenderness behind those harsh, sharp-sculpted shapes. His dark, fragmented face grew softer the more she looked, the eyes less fierce, more gentle.

She reached out with one hand to touch the bottom surface, her fingers following the line of whiteness where the figure faded into darkness. Below that line what at first seemed merely dark took on new forms, new textures – subtle variations of grey and black.

Buildings. Strange, architectural forms. Ghost images she had seen as real. All crowded there; trapped, pressed down beneath the thinnest line of white. Like a scar on the dark flesh of the canvas.

She tilted her head, squinting at the figure. It was stiff, almost lifeless in the chair, and yet there was the suggestion of pure force; of an intense, almost frightening vitality. A doubleness, there in everything: something she had not been aware of until he had shown it to her.

She relaxed, satisfied, and straightened her back, letting her hands drop to her knees. Then she stretched, her arms going up and back, her small, firm breasts lifting with the movement. She clawed the air with her fingers, yawning, then laughed to herself, feeling good.

Leaning forward, she activated the graphics keyboard beneath the painting's lower edge, then pressed one of the pads, making the canvas rotate through a full three hundred and sixty degrees.

Slowly the figure turned, presenting its left shoulder to the viewing eye, its face moving into profile.

She pressed PAUSE then sat back, looking. He was handsome. No, more than handsome: he was beautiful. And she had captured something of that. Some quality she had struggled at first to comprehend. A wildness – a fierceness – that was barely contained in him.

She shifted the focus, drawing out a detail of the wrist, the muscles there. She leaned forward, looking, touching the hard-edged textures of the projection, seeing what the machine had extrapolated from her intention.

She studied it a moment longer then got to work, bringing the pallet round into her lap and working at the projection with the light-scalpels, making the smallest of alterations, then shifting focus again, all the while staring at the canvas, her forehead creased in a frown of intense concentration, her body hunched, curled over the painting, her hands working the plastic surface to give it depth.

When she had finished it was almost eight and the artificial light of the wake hours showed between the slats of her blinds, but she had worked all the tiredness from her bones.

She felt like seeing him.

Her robe lay on the chair beside her bed. She put it on and went across to the comset, touching his code from memory. In a moment his face was there, on the flatscreen by her hand. She looked down at him and smiled.

'I need to see you.'

His answering smile was tender. 'Then I'll be over.'

The screen went dark. She sat there a moment, then turned away. Beside the bed she bent down, picking up the book she had left there only hours before. For a moment she stared at its cover as if bewitched, then opened it and, picking a passage at random, began to read.

She shuddered. It was just as Ben had said. There was no comparison. It was such a strange and wonderful book. Unseemly almost, and yet beautiful. Undeniably beautiful.

The novel she remembered had been a dull little morality tale – the story of a boy from the Clay who, taken in by a First Level family, had repaid their trust by trying to corrupt the upright daughter of the house. In that version filial piety had triumphed over passion. But this...

She shook her head, then set the book down. For all its excesses, it was so much more real, so much more *true* than the other. But what did it mean? What did all of these things mean? The paintings, the strange buildings beneath the City, and now this... this tale of wild moors and savage passions? What did it all add up to?

Where had Ben found these things? And why had she never heard of them before?

Why?

She sat, a small shiver – like an after-shock – rippling down her spine. Things that existed and yet had no existence. Things which, if Ben were right, were dangerous even to know about. Why should such things be? What did they mean?

She closed her eyes, focusing herself, bringing herself to stillness, calming the inner voices, then leaned back on her elbows.

He was coming to her. Right now he was on his way.

'Then I'll be over.'

She could hear his voice; could see him clearly with her inner eye. She smiled, opening her eyes again. He had not even kissed her yet. Had not gone beyond that first small step. But surely that must come? Surely? Else why begin?

She stood, looking about her, then laughed, a small thrill passing through her. Why, he hadn't even kissed her yet.

Ben stood there in the doorway, relaxed, one hand loosely holding the edge of the sliding panel, the other combing through his hair.

'Really...' he was saying, 'I'd much rather treat you to breakfast.'

He seemed elated, strangely satisfied; but with himself, not with her. He had barely looked at her as yet.

She felt herself cast down. A nothing.

'I'd like to cook you something...' she began again, knowing she had said it already. Again he shook his head. So definite a movement. Uncompromising. Leaving her nowhere. A bitter anguish clenched the muscles of her stomach; made her turn from him, lest he see. But she had seen how his eyes moved restlessly about the room, not really touching anything. Skating over surfaces, as if they saw nothing.

As if what he *really* saw was not in her room.

She turned and saw that he was looking at the covered canvas. But there was no curiosity in his eyes. For once he seemed abstracted from the world, not pressed right up against it. She had never seen him like this before; so excited and yet so cut off from things.

She looked at him a moment longer, then shrugged and picked up her slender clutch bag. 'All right. I'm ready.'

They found a quiet place on the far side of The Green from the Café Burgundy. At first they ate in silence, the curtain drawn about them in the narrow booth, giving the illusion of privacy. Even so, voices carried from either side. Bright, morning voices. The voices of those who had slept and came fresh to the day. They irritated her as much as his silence. More than that, she was annoyed with him. Annoyed for the way he had brought her here and then ignored her.

She looked across the table's surface to his hands, seeing how at ease they were, lying there either side of the shallow, emptied bowl. Through the transparent surface she saw their ghostly images, faint but definite, refracted by the double thickness of the ice. He was so self-contained. So isolated from the world. It seemed, at that moment, that it would be easier for her to reach through the surface and take those ghostly hands than reach out and grasp the warm reality.

She felt a curious pressure on her; something as tangible in its effect as a pair of hands pressed to the sides of her head, keeping her from looking up to meet his eyes. Yet nothing real. It was a phantom of her own creating – a weakness in her structure.

She looked away; stared down at her untouched meal. She had said nothing of her new painting. Of why she had called him. Of all she had felt, staring at that violent image of his face. He had shut her out. Cut off all paths between them. As she sat there she wished for the strength to stand up and leave him there, sitting before his empty bowl.

As if that were possible.

She felt her inner tension mount until it seemed unendurable. And then he spoke, reaching out to take her hands in his own; the warmth of them dissipating all that nervous energy, destroying the phantoms that had grown vast in his neglect.

'Have you ever tasted real food, Catherine?'

She looked up, puzzled, and met his eyes. 'What do you mean, *real?*'

He laughed, indicating her bowl. 'You know, I've never seen you eat. Not a morsel.' His hands held hers firmly yet without real pressure. There was a mischievous light behind his eyes. She had not seen him like this before.

'I eat,' she said, making him laugh again at the assertiveness of her simple statement. 'But I still don't understand you.'

'Ah,' he said. 'Then the answer is no.'

She shook her head, annoyed with him again, but in a different way. He was teasing her. Being unfair.

'It's strange what becomes important,' he said. 'For no apparent reason. Things take hold. Won't release you.'

He looked up again, all humour gone from his eyes. That intensity was back. That driven quality.

'And that's your obsession, is it? Food?'

She saw at once that her joke had misfired. In this, it seemed, he was vulnerable. Wide open.

Perhaps that was what obsession was. A thing against which there was no defence. Not even humour.

So, she thought. *And this is yours. The real.*

For a time he said nothing. She watched the movement in his dark, expressive eyes. Sea moods beneath the vivid green. Surface and undertow. And then he looked out again, at her, and spoke.

'Come with me. I want to show you something.'

Ben's apartment was to the north of Oxford Canton, on the edge of the fashionable student district. Catherine stood there in the main room, looking about her.

'I never imagined...' she said softly to herself, then turned to find him there in the doorway, a wine-filled glass in each hand.

'You're privileged,' he said, handing her a glass. 'I don't usually let anyone come here.'

She felt both pleased and piqued by that. It was hard to read what he meant by it.

It was a long, spacious room, sparsely decorated. A low sofa was set down in the middle of the plushly carpeted floor, a small, simply moulded coffee table next to it. Unlike the apartments of her friends, however, there were no paintings on the wall, no trinkets or small sculptures on the table-top. It was neat, almost empty.

She looked about her, disappointed. She had expected something more than this. Something like Sergey's apartment.

He had been watching her. She met his eyes and saw how he was smiling, as if he could read her thoughts. 'It's bleak, isn't it? Like a set from some dreadfully tasteful drama.'

She laughed, embarrassed.

'Oh, don't worry. This is' – he waved his hand in an exaggerated circle – 'a kind of mask. A front. In case I had to invite someone back.'

She sipped her wine, looking at him sharply, trying to gauge what he was saying to her. 'Well?' she said, 'What were you going to show me?'

He pointed across the room with his glass. There was a panel in the far wall. A sliding panel with the faint indentation of a thumb-lock.

'The mystery revealed,' he said. 'Come.'

She followed, wondering why he played these games. In all else he was so direct. So much himself. Then why these tricks and evasions? What was he hiding? What afraid of?

His fingers tapped out a combination on the touch-pad. The thumb-lock glowed ready and he pressed his right thumb into the depression. The door hissed back, revealing a second room, as big as the one they were in.

She stepped through, impressed by the contrast.

For all its size it was intensely cluttered, the walls lined with shelves. In the spaces between hung prints and paintings. A small, single bed rested against the far wall, its sheets wrinkled, a simple cover drawn back. Books were piled on a bedside table and in a stack on the floor beside the bed. Real books, not tapes. Like the one he had given her. Her mouth opened in a smile of surprise and delight. But what really grabbed her attention was the apparatus in the centre of the room.

She crossed the room and stood beside it.

'Is this what you do?' she asked, feeling the machine tremble, its delicate limbs quivering beneath her touch.

The scaffolding of the machine was laced with fine wires, like a cradle. Inside lay a life-size marionette, a mock human, no features on its face, its palms smooth and featureless. The morph was like the machine, almost alive, tremblingly responsive to her touch. Its white, almost translucent surfaces reflected the ceiling light in flashes and sparkles.

It was beautiful. Was a work of art in itself.

'Does it do anything?'

'By itself, no. But, yes, in a sense it's what I do.'

She looked quickly at him, then back at the machine, remembering what Sergey had said about him being a technician – a scientist. But how did that equate with what he knew about art? All that intuitive, deeply won knowledge of his? She frowned, trying to understand; trying to fit it all together. She looked down at the base of the machine, seeing the thick width of tape coiled about the spools, like some crude relic from the technological past. She had never seen anything like it.

She circled the machine, trying to comprehend its function. Failing.

'What is this?' she said finally, looking back at him.

He stood on the other side of the machine, looking at her through the fragile scaffolding, the fine web of wiring.

'It's what I brought you here to see.'

He was smiling, but behind the smile she could sense the intensity of his mood. This was important to him. For some reason very important.

'Will you trust me, Catherine? Will you do something for me?'

She stared back at him, trying to read him, but it was impossible. He was not like the others. It was hard to tell what he wanted, or why. For a moment she hesitated, then nodded, barely moving her head, seeing how much he had tensed, expecting another answer.

He turned away momentarily, then turned back, the excitement she had glimpsed earlier returned to his eyes, but this time encompassing her, drawing her into its spell.

'It's marvellous. The best thing I've done. You wait. You'll see just how marvellous. How *real*.'

There was a strange, almost childish quality in his voice – an innocence – which shocked her. He was so open at that moment. So completely vulnerable. She looked at him with eyes newly opened to the complexity of this strange young man. To the forces in contention in his nature.

Strangely, it made her want to hold him to her breast, as a mother would hold her infant child. And yet at the same time she wanted him, with a fierceness that made her shiver, afraid for herself.

Ben stood at the head of the frame, looking down at her. Catherine lay on her back, naked, her eyes closed, the lids flickering. Her breasts rose and fell gently, as if she slept, her red hair laid in fine, red-gold strands across her cheeks, her neck.

Stirrups supported her body, but her neck was encased in a rigid cradle, circled with sensitive filaments of ice, making it seem as if her head were caged in shards of glass. A fine mesh of wires fanned out from the narrow band at the base of her skull, running down the length of her body, strips of tape securing the tiny touch-sensitive pads to her flesh at regular intervals. Eighty-one connections in all, more than half of those directly into the skull.

The morph lay on the bed, inert. Ben glanced at its familiar shape and smiled. It was almost time.

He looked down at the control desk. Eight small screens crowded the left-hand side of the display, each containing the outline image of a skull.

Just now they flickered through a bright sequence of primaries, areas of each image growing then receding.

Beneath the frame a tape moved slowly between the reels. It was a standard work – an original *pai pi*, but spliced at its end was the thing he had been working on – the new thing he was so excited about. He watched the images flicker, the tape uncoil and coil again, then looked back at the girl.

There was a faint movement in her limbs; a twitching of the muscles where the pads were pressed against the nerve-centres. It was vestigial, but it could be seen. Weeks of such ghost movement would cause damage, some of it irreparable. And addicts had once spent months in their Shells.

The tracking signal appeared on each of the eight small screens. Fifteen seconds to the splice. He watched the dark mauve areas peak on six of the screens, then fade as the composition ended. For a moment there was no activity, then the splice came in, with a suddenness that showed on all the screens.

According to the screens, Catherine had woken up. Her eyes were open and she was sitting up, looking about her. Yet in the frame the girl slept on, her lidded eyes unmoving, her breasts rising and falling in a gentle motion. The faint tremor in her limbs had ceased. She was still now, perfectly at rest.

The seconds passed slowly, a countdown on the top right screen showing when the splice ended.

He smiled and watched her open her eyes, then go to shake her head and raise her hands. Wires were in her way, restraining her. She looked confused, for a brief moment troubled. Then she saw him and relaxed.

'How are you?' he asked.

Her eyes looked back questioningly at him. Green eyes, the same deep shade of green as his own. She looked quite beautiful, lying there. It was strange how he had not noticed it before. That he had *seen* it and yet not noted it.

'I don't understand...' she began. 'I woke up and you were sitting next to me at the Café Burgundy. I'd had too much to drink and I'd fallen asleep. I... I had been dreaming. We were talking... something about colours... and then I turned and looked across at the pagoda. You said something about all the birds escaping, and, yes, there, across The Green, I could see that it was so. There were birds flying everywhere. They'd broken out of their cage. Then, as I watched, one flew right at me, its wings brushing against my face even though I moved my head aside to avoid it. You were laughing. I turned and saw that you had caught the bird in your hands. I reached across and...'

She stopped, her brow wrinkling, her eyes looking inward, trying to fathom what had happened.

'And?'

She looked straight at him. 'And then I woke up again. I was here.' She tried to shake her head and was again surprised to find it encased, her movements restrained. She stared at the webbing trailing from her neck, as if it should dissolve, then turned, looking back at him.

'I shouldn't be here, should I? I mean, I woke up once, didn't I? So this...' confusion flickered in her face and her voice dropped to an uncertain whisper, 'this must be a tape.'

He smiled. 'Good,' he said softly. 'That's just what I wanted to hear.'

He moved around her and began to unfasten the connections, working quickly, methodically, his touch as sure and gentle as a surgeon's.

'I don't follow you, Ben. Which was which? I mean, this is real now, isn't it? But that part in the Café...'

He looked down into her face, only a hand's width from his own.

'That was the tape. My tape. The thing I've been working on these last four months.'

She laughed, still not understanding. 'What do you mean, your tape?'

He unclipped the band and eased it back, freeing her neck. 'Just what I said.' He began to massage her neck muscles, knowing from experience what she would be feeling with the restraint gone. 'I made it. All that part about the Café.'

She looked up at him, her head turned so that she could see him properly, her nose wrinkled up. 'But you can't have. People don't make tapes. At least, not like that. Not on their own. That thing before... that cartoon-like thing. That was a *pai pi*, wasn't it? I've heard of them. They used to have dozens of people working on them. Hundreds sometimes.'

'So I've been told.'

He moved behind her, operating the stirrup controls, lowering her slowly to the floor. Then he climbed into the frame above her, untaping the lines of wire and releasing the pads from her flesh one by one, massaging the released flesh gently to stimulate the circulation, every action of his carried out meticulously, as if long rehearsed.

'I don't like teams,' he said, not looking at her. Then, squatting, he freed the twin pads from her nipples, gently rubbing them with his thumbs. They rose, aroused by his touch, but he had moved on, working down her body, freeing her from the harness.

'I set myself a problem. Years ago. I'd heard about *pai pi* and the restrictions of the form, but I guess I realized even then that it didn't have to be like that. Their potential was far beyond what anyone had ever thought it could be.'

'I still don't follow you, Ben. You're not making sense.'

She was leaning up on her elbows now, staring at him. His hand rested on the warmth of her inner thigh, passive, indifferent to her, it seemed. She was still confused. It had been so real. Waking, and then waking again. And now this. Ben, crouched above her, his hand resting on her inner thigh, talking all this nonsense about what everyone knew had been a technological dead-end. She shook her head.

His eyes focused on her. 'What's the matter?'

'I still don't understand you, Ben. It *was* real. I *know* it was. The bird flying at me across The Green, the smell of coffee and cigars. That faint breeze you always get sitting there. You know, the way the air circulates from the tunnels at the back. And other things, too.'

She had closed her eyes, remembering.

'The faint buzz of background conversation. Plates and glasses clinking. The faint hum of the factories far below in the stack. That constant vibration that's there in everything.' She opened her eyes and looked at him pleadingly. 'It *was* real, Ben. Tell me it was.'

He looked back at her, shaking his head. 'No. That was all on the tape.'

'No!' She shook her head fiercely. 'I mean, I saw you there. Sitting there across from me. It *was* you. I know it was. You said...' She strained to remember, then nodded to herself. 'You said that I shouldn't be afraid of them. You said that it was their instinct to fly.'

'I said that once, yes. But not to you. And not in the Café Burgundy.'

She sat up, her hands grabbing at his arms, feeling the smooth texture of the cloth, then reaching up to touch his face, feeling the roughness of his cheeks where he had yet to shave. Again he laughed, but softly now.

'You can't tell, can you? Which is real. This or the other thing. And yet you're here, Catherine. Here, with me. Now.'

She looked at him a moment longer, then tore her gaze away, frightened and confused.

'That before,' he said, 'that thing you thought happened. That was a fiction. My fiction. It never happened. *I made it.*'

He reached out, holding her chin with one hand, gently turning her face until she was looking at him again. 'But this... this is real. This now.' He moved his face down to hers, brushing her lips with his own.

Her eyes grew large, a vague understanding coming into her face. 'Then...' But it was as if she had reached out to grasp at something, only to have it vanish before her eyes. The light faded from her face. She looked down, shaking her head.

He straightened up, stepping out from the frame. Taking his blue silk *pau* from the bed he turned back, offering it to her.

'Here, put this on.'

She took the robe, handling it strangely, staring at it as if uncertain whether it existed or not; as if, at any moment, she would wake again and find it all a dream.

He stood there, watching her, his eyes searching hers for answers, then turned away.

'Put it on, Catherine. Put it on and I'll make some coffee.'

She lay there on his bed, his blue silk *pau* wrapped about her, a mound of pillows propped up behind her, sipping at her coffee.

Ben was pacing the room, pausing from time to time to look across at her, then moving on, gesturing as he talked, his movements extravagant, expansive. He seemed energized, his powerful, athletic form balanced between a natural grace and an unnatural watchfulness, like some strange, magnificent beast, intelligent beyond mere knowing. His eyes flashed as he spoke, while his hands turned in the air as if they fashioned it, moulding it into new forms, new shapes.

She watched him, mesmerized. Before now she'd had only a vague idea of what he was, but now she knew. As her mind cleared she had found herself awed by the immensity of his achievement. *It had been so real...*

He paused beside the empty frame, one hand resting lightly against the upright.

'When I say I had a problem, I didn't realize how wrong it was to think of it as such. You see, it wasn't something that could be circumvented with a bit of technical trickery; it was more a question of taking greater pains. A question of harnessing my energies more intensely. Of being more watchful.'

She smiled at that. As if anyone could be more watchful than he.

'So... I began with a kind of cartoon. Ten frames a second, rough-cast. That gave me the pace, the shape of the thing. Then I developed it a stage further. Put in the detail. Recorded it at twenty-five a second. Finally I polished and honed it, perfecting each separate strand; re-recording at fifty a second. Slowly making it more real.'

His hands made a delicate little movement, as if drawing the finest of wires from within a tight wad of fibres.

'It occurred to me that there really was no other way of doing it. I simply had to make it as real as I possibly could.'

'But how? I can't see how you did it. It's...' She shrugged, laughing, amazed by him. 'No. It's not possible. You *couldn't* have!'

And yet he had.

'How?' He grew very still. A faint smile played on his lips, then was gone. For a moment she didn't understand what he was doing with his body, with the expression on his face. Then, suddenly, her mouth fell open, shocked by the accuracy of his imitation; his stance, the very look of him.

And then he spoke.

'But how? I can't see how you did it. It's...' He shrugged and laughed: a soft, feminine laugh of surprise. 'No. It's simply not possible. You *couldn't* have!'

It was perfect. Not *her* exactly, yet a perfect copy all the same – of her gestures, her facial movements, her voice. Every nuance and intonation caught precisely. As if the mirror talked.

She sat forward, spilling her coffee. 'That's...'

But she could not say. It was frightening. She felt her nerves tingle. For a moment everything slowed about her. She had the sensation of falling, then checked herself.

He was watching her, seeing how she looked: all the time watching her, like a camera eye, noting and storing every last nuance of her behaviour.

'You have to look, Catherine. Really look at things. You have to try to see them from the other side. To get right inside of them and see how they feel. There's no other way.'

He paused, looking at her differently now, as if gauging whether she was still following him. She nodded, her fingers wiping absently at the spilled coffee on his robe, but her eyes were half-lidded now, uncertain.

'An artist – any artist – is an actor. His function is mimetic, even at its most expressive. And, like an actor, he must learn to play his audience.' He smiled, opening out his arms as if to encompass the world, his eyes shining darkly with the enormity of his vision. 'You've seen a tiny piece of it. You've glimpsed what it can be. But it's bigger than that, Catherine. Much, much bigger. What you experienced today was but the merest suggestion of its final form.'

He laughed: a short, sharp explosion of laughter that was like a shout of joy.

'The art – that's what I'm talking about! The thing all true artists dream of!'

Slowly he brought down his arms. The smile faded on his lips and his eyes grew suddenly fierce. Clenching his fists, he curled them in towards his chest, hunching his body into itself like a dancer's. For a moment he held himself there, tensed, the whole of him gathered there at the centre.

'Not art like you know it now. No...' He shook his head, as if in great pain. 'No. This would be something almost unendurable. Something terrible and yet beautiful. Too beautiful for words.'

He laughed coldly, his eyes burning now with an intensity that frightened her.

'It would be an art to fear, Catherine. An art so cold it would pierce the heart with its iciness, and yet, at the selfsame time so hot that it would blaze like a tiny sun, burning in the darkness of the skull.

'Can you imagine that? Can you imagine what such an art would be like?' His laughter rang out again, a pitiless, hideous sound. 'That would be no art for the weak. No. Such an art would destroy the little men!'

She shuddered, unable to take her eyes from him. He was like a demon now, his eyes like dark, smouldering coals. His body seemed transfigured; horrible, almost alien.

She sat forward sharply, the cup falling from her hands.

Across from her Ben saw it fall and noted how it lay; saw how its contents spread across the carpet. Saw, and stored the memory.

He looked up at her, surprised, seeing how her breasts had slipped from within the robe and lay between the rich blue folds of cloth, exposed, strangely different.

And as he looked, desire beat up in him fiercely, like a raging fire.

He sat beside her, reaching within the robe to gently touch the soft warmth of her flesh, his hands moving slowly upward until they cupped her breasts. Then, lowering his face to hers, he let his lips brush softly against her lips.

She tensed, trembling in his arms, then, suddenly, she was pressing up against him, her mouth pushing urgently against his, her arms pulling him down. He shivered, amazed by the sudden change in her, the hunger in her eyes.

For a moment he held back, looking down into her face, surprised by the strength of what he suddenly felt. Then, gently, tenderly, he pushed her down, accepting what she offered, casting off the bright, fierce light that had held him in its grasp only moments before, letting himself slip down into the darkness of her, like a stone falling into the heart of a deep, dark well.

CHUNG KUO

Chapter 56

THE LOST BRIDE

'Well, Minister Heng, what was it you wished to see me about?'

Heng Yu had been kneeling, his head touched to the cold, stone floor. Now he rose, looking up at his T'ang for the first time.

Li Shai Tung was sitting in the throne of state, his tall, angular body clothed in imperial yellow. The Council of Ministers had ended an hour past, but Heng Yu had stayed on, requesting a private audience with his T'ang. Three broad steps led up to the presence dais. At the bottom of those steps stood the T'ang's Chancellor, Chung Hu-yan. In the past few months, as the old man had grown visibly weaker, more power had devolved on to the shoulders of the capable and honest Chung, and it was to Chung that Heng had gone, immediately the Council had finished. Now Chung gave the slightest smile as he looked at Heng.

'I am grateful for this chance to talk with you, *Chieh Hsia*,' Heng began. 'I would not have asked had it not been a matter of the greatest urgency.'

The T'ang smiled. 'Of course. But, please, Heng Yu, be brief. I am already late for my next appointment.'

Heng bowed again, conscious of the debt he owed the Chancellor for securing this audience.

'It is about young Shepherd, *Chieh Hsia*.'

The T'ang raised an eyebrow. 'Hal's boy? What of him?'

'He is at college, I understand, *Chieh Hsia*.'

Li Shai Tung laughed. 'You know it for a certainty, Heng Yu, else you would not have mentioned the matter. But what of it? Is the boy in trouble?'

Heng hesitated. 'I am not sure, *Chieh Hsia*. It does not seem that he is in any *immediate* danger, yet certain facts have come to my notice that suggest he might be in the days ahead.'

Li Shai Tung leaned forward, his left hand smoothing his plaited beard.

'I see. But why come to me, Heng Yu? This is a matter for General Nocenzi, surely?'

Heng gave a small bow. 'Normally I would agree, *Chieh Hsia*, but in view of the father's illness and the boy's possible future relationship with Prince Yuan...'

He left the rest unsaid, but Li Shai Tung took his point. Heng was right. This was much more important than any normal Security matter. Whatever Ben said just now of his intentions, he had been bred to be Li Yuan's advisor, and genes, surely, would out eventually? For anything to happen to him now was unthinkable.

'What do you suggest, Heng Yu?'

In answer, Heng Yu bowed, then held out the scroll he had prepared in advance. Chung Hu-yan took it from him and handed it up to the T'ang who unfurled it and began to read. When he had finished he looked back at Heng.

'Good. You have my sanction for this, Heng Yu. I'll sign this and give the General a copy of the authority. But don't delay. I want this acted upon at once.'

'Of course, *Chieh Hsia*.'

'And Heng Yu...'

'Yes, *Chieh Hsia*?'

'I am in your debt in this matter. If there is any small favour I can offer in return, let Chung Hu-yan know and it shall be done.'

Heng Yu bowed low. 'I am overwhelmed by your generosity, *Chieh Hsia*, but forgive me, it would not be right for me to seek advantage from what was, after all, my common duty to my lord. As ever, *Chieh Hsia*, I ask for nothing but to serve you.'

Straightening, he saw the smile of satisfaction on the old man's lips and knew he had acted wisely. There were things he needed; things the T'ang could have made easier for him; but none, at present, that were outside his own broad grasp. To have the T'ang's good opinion, however, that was another thing entirely. He bowed a second time, then lowered his head to Chung Hu-yan, backing away. One day, he was certain, such temporary sacrifices would pay off – would reap a thousandfold the rewards he now so lightly gave away. In the meantime he would find out what this business with the Novacek boy was all about. Would get to the bottom of it and then make sure that it was from him that the T'ang first heard of it.

As the great doors closed behind him, he looked about him at the great halls and corridors of the palace, smiling. Yes, the old T'ang's days were numbered now. And Prince Yuan, when his time came, would need a Chancellor. A younger man than Chung Hu-yan. A man he could rely on absolutely.

Heng Yu walked on, past bowing servants, a broad smile lighting his features.

So why not himself? Why not Heng Yu, whose record was unblemished, whose loyalty and ability were unquestioned?

As he approached them, the huge, leather-panelled outer doors of the palace began to ease back, spilling bright sunlight into the shadows of the broad, high-ceilinged corridor. Outside, the shaven-headed guards of the T'ang's elite squad bowed low as he moved between them. Savouring the moment, Heng Yu, Minister to Li Shai Tung, T'ang of City Europe, gave a soft, small laugh of pleasure.

Yes, he thought, looking up at the great circle of the sun. *Why not?*

Catherine stood in the doorway, looking across at him. Ben was sitting on the edge of the bed, his head pushed forward, his shoulders hunched, staring at the frame without seeing it.

He had woken full of life; had smiled and kissed her tenderly and told her to wait while he brought her breakfast, but he had been gone too long. She had found him in the kitchen, staring vacantly at his hands, the breakfast things untouched.

'What is it?' she had asked. 'What's happened?' But he had walked past her as if she wasn't there. Had gone through and sat down on the bed. So still, so self-engrossed that it had frightened her.

'Ben?' she said, setting the tray down beside him. 'I've cooked breakfast. Won't you have some with me?'

He glanced up at her. 'What?'

'Breakfast.' She smiled, then knelt beside him, putting her hand on his knee.

'Ah...' His smile was wan; was merely the token of a smile.

'What is it, Ben? Please. I've not seen you like this before. It must be something.'

For a moment he did nothing. Then he reached into the pocket of his gown and took something out, offering it to her.

It was a letter. She took it from him, handling it with care – with a feeling for its strangeness.

She sat on the floor beside his feet, handling the letter delicately, as if it were old and fragile like the book he had given her, taking the folded sheets and smoothing them out upon her lap.

For a moment she hesitated, a sudden sense of foreboding washing over her. What if it were another woman? Some past lover of his, writing to reclaim him – to take him back from her? Or was it something else? Something he had difficulty telling her?

She glanced at him, then looked back, beginning to read.

After only a few moments she looked up. 'Your sister?'

He nodded. 'She wants to come and visit me. To see what I'm up to.'

'Ah...' But, strangely, she felt no relief. There was something about the tone of the letter that troubled her. 'And you don't want that?'

Again he nodded, his lips pressed tightly together.

For a moment she looked past him at the books on the shelf beside his bed. Books she had never heard of before, with titles that were as strange as the leather binding of their covers; books like Polidori's *Ernestus Berchtold*, Helme's *The Farmer of Inglewood Forest*, Poe's *Eleanora*, Brown's *The Power Of Sympathy* and Byron's *Manfred*. She stared at them a moment, as if to make sense of them, then looked back at him.

Folding the sheets, she slipped them back inside the envelope, then held it out to him.

'I've come here to get away from all that,' he said, taking the letter. He looked at it fiercely for a moment, as if it were a living thing, then put it back in his pocket. 'This here...' He gestured at the frame, the books and prints on the walls, the personal things that were scattered all about the room, then shrugged. 'Well, it's different, that's all.'

She thought of Lotte and Wolf, beginning to understand. 'It's too close at home. Is that what you mean? And you feel stifled by that?'

He looked down at his hand – at the left hand where the wrist was ridged – then looked back at her.

'Perhaps.'

She saw how he smiled, faintly, looking inward, as if to piece it all together in his head.

'Your breakfast,' she said, reminding him. 'You should eat it. It's getting cold.'

He looked back, suddenly focusing on her again. Then, as if he had made his mind up about something, he reached out and took her hand, drawing her up towards him.

'Forget breakfast. Come. Let's go to bed again.'

'Well? Have you the file?'

Heng Chian-ye turned, snapping his fingers. At once his servant drew nearer and, bowing, handed him a silk-bound folder.

'I think you'll find everything you need in there,' Heng said, handing it across. 'But tell me, Novacek, why did you want to know about that one? Has he crossed you in some way?'

Sergey Novacek glanced at Heng, then looked back at the file. 'It's none of your business, but, no, he hasn't crossed me. It's just that our friend Shepherd is a bit of a mystery, and I hate mysteries.'

Heng Chian-ye stared at Novacek a moment, controlling the cold anger he felt merely at being in his presence. The *Hung Mao* had no idea what trouble he had got him into.

'You've made your own investigations, I take it?' he said, asking another of the questions his uncle had insisted he ask.

Novacek looked up, closing the file. 'Is this all?'

Heng smiled. 'You know how it is, the richer the man, the less there is on file. Those who can, buy their anonymity.'

'And you think that's what happened here?'

'The boy's father is very rich. Rich enough to buy his way into Oxford without any qualifications whatsoever.'

Novacek nodded, a hint of bitterness overspilling into his words.

'I know. I've seen the college records.'

'Ah...' Heng gave the briefest nod, noting what he had said.

'And the bronze?'

Heng Chian-ye turned slightly. Again the servant approached him, this time carrying a simple ice-cloth sack. Heng took the sack and turned, facing Novacek. His expression was suddenly much harder, his eyes coldly hostile.

'This cost me dear. If there had been any way I could have borrowed a million *yuan* I would have done so, rather than meet my uncle's terms. But before I hand it over, I want to know why you wanted it. Why you thought it worth a million *yuan*.'

Novacek stared at him a moment, meeting the Han's hostility with his own. Then he looked down, smiling sourly. 'You call us big-noses behind our backs, but you've quite a nose yourself, haven't you, Heng?'

Heng's eyes flared with anger, but he held back, remembering what his uncle had said. On no account was he to provoke Novacek.

'And if I say you can't have it?'

Novacek laughed. 'That's fine. You can pay me the million. In instalments, if you like. However, I'll charge you interest on it. A hundred and fifty thousand a year.' He looked up again, meeting Heng's eyes. 'But that's rather more than what you get, so I hear. You might find it... *difficult* to make ends meet. It takes a fair bit to live as richly as you do.'

Heng swallowed, then, almost brutally, thrust the sack into the other man's hands.

Sergey watched Heng a moment, noting how angry he was and wondering about it, then looked down at the plain white sack he held, feeling the shape of the bronze through the flesh-thin cloth, a clear, clean sense of satisfaction – of fulfilment – washing through him.

'Good,' he said. 'Then we're clear, Heng Chian-ye. I'd say your debt to me was settled, wouldn't you?'

Heng Chian-ye turned, taking three angry steps away from him before turning back, his face almost black with anger, his finger pointing accusingly at his tormentor.

'Take care, Novacek. Next time you might not be so lucky. Next time you could meet with someone who counts honour a lesser thing than I. And then you'll find out what the world really thinks of scum like you.'

Sergey stared back at him, smiling insolently. 'Go fuck yourself, Heng Chian-ye. You've no more honour than a Triad boss's cock. The only reason you paid up was your fear of losing face in front of your friends. But that's your problem. I've got what I want.'

Heng opened his mouth, as if to answer him in kind, then changed his mind. He laughed then shook his head, his voice suddenly colder, more controlled.

'Have you, my friend? Have you now?'

They went to the Café Burgundy and took a table close to The Green, paying to keep the three chairs empty. Catherine sat to Ben's right, the tiered cage of the central pagoda behind her, forming a frame to her pale, flame-like beauty. 'My bird' he called her now, and so it seemed fitting. He smiled, studying her profile, then turned and raised a hand to order wine.

He had been quiet all evening, pensive. A second letter had come. It lay inside his jacket pocket unopened. He could feel its gentle pressure against his chest; sense the hidden shape of it.

She too had been quiet, but for different reasons. Hers was a broody, jealous silence; the kind he had come to know only too well these last few days.

The waiter came and poured their wine, leaving the unfinished bottle in an ice bucket on the table between them. Ben leaned across and chinked his glass against hers.

She turned her head and looked at him. 'What does she want?'

He almost smiled at that, knowing what she really thought. His unexplained absences. The letters. Even his moods. He knew she took these things as signs of his infidelity. But she wasn't certain. Not yet, anyway. And so the brooding silence.

He sipped at his wine then set the glass down. 'Here.' He took the letter from his pocket and handed it to her.

She narrowed her eyes, suspicious of him, then took the letter. For a time she simply stared at it, not certain what he meant by giving it to her. Then she lifted it to her nose and sniffed.

'Open it,' he said, amused by her hesitation. 'Or give it back and I'll open it. It's from my sister, Meg.'

She nodded, only half convinced, but gave the letter back, watching as he slit it open with his thumbnail and drew out the four slender sheets of paper. Without even glancing at them, he handed them to her.

'Here...'

She lowered her eyes, beginning to read, reluctantly at first, but then with a growing interest. Finally, she looked up again, her face changed, more open to him.

'But why didn't you say? That was cruel of you, Ben, leaving me in the dark like that. I thought...'

She blushed and looked away. He reached across and took the letter from her.

'Aren't you pleased, Ben? I think it's sweet of her to worry about you. She could stay with me, if you'd like. I've a spare pull-down in my room. She could use that.'

He glanced at her, then returned to the letter. Finished, he folded it neatly and slipped it back into his pocket.

'Well?' she said, exasperated. 'It would be lovely to meet your sister. Really it would.'

He poured himself more wine, then drank deeply. She watched him, puzzled.

'What aren't you telling me?'

He shook his head.

'Don't you like her? Is that it?'

He laughed. 'What, Meg? No, she's...' He smiled strangely, looking down into his empty glass. 'She's just perfect.' He looked up at her, then reached across and, gently lifting her chin, leaned forward to brush his lips against hers.

She smiled. 'That's nice. But what about her?'

'She'll stay with me,' he said, dismissing the subject. 'Now... what shall we eat?'

She stared at him a moment, then let it go. 'I don't mind. Surprise me.' He laughed, suddenly, inexplicably, his old self. 'Oysters. Let's have oysters.'

'Just oysters?'

'No. Not just oysters, but a whole platter of oysters. The very best oysters. More than we could possibly eat.' He puffed out his cheeks and sat back in his chair, his hands tracing an exaggerated curve about his stomach, miming a grossly swollen gut. He laughed, then sat upright again and turned in his chair, snapping his fingers for a waiter.

The abruptness of the transformation both delighted and disturbed her. It hinted at a side of him she had not seen before, unless it was in that moment when he had mimicked her. She pushed her tongue between her teeth, watching him. Laughter at a nearby table distracted her momentarily, making her turn her head. When she looked back he was watching her again, a faint smile on his lips.

'Sometimes you're just plain strange,' she said, laughing. 'Like this business about your family. What's wrong with talking about them? You never tell me anything.'

He shrugged. 'It isn't important. That's home. This is here. I like to keep them separate.'

She looked down, wondering if he realized what he was saying. She felt hurt by his exclusion. Somehow lessened by it.

'It's too close there,' he went on. 'Too...' he laughed; a short, almost painful laugh, 'too intense. You'll find that difficult to understand, I know. I don't hate it, it's just that I need distance from all that. Need something other than what I get there.'

He had set down his glass and was pushing at the skin of his left hand with the fingers of his right; looking down at it as he smoothed and stroked the ridged flesh.

'And where, then, do I fit in? Am I real to you, Ben, or am I just something to be got?'

'Maybe,' he said, meeting her eyes candidly. 'Maybe that's all there is. Different kinds of getting.'

She was about to speak – about to say something she would have regretted later – when the laughter rang out again, louder this time. She felt herself go cold, realizing whose voice it was that led the cold, mocking laughter.

Sergey...

She turned, seeing him at once. He was no more than twenty *ch'i* away from where they were sitting.

He turned in his chair, smiling at her. 'Catherine! How *lovely* to see you!'

She could see that he was drunk. He pushed himself up unsteadily from his chair then came across, pulling out the empty chair beside her. Ignoring

Ben, he sat, leaning towards her unpleasantly, almost threateningly, as he spoke.

'How *are* you, Catherine, my dear? It's quite a while since we saw *you* here, isn't it?'

He belched, then turned, a sneering smile lighting his reddened face.

'And who's this?' He feigned startled surprise. 'My word, if it isn't our friend, the genius!' He made a mocking bow of politeness, but when he straightened up his face had hardened and his eyes were cold with malice. 'I've been wanting to have a few words with you, *friend*.'

There was an ugliness in the emphatic way he said the last word. A hint of violence.

She watched, her irritation with Ben transformed into fear for him. She knew just how dangerous Sergey could be when he was in this kind of mood.

Ben smiled and turned to call the waiter over. *Yes*, she thought, *that's best. End it now, before it gets out of hand.* But instead of asking the waiter to remove Sergey, Ben ordered a fresh bottle of the house wine and an extra glass. He turned back, facing his antagonist.

'You'll have a drink with us, I hope?'

Sergey gave a snort of surprise and annoyance. 'I really can't believe you, Shepherd. You're such a smooth shit, aren't you? You think you can buy the world.'

'Sergey...' she began, but he banged his fist down hard, glaring at her.

'Shut up, Catherine! You might learn a few things about smiling boy here.'

She turned away, shutting her eyes, wishing it would stop.

Sergey leaned forward, his whole manner openly hostile now. 'You're not from here, are you, Shepherd?'

Ben was silent, musing.

'You're not, are you?'

Catherine opened her eyes and looked across. There was a faint smile on Ben's lips: a wistful little smile.

'I've been doing a little digging,' Sergey said, leaning across the table towards Ben, his breath heavy with wine. 'And guess what I found out?' He laughed coldly. 'Our friend here bought his way into Oxford. Just like he buys up everything. They waived the rules to let him in.'

Catherine shook her head. 'I don't follow you...'

Sergey huffed, disgust writ large on his face. 'He's a charlatan, that's what he is. He shouldn't be here. He's like all the other parasites. The only difference is that he's not a Han.' He laughed brutally, then turned and looked at her again, angry now. 'Unlike the rest of us, Shepherd here has no qualifications. He's never passed an exam in his life. As for work...' The laugh was broken, the sneer in the voice pointed. At nearby tables people had broken off their own conversations to see what was going on. 'He's never attended a single tutorial. Never handed in a single essay. And as for sitting the end of year exams, forget it. He goes home before all that. He's above it, you see. Or at least, his money is.'

There was a flutter of laughter at that. But Sergey was not to be distracted by it. He was in full flow now, one hand pointing at his target as he spoke.

'Yes, he's a strange one, this one. He's rich and he's obviously connected. Right up to the top, so they say. But he's something of a mystery, too. He's not from the City. And that's why he despises us.'

She stared at Sergey, not understanding. What did he mean? Everyone came from the City. There was nowhere else to come from. Unless... She thought of the handwritten letters – of the strangeness of so many things connected with Ben – and for a moment felt uncertainty wash over her. Then she remembered what he was doing: recollected what she herself had experienced in the frame.

'You're wrong, Sergey. You don't understand...'

Sergey pulled himself up and went round the table, then stood there, leaning over Shepherd. 'No. I understand only too well. He's a fucking toad, that's what he is. A piece of slime.'

She watched the two of them anxiously, terrified of what was going to happen. 'He's drunk,' she said pleadingly. 'He doesn't mean it, Ben. It's the drink talking.' But she was afraid for him. He didn't know Sergey; didn't know how vicious his temper was.

Ben was looking at her, ignoring the other man. He seemed calm, unaffected by the words, by the physical presence of the other man above him.

'Let him have his say, my love. It's only words.'

It was the first time he had called her love, but she scarcely noticed it. All she could see was that the very mildness of Ben's words acted to inflame Sergey's anger.

'You're wrong,' he said icily. 'It's more than words.'

Ben turned and looked up at him, undaunted. 'When a fool tells you you're wrong, you rejoice.'

It was too much. Sergey lunged at him with both hands, trying to get a grip on his neck, but Ben pushed him away and stood, facing him. Sergey was breathing heavily, furious now. He made a second grab at Ben and got hold of his right arm, trying to twist it round behind his back and force him down on to his knees.

Catherine was on her feet, screaming. 'No! Please, Sergey! Don't hurt him! Please don't hurt him!'

Waiters were running towards them, trying to force a way through the crowd and break it up, but the press about the table was too great.

Using brute strength Sergey forced Ben down, grunting with the effort. Then, suddenly, Ben seemed to yield and roll forward, throwing his opponent off balance. Sergey stumbled and fell against a chair. When he got up there was blood running from beneath his eye.

'You bastard...'

With a bellow of rage he threw himself at Ben again, but Ben's reflexes were much quicker. As Sergey lunged past him, he moved aside and caught hold of Sergey's right hand, turning the wrist.

The snap of breaking bones was audible. Sergey shrieked and went down on to his knees, cradling the useless hand.

For a moment Ben stood over him, his legs planted firmly apart, his chest rising and falling erratically, then he shuddered.

'I didn't mean...'

But it was done. The sculptor's hand was crushed and broken. Useless, it began to swell. Sergey pushed at it tenderly with one finger of the other hand, then moaned and slumped forward, unconscious.

Ben stepped back, away, his eyes taking in everything. Then he turned and looked back at Catherine. She was standing there, her hands up to her mouth, staring down at the injured man.

'Ben...' she said softly, her voice barely in control. 'Oh, Ben. What have you done?'

★

Meg looked about her as they walked down Main towards the transit. The air was still, like the air inside a sealed box. It was the first thing she had noticed. There was no movement in the air, no rustling of leaves, none of the small, soft sounds that moving water makes, no hum of insects. Instead, small boys went between the flower boxes with spray cans, pollinating the flowers, or watered the huge oaks which rested in deep troughs set into the floor. From their branches hung cages: huge, ornately gilded cages filled with bright-coloured birds. But nothing flew here. Nothing bent and danced in the open wind.

'They like it like this,' Ben said, as if that explained it all. Then he frowned and turned to look at her. 'But it doesn't satisfy. Nothing here satisfies. It's all surfaces. There's nothing deep here. Nothing rooted.'

It was Meg's first full morning in the City, though morning here meant little more than a change in the intensity of the overhead lighting. Outside, beyond the City's walls, it was still dark. But here that fact of nature did not matter. Throughout City Europe, time was uniform, governed not by local variation but in accordance with the rising and setting of the sun over the City's eastern edge.

Morning. It was one more imperfect mimicry. Like the trees, the flowers, the birds, the word lost its sharp precision here without a sun to make it real.

They went up fifty levels to the college grounds. This was what they termed an 'open deck' and there was a sense of space and openness. Here there were no tight warrens of corridors, no ceiling almost within touch wherever one went; even so, Meg felt stifled. It was not like being in a house, where the door opened out on to the freshness of a garden. Here the eyes met walls with every movement. She had forgotten how awful it was. Like being in a cage.

'How can you stand it here?'

He looked about him, then reached out, taking her hand. 'I've missed you, you know. It's been... difficult.'

'Difficult?'

They had stopped in the central hexagonal space. On every side great tiers of balconies sloped back gently towards the ceiling, their surfaces transparent, reflecting and refracting light.

'You should come home, Ben. All this...' She looked about her, shaking her head. 'It's no good for you.'

'Maybe,' he said, looking away from her. 'And yet I've got to try to understand it. It may be awful, but this is what *is*, Meg. This is all that remains of the world we made.'

She went to shake her head, to remind him of home, but checked herself. It was not the time to tell him why she'd come. Besides, talking of home would only infuriate him. And perhaps he was right. Perhaps he did have to try to understand it. So that he could return, satisfied, knowing there was nothing else – nothing *missing* from his world.

'You seem depressed, Ben. Is it just the place? Or is it something else?'

He turned, half-smiling. 'No. You're right. It's not just the place.' He made a small despairing gesture, then looked up at one of the great tiers of balconies. Through the glass-like walls one could see people – dozens, hundreds, thousands of people. People, everywhere you looked. One was never alone here. Even in his rooms he felt the press of them against the walls.

He looked back at her, his face suddenly naked, open to her. 'I get lonely here, Meg. More lonely than I thought it possible to feel.'

She stared at him, then lowered her eyes, disturbed by the sudden insight into what he had been feeling. She would never have guessed.

As they walked on he began to tell her about the fight. When he had finished she turned to face him, horrified.

'But they can't blame you for that, Ben. He provoked you. You were only defending yourself, surely?'

He smiled tightly. 'Yes. And the authorities have accepted that. Several witnesses came forward to defend me against his accusation. But that only makes it worse, somehow.'

'But why? If it happened as you say it did?'

He looked away, staring across the open space. 'I offered to pay full costs. For a new synthetic, if necessary. But he refused. It seems he plans to wear his broken hand like a badge.'

He looked back at her, his eyes filled with pain and hurt and anger. And something else.

'You shouldn't blame yourself, Ben. It was *his* fault, not yours.'

He hesitated, then shook his head. 'So it seems. So I made it seem. But the truth is, I enjoyed it, Meg. I enjoyed pushing him. To the limit and then...' He made a small pushing movement with one hand. '*I enjoyed* it. Do you understand that, Meg?'

She watched her brother, not understanding. It was a side of him she had never seen, and for all his words she couldn't quite believe it.

'It's guilt, Ben. You're feeling guilty for something that wasn't your fault.'

He laughed and looked away. 'Guilt? No, it wasn't guilt. I snapped his hand like a rotten twig. Knowing I could do it. Don't you understand? I could see how drunk he was, how easily he could be handled.'

He turned his head, bringing it closer to hers, his voice dropping to a whisper.

'I could have winded him. Could have held him off until the waiters came to break things up. But I didn't. I *wanted* to hurt him. Wanted to see what it was like. I engineered it, Meg. Do you understand? I set it up.'

She shuddered, then shook her head, staring at him intently now. 'No.' But his eyes were fierce, assertive. What if he *had*?

'So what did you learn? What *was* it like?'

He looked down at her hand where his own enclosed it.

'If I close my eyes I can see it all. Can feel what it was like. How easily I led him. His weight and speed. How much pressure it took, bone against bone, to break it. And that knowledge is...' He shrugged, then looked up at her again, his hand exerting the gentlest of pressure on hers. 'I don't know. It's power, I guess.'

'And you enjoyed that?'

She was watching him closely now, forcing her revulsion down, trying to help him, to understand him.

'Perhaps you're right,' he said, ignoring her question. 'Perhaps I ought to go home.'

'And yet something keeps you...'

He nodded, his eyes still focused on her hand. 'That's right. I'm missing something. I know it. Something I can't see.'

'But there's nothing here, Ben. Just look about you. Nothing.'

He looked away, shrugging, seeming to agree with her, but he was thinking of the *Lu Nan Jen*, the oven man, and about Catherine. He had been wrong about those things – surprised by them. So maybe there was more.

He turned, looking back at her. 'Anyway, you'd better go. Your appointment's in an hour.'

She looked back at him, her disappointment clear. 'I thought you were coming with me.'

He had told Catherine he would meet her at eleven – had promised he would show her more of the old paintings – but seeing the look on Meg's face, he knew he could not let her go alone.

'All right,' he said, smiling, 'I'll come to the clinic with you. But then I've things to do. Important things.'

Ben looked about him at the rich decor of the anteroom and frowned. Such luxury was unexpected at this low level. Added to the tightness of the security screening it made him think that there must be some darker reason than financial consideration for establishing the Melfi Clinic in such an unusual setting.

The walls and ceiling were an intense blue, while underfoot a matching carpet was decorated with a simple yellow border. To one side stood a plinth, on which rested a bronze of a pregnant woman – *Hung Mao*, not Han – her naked form the very archetype of fecundity. Across from it hung the only painting in the room – a huge canvas, its lightness standing out against the blue-black of the walls. It was an oak, a giant oak, standing in the plush green of an ancient English field.

In itself, the painting was unsurprising, yet in context it was, again, unexpected. *Why this?* he asked himself. *Why here?* He moved closer, then narrowed his eyes, looking at the tiny acorn that lay there in the left foreground of the composition, trying to make out the two tiny initials that were carved into it.

AS. As what? he thought, smiling, thinking of all those comparatives he had learned as a very young child. As strong as an ox. As wily as a fox. As proud as a peacock. As sturdy as an oak.

And as long-lived. He stared at it, trying to make out its significance in the scheme of things, then turned, looking back at Meg. 'You've come here before?'

She nodded. 'Every six months.'

'And Mother? Does she come here, too?'

Meg laughed. 'Of course. The first time I came, I came with her.'

He looked surprised. 'I didn't know.'

'Don't worry yourself, Ben. It's women's business, that's all. It's just easier for them to do it all here than for them to come into the Domain. Easier and less disruptive.'

He nodded, looking away, but he wasn't satisfied. There was something wrong with all this.

He turned as the panel slid back and a man came through: a tall, rather heavily built Han, his broad face strangely nondescript, his neat black hair swept back from a polished brow. His full-length russet gown was trimmed with a dark green band of silk. As he came into the room he smiled and rubbed his hands together nervously, giving a small bow of his head to Meg before turning towards Ben.

'Forgive me, Shih Shepherd, but we were not expecting you. I am the Senior Consultant here, Tung T'an. If I had known that you planned to accompany your sister, I would have suggested...' He hesitated, then, not sure he should continue, smiled and bowed his head. 'Anyway, now that you *are* here, you had better come through, neh?'

Ben stared back at the Consultant, making him avert his eyes. The man was clearly put out that he was there. But why should that be if this were a routine matter? Why should his presence disturb things, even if this were 'women's business'?

'Meg,' the Consultant said, turning to her, 'it's good to see you again. We expected you next week, of course, but no matter. It will take us but a moment to prepare everything.'

Ben frowned. But she had said... He looked at her, his eyes demanding to know why she hadn't told him that her appointment was not for another week, but her look told him to be patient.

They followed Tung T'an into a suite of rooms every bit as luxurious as the first. Big, spacious rooms, decorated as if this were First Level, not the Mids. Tung T'an tapped out a combination on a doorlock, then turned, facing Ben again, more composed now.

'If you would be kind enough to wait here, Shih Shepherd, we'll try not to keep you too long. The tests are quite routine, but they take a little time. In the meantime, is there anything one of my assistants can bring you?'

'You want me to wait out here?'

'Ben...' Meg's eyes pleaded with him not to make trouble.

He smiled. 'All right. Perhaps you'd ask them to bring me a pot of coffee and a newsfax.'

The Consultant smiled and turned to do as Ben asked, but Meg was looking at him strangely now. She knew her brother well. Well enough to know he never touched a newsfax.

'What are you up to?' she whispered, as soon as Tung T'an was out of the room.

He smiled; the kind of innocuous-seeming smile that was enough to make alarm bells start ringing in her head. 'Nothing. I'm just looking after my kid sister, that's all. Making sure she gets to the Clinic on time.'

She looked down, the evasiveness of the gesture not lost on Ben.

'I'll explain it all, Ben. I promise I will. But not now.' She glanced up at him, then shook her head. 'Look, I promise. Later. But behave yourself while you're here. Please, Ben. I'll only be an hour or so.'

He relented, smiling back at her. 'Okay. I'll try to be good.'

A young girl brought him coffee and a pile of newsfax, then took Meg through to get changed. Ben sat there for a time, pretending to look at the nonsense on the page before him, all the while surreptitiously looking about him. As far as he could see he was not being observed. At the outer gates security was tight, but here there was nothing. Why was that? It was almost standard for companies to keep a tight watch on their premises.

He stood up, stretching, miming tiredness, then went across, looking closer at the walls, the vents, making sure. No. There was nothing. It was almost certain that he wasn't being observed.

Good. Then he'd delve a little deeper. Would answer a few of the questions that were stacking up in his head.

He went out into the corridor and made his way back to the junction. Doors led off to either side. He stopped, listening. There was the faintest buzz of voices to his right, but to his left there was nothing. He tried the left-hand door, drawing the sliding door back in a single silent movement. If challenged he would say he was looking for a toilet.

The tiny room was empty. He slid the door closed behind him, then looked about. Again there seemed to be no cameras. As if they had no need for them. And yet they must, surely, if they had a regular clientele?

He crossed the room and tried the door on the far side. It too was open. Beyond was a long, narrow room, brightly lit, the left-hand wall filled with filing cabinets.

Eureka! he thought, allowing himself a tiny smile. And yet it seemed strange, very strange, that he should be able to gain access to their files so easily.

As if they weren't expecting anyone to try.

His brow wrinkled, trying to work it out, then he released the thought, moving down the line of cabinets quickly, looking for the number he had glimpsed on the card Meg had shown at the gates. He found it without difficulty and tried the drawer. It opened at a touch.

Meg's file was missing. Of course... they would have taken it through. Like a lot of private clinics most of the work was of a delicate nature, and so records were kept in this old-fashioned manner, the reports handwritten by the consultants, no computer copy kept. Because it would not do...

He stopped, astonished, noting the name on the file that lay beneath his fingertips. A file that had a tiny acorn on the label next to the familiar name. *Women's business...*

And then he laughed, softly, quietly, knowing now why Tung T'an had been so flustered earlier. *They were here! They were all here!* He flicked through quickly and found it. *His* file, handwritten like all the rest, and containing his full medical record – including a copy of his genetic chart.

He shivered, a strange mixture of pain and elation coursing through his veins. It was as he'd thought – Augustus *had* been right. Amos's experiment was still going on.

He stared at the genetic chart, matching it to the one he held in memory – the one he had first seen in the back of his great-grandfather's journal that afternoon in the old house – the day he had lost his hand.

The two charts were identical.

He flicked through the files again until he came across his father's. For a time he was silent, scanning the pages, then he looked up, nodding to himself. Here it was – confirmation. A small note, dated 18 February 2185. The date his father had been sterilized. Sterilized without him knowing it, on the pretext of a simple medical.

A date roughly five years before Ben had been born.

He flicked through again, looking now for his mother's file, then pulled it out. He knew now where to look. Anticipated what it would say. Even so, he was surprised by what he read.

The implant had been made seven months before his birth, which meant that he had been nurtured elsewhere for eight weeks before he had been placed in his mother's womb. He touched his tongue to his teeth, finding the thought of it strangely discomfiting. It made sense, of course – by eight weeks they could tell whether the embryo was healthy or otherwise. His embryo would have been – what? – an inch long by then. Limbs, fingers and toes, ears, nose and mouth would have formed. Yes. By eight weeks they would have been sure.

It made sense. Of course it did. But the thought of himself, in utero, placed in a machine, disturbed him. He had always thought...

He let his hands rest on the edge of the drawer, overcome suddenly by the reality of what he had found. He had *known* – some part of him had believed it ever since that day when he had looked at Augustus's journal; even so, he had not been prepared. Not at core. It had been head-knowledge, detached from him. Until now.

So it was true. Hal was not his father, Hal was his brother. Like his so-called 'great-great-grandfather', Augustus, his 'great-grandfather', Robert and his 'grandfather', James. Brothers, all of them. Every last one the seeds of Old Man Amos. Yes. Sons of Amos and his wife, Alexandra.

He flicked through until he found her file, then laughed. Of course! He should have known. The name of the clinic – Melfi. It was his great-great-great-grandmother's maiden name. No. His *mother's* maiden name.

Which meant...

He tried another drawer. Again it opened to his touch, revealing the edges of files, none of them marked with that important acorn symbol. And inside? Inside the files were blank.

'It's all of a piece,' he said quietly, nodding to himself. All part of the great illusion Amos built about him. Like Augustus's town in the Domain, filled with its android replicants. Like the City Amos had designed to Tsao Ch'un's order. All a great charade. A game to perpetuate his seed, his ideas.

And this, here, was the centre of it. The place where Amos's great plan was carried out. That was why it was hidden in the Mids. That was why security was so tight outside and so lax within. No one else came here. No one but the Shepherd women. To be tested and, when the time was right and the scheme demanded it, to have Amos's children implanted into their wombs. No wonder Tung T'an had been disturbed to see him here.

He turned, hearing the door slide back behind him.

It was Tung T'an.

'What in hell's name...?' The Consultant began, then fell silent, seeing the open file on the drawer in front of Ben. He swallowed. 'You should not be in here, *Shih* Shepherd.'

'No, I shouldn't. But I am.'

'If you would leave now...'

'Of course. I've seen all I needed to see.'

The Han's face twitched. 'You misunderstand...'

Ben shook his head. 'Not at all, Tung T'an. You see, I knew. I've known for some time. But not how. Or where. All this...' He indicated the files. 'It just confirms things.'

'You *knew*?' Tung T'an shook his head. 'Knew what, *Shih* Shepherd? There's nothing to know.'

'As you wish, Tung T'an.'

He saw the movement in the man's eyes, the assessment and reassessment. Then Tung T'an gave a reluctant nod. 'You were never meant to see any of this. It is why...'

'Why you kept the Shepherd males away from here.' Ben smiled. 'Wise. To make it all seem unimportant. Women's business. But old Amos wasn't quite so thorough here, was he?'

'I'm sorry?'

Ben shook his head. No, Tung T'an knew nothing of just how thorough Amos could be when he wanted to. The old town was an example of that, complete down to every last detail. But this... In a sense this was a disappointment. It was almost as if...

He laughed, for the first time seriously considering the idea. What if Amos had *wanted* one of them to discover all this? What if that, too, were part of the plan? – a kind of test?

The more he thought of it, the more sense it made. The boarded-up old house, the hidden room, the enclosed garden, the lost journal. None of these were really necessary unless they were meant to act as clues – doors to be passed through until the last door was opened, the final revelation made. No. You did not preserve what you wished to conceal. You destroyed it. And yet he had stumbled on this by accident. Coming here had not been his doing, it had been Meg's. Unless...

She had come a week early. Why? What reason could she have had for doing that? A week. Surely it would have made no difference?

Tung T'an was still staring at him. 'You place me in an impossible situation, Shih Shepherd.'

'Why so, Shih Tung? You can't erase what I've seen, or what I know. Not without destroying me. And you can't do that.' He laughed. 'After all, it's what all of this here is dedicated to preserving, isn't it? You have no other function.'

Tung T'an lowered his head. 'Even so—'

Ben interrupted him. 'You need say nothing, Tung T'an. Not even that I was here. For my own part I will act as if this place did not and does not exist. You understand me?' He moved closer to the Han, forcing him by the strength of his will to look up and meet his eyes. 'I was never here, Tung T'an. And this conversation... it never happened.'

Tung T'an swallowed, aware suddenly of the charismatic power of the young man standing before him, then nodded.

'Good. Then go and see to my sister. She's like me. She doesn't like to be kept waiting. Ah, but you know that, don't you, Tung T'an? You, of all people, should know how alike we Shepherds are.'

Meg sat across from Ben in the sedan, watching him. He had been quiet since they had come from the clinic. Too quiet. He had been up to something. She had seen how flustered Tung T'an had been when he'd returned to her and knew it had to do with something Ben had said or done. When she'd asked, Ben had denied that anything had passed between him and Tung T'an, but she could tell he was lying. The two had clashed over something. Something important enough for Ben to be worrying about it still.

She tried again. 'Was it something to do with me?'

He looked up at her and laughed. 'You don't give up, do you?'

She smiled. 'Not when it concerns you.'

He leaned forward, taking her hands. 'It's nothing. Really, sis. If it were important, I'd tell you. Honest.'

She laughed. 'That doesn't make sense, Ben. If it's not important, then there's no reason for you not to tell me. And if it is, well, you say you'd tell me. So why not just tell me and keep me quiet?'

He shrugged. 'All right. I'll tell you what I was thinking about. I was thinking about a girl I've met here. A girl called Catherine. I should have met her, two hours back, but she's probably given up on me now.'

Meg looked down, suddenly very still. 'A girl?'

He squeezed her hands gently. 'A friend of mine. She's been helping me with my work.'

Meg looked up at him.

He was watching her, a faint, almost teasing smile on his lips. 'You're jealous, aren't you?'

'No...' she began, looking down, a slight colour coming to her cheeks, then she laughed. 'Oh, you're impossible, Ben. You really are. I'm curious, that's all. I didn't think...'

'That I had any friends here?' He nodded. 'No. I didn't think I had either. Not until a week ago. That's when I met her. It was strange. You see, I'd used her as a model for something I was working on. Used her without her knowing it. She was always there, you see, in a café I used to frequent. And then, one day, she came to my table and introduced herself.'

A smile returned to her lips. 'So when are you going to introduce her to me?'

He looked down at her hands, then lifted them to his lips, kissing their backs. 'How about tonight? That is, if she's still speaking to me after this morning.'

Ben was sitting with Meg in the booth at the end of the bar when Catherine came in. He had deliberately chosen a place where neither of them had been before – neutral ground – and had told Meg as much, not wanting his sister to feel too out of place. Ben saw her first and leaned across to touch Meg's hand. Meg turned, seeing how Catherine came down the aisle towards them, awkward at first, then, when she knew they had seen her, with more confidence. She had put up her flame-red hair so that the sharp lines of her face were prominent.

Looking at her in the half-light, Meg thought her quite beautiful.

Ben stood, offering his hand, but Catherine gave him only the most fleeting of glances. 'You must be Meg,' she said, moving round the table and taking the seat beside her, looking into her face. 'I've been looking forward to meeting you.' She laughed softly, then reached out to touch Meg's nose gently, tracing its shape, the outline of her mouth.

'Yes,' she said after a moment. 'You're like him, aren't you?' She turned, looking at Ben. 'And how are *you*?'

'I'm well,' he said noncommittally, taking his seat, then turning to summon a waiter.

Meg studied her in profile. Ben had said nothing, but she understood. The girl was in love with him.

She looked, as Ben had taught her, seeing several things: the fine and clever hands, the sharpness of the eyes that missed little in the visual field. An artist's eyes. And she saw how the girl looked at Ben: casual on the surface, but beneath it all uncertain, vulnerable.

Ben ordered then turned back, facing them. 'This, by the way, is Catherine. She paints.'

Meg nodded, pleased that she had read it so well. 'What do you paint? Abstracts? Portraits?' She almost said landscapes, but it was hard to believe that anyone from here would pick such a subject.

The girl smiled and glanced quickly at Ben before answering. 'I paint whatever takes my interest. I've even painted your brother.'

Ben leaned across the table. 'You should see it, Meg. Some of her work's quite good.'

Meg smiled. If Ben said she was 'good' you could take it that the girl was excellent. She looked at Catherine anew, seeing qualities she had missed the first time: the taut, animal-like quality of her musculature and the way she grew so very still whenever she was watching you. Like a cat. So very like a cat.

The waiter brought their drinks. When he had gone, Ben leaned forward, toasting them both.

'To the two most beautiful women in the City. *Kan pei!*'

Meg looked sideways at the girl, noting the colour that had come to her cheeks. Catherine wasn't sure what Ben was up to. She didn't know him well enough yet. But there was a slightly teasing tone in his voice that was unmistakable, and his eyes sparkled with mischief. His mood had changed. Or, rather, he had changed his mood.

'This painting...' Meg asked, 'is it good?'

Catherine looked down, smiling. There was no affectation in the gesture, only a genuine humility. 'I think it is.' She looked up, careful not to look at Ben, her cheeks burning. 'It's the best thing I've done. My first real painting.'

Meg nodded slowly. 'I'd like to see it, if you'd let me. I don't think anyone has painted Ben in years. If at all.'

The girl bowed her head slightly. There was silence for a moment, then Ben cleared his throat, leaning towards Meg. 'She's far too modest. I've heard they plan to put on an exhibition of her work, here in the college.'

Meg saw how the girl looked up at that, her eyes flying open, and knew it was not something she had told Ben, but that he had discovered it for himself.

She looked back at Catherine. 'When is it being held?'

'In the spring.'

'The spring...' Meg thought of that a moment, then laughed.

'Why did you laugh?' Catherine was staring back at her, puzzled, while from across the table Ben looked on, his eyes almost distant in their intensity.

'Because it's odd, that's all. You say spring and you mean one thing, while for me...' She stared down at her drink, aware of how strangely the girl was looking at her. 'It's just that spring is a season of the year, and here...' She looked up, meeting the girl's deeply green eyes. 'Here there are no seasons at all.'

For a moment longer Catherine stared back at her, seeking but not finding what she wanted in her face. Then she looked away, giving a little shrug.

'You speak like him, too. In riddles.'

'It's just that words mean different things to us,' Ben said, leaning back, his head pressing against the wall of the partition. It was a comment that seemed to exclude Catherine, and Meg saw how she took one quick look at him, visibly hurt.

Hurt and something else. Meg looked away, a sudden coldness in the pit of her stomach. It was more than love. More than simple desire. The girl was obsessed with Ben. As she looked back at Ben, one word formed clear in her head. *Difficult*. It was what he had said earlier. Now she was beginning to understand.

'Words are only words,' she said, turning back and smiling at the girl, reaching out to touch and hold her hand. 'Let's not make too much of them.'

★

Six hours later, Catherine finished wrapping the present, then stood the canvas by the door. That done, she showered, then dressed and made herself up. Tonight she would take him out. Alone, if possible; but with his sister, if necessary. For a moment she stood there, studying herself in the wall-length mirror. She was wearing a dark green, loose-fitting wrap, tied with a cord at the waist. She smiled, pleased by what she saw, knowing Ben would like it, then looked down, touching her tongue to her top teeth, remembering.

A card had come that afternoon. From Sergey. A terse, bitter little note full of recriminations and the accusation of betrayal. It had hurt, bringing back all she had suffered these last few weeks. But it had also brought relief. Her relationship with Sergey could not have lasted. He had tried to own her – to close her off from herself.

She shivered. Well, it was done with now. His clash with Ben had been inevitable and, in a sense, necessary. It had forced her to a choice. Sergey was someone in her past. Her destiny lay with Ben.

The bolt took her north, through the early evening bustle. It was after seven when she reached the terminal at the City's edge. From there she took a tram six stacks east, then two north. There she hesitated, wondering if she should call and tell him she was coming, then pressed on. It would give him less opportunity to make excuses. She had her own key now – she would surprise him.

She took the lift up to his level, the package under her arm. It was heavy and she was longing to set it down. Inside, she placed it against the wall in the cloakroom while she took off her cape. The smell of percolating coffee filled the apartment. Smiling, she went through to the kitchen, hoping to find him there.

The kitchen was empty. She stood there a moment, listening for noises in the apartment, then went through. There was no one in the living room. Two empty glasses rested on the table. For a moment she looked about her, frowning, thinking she had made a mistake and they were out. Then she remembered the coffee.

She crossed the room and stood there, one hand placed lightly against the door, listening. Nothing. Or almost nothing. If she strained, she thought she could hear the faintest sound of breathing.

She tried the door. It was unlocked. She moved the panel, sliding it back slowly, her heart pounding now, her hands beginning to tremble.

It was pitch black within the room. As she eased the panel back, light from the living room spilled into the darkness, breaching it. She saw at once that the frame had been moved from the centre of the room; pushed back to one side, leaving only an open space of carpet and the edge of the bed.

She stepped inside, hearing it clearly now – a regular pattern of breathing. At first it seemed single, but then she discerned its doubleness. Frowning, she moved closer, peering into the darkness.

Her voice was a whisper. 'Ben? Ben...? It's me. Catherine.'

She knelt, reaching out to touch him, then pulled her hand back sharply. The hair...

The girl rolled over and looked up at her, her eyes dark, unfocused from sleep. Beside her Ben grunted softly and nuzzled closer, his right arm stretched out across her stomach, his hand cradling her breast.

Catherine's breath caught in her throat. *Kuan Yin! His sister!*

Meg sighed, then turned her face towards the other girl. 'Ben?' she asked drowsily, not properly awake, one hand scratching lazily at the dark bush of her sex.

Catherine stood, the strength suddenly gone from her legs, a tiny moan of pain escaping her lips. She could see now how their limbs were entwined, how their bodies glistened with the sweat of lovemaking.

'I...' she began, but the words were swallowed back. There was nothing more to say. Nothing now but to get out and try to live with what she'd seen. Slowly she began to back away.

Meg lifted her head slightly, trying to make out who it was. 'Ben?'

Catherine's head jerked back, as if she had no control of it, and banged against the panel behind her. Then she turned and, fumbling with the door, stumbled out – out into the harsh light of the living room – then fell against the table. She went down, scattering the empty glasses, then lay there a moment, her forehead pressed against the table's leg.

She heard the panel slide back and turned quickly, getting up, wiping her hand across her face. It was Ben. He put his hand out to her, but she knocked it away, her teeth bared like a cornered animal.

'You bastard...' she whimpered. 'You...'

But she could only shake her head, her face a mask of grief and bitter disappointment.

He lowered his hand and let his head fall. It was an awkward, painful little gesture, one which Meg, watching from the other room, saw and understood. He hadn't told her. Catherine hadn't known how things were between Ben and her.

Meg looked beyond her brother. Catherine had backed against the door. She stood there a moment, trembling, her pale, beautiful face wet with tears, racked with grief and anger. Then she turned and was gone.

And Ben? She looked at him – saw how he stood there, his head fallen forward, all life, all of that glorious intensity of his, suddenly gone from him. He was hurt. She could see how hurt he was. But he would be all right. Once he'd got used to things. And maybe it was best. Yes, maybe it was, in the circumstances.

She went across and put her arms about him, holding him tightly, her breasts pressed against his back, her cheek resting against his neck.

'It's all right,' she said softly, kissing his naked shoulder. 'It's going to be all right. I promise you it will. It's Meg, Ben. I'm here. I won't leave you. I promise I won't.'

But when she turned him to face her, his eyes seemed sightless and his cheeks were wet with tears.

'She's gone,' he said brokenly. 'Don't you see, Meg? I loved her. I didn't realize it until now, but I loved her. And now she's gone.'

It was much later when Meg found the package. She took it through to the living room, then, laying it on the floor, she unwrapped it and knelt there looking down at it.

It was beautiful. There was no doubt about it. Meg had thought no one else capable of seeing it, but it was there, in the girl's painting – all of Ben's power; his harsh, uncompromising beauty. She too had seen how mixed, how gentle-fierce he was.

She was about to wrap it again, to hide it away somewhere until they were gone from here, when Ben came out of the bedroom.

'What's that?' he asked, looking across at her, the faintest light of curiosity in his eyes.

She hesitated, then picked it up and turned it towards him.

'The girl must have left it,' she said, watching him; seeing how his eyes widened with surprise; how the painting seemed to bring him back to life.

'Catherine,' he corrected her, his eyes never leaving the surface of the painting. 'She had a name, Meg, like you and I. She was real. As real as this.'

He came closer then bent down on his haunches, studying the canvas carefully, reaching out with his fingertips to trace the line and texture of the painting. And all the while she watched him, seeing how his face changed, how pain and wonder and regret flickered one after another across his features.

She looked down. Their lives had been so innocent – so free of all these complications. But now... She raised her head, then looked at him again. He was watching her.

'What is it?'

She shook her head, not wanting to say. They had both been hurt enough by this. Her words could only make things worse. Yet she had seen the change in him. Had seen that transient, flickering moment in his face when pain had been transmuted into something else – into the seed of some great artifice.

She shuddered, suddenly appalled. Was this all there was for him? This constant trading in of innocence for artifice? This devil's bargain? Could he not just *be*? Did everything he experienced, every living breath he took, have to be sacrificed on the bleak, unrelenting altar of his art?

She wished there were another answer – another path – for him, but knew it was not so. He could not *be* without first recording his being. Could not be free without first capturing himself. Nor did he have any choice in the matter. He was like Icarus, driven, god-defiant, obsessed by his desire to break free of the element which bound him.

She looked back at him, meeting his eyes.

'I must go after her, Meg. I must.'

'You can't. Don't you understand? She *saw* us. She'll not forgive you that.'

'But this...' He looked down at the painting again, the pain returned to his face. 'She saw me, Meg. Saw me clear. As I really am.'

She shivered. 'I know. But you can't. It's too late, Ben. Don't you see that?'

'No,' he said, standing. 'Not if I go now and beg her to forgive me.'

She let her head fall, suddenly very tired. 'No, Ben. You *can't*. Not now.'

'Why?' his voice was angry now, defiant. 'Give me one good reason.'

She sighed. It was what she had been unable to say to him earlier – the reason why she had come here a week early – but now it had to be said. She looked up at him again, her eyes moist now. 'It's Father. He's ill.'

'I know—' he began, but she cut him off.

'No, Ben. You don't know. The doctors came three days ago. The day I wrote to you.' There was a faint quaver in her voice now. She had let the painting fall. Now she stood there, facing him, the first tears spilling down her cheeks.

'He's dying.' She raised her voice suddenly, anger spilling over into her words. 'Goddammit, Ben, they've given him a month! Six weeks at most!' She swallowed, then shook her head, her eyes pleading with him now. 'Don't you see? That's why you can't go after her. You've got to come home. You must! Mother needs you. She needs you badly. And me. I need you too, Ben. Me more than anyone.'

Memorandum: dated 4th day of May, AD 2207

To His Most Serene Excellency, Li Shai Tung, Grand Counsellor and T'ang of *Ch'eng Ou Chou* (City Europe)

Chieh Hsia,
Your humble servant begs to inform you that the matter of which we spoke has now resolved itself satisfactorily. The girl involved, Catherine Tissan (see attached report, MinDis PSec 435/55712), has apparently returned to her former lover, Sergey Novacek (see attached report, MinDis PSec 435/55711), who, after pressure from friends loyal to Your Most Serene Excellency, has dropped his civil action against the Shepherd boy (see copies of documents attached).

Ben Shepherd himself has, as you are doubtlessly aware, returned home to tend his ailing father, abandoning his studies at Oxford, thus removing himself from the threat of possible attack or abduction.

This acknowledged, in view of the continuing importance of the Shepherd family to State matters, your humble servant has felt it his duty to continue in his efforts to ascertain whether this was, as appears on the surface of events, a simple matter of rivalry in love, or whether it was part of some deeper, premeditated scheme to undermine the State. Such investigations have revealed some interesting if as

yet inconclusive results regarding the nature of the father, Lubos
Novacek's business dealings. Results which, once clarified, will, if of
substance to this matter, be notified to Your Most Serene Excellency.

Your humble servant,
Heng Yu,
Minister Of Transportation, *Ch'eng Ou Chou* (City Europe)

Heng Yu read the top copy through then, satisfied, reached out and took his
brush from the ink block, signing his name with a flourish on each of the
three copies. One would go to Li Shai Tung. The second he would keep for
his own records. The third... well, the third would go to Prince Yuan, via his
contact in the palace at Tongjiang, Nan Ho.

Heng Yu smiled. Things could not have gone better. The boy was safe,
the T'ang pleased, and he was much closer to his ambition. What more
could a man ask for? Of course, not everything had been mentioned in the
documents. The matter of the bronze statue, for instance, had been left out
of the report on Sergey Novacek.

It had been an interesting little tale. One which, in spite of all, reflected
well on young Novacek. Investigations into the past history of the bronze
had shown that it had once belonged to his father, Lubos, who, to bail out
an old friend, had had to sell it. Sergey Novacek had heard of this and, hearing Heng Chian-ye talking of it, had set things up so that he might win
it back. The matter of Shepherd, it seemed, had been a secondary matter,
spawned of jealousy and tagged on as an afterthought. The statue had been
the prime mover of the boy's actions. From accounts, he had returned it to
his father on his sixtieth birthday.

And the father? Heng Yu sat back, stroking his beard. Lubos Novacek
was, like many of the City's leading tradesmen, a respectable man. His
trade, however, was anything but respectable, for Lubos Novacek acted as
a middleman between certain First Level concerns and the Net. Put crudely,
he was the pimp of certain Triad bosses, acting on their behalf in the Above,
buying and selling at their behest and taking his cut.

A useful man to know. And know him he would.

As for the Great Man – that pompous halfwit, Fan Liang-wei – Heng
had enjoyed summoning him to his Ministry and ordering him to desist

from his efforts to get Ben thrown out of the college. He had shown Fan the instrument signed by the T'ang himself and threatened him with instant demotion – even to the Net itself – should any word come back to him that Fan was pursuing the matter in any shape or form.

Yes, it had been immensely satisfying. Fan's face had been a perfect picture as he had attempted to swallow his massive pride and come to terms with the fact of the boy's influence. He had been almost apoplectic with unexpressed anger.

Heng Yu gave a little chuckle, then turned to face his young cousin.

'Something amuses you, Uncle?'

'Yes, Chian-ye. Some business I did earlier. But come now, I need you to take these documents for me.' He picked up two of the copies and handed them across. 'This first copy must be handed directly to Chung Hu-yan and no one else, and this to Nan Ho at Tongjiang. Both men will be expecting you.'

'Is that all, Uncle Yu?'

Heng Yu smiled. It was a moment for magnanimity. 'No, Chian-ye. I am pleased with the way you have served me this past week. In view of which I have decided to review the matter of your allowance. In respect of past and future duties as my personal assistant, you will receive an additional sum of twenty-five thousand *yuan* per year.'

Heng Chian-ye bowed low, surprised yet also greatly pleased. 'You are most generous, Uncle Yu. Be assured, I will strive hard to live up to the trust you have placed in me.'

'Good. Then get going, Chian-ye. These papers must be in the hands of their respective agents within the next six hours.'

Heng Yu watched his cousin leave, then stood, stretching and yawning. There was no doubting it, this matter – of little substance in itself – had served him marvellously. He laughed, then looked about him, wondering momentarily what his uncle, Chian-ye's father, would have made of it.

And the matter of the Melfi Clinic?

That, too, could be used. Was something to be saved until the time was ripe. For though his uncle, Heng Chi-po, had been a greedy, venal man, he had been right in one thing. Information was power. And those who had it wielded power.

Yes. And never more so than in the days to come. For Chung Kuo was changing fast. New things were rising from the depths of the City. Things he would do well to know about.

Heng Yu, Minister to the T'ang, nodded to himself, then reached across and killed the light above his desk.

Which was why, in the morning, he had arranged to meet the merchant, Novacek. To offer him a new arrangement – a new commodity to trade in; one he would pay handsomely to possess.

Information.

IN TIMES TO COME...

Chung Kuo: An Inch of Ashes is the sixth volume of a vast dynastic saga that covers more than half a century of this vividly realized future world. In the fourteen volumes that follow, the Great Wheel of fate turns through a full historical cycle, transforming the social climate of Chung Kuo utterly. Chung Kuo is the portrait of these turbulent – and often apocalyptic – times and the people who lived through them.

In Chung Kuo: The Broken Wheel the 'War of Two Directions' intensifies. Revolutionary activity is rife, culminating in an attack on Bremen stack, which kills over 15,000 citizens. Behind this, and behind a new splinter cult, the Yu, is our old friend DeVore – or at least a convincing copy of him – while at his side is Stefan Lehmann, son of an old Dispersionist leader, and as cold and cruel as DeVore himself.

Whereas once there was unanimity, now things are far from well within the Seven, with the odious Wang Sau-leyan sowing discord between the T'ang. For Prince Li Yuan, personal events overtake public considerations. When Fei Yen, heavily pregnant, defies him and goes riding, he kills all her horses. Furious, she leaves him, returning to her father's house. A week later, she tells him that the child she bears is not his.

This is not the only betrayal Li Yuan suffers. Ebert's scheme to work with DeVore is uncovered and reported to Marshal Tolonen, Ebert's future father-in-law. Horrified but convinced of Hans' guilt, the old man goes to Ebert's father, Klaus, his childhood friend, and gives him twenty-four hours to resolve the matter. Only things go wrong: Klaus is killed by one of his goat servants, while trying to choke his son to death, and Hans Ebert flees to Mars.

Kim Ward's true history of the world – his 'Aristotle File' – grows more influential with every year, undermining the work of the 'Thousand Eyes'. When his labs are attacked by assassins, everyone is killed bar Kim, who – using his darkest instincts from the Clay – savagely fights his way to freedom. He hides in the warren of ducts, traumatized, until the ancient sage and Master of *wei chi*, Tuan Ti Fo, led by a dream, rescues him.

With Li Shai Tung's death, Li Yuan becomes one of the Seven. His first act is to test the paternity of Fei Yen's child. He then divorces her, marrying three new wives. But his heart is empty, his mind numbed by what has happened.

But there is a new threat to the Seven, the 'Sons of Benjamin Franklin', a group of rich young Americans, heirs to their fathers' Companies, who want change as fiercely as any lower-level *Ko Ming* revolutionaries.

CHUNG KUO

CHARACTER LISTING

MAJOR CHARACTERS

Ascher, Emily
Trained as an economist, she joined the *Ping Tiao* revolutionary party at the turn of the century, becoming one of its policy-formulating 'Council of Five'. A passionate fighter for social justice, she was also once the lover of the *Ping Tiao*'s unofficial leader, Bent Gesell.

DeVore, Howard
A one-time major in the T'ang's Security forces, he has become the leading figure in the struggle against the Seven. A highly intelligent and coldly logical man, he is the puppetmaster behind the scenes as the great 'War of the Two Directions' takes a new turn.

Ebert, Hans
Son of Klaus Ebert and heir to the vast GenSyn Corporation, he is a captain in the Security forces, admired and trusted by his superiors. Ebert is a complex young man: a brave and intelligent officer, he also has a selfish, dissolute and rather cruel streak.

Fei Yen
Daughter of Yin Tsu, one of the heads of the 'Twenty Nine', the minor aristocratic families of Chung Kuo. The classically beautiful 'Flying Swallow', her marriage to the murdered Prince Li Han Ch'in nullified, marries Han's brother, the young Prince Li Yuan. Fragile in appearance, she is surprisingly strong-willed and fiery.

Haavikko, Axel
Smeared by the false accusations of his fellow officers, Lieutenant Haavikko has spent the best part of a decade in debauchery and self-negation.

	At core, however, he is a good, honest man, and circumstances will raise him from the pit into which he has fallen.
Kao Chen	Once an assassin from the Net, the lowest levels of the great City, Chen has raised himself from his humble beginnings to become an officer in the T'ang's Security forces. As friend and helper to Karr, he is one of the foot-soldiers in the War against DeVore.
Karr, Gregor	A major in the Security forces, he was recruited by Marshal Tolonen from the Net. In his youth he was an athlete and, later, a 'blood' – a to-the-death combat fighter. A giant of a man, he is to become the 'hawk' Li Shai Tung flies against his adversary, DeVore.
Lehmann, Stefan	Albino son of the former Dispersionist leader, Pietr Lehmann, he has become a lieutenant to DeVore. A cold, unnaturally dispassionate man, he seems to be the very archetype of nihilism, his only aim to bring down the Seven and their great City.
Li Shai Tung	T'ang of City Europe and one of the Seven, the ruling Council of Chung Kuo, Li Shai Tung is now in his seventies. For many years he was the fulcrum of the Council and unofficial spokesman for the Seven, but the murder of his heir, Han Ch'in, has weakened him, undermining his once strong determination to prevent Change at all costs.
Li Yuan	Second son of Li Shai Tung, he becomes heir to City Europe after the murder of his elder brother. Thought old before his time, his cold, thoughtful manner conceals a passionate nature, expressed in his wooing of his dead brother's wife, Fei Yen.
Shepherd, Ben	Son of Hal Shepherd, the T'ang's chief advisor, and great-great-grandson of City Earth's Architect. Shepherd is born and brought up in the Domain, an idyllic valley in the south-west of England where, deciding not to follow in his father's footsteps and become advisor to Li Yuan, he pursues instead his calling as an artist, developing a whole new art form, the Shell, which will eventually have a cataclysmic effect on Chung Kuo's society.
Tolonen, Jelka	Daughter of Marshal Tolonen, Jelka has been brought up in a very masculine environment, lacking a mother's influence. However, her genuine interest

in martial arts and in weaponry and strategy mask a very different side to her nature; a side brought out by violent circumstances.

Tolonen, Knut	Marshal of the Council of Generals and one-time General to Li Shai Tung, Tolonen is a big, granite-jawed man and the staunchest supporter of the values and ideals of the Seven. Possessed of a fiery, fearless nature, he will stop at nothing to protect his masters, yet after long years of war even his belief in the necessity of stasis has been shaken.
Tsu Ma	T'ang of West Asia and one of the Seven, the ruling Council of Chung Kuo, Tsu Ma has thrown off his former dissolute ways as a result of his father's death and become one of Li Shai Tung's greatest supporters in Council. A strong, handsome man, he has still, however, a weakness in his nature: one that is almost his undoing.
Wang Sau-leyan	T'ang of Africa; fourth and youngest son of Wang Hsien. The murder of his two eldest brothers has placed him closer to the centre of political events. Thought of as a wastrel, he is, in fact, a shrewd and highly capable political being who is set – through circumstances of his own devising – to become the harbinger of Change inside the Council of the Seven.
Ward, Kim	Born in the Clay, that dark wasteland beneath the great City's foundations, Kim has a quick and unusual bent of mind. His vision of a giant web, formulated in the darkness, has driven him up into the light of the Above. However, after a traumatic fight and a long period of personality reconstruction, he has returned to things not quite the person he was. Or so it seems, for Kim has lost none of the sharpness that has made him the most promising young scientist in the whole of Chung Kuo.

THE SEVEN AND THE FAMILIES

An Liang-chou	Minor Family prince
An Sheng	head of the An family (one of the 'Twenty-Nine' Minor Families)
Chi Hsing	T'ang of the Australias
Chun Wu-chi	head of the Chun family (one of the 'Twenty-Nine' Minor Families)

Fu Ti Chang	Minor Family princess
Hou Ti	Former T'ang of South America
Hou Tung-po	T'ang of South America
Hsiang K'ai Fan	Minor Family prince
Hsiang Shao-erh	head of the Hsiang family (one of the 'Twenty-Nine' Minor Families) and father of Hsiang K'ai Fan and Hsiang Wang
Hsiang Wang	Minor Family prince
Lai Shi	Minor Family princess
Li Ch'i Chan	brother and advisor to Li Shai Tung
Li Feng Chiang	brother and advisor to Li Shai Tung
Li Shai Tung	T'ang of Europe
Li Yuan	second son of Li Shai Tung and heir to City Europe
Li Yun Ti	brother and advisor to Li Shai Tung
Mien Shan	Minor Family princess
Pei Chao Yang	son and heir of Pei Ro-hen
Pei Ro-hen	head of the Pei family (one of the 'Twenty-Nine' Minor Families)
Tsu Ma	T'ang of West Asia
Tsu Tao Chu	third son of Tsu chang, deceased first son of Tsu Tiao
Wang Sau-leyan	T'ang of Africa
Wei Chan Yin	eldest son of Wei Feng and heir to City East Asia
Wei Feng	T'ang of East Asia
Wu Shih	T'ang of North America
Yi Shan-ch'i	Minor Family prince
Yin Chang	Minor Family prince; son of Yin Tsu and elder brother to Fei Yen
Yin Fei Yen	'Flying Swallow', Minor Family princess; daughter of Yin Tsu; widow of Li Han Ch'in; now wife of Li Yuan
Yin Sung	Minor Family prince; elder brother of Fei Yen and son and heir of Yin Tsu
Yin Tsu	head of Yin family (one of the 'Twenty-Nine' Minor Families)
Yin Wei	younger brother of Fei Yen
Yin Wu Tsai	Minor Family princess and cousin of Fei Yen

FRIENDS AND RETAINERS OF THE SEVEN

Auden, William	captain in Security
Chai	servant to Wang Hsien

Chang Li	Chief Surgeon to Li Shai Tung
Chang Shih-sen	personal secretary to Li Yuan
Ch'in Tao Fan	Chancellor of East Asia
Chu Ta Yun	Minister of Education for City Europe
Chuang Ming	Minister to Li Shai Tung
Chung Hsin	'Loyalty'; bondservant to Li Shai Tung
Chung Hu-Yan	Chancellor to Li Shai Tung
Ebert, Berta	wife of Klaus Ebert
Ebert, Hans	major in Security and heir to GenSyn, son of Klaus Ebert
Ebert, Klaus Stefan	head of GenSyn (Genetic Synthetics) and advisor to Li Shai Tung
Erkki	guard to Jelka Tolonen
Fan Liang-wei	painter to the court of Li Shai Tung
Fest, Edgar	captain in Security
Fischer, Otto	head of Personal Security at Wang Hsien's palace in Alexandria
Fu	servant to Wang Hsien
Haavikko, Axel	lieutenant in Security
Haavikko, Vesa	sister of Axel Haavikko
Helm	general in Security, City South America
Heng Yu	Son of Heng Fan and nephew of Heng Chi-Po
Hoffmann	major in Security
Hua	personal surgeon to Li Shai Tung
Hung Feng-chan	Chief Groom at Tongjiang
Hung Mien-lo	advisor to Wang Sau-leyan; Chancellor of City Africa
Kao Chen	captain in Security
Karr, Gregor	'blood', and, later, major in Security
Lautner, Wolfgang	captain in Security Personnel at Bremen
Little Bee	Maid to Wang Hsien
Lung Mei Ho	secretary to Tsu Ma
Mi Feng	see 'Little Bee'
Nan Ho	Li Yuan's Master of the Inner Chambers
Nocenzi, Vittorio	General of Security, City Europe
Panshin, Anton	colonel in Security
Pearl Heart	maid to Li Yuan
Rahn, Wolf	lieutenant in Security, City Africa
Russ	captain in Security
Sanders	captain of Security at Helmstadt Armoury
Scott	captain of Security
Shepherd, Ben	son of Hal Shepherd

Shepherd, Beth	wife of Hal Shepherd
Shepherd, Hal	advisor to Li Shai Tung and head of the Shepherd family
Shepherd, Meg	daughter of Hal Shepherd
Stifel	alias of Otto Fischer
Sun Li Hua	Wang Hsien's Master of the Inner Chambers
Sweet Rain	maid to Wang Hsien
Sweet Rose	maid to Li Yuan
Tender Willow	maid to Wang Hsien
Tolonen, Helga	aunt of Jelka Tolonen
Tolonen, Jelka	daughter of Knut Tolonen
Tolonen, Jon	brother of Knut Tolonen
Tolonen, Knut	Marshal of the Council of Generals and father of Jelka Tolonen
Wang Ta Chuan	Li Shai Tung's Master of the Inner Palace at Tongjiang
Wen	captain of Security on Mars
Wu Ming	servant to Wang Ta-hung
Ying Chai	assistant to Sun Li Hua
Ying Fu	assistant to Sun Li Hua
Yu	surgeon to Li Yuan

DISPERSIONISTS

Barrow, Chao	Representative of the House in Weimar
Berdichev, Ylva	wife of Soren Berdichev
Blake, Peter	head of personnel for Berdichev's SimFic Corporation
Cherkassky, Stefan	ex-Security assassin and friend of DeVore
DeVore, Howard	former major in Li Shai Tung's Security forces
Douglas, John	company head
Duchek, Albert	Administrator of Lodz
Ecker, Michael	company head
Kubinyi	lieutenant to DeVore
Lehmann, Stefan	albino son of former Dispersionist leader, Pietr Lehmann, and lieutenant to DeVore
Moore, John	company head
Moore, Paul	Senior Executive of Berdichev's SimFic Corporation
Parr, Charles	company head
Reid, Thomas	lieutenant to DeVore
Ross, Alexander	company head

Schwarz	lieutenant to DeVore
Scott	alias of DeVore
Turner	alias of DeVore
Wiegand, Max	lieutenant to DeVore
Weiss, Anton	banker

PING TIAO

Ascher, Emily	economist and member of the 'Council of Five'
Gesell, Bent	unofficial leader of the Ping Tiao and member of the 'Council of Five'
Mach, Jan	maintenance official for the Ministry of Waste Recycling and member of the 'Council of Five'
Mao Liang	Minor Family princess and member of the 'Council of Five'
Shen Lu Chua	computer expert and member of the 'Council of Five'
Yun Ch'o	lieutenant to Shen Lu Chua

OTHER CHARACTERS

Amandsun	friend of Sergey Novacek
Anton	friend of Kim Ward on the Recruitment Project
Barycz, Jiri	scientist on the Wiring Project
Beattie, Douglas	alias of DeVore
Chan Wen-fu	friend of Heng Chian-ye
Chuang Lian	wife of Minister Chuang
Ebert, Lutz	half-brother of Klaus Ebert
Ellis, Michael	assistant to Director Spatz
Fan Liang-wei	shanshui artist
Ganz, Joseph	alias of DeVore
Golden Heart	young prostitute bought by Hans Ebert for his household
Hammond, Joel	Senior Technician on the Wiring Project
Heng Chian-ye	son of Heng Chi-po and nephew of Heng Yu
Herrick	an illegal implant specialist
Janko	bully in the Casting Shop
Josef	friend of Kim Ward's on the Recruitment Project
Kao Ch'iang Hsin	infant daughter of Kao Chen
Kao Wu	infant son of Kao Chen
Kung Wen-fa	Senior Advocate from Mars
Ling Hen	henchman for Herrick

Lin Hou Ying	maintenance engineer for ProsTek
Liu Chang	brothel keeper/pimp
Loehr	alias of DeVore
Lotte	student at Oxford; twin of Wolf
Lo Wen	personal servant to Hans Ebert
Lo Yu-Hsiang	Senior Representative in the House at Weimar
Lu Cao	*amah* (maidservant) to Jelka Tolonen
Lu Ming Shao	'Whiskers Lu', Triad boss
Lu Nan Jen	the 'oven man'
Lu Wang-pei	murder suspect
Mu Chua	'Madam' of the House of the Ninth Ecstasy, a sing-song house, or brothel
Novacek, Lubos	merchant; father of Sergey Novacek
Novacek, Sergey	student at Oxford and sculptor
Reynolds	alias of DeVore
Schenck, Hung-li	Governor of the Mars Colony
Siang Che	martial arts instructor to Jelka Tolonen
Spatz, Gustav	Director of the Wiring Project
Sweet Flute	*mui tsai* to Madam Chuang Lian
Sweet Honey	sing-song girl in Mu Chua's
T'ai Cho	tutor and 'guardian' to Kim Ward
Tissan, Catherine	student at Oxford; artist
Tong Chou	alias of Kao Chen
Tsang Yi	friend of Heng Chian-ye
Tung T'an	Senior Consultant at the Melfi Clinic
Turner	alias of DeVore
Wang Ti	wife of Kao Chen
Ward, Kim	Lagasek, or 'Starer'; 'Clayborn', orphan and Scientist
White Orchid	sing-song girl in Mu Chua's
Wolf	student at Oxford and twin of Lotte
Wolfe	Security soldier
Yu, Madam	First Level socialite
Zhakar	Speaker of the House of Representatives

THE DEAD

Aaltonen	Marshal and Head of Security for City Europe
Anders	a mercenary
Anderson	Director of The Project
Ascher, Mikhail	junior credit agent in the Finance Ministry, the Hu Pu, and father of Emily Ascher

Bakke	Marshal in Security
Barrow, Chao	member of the House of Representatives; Dispersionist
Beatrice	daughter of Cathy Hubbard, granddaughter of Mary Reed
Berdichev, Soren	head of SimFic (Simulated Fictions) and leader of the Dispersionists
Big Wen	a 'landowner'
Boss Yang	an exploiter of the people
Buck, John	Head of Development at the Ministry of Contracts
Ch'eng I	Minor Family prince and son of Ch'eng So Yuan
Ch'eng So Yuan	Minor Family head
Chang Hsuan	Han painter from the eighth century
Chang Lai-hsun	nephew of Chang Yi Wei
Chang Li Chen	Junior Dragon, in charge of drafting the Edict of Technological Control
Chang Lui	woman who adopted Pavel
Chang Yan	Guard on the Plantations
Chang Yi Wei	senior brother of the Chang clan owners of MicroData
Chang Yu	Tsao Ch'un's appointment as First Dragon
Chao Ni Tsu	Grand Master of *wei chi* and computer genius. Servant of Tsao Ch'un
Chen So I	Head of the Ministry of Contracts
Chen Yu	steward to Tsao Ch'un in Pei Ch'ing
Cheng Yu	one of the original Seven, advisor to Tsao Ch'un
Chi Fei Yei	a usurer
Chi Lin Lin	legal assistant to Yang Hong Yu
Ching Su	friend of Jiang Lei
Chiu Fa	media commentator on the Mids news channel
Cho Hsiang	subordinate to Hong Cao and middleman for Pietr Lehmann
Cho Yi Yi	Master of the Bedchamber at Tongjiang
Chu Heng	*kwai* or hired knife; a hireling of DeVore
Chun Hua	wife of Jiang Lei
Chung Hsin	'Loyalty'; a bond-servant to Li Shai Tung
Croft, Rebecca	'Becky', daughter of Leopold, with the lazy eye
Curtis, Tim	Head of Human Resources GenSyn
Dag	a mercenary
Dick, Philip K.	American science-fiction writer
Duchek, Albert	Administrator of Lodz and Dispersionist

Ebert, Gustav	genetics genius and co-founder of GenSyn, Genetic Synthetics
Ebert, Ludovic	son of Gustav Ebert and a GenSyn director
Ebert, Wolfgang	financial genius and co-founder of GenSyn, Genetic Synthetics
Einar	a mercenary
Endfors, Jenny	wife of Knut Tolonen and mother of Jelka
Fan Chang	one of the original Seven, advisor to Tsao Ch'un
Fan Cho	son of Fan Chang
Fan Lin	son of Fan Chang
Fan Peng	eldest wife of Fan Chang
Fan Si-pin	Master of *wei chi* from the eighteenth century
Fan Ti Yu	son of Fan Chang
Feng I	Colonel in charge of Tsao Ch'un's elite force
Gosse	elite guard at the Domain
Grant, Thomas	captain in Security
Griffin, James B.	Sixtieth President of the United States of America
Haavikko, Knut	major in Security
Heng Chi-Po	Minister of Transportation for City Europe
Henrik	a mercenary
Ho	steward to Jiang Lei
Hong Cao	middle man for Pietr Lehmann
Hou Hsin-Fa	one of the original Seven, advisor to Tsao Ch'un
Hsu Jung	friend of Jiang Lei
Hubbard, Beth	daughter of Tom and Mary Hubbard
Hubbard, Cathy	daughter of Tom and Mary Hubbard
Hubbard, Mary	wife of Tom Hubbard and mother of Cathy. Second wife of Jake Reed
Hubbard, Meg	daughter of Tom and Mary Hubbard
Hubbard, Tom	farmer, resident in Church Knowle. Husband of Mary Hubbard and father of Beth, Meg and Cathy. Best friend to Jake Reed
Hui	receptionist for GenSyn
Hui Chang Ye	senior legal advocate for the Chang family
Hung	Tsao Ch'uns spy in Jiang Lei's camp
Hwa	'Blood', or fighter, beneath the Net
Jiang Ch'iao-chieh	eldest daughter of Jiang Lei
Jiang Lei	general of Tsao Ch'un's Eighteenth Banner Army, also known as Nai Liu
Jiang Lo Wen	granddaughter of Jiang Lei
Jiang San-chieh	youngest daughter of Jiang Lei

Jung	steward to Tobias Lahm
Kao Jyan	assassin
Karl	a mercenary
Kirov, Alexander	Marshal to the Seven, Head of the Council of Generals
Krenek, Henryk	Senior Representative of the Martian Colonies
Krenek, Irina	wife of Henryk Krenek
Krenek, Josef	company head
Krenek, Maria	wife of Josef Krenek
Ku	Marshal of the Fourth Banner Army
Kurt	Chief Technician for GenSyn
Lahm, Tobias	Eighth Dragon at the Ministry
Lao Jen	Junior Minister to Li Shai Tung
Lehmann, Pietr	Under Secretary of the House of Representatives and father of Stefan Lehmann and leader of Dispersionists
Li Chang So	sixth son of Li Chao Ch'in
Li Chao Ch'in	one of the original Seven, advisor to Tsao Ch'un
Li Fu Jen	third son of Li Chao Ch'in
Li Han Ch'in	first son of Li Shai Tung and heir to City Europe
Li Kuang	fifth son of Li Chao Ch'in
Li Peng	eldest son of Li Chao Ch'in
Li Po	T'ang dynasty poet
Li Shen	second son of Li Chao Ch'in
Li Weng	fourth son of Li Chao Ch'in
Lin Yua	first wife of Li Shai Tung
Ling	steward at the Black Tower
Ludd, Drew	biggest grossing actor in Hollywood and star of Ubik
Lung Ti	secretary to Edmund Wyatt
Lwo Kang	son of Lwo Chun-yi and Li Shai Tung's Minster of the Edict of Technological Control
Ma Shao Tu	senior servant to Li Chao Ch'in
Maitland (Fu Jen)	Stefan Lehmann's mother
Mao Tse T'ung	first Ko Ming emperor of China (ruled AD 1948–76)
Melfi, Charles	father of Alexandra Shepherd
Ming Hsin-far	senior advocate for GenSyn
Nai Liu	'Enduring Willow'; pen name of Jiang Lei and the most popular Han poet of his time
P'eng Chuan	Sixth Dragon at the Ministry ('The Thousand Eyes')
P'eng K'ai-chi	nephew of P'eng Chuan
Palmer, Joshua	'Old Josh', record collector

Pan Chao	the great hero of Chung Kuo, who conquered Asia in the first century AD
Pan Tsung-yen	friend of Jiang Lei
Pavel	Young worker on the Plantations
Pei Ko	one of the original Seven, advisor to Tsao Ch'un
Pei Lin-Yi	eldest son of Pei Ko
Ragnar	a mercenary
Raikkonen	Marshal in Security
Reed, Anne	first wife of Jake Reed; mother of Peter Reed and sister of Mary Hubbard (Jake's second wife)
Reed, Jake	'Login' or 'Webdancer' for Hinton Industries. Father of Peter Reed
Reed, Mary	sister of Jake Reed
Reed, Peter	son of Jake and Anne Reed. GenSyn Executive
Reed, Tom	son of Jane and Mary Reed
Rheinhardt	Media Liaison Officer for GenSyn
Schwartz	Aide to Marshal Aaltonen
Shao Shu	First Steward at Chun Hua's mansion
Shao Yen	major in Security, friend of Meng Hsin-far
Shen Chen	son of Shen Fu
Shen Fu	The First Dragon, Head of the Ministry ('The Thousand Eyes')
Shepherd, Alexandra	wife of Amos Shepherd and daughter of Charles Melfi
Shepherd, Amos	Great-great-grandfather of Hal Shepherd, advisor to Tsao Ch'un and architect of City Earth
Shepherd, Augustus Raedwald	Great-grandfather of Hal Shepherd
Shepherd, Beth	daughter of Amos Shepherd
Shu Liang	Senior Legal Advocate
Shu San	Junior Minister to Lwo Kang
Si Wu Ya	'Silk Raven'; wife of Supervisor Sung
Ssu Lu Shan	official of the Ministry, the 'Thousand Eyes'
Su Ting-an	Master of *wei chi* from the eighteenth century
Su Tung-p'o	Han official and poet of the eleventh century
Svensson	Marshal in Security
Tai Yu	Moonflower, maid to Gustav Ebert; a GenSyn clone
Teng	common citizen of Chung Kuo
Teng Fu	Guard on the Plantation
Teng Liang	Minor Family princess betrothed to Prince Ch'eng
Trish	Artificial Intelligence 'filter avatar' for Jake Reed's penthouse apartment

Ts'ao Pi	Number Three steward at Tsao Ch'un's court in Pei Ch'ing
Tsao Ch'l Yuan	youngest son of Tsao Ch'un
Tsao Ch'un	ex-member of the Chinese politburo and architect of 'the Collapse'. Mass murderer and tyrant; 'creator' of Chung Kuo
Tsao Heng	second son of Tsao Ch'un
Tsao Hsiao	Tsao Ch'un's elder brother
Tsao Wang-po	eldest son of Tsao Ch'un
Tsu Chen	one of the original Seven, advisor to Tsao Ch'un
Tsu Lin	eldest son of Tsu Chen
Tsu Shi	steward to Gustav Ebert, a GenSyn clone
Tsu Tiao	T'ang of West Asia
Tu Mu	assistant to Alison Winter at GenSyn
Wang An-Shih	Han official and poet of the 11th century
Wang Chang Ye	eldest son of Wang Hsien
Wang Hsien	T'ang of Africa
Wang Hui So	one of the original Seven, advisor to Tsao Ch'un
Wang Lieh Tsu	second son of Wang Hsien
Wang Lung	eldest son of Wang Hui So
Wang Ta-hung	third son of Wang Hsien
Wang Yu-lai	'Cadre', servant of the Ministry, 'The Thousand Eyes', instructed to report back on Jiang Lei
Wei	a judge
Weis, Anton	banker and Dispersionist
Wen P'ing	Tsao Ch'un's man. A bully
Weo Shao	chancellor to Tsao Ch'un
Winter, Alison	Jake Reed's girlfriend at New College and evaluation executive at GenSyn
Winter, Jake	son of Alison Winter
Wolfe	elite guard in the Domain
Wu Chi	AI (Artificial Intelligence) to Tobias Lahm
Wu Hsien	one of the original Seven, advisor to Tsao Ch'un
Wyatt, Edmund	businessman and (unknown to him) father of Kim Ward
Yang Hong Yu	legal advocate
Yang Lai	Minister under Li Shai Tung
Yo Jou His	a judge
Yu Ch'o	family retainer to Wang Hui So

GLOSSARY OF MANDARIN TERMS

I t is not intended to belabour the reader with a whole mass of arcane Han expressions here. Some – usually the more specific – are explained in context. However, as a number of Mandarin terms are used naturally in the text, I've thought it best to provide a brief explanation of those terms.

aiya!	a common expression of surprise or dismay
amah	a domestic maidservant
Amo Li Jia	the Chinese gave this name to North America when they first arrived in the 1840s. Its literal meaning is 'The Land Without Ghosts'
an	a saddle. This has the same sound as the word for peace, and thus is associated in the Chinese mind with peace
catty	the colloquial term for a unit of measure formally called a *jin*. One catty – as used here – equals roughly 1.1. pounds (avoirdupois), or (exactly) 500 gm. Before 1949 and the standardization of Chinese measures to a metric standard, this measure varied district by district, but was generally regarded as equalling about 1.33 pounds (avoirdupois)
ch'a	tea; it might be noted that *ch'a shu*, the Chinese art of tea, is an ancient forebear of the Japanese tea ceremony *chanoyu*. *Hsiang p'ien* are flower teas, *Ch'ing ch'a* are green, unfermented teas
ch'a hao t'ai	literally, a 'directory'
ch'a shu	the art of tea, adopted later by the Japanese in their tea ceremony. The *ch'a* god is Lu Yu and his

	image can be seen on banners outside teahouses throughout Chung Kuo
chan shih	a 'fighter', here denoting a *tong* soldier
chang	ten ch'i, thus about 12 feet (Western)
Chang-e	the goddess of the Moon, and younger sister of the Spirit of the Waters. The moon represents the very essence of the female principal, *Yin*, in opposition to the Sun, which is *Yang*. Legend has it that Chang-e stole the elixir of immortality from her husband, the great archer Shen I, then fled to the Moon for safety, where she was transformed into a toad, which, so it is said, can still be seen against the whiteness of the moon's surface
chang shan	literally 'long dress', which fastens to the right. Worn by both sexes. The woman's version is a fitted, calf-length dress similar to the *chi pao*. A south China fashion, it is also known as a *cheung sam*
chao tai hui	an 'entertainment', usually, within *Chung Kuo*, of an expensive and sophisticated kind
chen yen	true words; the Chinese equivalent of a mantra
ch'eng	The word means both 'City' and 'Wall'
Ch'eng Ou Chou	City Europe
Ch'eng Hsiang	'Chancellor', a post first established in the Ch'in court more than two thousand years ago
ch'i	a Chinese 'foot'; approximately 14.4 inches
ch'i	'inner strength'; one of the two fundamental 'entities' from which everything is composed. Li is the 'form' or 'law', or (to cite Joseph Needham) the 'principal of organization' behind things, whereas *ch'i* is the 'matter-energy' or 'spirit' within material things, equating loosely to the *Pneuma* of the Greeks and the *prana* of the ancient Hindus. As the sage Chu Hsi (AD 1130–1200) said, 'The li is the *Tao* that pertains to "what is above shapes" and is the source from which all things are produced. The *ch'i* is the material [literally instrument] that pertains to "what is within shapes", and is the means whereby things are produced... Throughout the universe there is no *ch'i* without li. Or li without *ch'i*.'
chi ch'i	common workers, but used here mainly to denote the ant-like employees of the Ministry of Distribution
Chia Ch'eng	Honorary Assistant to the Royal Household

chi'an	a general term for money
chiao tzu	a traditional North Chinese meal of meat-filled dumplings eaten with a hot spicy sauce
Chieh Hsia	term meaning 'Your Majesty', derived from the expression 'Below the Steps'. It was the formal way of addressing the Emperor, through his Ministers, who stood 'below the steps'
chi pao	literally 'banner gown', a one-piece gown of Manchu origin, usually sleeveless, worn by women
chih chu	a spider
ch'in	a long (120 cm), narrow, lacquered zither with a smooth top surface and sound holes beneath, seven silk strings and thirteen studs marking the harmonic positions on the strings. Early examples have been unearthed from fifth century BC tombs, but it probably evolved in the fourteenth or thirteenth century BC. It is the most honoured of Chinese instruments and has a lovely mellow tone
Chin P'ing Mei	*The Golden Lotus*, an erotic novel, written by an unknown scholar – possibly anonymously by the writer Wang Shih-chen – at the beginning of the seventeenth century as a continuation of the *Shui Hui Chuan*, or 'Warriors of the Marsh', expanding chapters 23 to 25 of the *Shan Hui*, which relate the story of how Wu Sung became a bandit. Extending the story beyond this point, *The Golden Lotus* has been accused of being China's great licentious (even, perhaps, pornographic) novel. But as C.P. Fitzgerald says, 'If this book is indecent in parts, it is only because, telling a story of domestic life, it leaves out nothing.' It is available in a three-volume English-language translation
ch'ing	pure
ching	literally 'mirror', here used also to denote a perfect GenSyn copy of a man. Under the Edict of Technological Control, these are limited to copies of the ruling T'ang and their closest relatives. However, mirrors were also popularly believed to have certain strange properties, one of which was to make spirits visible. Buddhist priests used special 'magic mirrors' to show believers the form into which they would be reborn. Moreover, if a man looks into one of these mirrors and fails to recognize his own face, it is a

	sign that his own death is not far off. [See also *hu hsin chung.*]
ch'ing ch'a	green, unfermented teas
Ch'ing Ming	the Festival of Brightness and Purity, when the graves are swept and offerings made to the deceased. Also known as the Festival of Tombs, it occurs at the end of the second moon and is used for the purpose of celebrating the spring, a time for rekindling the cooking fires after a three-day period in which the fires were extinguished and only cold food eaten
Chou	literally, 'State', but here used as the name of a card game based on the politics of Chung Kuo
chow mein	this, like chop suey, is neither a Chinese nor a Western dish, but a special meal created by the Chinese in North America for the Western palate. A transliteration of *chao mian* (fried noodles), it is a distant relation of the *liang mian huang* served in Suchow
ch'u	the west
chun hua	literally, 'Spring Pictures'. These are, in fact, pornographic 'pillow books', meant for the instruction of newly-weds
ch'un tzu	an ancient Chinese term from the Warring States period, describing a certain class of noblemen, controlled by a code of chivalry and morality known as the *li*, or rites. Here the term is roughly, and sometimes ironically, translated as 'gentlemen'. The *ch'un tzu* is as much an ideal state of behaviour – as specified by Confucius in the *Analects* – as an actual class in Chung Kuo, though a degree of financial independence and a high standard of education are assumed a prerequisite
chung	a lidded ceramic serving bowl for *ch'a*
chung hsin	loyalty
E hsing hsun huan	a saying: 'Bad nature follows a cycle'
er	two
erh tzu	son
erhu	a traditional Chinese instrument
fa	punishment
fen	a unit of currency; see *yuan*. It has another meaning, that of a 'minute' of clock time, but that usage is avoided here to prevent any confusion

feng yu	a 'phoenix chair', canopied and decorated with silver birds. Coloured scarlet and gold, this is the traditional carriage for a bride as she is carried to her wedding ceremony
fu jen	'Madam', used here as opposed to *t'ai t'ai*, 'Mrs'
fu sang	the hollow mulberry tree; according to ancient Chinese cosmology this tree stands where the sun rises and is the dwelling place of rulers. *Sang* (mulberry) however has the same sound as *sang* (sorrow) in Chinese
Han	term used by the Chinese to describe their own race, the 'black-haired people', dating back to the Han dynasty (210 BC–AD 220). It is estimated that some ninety-four per cent of modern China's population are Han racially
Hei	literally 'black'. The Chinese pictogram for this represents a man wearing war paint and tattoos. Here it refers specifically to the genetically manufactured half-men, made by GenSyn and used as riot police to quell uprisings in the lower levels of the City
ho yeh	*Nelumbo Nucifera*, or lotus, the seeds of which are used in Chinese medicine to cure insomnia
Hoi Po	the corrupt officials who dealt with the European traders in the nineteenth century, more commonly known as 'hoppos'
Hsia	a crab
hsiang p'en	flower *ch'a*
hsiao	filial piety. The character for *hsiao* is comprised of two parts, the upper part meaning 'old', the lower meaning 'son' or 'child'. This dutiful submission of the young to the old is at the heart of Confucianism and Chinese culture generally
Hsiao chieh	'Miss', or an unmarried woman. An alternative to *nu shi*
hsiao jen	'little man/men'. In the *Analects*, Book XIV, Confucius writes, 'The gentleman gets through to what is up above; the small man gets through to what is down below.' This distinction between 'gentlemen' (*ch'un tzu*) and 'little men' (*hsiao jen*), false even in Confucius's time, is no less a matter of social perspective in Chung Kuo

hsien | historically an administrative district of variable size. Here the term is used to denote a very specific administrative area, one of ten stacks – each stack composed of 30 decks. Each deck is a hexagonal living unit of ten levels, two *li*, or approximately one kilometre, in diameter. A stack can be imagined as one honeycomb in the great hive that is the City. Each *hsien* of the city elects one Representative to sit in the House at Weimar

Hsien Ling | Chief Magistrate, in charge of a *Hsien*. In Chung Kuo these officials are the T'ang's representatives and law enforcers for the individual *hsien*. In times of peace each *hsien* would also elect one Representative to sit in the House at Weimar

hsueh pai | 'snow white', a derogatory term here for *Hung Mao* women

Hu pu | the T'ang's Finance Ministry

hu hsin chung | see *ching*, re Buddhist magic mirrors, for which this was the name. The power of such mirrors was said to protect the owner from evil. It was also said that one might see the secrets of futurity in such a mirror. See the chapter 'Mirrors' in *The White Mountain* for further information

hu t'ieh | a butterfly. Anyone wishing to follow up on this tale of Chuang Tzu's might look to the sage's writings and specifically the chapter 'Discussion on Making All Things Equal'

hua pen | literally 'story roots', these were précis guidebooks used by the street-corner storytellers in China for the past two thousand years. The main events of the story were written down in the *hua pen* for the benefit of those storytellers who had not yet mastered their art. During the Yuan or Mongol dynasty (AD 1280–1368) these *hua pen* developed into plays, and, later on – during the Ming dynasty (AD 1368–1644) – into the form of popular novels, of which the *Shui Hu Chuan*, or 'Outlaws of the Marsh', remains one of the most popular. Any reader interested in following this up might purchase Pearl Buck's translation, rendered as *All Men Are Brothers* and first published in 1933

Huang Ti | originally Huang Ti was the last of the 'Three Sovereigns' and the first of the 'Five Emperors' of ancient Chinese tradition. Huang Ti, the Yellow

Emperor, was the earliest ruler recognized by the historian Ssu-ma Ch'ien (136–85 BC) in his great historical work, the Shih Chi. Traditionally, all subsequent rulers (and would-be rulers) of China have claimed descent from the Yellow Emperor, the 'Son of Heaven' himself, who first brought civilization to the black-haired people. His name is now synonymous with the term 'emperor'

hun · the higher soul or 'spirit soul', which, the Chinese believe, ascends to Heaven at death, joins Shang Ti, the Supreme Ancestor, and lives in his court for ever more. The hun is believed to come into existence at the moment of conception (see also p'o)

hun tun · 'the Chou believed that Heaven and Earth were once inextricably mixed together in a state of undifferentiated chaos, like a chicken's egg. Hun Tun they called that state' (The Broken Wheel, Chapter 37). It is also the name of a meal of tiny sack-like dumplings

Hung Lou Meng · The Dream of Red Mansions, also known as The Story Of The Stone, a lengthy novel written in the middle of the eighteenth century. Like the Chin Ping Mei, it deals with the affairs of a single Chinese family. According to experts the first eighty chapters are the work of Ts'ao Hsueh-ch'in, and the last forty belong to Kao Ou. It is, without doubt, the masterpiece of Chinese literature, and is available from Penguin in the UK in a five-volume edition

Hung Mao · literally 'redheads', the name the Chinese gave to the Dutch (and later English) seafarers who attempted to trade with China in the seventeenth century. Because of the piratical nature of their endeavours (which often meant plundering Chinese shipping and ports) the name continues to retain connotations of piracy

Hung Mun · the Secret Societies or, more specifically, the Triads

huo jen · literally, 'fire men'

I Lung · the 'First Dragon', Senior Minister and Great Lord of the 'Ministry', also known as 'The Thousand Eyes'

jou tung wu · literally 'meat animal': 'It was a huge mountain of flesh, a hundred ch'i to a side and almost twenty ch'i in height. Along one side of it, like the teats of a giant pig, three dozen heads jutted from the flesh,

long, eyeless snouts with shovel jaws that snuffled
and gobbled in the conveyor-belt trough...'

kai t'ou | a thin cloth of red and gold that veils a new bride's
face. Worn by the Ch'ing empresses for almost three
centuries

kan pei! | 'good health!' or 'cheers!' – a drinking toast

kang | the Chinese hearth, serving also as oven and, in the
cold of winter, as a sleeping platform

k'ang hsi | a Ch'ing (or Manchu) emperor whose long reign
(AD 1662–1722) is considered a golden age for the
art of porcelain-making. The lavender-glazed bowl
in 'The Sound Of Jade' is, however, not kang-hsi but
Chun chou ware from the Sung period (960-1127) and
considered amongst the most beautiful (and rare)
wares in Chinese pottery

kao liang | a strong Chinese liquor

Ko Ming | 'revolutionary'. The Tien Ming is the Mandate of
Heaven, supposedly handed down from Shang Ti,
the Supreme Ancestor, to his earthly counterpart, the
Emperor (Huang Ti). This Mandate could be enjoyed
only so long as the Emperor was worthy of it, and
rebellion against a tyrant – who broke the Mandate
through his lack of justice, benevolence and sincerity
– was deemed not criminal but a rightful expression
of Heaven's anger

k'ou t'ou | the fifth stage of respect, according to the 'Book
of Ceremonies', involves kneeling and striking the
head against the floor. This ritual has become more
commonly known in the West as kowtow

ku li | 'bitter strength'. These two words, used to describe
the condition of farm labourers who, after severe
droughts or catastrophic floods, moved off their
land and into the towns to look for work of any kind
– however hard and onerous – spawned the word
'coolie' by which the West more commonly knows
the Chinese labourer. Such men were described as
'men of bitter strength', or simply 'ku li'

Kuan Hua | Mandarin, the language spoken in mainland China.
Also known as kuo yu and pai hua

Kuan Yin | the Goddess of Mercy. Originally the Buddhist male
bodhisattva, Avalokitsevara (translated into Han as
'He who listens to the sounds of the world', or 'Kuan
Yin'), the Han mistook the well-developed breasts of

the saint for a woman's and, since the ninth century, have worshipped Kuan Yin as such. Effigies of Kuan Yin will show her usually as the Eastern Madonna, cradling a child in her arms. She is also sometimes seen as the wife of *Kuan Kung*, the Chinese God of War

Kuei Chuan 'Running Dog', here the name of a Triad

kuo yu Mandarin, the language spoken in most of Mainland China. Also rendered here as *kuan hua* and *pai hua*

kwai an abbreviation of *kwai tao*, a 'sharp knife' or 'fast knife'. It can also mean to be sharp or fast (as a knife). An associated meaning is that of a 'clod' or 'lump of earth'. Here it is used to denote a class of fighters from below the Net, whose ability and self-discipline separate them from the usual run of hired knives

Lan Tian 'Blue Sky'

Lang a covered walkway

lao chu sing-song girls, slightly more respectable than the common *men hu*

lao jen 'old man' (also *weng*); used normally as a term of respect

lao kuan a 'Great Official', often used ironically

lao shih term that denotes a genuine and straightforward man – bluff and honest

lao wai an outsider

li a Chinese 'mile', approximating to half a kilometre or one third of a mile. Until 1949, when metric measures were adopted in China, the li could vary from place to place

Li 'propriety'. See the Li Ching or 'Book Of Rites' for the fullest definition

Li Ching 'The Book Of Rites', one of the five ancient classics

liang a Chinese ounce of roughly 32gm. Sixteen *liang* form a *catty*

liu k'ou the seventh stage of respect, according to the 'Book of Ceremonies'. Two stages above the more familiarly known 'k'ou t'ou' (kowtow) it involves kneeling and striking the forehead three times against the floor, rising to one's feet again, then kneeling and repeating the prostration with three touches of the forehead to the ground. Only the *san* kuei chiu k'ou – involving three prostrations – was more elaborate and was reserved for Heaven and its son, the Emperor (see also san k'ou)

liumang — punks

lu nan jen — literally 'oven man', title of the official who is responsible for cremating all of the dead bodies

lueh — 'that invaluable quality of producing a piece of art casually, almost uncaringly'

lung t'ing — 'dragon pavilions', small sedan chairs carried by servants and containing a pile of dowry gifts

Luoshu — the Chinese legend relates that in ancient times a turtle crawled from a river in Luoshu province, the patterns on its shell forming a three by three grid of numeric pictograms, the numbers of which – both down and across – equalled the same total of fifteen. Since the time of the Shang (three thousand-plus years ago) tortoise shells were used in divination, and the Luoshu diagram is considered magic and is often used as a charm for easing childbirth

ma kua — a waist-length ceremonial jacket

mah jong — whilst, in its modern form, the 'game of the four winds' was introduced towards the end of the nineteenth century to Westerners trading in the thriving city of Shanghai, it was developed from a card game that existed as long ago as AD 960. Using 144 tiles, it is generally played by four players. The tiles have numbers and also suits – winds, dragons, bamboos and circles

mao — a unit of currency. See yuan

mao tai — a strong, sorghum-based liquor

mei fa tzu — common saying, 'It is fate!'

mei hua — 'plum blossom'

mei mei — sister

mei yu jen wen — 'subhumans'. Used in Chung Kuo by those in the City's uppermost levels to denote anyone living in the lower hundred

men hu — literally, 'the one standing in the door'. The most common (and cheapest) of prostitutes

min — literally 'the people'; used (as here) by the Minor Families in a pejorative sense, as an equivalent to 'plebeian'

Ming	the dynasty that ruled China from 1368 to 1644. Literally, the name means 'Bright' or 'Clear' or 'Brilliant'. It carries connotations of cleansing
mou	a Chinese 'acre' of approximately 7,260 square feet. There are roughly six mou to a Western acre, and a 10,000-mou field would approximate to 1,666 acres, or just over two and a half square miles
Mu Ch'in	'Mother', a general term commonly addressed to any older woman
mui tsai	rendered in Cantonese as 'mooi-jai'. Colloquially, it means either 'little sister' or 'slave girl', though generally, as here, the latter. Other Mandarin terms used for the same status are pei-nu and yatou. Technically, guardianship of the girl involved is legally signed over in return for money
nan jen	common term for 'Man'
Ni Hao?	'How are you?'
niao	literally 'bird', but here, as often, it is used euphemistically as a term for the penis, often as an expletive
nu er	daughter
nu shi	an unmarried woman, a term equating to 'Miss'
Pa shi yi	literally 'Eighty-One', here referring specifically to the Central Council of the New Confucian officialdom
pai nan jen	literally 'white man'
pai pi	'hundred pens', term used for the artificial reality experiments renamed 'Shells' by Ben Shepherd
pan chang	supervisor
pao yun	a 'jewelled cloud' ch'a
pau	a simple long garment worn by men
pau shuai ch'i	the technical scientific term for 'half-life'
p'i p'a	a four-stringed lute used in traditional Chinese music
Pien Hua!	Change!
p'ing	an apple, symbol of peace
ping	the east
Ping Fa	Sun Tzu's The Art Of War, written over two thousand years ago. The best English translation is probably Samuel B. Griffith's 1963 edition. It was a book Chairman Mao frequently referred to

Ping Tiao	levelling. To bring down or make flat. Here, in Chung Kuo, it is also a terrorist organization.
p'o	The 'animal soul' which, at death, remains in the tomb with the corpse and takes its nourishment from the grave offerings. The p'o decays with the corpse, sinking down into the underworld (beneath the Yellow Springs) where – as a shadow – it continues an existence of a kind. The p'o is believed to come into existence at the moment of birth (see also hun)
sam fu	an upper garment (part shirt, part jacket) worn originally by both males and females, in imitation of Manchu styles; later on a wide-sleeved, calf-length version was worn by women alone
san	three
San chang	the three palaces
san kuei chiu k'ou	the eighth and final stage of respect, according to the 'Book Of Ceremonies', it involves kneeling three times, each time striking the forehead three times against the ground before rising from one's knees (in k'ou t'ou one strikes the forehead but once). This most elaborate form of ritual was reserved for Heaven and its son, the Emperor. See also liu k'ou
san k'ou	abbreviated form of san kuei chiu k'ou
San Kuo Yan Yi	The Romance of The Three Kingdoms, also known as the San Kuo Chih Yen I. China's great historical novel, running to 120 chapters, it covers the period from AD 168 to 265. Written by Lo Kuan-chung in the early Ming dynasty, its heroes, Liu Pei, Kuan Chung and Chang Fei, together with its villain, Ts'ao Ts'ao, are all historical personages. It is still one of the most popular stories in modern China
sao mu	the 'Feast of the Dead'
shang	the south
shan shui	the literal meaning is 'mountains and water', but the term is normally associated with a style of landscape painting that depicts rugged mountain scenery with river valleys in the foreground. It is a highly popular form, first established in the T'ang Dynasty, back in the seventh to ninth centuries AD
shao lin	specially trained assassins, named after the monks of the shao lin monastery

shao nai nai	literally, 'little grandmother'. A young girl who has been given the responsibility of looking after her siblings
she t'ou	a 'tongue' or taster, whose task is to safeguard his master from poisoning
shen chung	'caution'
shen mu	'she who stands in the door': a common prostitute
shen nu	'god girls': superior prostitutes
shen t'se	special elite force, named after the 'palace armies' of the late T'ang dynasty
Shih	'Master'. Here used as a term of respect somewhat equivalent to our use of 'Mister'. The term was originally used for the lowest level of civil servants, to distinguish them socially from the run-of-the-mill 'Misters' (*hsian sheng*) below them and the gentlemen (*ch'un tzu*) above
shou hsing	a peach brandy
Shui Hu Chuan	*Outlaws of the Marsh*, a long historical novel attributed to Lo Kuan-chung but re-cast in the early sixteenth century by 'Shih Nai-an', a scholar. Set in the eleventh century, it is a saga of bandits, warlords and heroes. Written in pure *pai hua* – colloquial Chinese – it is the tale of how its heroes became bandits. Its revolutionary nature made it deeply unpopular with both the Ming and Manchu dynasties, but it remains one of the most popular adventures among the Chinese populace
siang chi	Chinese chess, a very different game from its Western counterpart
Ta	'Beat', here a heavily amplified form of Chinese folk music, popular amongst the young
ta lien	an elaborate girdle pouch
Ta Ssu Nung	the Superintendency of Agriculture
tai	literally 'pockets' but here denoting Representatives in the House at Weimar. 'Owned' financially by the Seven, historically such *tai* have served a double function in the House, counterbalancing the strong mercantile tendencies of the House and serving as a conduit for the views of the Seven. Traditionally they had been elderly, well-respected men, but more recently their replacements were young, brash and

	very corrupt, more like the hoppoes of the Opium Wars period
t'ai chi	the Original, or One, from which the duality of all things (yin and yang) developed, according to Chinese cosmology. We generally associate the t'ai chi with the Taoist symbol, that swirling circle of dark and light supposedly representing an egg (perhaps the Hun Tun), the yolk and the white differentiated
tai hsiao	a white wool flower, worn in the hair
Tai Huo	'Great Fire'
T'ai Shan	Mount T'ai, the highest and most sacred of China's mountains, located in Shantung province. A stone pathway of 6,293 steps leads to the summit and for thousands of years the ruling emperor has made ritual sacrifices at its foot, accompanied by his full retinue, presenting evidence of his virtue. T'ai Shan is one of the five Taoist holy mountains, and symbolizes the very centre of China. It is the mountain of the sun, symbolizing the bright male force (yang). 'As safe as T'ai Shan' is a popular saying, denoting the ultimate in solidity and certainty
Tai Shih Lung	Court Astrologer, a title that goes back to the Han dynasty
T'ang	literally, 'beautiful and imposing'. It is the title chosen by the Seven, who were originally the chief advisors to Tsao Ch'un, the tyrant. Since overthrowing Tsao Ch'un, it has effectively had the meaning of 'emperor'
Ta Ts'in	the Chinese name for the Roman Empire. They also knew Rome as Li Chien and as 'the land West of the Sea'. The Romans themselves they termed the 'Big Ts'in' – the Ts'in being the name the Chinese gave themselves during the Ts'in dynasty (AD 265–316)
te	'spiritual power', 'true virtue' or 'virtuality', defined by Alan Watts as 'the realization or expression of the Tao in actual living'
t'e an tsan	'innocent westerners'. For 'innocent' perhaps read naive
ti tsu	a bamboo flute, used both as a solo instrument and as part of an ensemble, playing traditional Chinese music

ti yu	the 'earth prison' or underworld of Chinese legend. There are ten main Chinese Hells, the first being the courtroom in which the sinner is sentenced and the last being that place where they are reborn as human beings. In between are a vast number of sub-Hells, each with its own Judge and staff of cruel warders. In Hell, it is always dark, with no differentiation between night and day
Tian	'Heaven', also, 'the dome of the sky'
tian-fang	literally 'to fill the place of the dead wife'; used to signify the upgrading of a concubine to the more respectable position of wife
tiao tuo	bracelets of gold and jade
T'ieh Lo-han	'Iron Goddess of Mercy', a *ch'a*
T'ieh Pi Pu Kai	literally, 'the iron pen changes not', this is the final phrase used at the end of all Chinese government proclamations for the last three thousand years
ting	an open-sided pavilion in a Chinese garden. Designed as a focal point in a garden, it is said to symbolize man's essential place in the natural order of things
T'ing Wei	the Superintendency of Trials, an institution that dates back to the T'ang dynasty. See Book Eight, *The White Mountain*, for an instance of how this department of government – responsible for black propaganda – functions
T'o	'camel-backed', a Chinese term for 'hunch-backed'
tong	a gang. In China and Europe these are usually smaller and thus subsidiary to the Triads, but in North America the term has generally taken the place of Triad
tou chi	Glycine Max, or the black soybean, used in Chinese herbal medicine to cure insomnia
Tsai Chien!	'Until we meet again!'
Tsou Tsai Hei	'the Walker in the Darkness'
tsu	the north
tsu kuo	the motherland
ts'un	a Chinese 'inch' of approximately 1.4 Western inches. Ten ts'un form one *ch'i*
Tu	Earth
tzu	'Elder Sister'

wan wu	literally 'the ten thousand things'; used generally to include everything in creation, or, as the Chinese say, 'all things in Heaven and Earth'
Wei	Commandant of Security
wei chi	'the surrounding game', known more commonly in the West by its Japanese name of *Go*. It is said that the game was invented by the legendary Chinese Emperor Yao in the year 2350 BC to train the mind of his son, Tan Chu, and teach him to think like an emperor
wen ming	a term used to denote civilization, or written culture
wen ren	the scholar-artist; very much an ideal state, striven for by all creative Chinese
weng	'Old man'. Usually a term of respect
Wu	a diviner; traditionally, these were 'mediums' who claimed to have special psychic powers. *Wu* could be either male or female
Wu	'non-being'. As Lao Tzu says: 'Once the block is carved, there are names.' But the Tao is unnameable (*wu-ming*) and before Being (*yu*) is Non-Being (*wu*). Not to have existence, or form, or a name, that is *wu*
Wu ching	the 'Five Classics' studied by all Confucian scholars, comprising the *Shu Ching* (Book Of History), the *Shih Ching* (Book of Songs), the *I Ching* (Book of Changes), the *Li Ching* (Book of Rites, actually three books in all), and the *Ch'un Chui* (The Spring and Autumn Annals of the State of Lu)
wu fu	the five gods of good luck
wu tu	the 'five noxious creatures' – which are toad, scorpion, snake, centipede and gecko (wall lizard)
Wushu	the Chinese word for Martial Arts. It refers to any of several hundred schools. *Kung fu* is a school within this, meaning 'skill that transcends mere surface beauty'
wuwei	nonaction, an old Taoist concept. It means keeping harmony with the flow of things – doing nothing to break the flow
ya	homosexual. Sometimes the term 'a yellow eel' is used
yamen	the official building in a Chinese community
yang	the 'male principle' of Chinese cosmology, which, with its complementary opposite, the female *yin*,

	forms the *t'ai ch'i*, derived from the Primeval One. From the union of *yin* and *yang* arise the 'five elements' (water, fire, earth, metal, wood) from which the 'ten thousand things' (the *wan wu*) are generated. Yang signifies Heaven and the South, the Sun and Warmth, Light, Vigor, Maleness, Penetration, odd numbers and the Dragon. Mountains are *yang*
yang kuei tzu	Chinese name for foreigners, 'Ocean Devils'. It is also synonymous with 'Barbarians'
yang mei ping	'willow plum sickness', the Chinese term for syphilis, provides an apt description of the male sexual organ in the extreme of this sickness
yi	the number one
yin	the 'female principle' of Chinese cosmology (see *yang*). Yin signifies Earth and the North, the Moon and Cold, Darkness, Quiescence, Femaleness, Absorption, even numbers and the Tiger. The *yin* lies in the shadow of the mountain
yin mao	pubic hair
Ying kuo	English, the language
ying tao	'baby peach', a term of endearment here
ying tzu	'shadows' – trained specialists of various kinds, contracted out to gangland bosses
yu	literally 'fish', but, because of its phonetic equivalence to the word for 'abundance', the fish symbolizes wealth. Yet there is also a saying that when the fish swim upriver it is a portent of social unrest and rebellion
yu ko	a 'Jade Barge', here a type of luxury sedan
Yu Kung	'Foolish Old Man!'
yu ya	deep elegance
yuan	the basic currency of Chung Kuo (and modern-day China). Colloquially (though not here) it can also be termed *kuai* – 'piece' or 'lump'. Ten *mao* (or, formally, *jiao*) make up one *yuan*, while 100 *fen* (or 'cents') comprise one *yuan*
yueh ch'in	a Chinese dulcimer, one of the principal instruments of the Chinese orchestra
Ywe Lung	literally 'The Moon Dragon', the wheel of seven dragons that is the symbol of the ruling Seven throughout Chung Kuo: 'At its centre the snouts

of the regal beasts met, forming a rose-like hub,
huge rubies burning fiercely in each eye. Their lithe,
powerful bodies curved outward like the spokes
of a giant wheel while at the edge their tails were
intertwined to form the rim.' (Chapter 4 of *The Middle
Kingdom*)

AUTHOR'S NOTE

The transcription of standard Mandarin into European alphabetical form was first achieved in the seventeenth century by the Italian Matteo Ricci, who founded and ran the first Jesuit Mission in China from 1583 until his death in 1610. Since then several dozen attempts have been made to reduce the original Chinese sounds, represented by some tens of thousands of separate pictograms, into readily understandable phonetics for Western use. For a long time, however, three systems dominated – those used by the three major Western powers vying for influence in the corrupt and crumbling Chinese Empire of the nineteenth century: Great Britain, France, and Germany. These systems were the Wade-Giles (Great Britain and America – sometimes known as the Wade System), the *École Française de l'Extrême Orient* (France) and the Lessing (Germany).

Since 1958, however, the Chinese themselves have sought to create one single phonetic form, based on the German system, which they termed the *hanyu pinyin fang'an* (Scheme for a Chinese Phonetic Alphabet), known more commonly as *pinyin*, and in all foreign language books published in China since 1 January 1979 *pinyin* has been used, as well as being taught now in schools alongside the standard Chinese characters. For this work, however, I have chosen to use the older and to my mind far more elegant transcription system, the Wade-Giles (in modified form). For those now used to the harder forms of *pinyin*, the following may serve as a basic conversion guide, the Wade-Giles first, the *pinyin* after:

p for b	ch' for q
ts' for c	j for r
ch' for ch	t' for t
t for d	hs for x
k for g	ts for z
ch for j	ch for zh

The effect is, I hope, to render the softer, more poetic side of the original Mandarin, ill-served, I feel, by modern *pinyin*.

The translation of Li Shang-Yin's 'untitled poem' is by A. C. Graham from his excellent *Poems of the Late Tang*, published by Penguin Books, London, 1965.

The translation of Wu Man-yuan's 'Two White Geese' (Fei Yen's song in Chapter 49) is by Anne Birrell from *New Songs from a Jade Terrace: An Anthology of Early Chinese Love Poetry*, published by George Allen & Unwin, London, 1982.

The quotations from Sun Tzu's *The Art of War* are from the Samuel B. Griffith translation, published by Oxford University Press, 1963.

The translation from Nietzsche is by R. J. Hollingdale and is taken from *Beyond Good and Evil* (Prelude to a Philosophy of the Future), published by Penguin Books, London, 1973; *Ecce Home* (How One Becomes What One Is), published by Penguin Books, London, 1979.

D. H. Lawrence's 'Bavarian Gentians' can be found in *Last Poems* (1932) but the version here is taken from an earlier draft of the poem.

The game of *wei chi* mentioned throughout this volume is, incidentally, more commonly known by its Japanese name of *Go*, and is not merely the world's oldest game but its most elegant.

David Wingrove
April 1990
January 2013

CHUNG KUO

ACKNOWLEDGMENTS

Thanks must go, once again, to all those who have read and criticized parts of *An Inch of Ashes* during its long gestation. To my editors – Nick Sayers, Brian DeFiore, John Pearce and Alyssa Diamond – for their patience as well as their enthusiasm; to my Writers Bloc companions, Chris Evans, David Garnett, Rob Holdstock, Garry Kilworth, Bobbie Lamming and Lisa Tuttle; to Andy Sawyer, for an 'outsider's view' when it was much needed, and, as ever, to my stalwart helper and first-line critic, Brian Griffin, for keeping me on the rails.

Thanks are due also to Rob Carter, Ritchie Smith, Paul Bougie, Mike Cobley, Linda Shaughnessy, Susan and the girls (Jessica, Amy and baby Georgia), and Is and the Lunatics (at Canterbury) for keeping my spirits up during the long, lonely business of writing this. And to 'Nan and Grandad', Daisy and Percy Oudot, for helping out when things were tight... and for making the tea!

Finally, thanks to Magma, IQ and the Cardiacs for providing the aural soundtrack to this.